COLD TRUTH

ELLIE KLINE SERIES: BOOK ONE

MARY STONE
DONNA BERDEL

Copyright © 2020 by Mary Stone

All rights reserved.

No part of this book may be reproduced in any form or by any electronic or mechanical means, including information storage and retrieval systems, without written permission from the author, except for the use of brief quotations in a book review.

❀ Created with Vellum

Mary Stone
To my husband.
Thank you for taking care of our home and its many inhabitants while I follow this dream of mine.

Donna Berdel
First, a big thank you to Mary Stone for taking a chance on me by collaborating on this story. I'm honored and indebted!And, of course, to my husband. Thank you for being you. You're my rock.

DESCRIPTION

Say the words...

In a dark basement, a cold-blooded killer pits friend against friend, torturing one until the other says the horrible words that will end their friend's suffering. He's gotten away with murder for years. Until now...

Ellie Kline can't remember most of her kidnapping when she was fifteen, but that night has shaped her life. Instead of cowering, that horrible night made her strong. Determined to prove herself as a cop despite being heir to the Kline fortune, she never backs down, and she never takes no for an answer. When the daring takedown of a suspect catapults her into the spotlight, it earns her a promotion...and the admiration of a killer.

Now a detective assigned to the Cold Case Unit, Ellie is drawn into the mysterious murder of a young, unidentified college-age woman with no missing persons' report, no leads, and no evidence. Even more shocking is that, while she was tortured extensively, her death was quick. But as Ellie delves deeper, she discovers a startling connection between the woman found dismembered in a park and another Jane Doe case. Is there more?

As hazy memories of her own past begin to surface, it's not only her family and the brass at Charleston PD who are watching her every move. Someone lurks in the shadows, ready to kill if Ellie's journey into history gets too close to the cold truth.

A riveting roller coaster ride of a psychological thriller, Cold Truth is the first book of the Ellie Kline Series that will make you consider adding a second lock to your door.

1

Dark.

Damp.

Cold.

Tabitha forced her eyes open.

Joyful humming was like a whisper, and Tabitha fought to locate the source. He was there, in the corner, puttering around in the deep shadows the single lightbulb couldn't chase from the dank room.

She squeezed her eyelids shut again. Hot tears spilled down her cheeks, racing to her chin and down her neck, the liquid warm against her cool skin.

Frozen by the knowledge that *he* was near, she couldn't stop her eyes from opening just enough to watch him.

Fingers tingling, she tried to flex her hands to bring the blood flow back to her frozen flesh. But the ropes were too tight, and the heavy iron chair's arms curved unnaturally, turning her wrists at a painful angle. She forced herself to focus on the pain, willing her anger to build.

Without light from the outside world to mark the sun's travels, she'd lost track of how long they'd been in the old basement. An eternity? She was starting to wonder if her memories from before were just dreams. Had she always been here—trapped and starving—staring at a woman tied up just like her? Had she possessed a life before this happened? Had she really gone to college, or had that been a dream?

At first, she'd thought the woman was her reflection in a mirror. Her hair was even almost the color of her own, except it had that freshly colored hue of a first time bleach job, glinting in the light from the bulb so it seemed like coppery strands ran through the golden brown. Tabitha had woken up before the woman, who had been unconscious still, blissfully dead to the world. Sleeping through this ordeal seemed to be her superpower.

Or was it from blood loss?

The woman's outfit was exactly like the one he'd dressed Tabitha in—a lavender shirt and jeans. The exception was the pool of black blood surrounding this stranger, crusted on the rough concrete. In the middle of the pool lay a decaying finger. Beside it, one that appeared a little fresher.

Tabitha took stock of herself. Ten fingers. Ten toes. A detached feeling brought on by shock and low levels of ketamine numbed her senses. The man had earlier told her the name of the drug and why it had been the perfect choice. Low levels of ketamine deadened the senses and slowed down the reflexes. The purest torture, he'd called it, just before he'd demanded that she beg him for more.

Her head was still tender where it had bounced off the wall when she'd spit in his face, and he'd backhanded her so hard she felt her brain slam against her skull. Her neck was sore, stiff, and cricked to the side from being held in one position for so long. Shivers wracked her body—a futile attempt to bring warmth. She slid into merciful blackness again.

When she next woke, the man was gone. For a moment, she and the woman were alone.

"Mabel," Tabitha whispered, her voice echoing in the almost empty dark space. "Mabel, wake up."

Mabel groaned, and a single red dot to her left clicked on in the darkness, then turned green.

Another one appeared to Tabitha's left.

She whimpered. *Not again*, she prayed silently, fresh tears gushing from her itchy eyes. *Please, not again.*

Mabel blinked, her expression showing how much her alertness had been muddled by sleep and the cocktail of pharmaceutical-grade poison that did nothing to ease her pain. Realization snapped her eyes open wide with fear as her befuddled brain made sense of what she was seeing. She started blubbering, her words senseless and heart-wrenching.

Tabitha could tell that Mabel knew what was coming, even if she couldn't form the words. The horror was no less for her failing. Having all of her tongue in her mouth wouldn't bring clarity…or freedom.

"Mabel, please, look at me. We're going to make it out of this. I promise."

A *buzzzz* from the ceiling made Tabitha's pulse leap, drawing her attention to the clear IV tubes that were always there. She fought her restraints, but the liquid made its way to the line that was duct taped to her forearm. She watched in horror, then screamed when the fire entered her arm and found its way through the vein, spreading out and scorching every capillary it passed.

She tried to focus on Mabel, but the woman was convulsing, head lulling to the side. Suddenly, she snapped upright, eyes wide and unblinking. Whatever he'd given her, it had forced her into what she'd worked so hard to pull away from

—clarity, alertness. Her line was a putrid green that made Tabitha gag.

She wretched, her stomach cramping and trying desperately to expel the emptiness.

"You'll stop that in a minute." The man's voice was soft, reassuring, but Tabitha jerked. She hadn't heard him enter. "Tell me, what colors do you see?" The casual way he addressed her threatened to drive her mad.

Turning feral, Tabitha growled at him, her hatred visceral and overwhelming. The entire room began to drip with a viscous green liquid, a shade darker than her favorite color. She would never like lime green again. An instant later, it dried up with an audible *pop* that hurt her eyes instead of her ears, and the green was gone. Even Mabel's IV line held clear liquid, and Tabitha realized that it had never been green.

A low, keening sound tumbled from Mabel's lips. She'd given up hope.

Tabitha didn't blame her. He'd tortured her mercilessly. Tabitha's only pain had been in being forced to watch. She didn't know why he'd chosen her over Mabel, but Tabitha refused to do the horrible thing he'd asked her to.

She couldn't.

He appeared in the light, standing out of sight of both cameras, like he always did.

Mabel was trying to move, but she couldn't overpower his concoction.

Besides, it wasn't Mabel he was looking at. It was *her*.

"Tabitha, Tabitha, Tabitha," he tsked, sharpening the already razor-edged butcher knife. His tongue glided over his teeth in time with each swipe.

Did he know that he did such a thing? Had he been bullied for being the weird one? Was that what turned him into a monster, or had he always been soulless, excited by fear and the smell of blood?

"Nothing pretty rhymes with Tabitha. It's such a pointless name. Now, Mabel. That's a beautiful name with so much potential. I wonder if someone will write a poem about her? Sable, table, able, stable, fable, cable." He sucked in air through clenched teeth, his eyes closing as if he were savoring fine wine. "It's almost prophetic. Like the gods themselves created her just for me. A shame I won't have her to play with much longer."

"You're letting her go?" Tabitha asked before she could stop herself. She blinked, bit her lip hard, trying to hold in the words that wanted to spill out. "I'm not telling you that I'm thinking about killing you when I'm untied. You can't make me do it." She gasped as a hard shudder ran through her. "What did you give me?"

"My own concoction. Aside from the nausea, do you like it? Did it fill you with rage?"

"Your face does that for me," she spat out. "I hope you fall on that knife and die."

"Ooh," he giggled, clearly delighted. The girlish laugh grated on Tabitha's nerves like a knife. "I like *this* Tabitha. I may have to change my plans for you."

"I don't want to die." The last word cracked, and as it exited her throat, a sudden sob made her sound just as miserable and afraid as she felt.

"Of course you don't, but I'm not talking about that. Tell me, what are you thinking about right now?"

She fought, trying to keep the words inside, but they still came. Sobbing, she described exactly how she'd planned to kill him and escape.

His eyebrows arched slightly, and he nodded. "If you hadn't told me, that might have worked. That's why I want to hear your every thought. You see, some women are so smart they make my job difficult."

"This isn't a job," Tabitha sneered, kicking at the chair,

rage thundering over the fear.

"Not to you, but to me, this is everything." He swept his arms wide, as if presenting the room for her appraisal. "I don't function well if I don't have my pets. You're doing this for the greater good. I have to release the valve to be at my best. And the world needs me at my best. Don't you care about anyone but yourself, Tabitha?"

"I'm not a pet."

"Tomato, to-mah-toe." He pulled a hair from Tabitha's head and ran it across the blade. It split in two. "Now, for today's challenge. We'll pick up where we left off."

"No!" Her scream echoed off the cinderblock walls.

Mabel wailed in response, the sound so pitiful it filled Tabitha with a sadness she'd never known.

"You can be that way." A pouty tone entered his voice. "Or you can be a team player."

"I'll never play your game."

He smiled and shrugged, running his tongue over his teeth again. "Tabitha," he said, and pretended to gag. "What an ugly name. Did you ever consider changing it? I'm wondering, since you cannot tell a lie right now."

"I love my name."

"Huh." He appeared to be desperately disappointed in her. "Okay, then. Anyway, as I was saying. Choosing *not* to play the game is playing the game. So, you're still playing."

"I hate you." Her teeth were clenched again, the hatred so thick in her chest she could barely draw in a breath.

"Oh, there's where we agree. I hate me too. That's why I do this. To feel alive."

She blinked, tilting her chin up slightly, imagining what her daddy would do once she got free. "My father is going to find you and make you wish you'd never been born."

"It's so cute that you truly believe that. It's inspiring, really. But your noble spirit is tiresome. I'm ready to play."

He took his place beside Mabel, who was shaking so forcefully her teeth chattered.

A hysterical laugh bubbled up from Tabitha's chest. She slammed her head back, connecting with the wall hard enough to clack her teeth together. The laughter spilled out anyway.

He waited until she was quiet again before demanding her to, "Say the words."

"Never!" Tabitha snarled the refusal through clenched teeth.

"This won't end until you do."

"I won't do it." She tried to look away. Her eyes wouldn't cooperate.

"That's a lovely side effect," he cooed just before slamming the knife down on Mabel's wrist, severing her hand. With a sickening *plop*, the appendage landed in the puddle of blood. Her screams filled the claustrophobic space.

"No," Tabitha whimpered, the only sound her tight throat would make.

"You really shouldn't torture her like that." He tsked. "She deserves so much better, don't you think? She colored her hair and changed her clothes to look like you, and you appreciate none of her efforts."

"*You* colored her hair."

"Details." He waved the knife nonchalantly then held the blade poised over the middle of the same arm. "Say it."

Tabitha shook her head.

The knife plunged.

Mabel screamed, more alert than Tabitha'd ever seen her.

"H-how…?" What Tabitha wanted to ask but couldn't was…shouldn't Mabel be passed out by now? How could she still be awake with so much pain?

The psychopath seemed to understand because he smiled.

"She'll stay awake and alert for everything. Wouldn't want her to miss the grand finale."

"Ta-ta-tabita," Mabel cried, each syllable ending on a sob. "Plea…"

Tears cascaded down Tabitha's face as she felt the words building in her belly. "Mabel, I can't. Please don't ask me to."

He moved the knife over to Mabel's other wrist.

The horrified woman's eyes were locked on Tabitha's. Her mouth worked, and she finally managed to form a word that made sense. "Love me," she pleaded, her request stronger now. "Please."

Tabitha knew what she was asking. The knife glinted, distorted by her tears.

"I love you too," Tabitha said on a strangled sob, her chest squeezing so hard it was difficult to breathe let alone speak. "Please forgive me."

The man's smile was villainous, his glee rabid. "Is she going to say it, sweet Mabel? Is she going to say it and save you from this horror?"

Tabitha took a breath, then another. Her heart was pounding, but she couldn't force herself to speak the words that would release her friend from this misery. She needed to close her eyes. She didn't want to see Mabel's face when she said it. She couldn't live with that memory. But her eyes wouldn't close, no matter how hard she tried.

With Tabitha's heartbeat and breathing so loud they seemed to bounce around the room, she finally choked out the words he wanted to hear. "Die. Bitch. Die."

Another obscene giggle, and his arm swung wide.

Desperate, Tabitha squeezed her eyes shut, and this time, the lids closed together.

Mabel's screams went silent.

Over the pounding of her heart, the only sound she could hear was a heavy, wet thud.

Tabitha's eyeballs rolled back in her head as she realized what he'd done.

"Do you want to see her?" he taunted. "It's a trip. Her neck is bleeding. I bet her heart is *still* beating. I wonder if she can see you from down there on the floor."

"I did it." She turned as far to the side as her bindings would allow, squeezing her eyelids tight so she wouldn't be tempted to look. Why did she want to look? "What more do you want from me?"

"Oh Tabitha of the ugliest name in the world, we aren't quite done."

"W-why," the word hiccupped from her throat, "are you doing this?"

"So I could record it. Share it. Do you know what a snuff film is?"

"No." She sniffled, focusing on his words rather than the horror that would be right before her eyes should she open them.

"It's the final moments of someone's life captured for all eternity. So beautiful. So powerful. This day will be replayed millions of times. You'll be famous."

"Just end this, please." The plea in Tabitha's voice was pitiful as it bounced off the walls and back to her.

"I will, but not before you do one more thing."

A glimmer of hope streaked through her even as she wondered how she would ever be brave enough to tell Mabel's parents what she'd done. "What?"

"You see, Mabel wasn't the star of this film."

Her heart thrummed faster at the hint of excitement in his voice. "I-I d-don't understand." Her eyes flew open, and she forced them to focus on him, not the mutilated body or the round object that shouldn't be lying on the floor.

"I don't expect you to. You're so sweet and innocent. I knew right away that you were the better person. You did all the work. You made all the sacrifices." He wiped the blood from the knife with an old rag. "That's why you're sitting in this chair and not the other one, with your head at your feet. Mabel coasted by on your hard work, so it was only fitting that she would end her worthless life that way."

Anger fired to life. "Don't talk about her like that."

"Why not?" He giggled again. "You called her a bitch. Do you suddenly care about her?"

"You made me call her that." It was so stupid to argue with him, but she couldn't hold the words in.

"I didn't have a gun to your head." He was enjoying their exchange, the glint in his eyes brighter.

"I'll kill you if I get the chance."

"That's what I love about you. I'm going to be sad to let you go, but I make more money this way." His demeanor was so calm, his voice so matter-of-fact. As if he hadn't just murdered Mabel right in front of her. As if he hadn't fooled them both.

"It's my fault Mabel is dead," she said, her emotions turning from anger to misery in an instant. "I deserve to die."

"What would you do to have one more chance?" He took a half step closer, his eagerness palpable.

"I'd do anything you want," she answered automatically, appalled by how easily the words tumbled from her mouth.

"I can see that. You're not the person you thought you were. If you were stronger, my concoction wouldn't work on you."

"That's not true." How could any of this be true?

He seemed pleased. "Isn't it?"

Desperation took misery's place. "Please, let me go. I won't tell anyone what happened."

"Of course you wouldn't." He rolled his eyes, the gesture taking many more seconds longer than necessary. "What would you tell them? That you demanded I kill Mabel? There is no version of this story that looks good for you."

"I'll do anything." If her hair wasn't taped to prevent her head from falling forward, Tabitha would've hung her head in the deepest shame. But her head would only go back, and her skull already felt like mush. She pictured it pounded to a pulp after she tried to put herself out of her misery, and another laugh burst from her lips.

"Just one more thing, then you're free, Tabitha." He spat on the floor. "Maybe you should pick another name."

"You can call me whatever you want." Her stomach turned at the wheedling in her tone, but her survival instinct was too strong to shut off. She wanted to live, even if she would never be okay again.

"That's cute, but I'll pass. I don't think you'll want to do what I need you to."

"Anything." And she would, but she wished he didn't know that.

"You choose how the next one dies."

"Please…" The sound was an anguished moan. "Please, I can't do it again."

"You will."

The line suspended from the ceiling jerked and fluid poured down and into her veins. This time, the sensation it caused felt weird, like she was floating outside herself, but every thought was excruciating. Every thought caused her head to rip with real, physical pain.

"If you do what I ask, this won't hurt."

"Whatever you want." To her shock, the pain was gone in an instant, and she immediately regretted folding to it.

"Perfect. Now, it's time for you to choose how the next one dies. So, what do you prefer? Quick and painless, or long and drawn out? I prefer drawn out, if you need a suggestion."

"Quick. Painless." Tabitha's voice wasn't her own, her tone indifferent.

"Do you want to know whose death you'll be choosing this time?"

"Sure," she said in a detached voice. As if she were unbothered by the horror of the scene in front of her.

"All you have to do is say the words one last time, and you'll know."

Tabitha's mouth was so dry, her tongue stuck to the back of her teeth. She swallowed, not in fear, but to wet it so she could speak. What was wrong with her? Oh, the drugs.

She laughed, then looked him right in the eye and said it again, this time with a giggle that sounded so much like his. "Die. Bitch. Die."

The silver glint of the knife as it sliced the air in front of her was the last thing she ever saw.

2

"Ellie!" Jacob shouted as two onlookers leaned so far over the crime scene barricade that it collapsed to the ground. He cursed under his breath. It had already been a busy morning.

A half-dozen gawkers moved closer to the house on the corner.

Ellie scowled at the realization that she'd let her concentration shift from crowd control to what the detectives were doing. "Sorry!" Grimacing as she shifted to help with the barricade, early morning sun reflected off her Charleston Police Department badge, obscuring part of her name.

He couldn't help but admire her uniform's ironing job—so crisp, the telltale perfection an obvious sign of a higher quality cleaner than he could afford. He turned his uniforms in for the cleaning service once a week like everyone else, exchanging them for another week's worth. But Ellie lived differently than most. She always had.

"That's the third time you've turned to watch them, Kline," he chided, as he had many times during the six months they'd been partners. "We're on crowd control. You're not a detective."

She rolled her moss-green eyes, her fiery red French braid wrapped into a bun sparking in the sunlight as she jutted out her chin. She was tall and lean, but her brilliant red hair and bright green eyes only accentuated her soft features. "Not yet, but I want to be. It's so much more interesting than standing here." She scoffed then gestured at the crowd. "One of us could handle watching a few people."

"There are way more than a few people, but that's not the point. Sergeant Danver is already on your case, which means he's also on my case. Keep pissing him off, and you'll never make detective."

Her eyes lit for a second, glinting brighter than the sea at Folly Beach on a sunny day. Just as quickly, Ellie covered her reaction, pulling at the starched collar close to her neck with a tight grimace. "It's hot today. I think I'm getting a sunburn."

"You should've worn sunscreen."

She wrinkled her nose. The expression drew his attention to the light smattering of freckles across the bridge. "I'll pass. Don't want to be so greasy I can't hold on to handcuffs."

"You'll change your tune when you can't move, you're so crispy."

"I get crispy every year." She lifted one shoulder and let it drop, as if her three years on the force was forever. "It's October, almost fall. It shouldn't be so hot."

"Suit yourself. But don't think I'm going to freeze in the car with the air-conditioning just because you care more about looking pretty than common sense."

"Made you say 'freeze.'"

He rolled his eyes, shaking his head. His partner was something else, and yet she still surprised him every day. The world underestimated her, but Officer Jacob Garcia knew better.

Movement behind the barrier once again drew her gaze away from the detectives squatting near the covered bodies. She reached a hand out to a man who had moved forward, all business. "Sir, I'm going to have to ask you to take a step back."

The man scowled at her, his face reddening almost instantly. "I ain't crossed the line, *ma'am*." The last word dripped so much disdain from his lips, Jacob could almost see the ugliness hanging in the steamy air.

"You're touching police property," Ellie said, her voice steady, but Jacob caught the way she carefully weighed the man. She was ready if he escalated the situation, and he knew her well enough to know she was hoping the man would take a swipe at her. "I'll ask you one last time, hands off the barricade and take three large steps back."

"You said one," the man countered.

"Now, it's three." Jacob stepped closer, hand going to hover over his taser.

The man glared at Ellie, then at Jacob before he took a step back. "Good thing they don't send you on patrol without a man to back you up."

"Someone's got to rescue you from your stupidity before you get hurt," Jacob countered without missing a beat. He let a slow, threatening smile spread across his face. "Walk away, sir. She's not going to warn you again."

The man blew out an angry breath and spun on his heel, stomping away and grumbling under his breath. He wasn't the first citizen who made patrolling the streets of Charleston, South Carolina a pain. Each year there were more and more like him—entitled assholes who behaved like spoiled children—smarter than the police in their own estimation. Yet they called emergency services every time a child dared set up a lemonade stand without a permit. Jacob was happy this man had gotten exactly what he deserved.

But as soon as the angry man cleared the crowd, someone else took his place. The new spectator stayed back three feet, and when Ellie looked at him, he nodded slowly, eyes crinkled at the corner. He'd heard the exchange and wasn't about to step out of line and risk having his ass handed to him by a woman in front of all these people.

Smart man, Jacob mused.

Ellie nodded back, but she didn't crack a smile. During her time as his partner, she'd developed the fierce, no-nonsense expression she now wore. It was one of the things that kept people from walking all over her. Not that she deserved it. Even with the uniform and the way she carried herself, she still held an aura that screamed Charleston elite.

More than once since he'd been assigned to partner with her, a perp had found out the hard way that Eleanor Kline was not a cop you wanted to underestimate. She was fast, proficient in more than one style of hand-to-hand combat, and she had a sharp tongue that could put a man in his place faster than he could say *yes, ma'am.*

There was movement behind them, and Jacob turned to see the crime techs carrying out their equipment. The coroner was thankfully gone, the two murder victims having been photographed, processed, and wheeled out before the crowd had gathered. If nothing else, the victims' privacy had been protected an iota.

"They're about done." Ellie nodded at the onlookers, who were slowly moving away and on with their lives.

"There's the hazmat team," Jacob noted. They stepped forward in sync, directing the crowd to move out of the way to let the plain white van through.

The crowd scattered, then dispersed.

Ellie snorted and adjusted the heavy gunbelt at her waist. "Guess they don't want to see the cleanup."

"No one ever does."

A man in white coveralls stepped out of the passenger side with a clipboard. "Who do I give this to?"

Jacob motioned to Ellie, whose face lit up for the first time since they'd arrived. But the man was already sizing up the scene and didn't notice Ellie's enthusiasm, or the careful way she chose her path through the numbered yellow crime scene markers that were scattered in the alley behind the house.

The lead detective took a few steps to meet her, signed the authorization sheet, then handed it off as he chatted with Ellie.

Jacob couldn't hear what they were saying, but Ellie's entire demeanor had changed. She was smiling, her hands moving like they did when a subject excited her. It was only a matter of time before he lost his favorite partner to the Homicide Division. She was an excellent officer, and the citizens of Charleston loved her. Especially the children they tried hard to make friends with. But her heart was in detective work, and he knew this was only a step on her way to the top.

If she can keep her nose clean, he amended with an inward sigh. The passion that had her lighting up as she talked shop with the detective got her in trouble with Sergeant Danver on a regular basis. Danver was jockeying for retirement, and every wrong move was scrutinized.

Jacob was getting antsy when Ellie finally returned the clipboard to the crime scene cleanup crew, authorizing them to strip the alley and brick wall of all evidence of the heinous crime committed just a few hours before.

The two men unloaded their equipment, leaving the crime scene tape up to deter any looky-loos who might show up before they were done.

"You ready?" she asked Jacob, grinning wide when he tapped his watch. "What? You knew what you were doing when you sent me in there. If you were in a hurry, you should've done it yourself."

"And deprive you of the chance to rub elbows with your future colleagues? Not a chance. You get any inside information?"

"Not much. There's a witness with a solid lead, and a person of interest."

"I wouldn't want to be in their shoes."

"Tell me about it. That's more than they usually have at this point." They got into the cruiser, and Ellie cranked the air up all the way. "I don't know how you're not burning up," she muttered as she buckled up.

He put the car in gear. "Because I'm cool like that."

"Whatever." On the computer, Ellie logged information from the crime scene and updated their status from "on a call" to "on patrol." When he glanced in her direction, she was watching him. "I wish my family was as supportive as you are."

"They've been trying to get you to quit the force again? They'll come around. Eventually."

She pushed a loose lock of hair behind her ear. "My mom is still appalled that I chose police work instead of a nice office job at a charity."

"But Wesley has your back, right?"

"My brother says whatever ruffles Mom's feathers the most." She scanned the sidewalks and housefronts as Jacob turned at the intersection, weaving through the streets at a leisurely pace. "He's one of my biggest supporters besides you and Nick."

Jacob scowled. "Are you sure Nick isn't just taking your side because he wants an in with you? You're the only female heir to the Kline fortune."

Her laughter filled the squad car. "Not a chance. I've known him all my life. He doesn't let his feelings get in the way of being my best friend. Besides, his family has loads more than we do."

"That's why your mother still adores him, I gather?"

She shrugged. "One of the reasons."

A group of kids waved from the sidewalk where they were shooting hoops around a portable basket. When the ball bounced into the road in front of the car, Jacob stopped and Ellie got out. She scooped the ball up and dribbled, rushing and ducking before leaping up and sinking it with effortless grace.

Jacob took a headcount and grabbed enough sticker badges for all the kids, which he stuffed in his shirt pocket before joining the melee.

They played a few rounds, high-fiving the jubilant kids when they were done. Jacob was putting the last Junior Police badge on the littlest boy's shirt when a call came over the radio.

The kids went silent, listening to the detached voice coming from the cruiser's open window. "Code ten…"

Shit.

Jacob didn't need to hear anything else. There had been a murder, but as he ran to the driver's door, he made out that the murder suspect was fleeing in a vehicle. They were armed and considered dangerous.

No surprise there.

Before Jacob could get to the car, Ellie was in the passenger seat with the radio in her hand. Her eyes wide and bright with excitement. "Adam twelve responding," she said and gave their location as Jacob backed into the nearest driveway and waved out the window to the kids as he flipped on the sirens and hurried toward South Carolina Highway 7.

"Suspect is described as five-foot-ten, black hair and brown eyes, two hundred pounds driving an older model, brown four-door." The dispatcher rattled off the license plate number and last known location, which was less than a block away.

Jacob cruised the street, keeping a sharp eye on traffic.

Ellie pointed at something up ahead. "Right there, just passing the Ashley Landing Mall."

Jacob slammed the accelerator down, weaving in and out of the late morning traffic. Thankfully, it was the end of rush hour, and he sped past a frazzled-looking woman pulling off to the side of the road. "How far away is backup?"

Ellie relayed the question to dispatch, and when the answer came back, Jacob groaned.

Ellie said what he'd already gathered. "It's just us."

"We need to keep him in sight and wait for backup." Jacob eased his foot off the accelerator a fraction.

"If he gets across the river, we're going to lose him."

"Ellie, we don't have many options here." The long bridge was already in view in the distance.

"You can pit him."

He took his eyes off the road for a second to stare at her. "On the bridge? Are you crazy?"

"We're running out of options. SC-7 dumps right into the cloverleaf at I-26. If he gets there, he could get away. I bet I-26 is still packed with commuters."

They flew past the Elks Lodge. Jacob was only three car lengths behind the older sedan, and with every passing second, he was gaining. The way in front of them was nearly clear, the bridge almost deserted.

"Fine," he muttered, then glanced at her. "Hold on."

His heart was racing, pounding in his ears, but he focused, readying himself for what was coming. The brown sedan was still racing down the highway, but its engine wasn't made for high-speed chases. The police cruiser was.

Next to him, Ellie braced herself when they got close, holding her breath, eyes wide.

Jacob pulled the nose of the cruiser even with the suspect's back panel, lining up the squad car's front tires with the sedan's rear ones.

Yanking the wheel slightly, he guided the cruiser into contact with the sedan, then accelerated, sending the fleeing car sideways.

Jacob caught a glimpse of the man's face as he fought to control the car, careening across the bridge and skidding backward. The driver's door dragged along the cement wall. Jacob turned his car into the sedan, initiating contact between the passenger side of both front bumpers as the fleeing car slowed.

The suspect shouted profanity through the passenger's window, revving his engine and trying to force the car forward and the cruiser out of the way. His car's rear was pinned against the wall at an angle, and he was trapped inside by the crumpled driver's door.

"Gun!" Ellie shouted as she ducked.

Bullets zinged off the front of the cruiser.

Ellie released her seatbelt just as the sound of breaking glass filled the air.

"Stay in the car," Jacob ordered, his ears ringing.

"He's out of bullets, and he's climbing out the window." She wrapped her fingers around the release for the door.

"We need to wait for backup."

"There's no way I'm letting this guy get away." Ellie flung open her door, and she was gone.

"Ellie, wait." He put it in park, but by the time he yanked on his door handle, the perp was already out of the car, running down the bridge. Ellie was on his heels.

Jacob's heart caught when the man turned and pointed the gun at Ellie, his own hand going to his police-issued gun as he ran. She was in his line of fire.

The bastard with the gun pulled the trigger.

"Shit!" Jacob kicked it up a notch.

But the perp's gun didn't fire. She'd been right; he was out of bullets and hadn't had the chance to reload.

With a disgusted look on his face, sweat shining on his brow, the dark-haired criminal launched the gun at Ellie and took off, the waistband of his oversized Dickies gathered in one hand to keep them from falling. His open plaid work shirt caught the wind as he ran. Even with his billowing garments slowing him down, he made it almost halfway across the bridge over the Ashley River, Ellie still behind him.

Unless Ellie managed to tackle the man before he got off the bridge and disappeared beneath the highway, he could get lost in the neighborhood, and if so, likely be gone for good. A door-to-door search would take too long to organize, and with instant car services available at the touch of a finger, the man could be halfway to the state line while they were still chasing their tails.

A chopper overhead caught Jacob's attention.

But it was only the news helicopter that hovered over the freeways during rush hour—probably filming to air the story on tonight's news.

With no help from above, he and Ellie were on their own.

3

Ellie's footfalls were hollow on the smooth concrete of the bridge. She could hear Jacob running behind her, but she was focused, gaze locked on the fleeing man.

It would be pointless to waste her breath commanding him to stop, but it was procedure, so she wasted some breath screaming at him. He'd already tossed his gun at her, and she hadn't seen an additional weapon. Drawing her weapon on an unarmed man wasn't an option, and she was out of range for the Taser.

They were running north in the northbound lane, which was empty since traffic was stopped behind their cars. A trickle of southbound traffic crept by with drivers doing double takes and gawking at them as they cruised by—one giving her a wolf whistle. There was nothing more than a small curb and flexible delineator posts to mark the division of the highway, and luckily, the man was smart enough not to cross into oncoming traffic. But Ellie knew that could change in an instant. Men fleeing murder charges rarely made intelligent decisions.

She pushed her legs to pump harder, so fixated on the

pursuit that the whop-whop of the news chopper barely registered.

The suspect heard it and stumbled as he turned to look overhead.

Her eyes met angry brown ones, and he let out another string of curse words before he made a sharp right, straight for the railing.

"You've gotta be kidding me," she whispered, her hands already on the buckle to release her gun belt.

"Wait!" Jacob's warning reached her over the whirring blades of the chopper and squealing tires of the onlookers who were stopping to gape, but it was too late.

The runner's hands were on the railing, then he was over the side. The splash was loud when he hit the water and frantically swam north toward the shore.

"Don't do it!" Jacob called out as she kicked off her shoes and dropped her gun belt on top of them. He was only a few yards back, face red with effort, brown eyes more worried than she'd ever seen them.

She lifted her hands in the air, palms up, grabbed the railing and launched herself over the side before she could change her mind.

His "damn it, Ellie," was whipped away as wind rushed past her ears. Then her stocking feet hit the cool water, which opened to swallow her whole. The instant her head was beneath the surface, the water slammed back together, slapping her so hard her head jerked to the side. There was nothing but the muted sound of air bubbles as she kicked and flailed her arms to slow her descent.

She pushed past the surface, taking in a lung full of precious oxygen, ears popping from the sudden pressure, then release. It took less than a second to catch sight of her target, closer than she'd expected him to be.

Ellie's practiced strokes cut through the current, carrying

her across the surface quickly. She caught up to him about halfway to the shore, but before she could grab his collar, he shrieked and started sputtering. When he turned around and saw her, rather than trying to get away, he grabbed at her shoulders. He was hysterical, screaming the same syllable over and over.

Ellie went under when he managed to grab on to her arm, pressing his weight into hers. He dunked her again as he tried to crawl into her arms, eyes wide, the whites as red as if he'd been crying.

Kicking to the surface, she freed herself, coughing up the water she'd swallowed, clearing her lungs as she tried to see what he was screaming about.

His voice rising nearly two octaves higher than before, it took Ellie a beat to realize that he was screaming "croc!" and pointing at an object in the water. He grabbed her again, taking her under once more, and pulling her hair in the process.

When they resurfaced, she punched him hard in the jaw, knocking him back and quieting him long enough to get a word in.

"Calm down, or we're both going to drown," she ordered, turning him until she was facing his back. She grabbed his collar in one hand and started kicking toward shore. "If you fight me again, I'll have to let that gator get you." She took in a few deep breaths, the exertion making it hard to speak. "Relax, let your body float, and we'll get to shore just fine."

He was crying now, huge wracking sobs that echoed off the underside of the bridge. Was there really a croc nearby? She scanned the water until she spotted the reptile that had set the man off. Floating lazily near the surface and watching them with interest was…a large river turtle.

If Ellie had possessed enough air for the effort, she would have laughed.

"Please don't let me get eaten," the man blubbered, kicking and trying to roll back onto his stomach.

"Stop, or you will," she said without a twinge of guilt for lying. They were almost to the edge of the marshy shore. She needed him to cooperate. "It's not interested in you right now. But if you keep flailing around, you'll attract his attention again. He'll eat us both."

The man's breaths came faster, and his body went stiff as a board. He began praying in a low voice, pleading with a higher power to keep him from becoming gator bait.

Ellie was tempted to suggest he confess to the murders, but without Mirandizing him, anything he said would be thrown out in court.

Jacob was running along the bridge, his eyes on them, her shoes and gun belt tucked under his arm. When he was even with the shore, he lowered himself over the edge and dropped to his feet. Dumping her belongings in a pile, he waded out to help her.

Once the suspect's soggy shoes met with the riverbank, Jacob hauled the man onto his feet and cuffed him, then offered a hand to Ellie.

She took it, both exhaustion and her wet clothes dragging her down as the earth sank beneath her feet with every step. Once on shore, she picked her way over the wetland, testing the ground before each step.

"What is he going on about?" Jacob growled, half dragging, half carrying the weeping man toward the bridge.

A pair of cruisers screeched to a stop, and three officers jumped out and scrambled over the railing.

"Gator," Ellie said, raising both arms over her head to increase her lung capacity.

Jacob glanced back out at the water, concern in his expression. "Where?"

The man moaned. "It was right there. I think I crapped myself. Oh man, where are my pants?"

Ellie and Jacob looked down at the man's naked legs in unison, and Ellie choked on the laugh that bubbled up. A quick look back revealed his lost pants floating in the water near the same large turtle that was still watching them, too interested in what was going on to hide beneath the surface.

"If you cared about people seeing your boxers, you wouldn't wear pants that don't stay up." Ellie tried to keep a straight face and failed.

"Don't kick a man when he's down, okay?" the man shot back. "I almost died today."

"Yeah, that turtle looked really hungry," Ellie teased.

The man's face went blank before his brows drew together, and he looked out over the river, shaking his head vehemently. "No. I saw it. It was a gator."

The other officers had formed a chain and handed the suspect off to the next until he was back on the bridge. He was still ranting about the gator, jaw quivering as he was loaded into the back of a squad car.

Ellie swung onto the bridge and over the railing, wet socks squishing on the roadway.

"You're shivering," Jacob said when he handed her gun belt and shoes to her.

"I'm fine. The water was great, it's just the wet clothes."

He eyed the circling chopper. "I guess there's no use trying to play this one down for Danver."

Ellie sighed. "My mom is going to be thrilled. I'm sure it's live all over Charleston."

"There's plenty of cell phone video too."

She blinked, noticing the crowd that had parked on the bridge and gathered nearby. Every one of them held a cell phone trained on her and Jacob or the suspect, mouths open in awe as they captured every minute.

"Danver is going to kill you."

"Better than getting eaten by a gator." She laughed, shrugging, her wet shirt sticking to her back.

Jacob put his arm around her and led her to the back of an ambulance parked near the end of the bridge. She sat down on the floor of the ambulance, perching on the edge with her legs dangling, and the paramedic wrapped a hot blanket around her shoulders. She shivered as the heat sank into her muscles, and answered each of his questions as honestly as she could while Jacob tried to block the onlookers' view.

Her partner's uniform pants had wicked water all the way up above his knees, and the marsh had claimed one of his shoes. But even covered with mud, which had spattered up his arms when he jumped into the sinking mud to help her, he still looked completely in his element. His brown hair was cut so short the wind whipping around them left it undisturbed. His deep brown eyes narrowed, taking every detail in and logging it all.

Ten years her senior, he was everything she hoped to be at thirty-seven. Cool, collected, and completely comfortable with who he was, Jacob Garcia was the fourth partner she'd had, and when she moved on to detective, the only one she was going to miss. She smiled and squinted up at the chopper that still hovered over the bridge. If she didn't make detective after this—

The paramedic pulled the blood pressure cuff off her arm, the Velcro making a sharp ripping sound. "You're good to go, if you're sure nothing hurts."

She shook her head.

"You'll probably feel fine tonight, but I would take some ibuprofen and soak in a hot bath before bed. Under the best circumstances, hitting the water from the distance you did is jarring. The day after is usually the worst. Kind of like being in a car accident."

"I'm fine." She stood, gritting her teeth when she took the first step, and her wet foot hit concrete.

She handed the blanket back to the paramedic and immediately wished she hadn't. With the wind on the bridge and soaked head to toe, she was freezing immediately.

"Get into something dry, and take a load off," the paramedic said, ducking into the back of the ambulance.

"What's wrong?" Jacob asked, lowering his head until they were close enough to whisper. "I was starting to think they were going to transport you. Good job, though." He elbowed her playfully. "Most of the evidence has already been collected, and someone else will be transporting him to the station."

"I hate when my feet are wet." She gritted her teeth and searched the bridge for their patrol car.

Jacob wrapped his hand around her arm and guided her in the opposite direction. "Are you serious? All that, and your feet being wet is what's bothering you most?"

"I'm not a big complainer."

"I've noticed. Luckily, our ruthless thug does enough complaining for two people."

Ellie followed his gaze to the back of one of the police cruisers, where the man was still yelling about the gator, his voice only slightly muted by the closed windows.

Shaking her head, Ellie motioned to Jacob's missing shoe. "You have a backup?"

"At home." He shrugged. "Our shift is almost over anyway."

She looked down at her watch, surprised to see that it was well after lunchtime. "How's the car?"

"It's drivable, but they're putting it onto a flatbed with his car." He nodded toward the truck.

She stopped, surveying the damage. "Bullet holes?"

Jacob's face grew serious. "More than a few. They'll tack on attempted murder of two officers."

"He's in a lot of trouble."

"He is, but he's better off in jail."

She tilted her head. "How so?"

"His street cred went out the window when he started shrieking about a gator so loud I'm sure someone got it on film."

"Could you see it? I only saw the turtle, but this is South Carolina."

He shook his head, his lips twitching. "There was no gator. You could see the turtle clearly from up here." He pointed skyward, at the helicopter. "And I'd be willing to bet that it's on the news footage too."

"Oh boy."

"Exactly. He'll be the laughingstock of Charleston." He didn't look like he felt sorry for the guy.

"Hey, it made him easier to drag out of the water."

Jacob's dark eyes zeroed in on hers. "He almost drowned you."

"I was there," she teased, closing her eyes to block out his concern. She shuddered and rubbed her arms. "I need to go home. I have a hair appointment in a little over two hours, and I have to wash the marsh stink from my body before I go."

"Are you going to the gala tonight? Still?" He handed her phone to her.

"Glad it survived your PIT maneuver. That was excellent, by the way. Let me know whenever you need to practice that again." He rolled his eyes, and she winked at him. "And I have to go to the gala. My family is hosting it. If I don't show up, my parents will disown me." She stood on her toes and waved at a cab in the single lane of cars creeping by the scene. "You got this?"

"Sure," he said. "But you realize that Danver is going to be pissed when you don't go in after this?"

"I have Danver under control. I get off in forty-five minutes, and the paramedic said to get out of these clothes and get some rest." She poked him on the arm. "You heard him."

He poked her right back. "You're on your own, Kline. I'm not taking the fall for this."

"You don't have to." She smiled as she stepped toward the cab. "I'm leaving against your advice. I'm sure they have this on camera too."

He sighed and shook his head, but his lips were trying not to curl up at the edges. She knew her partner, and no matter what he claimed, they had each other's backs. She knew she could count on him. Danver would get over it.

She leaned in the passenger side window and smiled at the Hispanic man in the driver's seat.

He smiled back. "You need a ride?"

"Can't patrol with a layer of Ashley River mud weighing me down. State Street and Queen?"

He blinked. "That where you live?"

She slid into the back and flashed him a smile. "Home sweet home."

"How does a cop afford an apartment in the French Quarter?"

She quirked a brow at him. "The same way I can afford to make the trip worth your while."

He grinned at her from the rearview mirror and put the cab in gear. She didn't have to ask him to turn the rear ventilation up on high heat.

"Thank you." She slumped against the back of the seat. "I'll pay you for detailing. I'm sure I smell like a swamp."

"More like marsh mud, but yeah, I'll have to detail the car before I pick up another fare." He rattled off his email address and the cost of the fare. "I'll probably spend that much steaming my seats."

She nodded, sending him a thousand dollars through fast cash on her phone. The amount popped up on his phone's lock screen, which was attached to the dash to double as a GPS. He eyed her in the rearview mirror, and she shrugged. "I thought a generous tip was in order."

"I appreciate it," he said as he pulled the cab to a stop in front of her apartment. He actually looked like he was going to cry, and she was tempted to add another thousand to really make his day.

"Not as much as I appreciate you. Thank you again."

She was out before he could utter another word, rushing up to the side entrance and jogging up the stairs to the third floor. Her socks squished around her toes with each step, but she kept her thoughts on the hot shower she was going to take the second she walked through the door.

Using the keyless entry pad, she typed in the code and opened the door, stepping through and letting it close behind her. She stripped in the entryway, carrying her clothes under her arm, the hardwood floor cold under her bare feet. She tossed her uniform into a dry cleaning bag and hung her Kevlar vest in the laundry room. The dry cleaner could salvage the uniform, but she had a feeling the vest was ruined. "I'll probably have to buy the department another one," she mumbled, turning on the water and stepping under the spray.

Yellow water swirled down the drain, and by the time it ran clear, she'd finally stopped shivering. Her muscles were already starting to ache, but she didn't have time to rest just yet. The stylist expected her in the chair in an hour, and he didn't tolerate lateness. She scrubbed herself clean three times before stepping out of the shower and drying off quickly.

By the time she dragged herself into her bedroom, she was too tired to think. She swallowed four ibuprofen tablets and eyed her bed with longing.

Just a short nap, she promised herself as she snuggled under the heavy duvet and pulled the sheet up around her ears. She would do her own hair and save some time.

She texted the hairdresser and paid him for the appointment, then she rolled over and burrowed into the mattress. Two hours. She had two hours before she had to get up and get dressed. It was more than enough time to recharge and be ready to face her parents.

The news coverage would have people talking, but they wouldn't dare cause a scene at such an important event. *Any exposure is good exposure,* her father would say while ignoring her mother's grumblings. Helen Kline preferred to maintain the family's dignity in the public eye, but Ellie wasn't about to start beating herself up for doing her job. She'd caught a dangerous suspect, and she had no doubt the footage would be just the leverage she needed to get one step closer to Homicide Division.

Today had been an exciting day, and she wasn't going to let anyone ruin it for her. Not Danver, not her own doubts, and especially not her mother.

Ellie had big dreams.

After today, they were closer to becoming a reality.

4

An attendant rushed forward when Ellie's Uber driver pulled up to the curb in front of the massive four-story building on the waterfront of the French Quarter. Her youngest brother, Wesley, was standing outside and immediately waved.

Wesley helped her out of the car, grinning from ear to ear. Bright green eyes the same shade as hers twinkled with mischief, not a single auburn-colored hair out of place. "Too bad Mom and Dad didn't see you pull up in Bubba's Mini Cooper."

"I think his name was Tom, but I'm not sure." She sighed and smoothed the skirt of her deep blue slit dress. She arranged her curls around her shoulders, suddenly hot and regretting not putting her hair up. "All the car services were booked, and I didn't feel like driving."

"Gee, I wonder why."

She laughed. "I know, I know. I've had a rough day."

"I saw."

Cringing, she was thankful she had put something in her

stomach, or she might've dry heaved right there on the sidewalk. "Mom and Dad too?"

"Are you kidding? Everyone has their cell phone out, ready to show them the video. Like the local stations didn't cut to the live feed." He snickered, reminding Ellie of the playful cohort he'd been when they were younger. For an instant, she could almost see him running around the house, chasing her with a frog, and the exhausted expression on their mother's face as she pleaded with them to stop acting like heathens. Her mom had wanted another girl. Instead, she'd been gifted with Wesley.

She groaned. "Was it live on every channel?"

"Every last one. Just you with your name plastered all over the screen." He lowered his voice to a whisper. "Mom is not amused."

Ellie took the elbow he offered, leaning on him for a moment. "Did you see the whole ordeal?" she asked as they made their way up the steps. Her heels pinched her feet, and she wished she'd worn flats, but she'd needed the extra boost to her already tall frame to give her the confidence to get through the night.

"You jumping over the railing like a wild woman? Yeah, I did. Ellie, it was the best thing I've ever witnessed. What was it like? Were you scared? Cause it didn't look like it."

She pursed her lips, trying not to grin. "You better rein that in before we get inside."

"I will, but come on. I'm proud of my little sister."

She tried to elbow him, but he was too close, and she only succeeded in nearly tripping in her gown. "I'm five years older than you."

He gave her a playful shove. "And five inches shorter."

She pushed out her bottom lip, pretending to be hurt. "Haven't I been through enough today?"

Wesley only rolled his eyes. "Please. You enjoyed it. The

look on your face when you put your hands on the railing just before you jumped was pure joy. I've never seen you happier."

Ellie blew out a long breath when they reached the top step. Gilded double doors with artfully carved phoenixes on each swung open wide. The doormen were dressed in matching uniforms that made them look so similar, Ellie wondered aloud if they were twins.

"How much of the Ashley River did you drink?"

"Far too much. That fool almost drowned me."

"I wonder if his new nickname is Michaelangelo." He raised his brows, waiting for her to laugh at his reference to the Teenage Mutant Ninja Turtles. "I bet that's going over well in prison. You could hear him screaming on the video. At first, I thought it was you, but you're not afraid of turtles."

She nudged him with her elbow. "Can we change the subject?"

"Sure, but no one else will."

"What do you mean?"

They stepped into the ballroom, and every head turned her way. The string quartet on the stage in front of the dance floor played on, but Ellie caught a few sour notes. Several dancing couples were frozen in place, their arms still in position, faces registering varying stages of disdain.

"You should bow," Wesley said close to her ear.

"I'm not bowing," she said through gritted teeth as silence settled over the room. She'd been through this song and dance enough times to know that everyone present was waiting for her mother to reel her in.

Please let the floor open up and swallow me whole.

But the marble beneath her feet remained firm. Her heart rate quickened, and the urge to run had built to a fever pitch when the first slow clap began. Ellie searched the crowd, but before her eyes settled on the familiar face and sea blue eyes, she knew who it was.

"Leave it to Nick to save the day," Wesley muttered as the attendees began to applaud.

Bewildered expressions spread into welcoming smiles, and strangers called out their congratulations for a job well done as she and Wes strolled through the gathering.

Ellie smiled, hoping she didn't look like the gator of her suspect's imagination. "Where are Mom and Dad? I don't want to dread this encounter all night."

"Looks like they found us."

Ellie followed his gaze. Sure enough, their parents were making their way through the crowd toward them, which parted to let them pass. Daniel Kline's full head of silver hair was perfectly styled, and he carried a hand-carved cane, which only added to the air of dignity that seemed to cling to the tall man.

Helen Kline looked stunning in a simple chocolate-brown sheath that matched the color of her eyes and accentuated the bright red hair Ellie had inherited from her. She was pale, and beneath a layer of professionally applied makeup, Ellie could see she was exhausted.

"Oh boy," Ellie groaned under her breath.

"Eleanor, darling." Her mother kissed Ellie on both cheeks, then guided her away from the dance floor to one of the tables set up near the wall. "We should sit," Helen insisted. She gave Daniel a pointed look, and he sighed before lowering himself into a chair and settling in.

"I'd rather stand." Ellie tried not to feel like a teenager who had been caught doing something naughty, but her mother always made her feel that way, no matter what she had done.

"Oh my. I suppose we'll have to stand. I didn't notice your dress was so daring. With the slits nearly reaching your hips,

I guess there's really no ladylike way to sit." Helen's sniff said more than a million words could.

The jab was intentional. Ellie knew her mother wanted to have a sit-down, even in full view of the public she was so eager to impress. Helen Kline never caused a scene, and she rarely raised her voice. But Ellie already knew what was coming. People out of earshot would never guess when Helen tore down Ellie's "hobby" in favor of something more fitting for a woman of Ellie's "station in life." The words were always spoken with kindness, but Ellie wasn't in the mood for the underlying barbs.

Standing, Ellie towered over her petite mother. It didn't level the field, but it was enough for Ellie not to feel like she was a young girl again.

Before Ellie could defend her choice of dress, her two oldest brothers showed up, taking their place behind Daniel Kline and making their position clear. Unlike Helen, they were scowling, perturbed that, once again, their little sister had run amok.

Ellie gave each of them a megawatt smile that bared all her teeth, and Wesley did nothing to stifle his laughter.

Daniel Jr. stiffened, and Blake shook his head in disapproval. The two weren't twins, but they could pass for it, both dark-haired and dark-eyed.

Their mother sighed, looking to her husband for help, then back at Ellie. "I'm sure you're aware we saw the news."

"It seems like everyone did. I saved the video to my desktop."

Helen scowled delicately for an instant, then her face smoothed out again. Controlled, kind, and proper. "What happened is nothing to boast about. You could have been killed."

"Those Carolina turtles will get you," Wesley interjected.

Helen didn't even glance his way. She'd had plenty of

practice ignoring his antics over the past twenty-two years, but that never stopped Wesley from trying. "I talked to Violet about a position at the Kline House. The residents aren't criminals, but perhaps you can throw your energy into helping young families recovering from a loss. It will give that civil servant's heart of yours something to focus on, and you can make a difference in a safer manner."

A more *dignified* manner was what her mother didn't say.

"Kline House is your thing. I'm fine where I am." Ellie bit on the inside of her lip. She'd help out at the house when she was a kid and insisted on working there in the summers as a teen. But it broke her heart to see the families come in, having lost their home to a fire or worse. Kline House helped them get on their feet and find a new home. She loved what it stood for, but working there was too constrictive for her. "I'm not working for Kline House. I want to make a real difference."

"We do make a difference. So many of our families have left Kline House in much better circumstances than when they moved in. You can make a difference in so many lives, and there are children. Darling, I know how you love children, and—"

"Mother, please."

"I'm sorry, honey." Her mother clutched her neck in the perfect Southern belle pose. "Seeing you fall off that bridge terrified me to no end."

"I jumped."

Her mother sucked in a sharp breath. "Fell or jumped, the outcome was the same."

"Not really," Wesley said.

"Quiet," their father hissed, then coughed and wiped his face with a handkerchief, even as his green eyes shone with pride. "Wesley, your sister doesn't need your help expressing herself. Your mother and I have raised her well. She can handle herself."

Ellie smiled warmly at her father, then turned her attention back to Helen. "Mom, I jumped, and I would do it again. I protect and serve, and it was the only way to bring in a dangerous suspect."

Helen's eyes sparkled with outrage. "Eleanor, this is not who we are."

"It's not who *you* are. This job is what I've dreamed of for as long as I can remember." *Not exactly,* she amended silently, but it was close enough for now. "I'm not meant to sit on a phone all day, collecting donations from people who have more money than God. I need to be in the midst of it, and being a police officer is what makes me happy." She reached out and touched Helen's hand. Helen sighed and squeezed Ellie's fingers in a gesture of affection. "Mom, I know you want what's best for me. I just need you to understand that I'm doing it."

"I know, sweetheart. I just worry."

"Don't worry about me. I'll be fine."

Nick stepped into her line of sight, a smile on his face and two glasses of champagne in one hand. Handsome in his tuxedo, his light brown hair perfectly groomed, his piercing blue eyes ran over her dress with a look of approval.

Helen followed Ellie's gaze and smiled. "Oh, there's Nick. I was wondering when he'd find you." She blew out a soft breath. "Eleanor, dear, please do consider what we've talked about. There's no reason for you to work unless you want to, but at least think about something a bit less dangerous."

"Everything will be fine, Mom."

Helen nodded, but when Ellie eyed her father, he was still pale. "Is Dad all right?"

Helen pressed her lips together, stepping closer. "His heart is weaker. He'll need another surgery soon." She hugged Ellie and held her tight, whispering so only she could hear. "Darling, please think about Kline House. Your father isn't doing well, and you know how he worries about you."

Ellie knew her mother was using her father's condition to guilt her, and for a moment, she was overwhelmed by the emotion. But she forced a smile. "Daddy will be all right. He always is."

"This time, I'm not so sure." Helen released Ellie and motioned to Nick. "You two have a lot to chat about. Maybe Nick can talk some sense into you."

"It's a party, Mom. Let's have a little fun."

"Think about what I said." She turned toward her eldest sons.

"I will," Ellie lied.

Ellie took Nick's arm and one of the glasses. She sipped as they strolled across the room, and when the crowd was between her and her parents, she tossed back the contents.

"Need another?" He flashed perfect white teeth at her. "Sorry I took so long to rescue you. Tessa waylaid me."

Ellie wrinkled her nose and grabbed a glass of wine as a waiter passed with a tray. "I'm not sure who had it worse."

"Definitely you. Did your mother lay a guilt trip on you?"

She sipped from the glass, the sour, thick wine not going down as easy as the sweet champagne. "The biggest."

"Sorry."

She shook her head, thankful the alcohol was already making her feel lighter. "I don't get it. I thought they'd be relieved to see I was okay, but Mom seemed freaked out."

"Helen Kline freaked out?" Nick scoffed playfully.

"You know what I mean."

"I'd ask if you would be in her place, but we both know the answer." He set the empty glasses on a table and gathered her into his arms. "I know you've probably heard this all day, but I'm proud of you." He kissed her lightly on the lips, then pressed his forehead against hers for a moment, sighing. "When you went over that railing, you were on fire. I knew that man wasn't getting away. If he was smart, he would've seen it too."

"Thank you. I can't tell you how much it means to hear you say those words."

He moved her toward the edge of the dance floor and swayed her back and forth to the soft music. "Wesley was obviously enjoying the talk."

"Wesley enjoys anything that gets our parents riled up. If Dan and Blake lose their cool, too, even better."

"Wesley was always your smartest brother."

Ellie giggled, thoroughly enjoying herself now that she had shed the nerves. "I'm glad you're here. I've missed you."

He spun her gently and dipped her, careful not to make the movement too deep. "You want to get some air?"

"Yeah, that sounds good."

He spun her one more time, and as the song ended, he took her hand and led her toward the balconies. Outside, she inhaled the fresh, humid air steeped in the fragrance of Confederate Roses that were planted in the expansive flowerbeds. She took in the sweeping view of the Cooper River and squinted into the distance to see if she could spot Fort Sum ter.

Leaning against the stone railing, she closed her eyes and sighed when Nick's arm came around her. His comfortable warmth drew her in, and she snuggled against him as he held her tight to his side. "I wish my parents could see things the way I do."

"Don't we all."

"Yeah, but your parents don't bat an eye when you spend all day out at a construction site. Even if you are on the developmental end of real estate and don't actually build the houses yourself, if you pitched in, they wouldn't balk." She lifted a hand to fiddle with the curls she'd left cascading down her back. "If I picked up a hammer, even that would be too much for a 'cultured lady' in my mom's eyes. She would swoon if she saw me with my gun. I don't know how she can feel that way. I want to change lives and see that change in the community I serve. She acts like I'm on a garbage pick-up crew."

"Garbage men make decent money, and there's the added bonus of finding treasures." Nick smiled down at her, letting her know he didn't mind listening to her vent.

"You know what I mean. It's like my uniform is shameful to her. But she always donates to police fundraisers, and she loves Captain Browning and Chief Johnson. Why can't she accept what I do?"

"If you become the Chief of Police, she might change her tune."

"Even I know that's farfetched. I had to turn my phone off. Danver has been calling nonstop."

"Maybe he misses you."

Ellie laughed. It was just like Nick to give her one-liners until she finally cracked a smile. "Danver is riding the desk until retirement. The only thing he misses is *not* having me to babysit." She blew out a breath. "Between my colleagues and my mother, I'm either a spoiled rich girl playing cops and robbers or a delicate rose to be protected."

Nick's blue eyes took on a serious note. "You know they have their reasons."

"I know they do. But I guess I just want them to see me for who I am. I'm not Helen Kline, and I won't ever be. Dan Jr. and Blake jumped into the family investment business with both feet. That should be enough, right?"

"You would think. But you are their only daughter."

"That's Wesley's fault." She laughed. "My mom never got

over him being a boy. All those pink clothes she bought when the ultrasound was wrong."

"I'm surprised she didn't sue."

"Or name him Wendy anyway." Ellie snorted lightly, then giggled.

Nick touched the underside of her chin and ran his thumb over her cheek. Though they'd kissed a thousand times, her heart still fluttered when their lips met. His touch was light, achingly tender. And when he pulled away, she found herself wishing they were somewhere else. Anywhere else.

He held her as she melted against him, letting the gurgling of the river calm her soul and erase her troubles. Things were going to work out. And if they didn't, she would find a way to make them work out. Her dreams were in reach, and no amount of guilt would weigh her down. She was going to do what she set out to do and more.

And anyone who stood in her way would find out exactly what type of woman she was.

A woman who refused to live in fear.

5

Nick stood beside Ellie on the balcony, the soft Charleston air dancing around them, her dress and the water below shimmering in the bright light of the full moon.

Her hair was loose, tightly coiled curls brushing her bare back. Her dress was daring, but carefully so. A slit on each side showed off more of her long legs than a mini skirt while somehow still being classy, and the plunging back made up for any sense of modesty the conservative front gave. Ellie was slender with toned muscles, but the cut of the dress softened her curves.

On the balcony, away from the party and the Charlestonians who had stared at them both openly, he could almost forget the way his stomach had dropped when the man in the river had tried to climb on top of her.

"You make Mother happy," Ellie told him, plopping down gracefully onto a wicker loveseat and spreading her knees so the fabric of her dress fell between them.

He tilted his chin in the direction of her unladylike pose

with a laugh. "Why don't you get comfortable? Is that why you chose the dress?"

She shot him a look. "Hey, if I'm going to sit down at one of these events, at least I can be comfortable."

"Your mother would be appalled."

"Everything appalls my mother." She glared at the towering silver heels and rolled her ankle with tight lips. "At least my Louboutins should please her."

Nick sat down beside her and patted his lap. "Give it here."

"It's all right."

"Don't argue. You know I'm going to win this one." He pointed at his thigh, insisting. If he couldn't make out with her on the balcony, he knew the second best way to make her melt in his hands.

"Fine." She sighed, turning so the high arm of the sofa was at her back and placed her feet on his thighs. She rested her temple against the back of the sofa and watched him.

"What?" He unbuckled the straps and slipped her shoes off.

She threw her head back when he pressed his thumb into her arch. "You're so good at that."

"Maybe I raid your closet while you're gone," he teased.

"You don't have a key."

He kept his gaze on her feet as he said, "We should fix that."

"Hard pass."

He laughed, hoping it sounded genuine. "It was worth a shot."

"I'm surprised my parents haven't given you one. It is their building, after all."

She flinched as his fingers loosened the tight muscles in her feet that begged for relief. "Come on, they're not that overbearing."

"Just protective. And they ask about you all the time."

That piqued his interest, and he looked up. The drinks had definitely gone to her head. "About what?"

"If you've proposed yet, and…" She tilted her head. "Well, I guess that's it."

"You'd have to accept my request to go steady first."

She laughed, her green eyes shining like precious gems. His heart clenched, and he wondered how many trips to the "friend zone" it would take before that feeling faded. "Go steady? What an archaic concept. I like the way we are. What we have is good, right?"

He smiled and nodded. "It is." It was, but he still wanted more. She let her head fall back against the cushion, eyes closed, and a tender smile on her lips. "Feeling a little fuzzy?"

"Not buzzed, just good."

"You look tired." She moaned when he took one foot in each hand and started rubbing.

"You know how to make a girl feel pretty," she shot back, rolling her eyes. "I busted my ass today."

"You did. And you still made an appearance tonight. If you wanted to leave, no one would blame you."

This perked her up a little, then she sagged against the sofa, and her head rolled back. "I'm not sure I want this to end right now."

"We can pick up where we leave off at my place." He shrugged. "Or yours."

"I'd rather be alone tonight."

He held in a sigh, working his way up her ankle to her calf, but he couldn't hold in the words. "Isn't that every night?"

"You know what I mean."

"Of course I do. That doesn't mean I can't hope to change your mind."

Her expression turned serious. "I hope you don't think I'm leading you on."

"No, of course not. I know who you are, Ellie, and your quirks. Part of loving you is embracing that."

She was silent for a moment as she frowned. "I...appreciate that."

"I'm glad, because it's not easy."

"I know there are plenty of eligible bachelorettes fawning over you, and yet you sit here with me in the dark, rubbing my feet. That golden-brown hair of yours and those dark blue eyes drive all the girls mad."

"They're mad if they think they measure up to you." He leaned over and kissed her, resting one hand on her bare thigh.

She leaned into his kiss, then broke away and bit her lip. "I'm really exhausted, and the aches are setting in. Can you take me home? I rode here in an Uber."

Nick laughed. "An Uber? Do your parents know?"

"I'm sure they've already heard about it. It was a particularly obnoxious shade of bright yellow."

He stood and held out his hand, holding her strappy heels in his other. Barefoot, she let him lead her through the crowd and toward the exit. He caught sight of Helen Kline, who beamed when he nodded in her direction. Her smile faltered when she took in her daughter traipsing across the dance floor in bare feet sans stockings, but she hid her feelings with the same practiced precision his own mother employed—nothing but contentment on the woman's face.

"My mother can overlook anything when you're involved," Ellie said as if reading his thoughts. "Maybe you should join Charleston PD."

"And risk being disowned while my parents funnel every cent of my vast inheritance to charities?" He smiled and winked at her. "I'll consider it."

"You're a mess."

"And you're not stepping onto that nasty sidewalk without shoes on." He scooped her up, careful to preserve her modesty despite the dress's attempts to foil him. She was light, the skin of her arms soft as they went around his neck, and she leaned against him.

The valet noticed them long before Nick started down the stairs. By the time he was at the bottom, his Porsche Cayenne was at the curb, passenger door already open.

He sat Ellie down on the butter-soft leather, then kissed her forehead as he buckled her in.

"Is this another new one?" she asked as he pulled away from the curb.

"I donated the last one. It brought quite a bit at auction."

"And the one before that."

He shrugged, gripping the steering wheel that still felt a bit alien in his hands. "As long as it's for a good cause, right?"

"Wouldn't it be simpler to just keep what you have and donate the money?"

"The cars bring in more than they're worth at charity auctions. Besides, I love that new car smell."

She relaxed in the seat, stretching her long legs. "They make those little trees to hang from the mirror in that exact scent."

"It's not the same." He gestured at the line of restaurants out the window. "You want dessert? Coffee?"

"I'm sorry. I just want to go home. Rain check?"

"I'll add it to the growing pile." He winked at her when she rolled her eyes. "At this rate, I'll have to take you on a year-long vacation in Fiji to use all those rain checks."

"You're the best," she said when he turned down Queen Street.

"You deserve that and more."

She shifted in her seat, but when he reached for her hand,

she took it. He'd known Ellie since they were in high school, and he'd loved her from that first look. But she was different from most Charleston-born women, who were taught from birth to bow to the old ways—engagement, marriage, babies. Ellie was fierce, independent, strong, and stubborn. No man was going to tame her against her will, and Nick wasn't fool enough to try. She had enough people in her life telling her how to act and who to be. And Nick wasn't interested in clipping her wings.

Even if that meant waiting an eternity for Ellie to take the next step. Like fine wine, she was worth the wait.

❄

Ellie closed the door of her apartment and waited until Nick's footsteps faded down the hallway.

The urge to invite him in had been strong, but tonight wasn't the night for that. She was exhausted and raw from challenging her parents, not to mention needing some space before she got the ass-chewing she knew was coming tomorrow.

She made sure he was long gone before she finished locking the door for the night. Nick had commented on the extra locks before, but she'd had a floor bolt installed since then, and she didn't want to explain. They weren't because of fear or paranoia, but the reality of the situations she'd witnessed since graduating from the police academy and working the streets.

Charleston, for the most part, was a vibrant tourist town. But under the cover of night, the city had secrets just like every city did, and Ellie knew the only way she'd get any sleep was to make sure no one could surprise her when she was at her most vulnerable. The locks wouldn't prevent every determined criminal, but they were enough to give her peace of mind.

Her muscles screaming with every step, she moved through her apartment slowly. Surprised to see it was only quarter 'til eight, she stepped out of her dress and hung it by the bedroom door so she wouldn't forget to send it to the cleaners over the weekend. The basket of laundry she'd washed days ago was still on the couch. She grabbed a loose t-shirt and pulled it over her head and padded through the house in her bare feet to make herself something to eat. The grocery service delivered on Saturdays, and her large, brightly lit refrigerator held just enough to last until then. She settled for a turkey sandwich with artisan Havarti cheese paired with a large glass of water.

She checked her messages, wincing when Danver's angry voice echoed in the rafters, then she skipped through a dozen messages from news outlets that wanted an official interview. Like everything and everyone else, they were going to have to wait until tomorrow. It was only Thursday, which meant she had one more day of work before she could take off, and she needed her rest so she could placate Sergeant Danver in the morning.

She wasn't in the least bit interested in on-camera interviews. With any luck, she'd be able to dodge them long enough for something else to grab their attention and make them forget about the police officer who was only doing her job.

The fact that all of Charleston was in awe of what she'd done got under her skin. Yes, she'd gone above and beyond to get a dangerous man off the streets, but would a male officer who did the same attract this much attention? Or was it that she was a Kline? Whatever the reason, she wanted nothing more than to lose herself in a good book and a warm bath. Tomorrow was a new day. The world could wait until then.

By the time she made it across the four-bedroom apartment to the master bedroom, she'd finished the last bite of sandwich, and the glass was half-empty. She set it on the edge of the jet tub and turned on the water to steaming in hopes of working most of the stiffness out of her body before bed. The paramedic's warning played in her head, and as much as she wanted to deny it, she knew he was right. Tomorrow was going to hurt.

"It was worth it," she whispered with a smile as she sank below the jasmine and vanilla scented bubbles.

The book she'd left on the edge of the tub the last time she'd soaked beckoned. She tried to read, but the true crime novel couldn't hold her attention. Her mother's voice kept interrupting, and after reading the same sentence fifteen times, Ellie gave up.

Her mother wasn't going to change, and after dealing with Helen's intrusions for twenty-seven years, Ellie knew she should've made peace with it. Helen Kline came from old money—the Cushing side of the family—and in their circle, women ran houses and charities, and they did it smelling like a freshly plucked rose, not a swampy river.

Despite how offensive Helen's views on a woman's place in the world could be, Ellie knew deep down that her mother truly believed the rich did the most good from the safety of a desk with a landline. Collecting donations and organizing events were Helen's forte, and though Ellie had spent most of her teen years making up for her mistakes, there was no amount of guilt that could force her to enjoy stamping envelopes and calling bored, rich housewives to donate to a cause. She didn't have it in her, not the way she had policework coursing through her veins.

Helen would never understand, and her mother's steadfast belief that she was right prevented her from accepting Ellie's path in the world. Blake and Dan Jr. were comfortable following their parents' lead, but Ellie wasn't her brothers. Even Wesley was too easily molded into their vision for him. He always stood up for Ellie, but in the end, their mother would force an end to the conversation when she wasn't winning. For once, she wanted her mother to focus on listening to what she had to say and not plan her next rebuttal.

"I'm not going to change," Ellie declared to the empty bathroom. "This is my life, and no one is going to tell me how to live it."

But her mother's voice haunted her. Ellie had defied her parents once before with a disastrous outcome, and Helen had never let her forget it. Not that her father's failing health didn't slap her in the face every time she looked at him. Every time she saw him, he was more frail—a fragile shadow of the man he once was, before that night. No matter how she framed it, her rebellious nature had and still did cause him great stress. Short of quitting the force, nothing was going to change that.

She drained the tub, dried off, and put on her softest pajamas. She threw herself on the bed, red hair still damp, the sheets soft against her skin. She intended to sleep until the last possible second before she had to be at work in the morning.

In the dark room, the light from the moon bled through the blinds and shimmered on the polished wood floors. She blinked, her heart leaping one beat, fighting sleep for an instant before she gave in to the darkness that crept in.

She thought about the man in the river, his voice thin and high like a little girl's, screaming about gators.

At least someone is having a worse day than me, she mused, a smile touching her lips as her eyes grew heavy.

No matter what Helen said, and no matter how much Danver yelled at her in the morning, one thing was certain.

A jail cell held a man whose most embarrassing moment had been broadcast live for all the world to see. If he could survive that, Ellie could handle her parents.

She reminded herself that she'd been kidnapped and hit by a police car, all at the age of fifteen. At least that was what she'd been told.

If she could only remember.

If she could only see past the darkness of that memory, see the cold truth of what happened during those hours after she'd lied to her parents. See…him. The man whose voice sometimes rang in her ear.

Try as she might, the memories wouldn't come. They taunted her. Teased her. Played with her emotions. Threatened to sometimes drive her mad.

6

One cup of coffee in each hand, Ellie nodded at the officer who stopped to hold the door open for her at the Charleston PD Headquarters early the next morning.

"Helluva collar," he said with a wide smile.

"Thanks." She slipped through the door, trying to avoid eye contact as the briefing room she entered went silent. Several officers wore admiration on their faces, mixed with something else she couldn't quite put her finger on.

Her stiff shoulders screamed even under the small weight of the large cups of steaming liquid, but she forced her face to remain passive. She was going to get through this day if it killed her.

As soon as he spotted her, Jacob rushed forward and took the cup with his name on it. His smile was a welcome relief. His eyes closed when he took the first sip, then he nodded toward the hallway that led to the bathrooms, and she followed him back there.

"Have you turned on your cell phone yet?" he asked, his voice low.

She shook her head. "I barely got out of the apartment on

time today." She shrugged one shoulder, and it popped loudly. She grimaced.

Jacob's eyebrows knitted together. "Maybe you should see a doctor."

"I'm just stiff. More from battling him in the water than anything. The jump from the bridge was a cakewalk."

Jacob chuckled. "He *was* trying to climb on top of your head to escape the vicious turtle."

"Funny." She was almost starting to feel sorry for the guy.

"Really. You should take the day off." His eyes flicked to the right, then back again.

"No way." She scowled. "What are you not telling me?"

"Danver is on the warpath. He's been stomping around his office all morning, and he keeps poking his head out to see if you're here yet. Maybe you should call in sick and pretend you were never here." Jacob glanced down the hall as if he expected Danver to appear at any second.

She snorted. "And miss the chance to have Danver hand me my ass for the greatest collar of my career? Not a chance."

"You're out of your mind." Jacob placed his hands on his duty belt, an obvious sign he wasn't finished giving her his opinion. "He can fire you for what happened yesterday. You know that, right?"

"If he does, I'll find a job somewhere else. There are plenty of other departments that would be happy to have me."

"Not if you're a liability. It's one thing for you to risk your life to save another person, but a pattern of reckless behavior can really limit your options." His dark brown eyes bored into hers, making sure she understood his meaning.

His words stung, but Ellie brushed them off, knowing he just wanted the best for her. "There's no pattern of reckless behavior. I take my job seriously, and playing it safe loses suspects."

"You can do your job *and* stay safe. It's not an either-or situation."

"Did you pull me out here to get a dig in before Danver gets ahold of me, or what?"

He recoiled a little, then pursed his lips. "You can be so frustrating sometimes, you know that? I brought you out here so you could prepare for what was about to happen. If you'll at least pretend to be apologetic, Danver might let this incident slide. Then you have to be on your best behavior."

"Well-behaved women don't change the world."

He quirked up one brow. "And cops who get fired don't make detective. Think of your future. Please."

The men's bathroom door beside them burst open and Danver appeared, his displeasure written on every millimeter of his face. "Kline, my office. Now!" He was gone as quickly as he'd arrived.

Jacob gave her a *sorry, not sorry* look. "Told ya. Good luck, Kline. You were my favorite partner."

"Stop." She elbowed him hard in the ribs. "It's not that bad."

But it was that bad, and by the time she walked into Danver's office and closed the door, he was red-faced and pacing. The flush of his face contrasted sharply with his gray hair. "Have a seat."

"I'm fine."

"Sit. Down," he ordered through gritted teeth.

She plopped down into the stiff chair and winced, immediately regretting it. Her body ached all over, and even brushing her teeth last night and this morning, then drinking coffee had done nothing to wash away the odd aftertaste the river water had left in her mouth. "Sergeant, I—"

"Don't," he hissed before dropping his massive body into his own chair. He leaned back and closed his eyes. Fingers pinching the bridge of his nose, he was still for so long, Ellie worried he'd passed out or had a stroke. Finally, he sighed and leveled a cold, angry glare in her direction, his dark eyes boring into her. "You know jumping off bridges is dangerous, right? I just want to establish that you're aware you could have died."

"The perp went over first, and it's not like I jumped off the Ravenel Bridge."

"No. Then I'd be having this conversation with your next of kin." Somehow, he'd both agreed with her and made his point.

"I made a decision based on the situation at hand, and I took action. I captured the perp and didn't ruin my service piece *or* my Taser."

"This time," Sergeant Danver muttered. "Let's not revisit what happened to your last gun belt."

She nodded, trying not to grimace at the memory of her gun belt being trampled by the team of horses pulling a tourist carriage. "I've learned from my mistakes and adjusted my behavior. If I hadn't jumped, he would've gotten away."

"And if he'd hurt you in the process?"

Damn, she was tired of talking about the suspect—who was sitting in a jail cell—possibly drowning her. He hadn't. End of story. "Would you ask Garcia the same question?"

Danver scowled then shook his head. "No. But I also don't have to worry about him putting his life at risk once a week."

"It's not that often," she countered.

"Really?" He picked up a piece of paper from his desk that was covered with his sloppy handwriting scrawled in haphazard lines. "By my estimation, this is the third time in October. It's only halfway through the month." She stiffened when he moved the paper, and she caught a glimpse of the form beneath it. "And then there's this. Did you think I wouldn't find out?"

"I can explain."

"I'm sure you can."

Shit. Maybe Jacob had been right. Maybe she was going to get fired. She didn't have time to go there, though, she needed to pull her thoughts together.

"Captain Browning and I were chatting at an event, and when I mentioned that I always wanted to join Homicide, he told me to put in my application. That's it."

"You should've put it in with *me*. But the fact is, whether you went over my head or not, you still need my signature to be considered for Homicide Division. Do you honestly think I'd suggest someone as hotheaded and reckless as you?"

She wanted to squirm in her seat, but she forced herself to remain rigid. "I think it's exactly what you should do. Detective work requires out-of-the-box thinking. Cops who play it safe don't catch criminals."

Danver shook his head, laughing without a hint of humor. "I'd ask if you were serious, but I know you are." He leaned forward over his desk, his thin, closely cropped gray hair sticking straight up, his expression almost threatening. "Reckless cops lose cases. If you screw up in Homicide and they have to let someone walk because you're too busy showboating to make good choices, the captain will be the first after your head. Being a Kline won't change that."

She remained passive, though beneath the surface, her blood heated.

But Danver wasn't the first to insinuate that any success she achieved was because of her family's influence, and he likely wouldn't be the last. She just had to get through this, and she'd be back on patrol with Jacob, biding her time until she found a way into Homicide.

"Is there anything else?" she asked, working to keep her tone cool and unaffected.

His eyebrows shot up, then he chuckled. And this time, when he reached into the stack of papers, her heart jumped into her throat. Would he fire her? Was his smile proof that he'd already put her termination in?

She took the paper when he slid it toward her. As she read the words, it took a moment for the wording she'd been dreading to make sense in her brain.

Her head snapped up. "You wrote me a letter of recommendation?"

"Glad to see that you can read." He was smiling, looking like he'd just given his favorite niece a Christmas present that he'd bought for himself too.

"I thought you didn't like me?"

"I don't." He laughed when she scrunched up her nose. "But I didn't get this close to retirement by letting loose cannons like you run amok on my watch. I'm not a babysitter, but if you want to play cop and run around solving crimes during the day and attend charity balls at night, be my guest." His eyes crinkled at the corners, and his expression warmed. "I honestly wish you the best. It's really the only way to keep you out of my hair. Good day, Officer Kline." He smiled and winked. "*Detective* Kline."

She stood, and he held up his hand. "One more thing." He turned the computer monitor around so the screen faced her, then he highlighted a number with the mouse.

"What's this?"

"The stats on the recruitment page. See that number in the corner?" He clicked over to another tab on his desktop. "This is the stats from the past week." He clicked back to the first page. "This is how high the number has leaped since you were on the news, jumping off a bridge, then dragging a screaming, half-naked thug out of the water."

"That's almost four times as many." She sucked in a breath, shocked. "Maybe it's a glitch."

"Not a glitch. We only get an email if the prescreening online is completed. HR has more emails to sort through since yesterday than they usually have in a month. Many of them are good quality." He groaned. "A few of them remind me of you."

She couldn't wipe the grin off her face. "Why, Sergeant Danver, I do believe you're going to miss me."

"I'm looking forward to it. Enjoy the rest of the day off. You start Homicide Monday morning."

"I just got here," she said in an awed whisper.

"I know. You're getting a paid day off. If you want, though, head on over to Homicide and introduce yourself to the lead detective. He should probably be warned, but we'll let him figure you out on his own. Otherwise, enjoy your weekend."

"I appreciate you giving me a chance to make a good first impression."

"That ship has sailed. There isn't anyone alive in Charleston who doesn't know who you are by now." His eyes crinkled at the corners as he smiled. "Congratulations."

"Thank you," she gushed, thrusting her hand across the desk and shaking Danver's hand vigorously. "I can't tell you how much…I can't believe that I'm going to be a detective." She quickly composed herself, then nodded. "Thank you, Sergeant," she amended. "It's an honor to have worked with you."

She turned and exited his office before he could change his mind, walking on the balls of her feet, light as air.

Jacob was waiting for her, and he motioned in the direction of the back exit.

She followed him out, buzzing with excitement.

"I can see you're about to burst," Jacob said. "What happened? I'm guessing you still have a job."

"Better," she retorted.

"Okay. Care to elaborate?"

"I made detective, effective immediately."

He skidded to a halt on the pavement and blinked at her. "What?"

"I put in for detective after meeting with Captain Browning, and he sent it over for Danver to sign off on."

His eyes went wide. "You went over his head, he found out, and he *still* signed off on it? How the hell did you manage that?"

She shrugged, a little embarrassed to admit the reason he'd given for his sign-off. "Apparently, he's tired of my antics."

"Who isn't? But come on. You don't give a promotion for that."

"I thought you'd be happy for me." Her eyes narrowed. "I didn't know you were tired of me already."

He sighed. "It's not like that, Ellie. I just never know when you're going to go off-script, and it's exhausting. Your job isn't the only one at stake, you know?"

"I guess I didn't think of that." She'd gone from flying high to feeling like she had been shuffled over to Homicide to get rid of a problem.

"Don't worry about it now," he said with a shake of his head. "At least working with you was never dull. I'm going to miss that."

"But you're not going to miss my 'antics.'" She held her fingers up in air quotes.

"That came out wrong. This is all so sudden, I'm just a little shocked is all. How am I going to get used to a new partner after you? Maybe I should put in for PTO so I can adjust to losing you."

The smile slowly returned to her face. "I'm sure you'll be fine."

"What if my new partner doesn't run as fast as you?"

"Then you'll have to start catching the bad guys yourself. Like me."

He snorted. “And what if they want to drive?”

“I wouldn’t let them.”

His chocolate-brown eyes softened. “It’s going to be quiet without you, Kline.”

“I’ll visit.”

He held up a hand. “Please don’t. I don’t think Danver can handle it.”

They both laughed, then went silent. For a moment, they were both sullen, the stillness of the back lot magnifying the finality of the moment.

Ellie was the first to crack under its weight. “I’m going to miss you.” She slid her arms around his neck and hugged him tight. “You’ll always be my fourth and favorite partner.”

He chuckled. “You’ll always be my favorite.”

“I know.”

His body shook long before the first note of laughter left his lips. “You’re something else,” he told her. “I hope your future partner is prepared for you. When do you start?”

“I have the rest of the day off, and I start Monday.”

“Danver gave you the day off?”

“He gave the impression that it was more for him than me.”

Jacob shook his head, a grin overtaking his face. “I don’t doubt that. I guess I’ll suck it up and go find out who my new partner is going to be.”

“Whoever she is, don’t underestimate her.”

“I’ve learned that lesson,” he teased. “As long as I don’t end up with another fiery redhead, I’ll be fine.”

They reentered the building, Jacob heading for the briefing room as the door opened, and someone announced it was time for the morning’s patrol assignment.

“I’ll see you around, Garcia.”

“Good luck, *Detective* Kline.”

They held eye contact for a second, then Ellie gave him a sad smile and turned away, walking down the hall.

Yesterday, when she'd sat next to Jacob in the high school style desk, writing down their duties for the day, she'd had no idea it would be the last time she rode with Jacob Garcia. The promotion to Homicide was everything she'd ever wanted, but the moment was bittersweet. She knew she would never have another partner like Garcia, and to her surprise, her eyes filled with tears.

Swiping angrily with the sleeve of her shirt, she wiped them away and blinked until the moment passed. She would not cry over Jacob. This was a new and exciting time in her life, and she wasn't going to ruin it by pining over losing the first partner who hadn't dumped her.

Instead of getting a jump on her weekend, she took a detour.

Climbing the stairs to the second floor, she made her way down the long hallway.

There was only one thing that could chase away her blues.

It was time to pay her new boss a visit.

7

The room had an entirely different energy than the main office when Ellie stepped through the door that read "Violent Crimes."

Six desks were placed strategically throughout the space, each covered with framed photographs of family, stacks of files, and computers with two monitors. In the back of the room, on the other side of a glass-paneled wall, a man in his mid-forties with tanned skin and tight, coarse brown curls cut close to his head worked behind a desk. When she moved closer, he looked up, and his piercing hazel eyes, gold like rich honey, drew her in until she'd crossed the entire room, and her hand was on the door.

The man tilted his head and beckoned her into his office, setting aside the file he'd been holding. He stood, and a tentative smile spread across his face. Warm, but not too inviting. Cautious. "With hair that red, I'm going to bet you're Eleanor Kline."

He reached his hand out, and when she took it, his large fingers curled around hers, completely engulfing her smaller hand. "Yes, sir. Please call me Ellie."

"You can call me Fortis. Lead Homicide Detective Harold Fortis." Gesturing to the chair across from him, he sat down and leaned back. When she didn't sit right away, he continued as if it didn't matter.

He's nothing like Danver, she mused, then slowly, she sank down into the chair. "I'm sorry to barge in. I just wanted to introduce myself and see where I would be working."

He nodded. "I'd be lying if I said your reputation didn't beat you in here, but it's nice to meet you all the same. You're a bit taller than I imagined, but it's hard to judge a person's height when they're jumping off a bridge on live television."

Her cheeks heated. "All in the line of duty, sir."

"You can cut that out. Homicide isn't like working the beat. We're a family here. The sooner you get comfortable with that, the better."

"I understand, sir, I mean, Fortis."

"You'll get there." He opened a folder with her name on the front, glanced at it, then closed it again. "You do realize you don't start 'til Monday?"

"I do, but I wanted to swing by first. Get a look at my desk and maybe meet my partner."

His smile was dazzling. "That'll be easy. You're your partner."

"Oh."

"And I don't have a desk for you yet. This was all pushed through late yesterday afternoon, so I didn't have a chance to get things situated." He pointed to a corner table along the outer wall in the main room. "I hope you like a window seat because this office wasn't set up to house this many detectives."

"That's perfect," she said, but couldn't keep herself from wrinkling her nose slightly. "Any idea when I'll have a desk?"

He shrugged. "You know how much red tape it takes to

get things done around here, right? Could be Monday, could be next year." He opened a drawer and handed her a gold badge. "You can keep your silver one as a souvenir. You'll receive a badge with your number on it when it comes in."

She accepted the heavy gold badge with "Detective" stamped on it, trying to keep her excitement at bay. "Thank you."

"You'll have plenty of space to work while you're waiting for a desk. Since you're here already, I guess I can show you what you'll be working on."

"I already have a case? Shouldn't I work on it now, then? I know the first forty-eight hours are crucial, so I don't think sitting on it all weekend—"

He held up his hand. "It won't make a bit of difference when you start." Shrugging, he pursed his lips. "I'll get together a list of priorities, but honestly, it doesn't matter which case you do first. If you need guidance, I'll help you out, but for the most part, you'll be flying solo."

When he stood and walked around the desk to open the door for her, his presence was imposing. He was quite a bit taller than she'd realized. As soon as they'd cleared the doorway, he took a sharp left and took her to a door opposite Violent Crimes in the main hallway.

"This is the way to the service elevator. If you see any civilians wandering down this hall, send them back toward the main entrance. Authorized personnel only." He stepped into a dingy elevator that was about half the size of the main one that served the public area, and pushed the button for the basement before leaning against the wall. "It can get a little bumpy."

The elevator lurched downward, and Ellie's hand shot out to grab the railing. Detective Fortis smiled. A few moments later, the doors scraped open, and Ellie hurried off the lift. It shuddered, then the doors closed with a loud *clank*.

"That was an experience," she muttered.

"You'll get used to it." He gestured down a dimly lit hall. "The evidence locker is this way. Our clerk is on lunch, but you'll be issued a key code Monday." He gave her what passed for a stern look as he typed in his own code, his body obscuring her view. "Only a select few have a code, but every time you use your code, it's noted, and the video log for the time you're in evidence is tagged to that timeframe. When things have gone missing in the past, the situation has been corrected very quickly."

She nodded. "I understand."

"You can check evidence out as needed, but only with the clerk, and don't abuse the privilege."

"Got it."

He shot her a smile. "Honestly, you'd have to really *try* to mess this up."

"I've been told I can throw a wrench into any plan," she joked.

Fortis chuckled with a shake of his head. "I really didn't want to like you, what with you going over everyone's head to get what you wanted, but you're a trip. I can see why Cap likes you."

"He likes the family name," she said, then covered her mouth, horrified she'd spoken her thoughts. "Sorry, I shouldn't have said that out loud."

"You only said what we're all thinking. At least you're aware of Cap's," he searched for the right word, "motives. The man is driven to succeed, and everything he does is a calculated effort to get what he wants. Right down to having his hair dyed weekly so no one realizes he's pushing sixty."

"His hair is dyed?"

"How did you not notice?"

She shrugged. "I don't know, but now that you mention it, it's an unnatural shade of black."

"Captain Browning is so bent on looking the part and rubbing elbows with all the right people, he doesn't see how asinine it looks." He winked. "But you didn't hear that from me."

"Understood," she said, following him into the cold room.

There was a large desk near the door, stacked with neatly arranged piles of files and a rubber stamp that was comically large. The light above it was outrageously bright, as if someone had wished for natural light, and installed it to give off as much as the sun. There were no windows, and the air was only as fresh as the filters in the building's air-conditioning unit.

A small collection of unicorn figurines were lined up under the huge computer monitor, and next to that, a frame depicting a dog running down the beach carrying a piece of driftwood nearly twice its size. The dog was dirty and wet with sand stuck to its fur, obscuring most of its black coloring. Ellie could tell it was some kind of mutt, but it was the happiest dog she'd ever seen.

"You'll like Clerk Reed. Friendly and helpful, but not overbearing. Nice combination." Fortis went to another metal door to the right and typed in his code again. Inside the large storage room, he flipped on a light switch and walked to another doorway, this one without a door. A sign hanging on the wall nearby caught her attention.

"Cold cases?"

"Yep, that's you." He gave a grand gesture to the rows upon rows of standard white evidence boxes inside the second room. "They go back from two to twenty years or so. How many boxes they fill just depends on how much evidence we were able to collect before we had to shelve them. Like I said, for now, which cases you tackle first is up to you, but this should keep you busy. Don't worry about checking in Monday morning. I get an alert when anyone from my unit enters the evidence locker, so you can head straight in."

"This is it?" She couldn't keep the note of trepidation out of her voice. She'd been looking forward to her first case as a detective, and now she had more cases than she could familiarize herself with within a year.

"It is. All yours. If you need help, feel free to come upstairs, and once I get your desk, I'll get you set up in that corner. But you'll spend most of your time down here." He frowned. "I should probably get you a laptop for your desk so you can move from one place to another." He led her down one row and pointed to an empty tabletop. "There are several workspaces like this you can use. Just make sure you put the boxes back where you find them."

"How many cases are there?"

"Couple hundred. Maybe more." He gestured toward the open door. "Reed is really good at keeping up with them and will help you find anything you need. We cover all violent crimes, but I want you to stick with the unsolved murders."

"And how many of those are there?"

"You don't want to know."

"What's the protocol when I solve a case?" She glanced down a row of boxes and imagined solving one after the other.

"Write up a report and leave it on my desk. If the perp is still alive, have patrol bring them in for questioning. You can question witnesses alone, but I don't want you picking up persons of interest without a patrol officer."

She stiffened, about to object that she'd been a patrol officer until this morning.

He pinned her with a stern look. "We do things my way here. I like you, but don't think I'll hesitate to knock you down a few pegs if I think you need it."

Was there something lower than cold cases? she wondered,

then thought better of asking outright. Detective Fortis didn't seem like the kind of guy who played around.

"That's the tour," he declared, ushering her out and securing both doors behind him.

He led the way to the elevator and pushed the up button. When the door opened, he tipped his chin in an informal farewell and pointed down the hallway.

"That door goes straight out to the parking lot." The square pane of reinforced glass was the only place sunlight could peek into the basement. "The clerk is here nine to five, Monday through Friday. There's a cap on hours for clerks, but you're salary, and as long as you're here doing your job, you can set your own hours. Until you get the lay of the land, I would suggest taking advantage of Reed's expertise. You can work more than one case each week, but if you're not making headway within thirty days, I'd like you to note it, shelve it, and move on to the next case."

She nodded, ready for him to depart so she could get her hands on her first case after the clerk came back from lunch. Her fingers were itching to have a file in them.

The doors started to creep shut even though Detective Fortis was standing on the threshold. He didn't flinch when the door bumped his leg and skittered back open again. "I guess I'll see you on Monday?"

"Yes, sir."

He tipped his head and stepped into the elevator. "I look forward to it. I'll let Reed know to expect you."

Ellie stood in the hallway for a few moments after the door closed and the elevator light indicated the car had made it back to the second floor. She waited by the evidence room door for a few minutes, but the basement was like being in a cave. A cold, dark, boring cave.

Was this some type of punishment? A move just to get her out of the way? She decided to soak up some sunlight, maybe wait until Monday for her first case after all. Heading for the exit, she pushed open the outer door and stepped out into the brilliant sunlight.

Jacob was standing a few yards away, leaning against his car, which was parked next to hers.

"Were you waiting for me?" She heard the locks of her Audi Q3 click open as she approached. She loved technology.

"I saw you through the window and figured you'd be out soon. How was it?"

She blew out a frustrated breath. "I think I know why Danver was happy to be rid of me."

"Besides the obvious?"

"Very funny." She shoved his shoulder playfully. "I'm not working active homicide. I'm working cold cases."

"Cold cases." He appeared to be studying the words. "That could be interesting, right?"

"Sure," she huffed. "If you like looking at old cases that no one was able to solve."

"Maybe they thought you'd enjoy the challenge."

She laughed. All those boxes certainly looked like a challenge to her. "He didn't say it, but Detective Fortis acted like he'd been saddled with babysitter duties. He's nicer about it than Danver was, but it was pretty clear he wasn't happy about the change."

"Fortis is a good man. You'll get along, and soon you'll be totally in sync like you and me."

"He's not my partner," she scoffed, feeling mutiny to her marrow.

Jacob's forehead wrinkled. "Who are you partnered with?"

"The evidence clerk."

Jacob blinked. "The evidence clerk?"

"Yep. And my workspace is in the evidence locker. Or a table in the corner upstairs." She blew out a breath, and a stray lock of curly hair floated a few inches off her cheek then settled in the same place again. "It's busywork, Jacob. I don't know why they didn't just put me there in the first place. It would've saved Danver a lot of gray hair."

"Don't let them get to you."

"Why not? That's what they want, isn't it?"

"No. They want to prove you can't hack it. That you're just some rich girl playing cops and robbers." He clamped his hand on her shoulder, and she met his dark gaze. "Don't let them screw with you. You're stronger than this. Monday morning, you find a case that speaks to you, and you work it until every angle is exhausted. They'll take notice when you start solving cases their guys couldn't."

"It's such bullshit."

"It is, but you've got this. Prove them wrong and make them sorry they doubted you."

His confidence in her shook her out of her mood. She stepped back, breathing out the breath that had felt locked in her lungs. "You're right. I'm not going down without a fight."

"You can do this. Hell, you jumped off a bridge yesterday to catch a thug and braved turtle infested waters for justice."

It felt good to laugh. "I wonder if gator guy knows he made the news."

"I'm sure he does by now. Every time they showed the footage, they used a stylus to highlight the 'killer turtle,' then his mugshot was added to the frame."

"At least someone is having a worse day than me."

"Worse day?" He grabbed her shoulders and shook her gently. "This is the best day. You made detective! Let's celebrate?"

He was right. "It's too early to hit Charlie's Pub."

"Later then, after my shift?"

She scrunched her nose, and a slow smile spread across

her face. "I don't know..." she said, enjoying teasing him because she wouldn't be seeing him that much after today.

"Come on. For old time's sake."

She kicked at the ground. "Fine, but I hope your new partner never lets you drive. Text me when you get off."

He was laughing when she pushed the start button in her car, and the engine roared to life. "What are you laughing about?" she demanded.

"I guess they felt sorry for me, you know, since my last partner was so reckless." His eyes were shining with the bit of info he was clearly withholding.

She ignored the bait. "Do you know who your partner is already? Is it Davis?"

"Close."

She narrowed her eyes and revved the engine. "Spill it. I have pressing matters on my day off."

He turned toward his squad car, throwing a grin back at her. "I'll be driving for the next five years, at least." He paused at the door, then laughed when Ellie only gave him a questioning look. "My new partner is a K-9."

Mercy. Did the insults never cease?

Ellie flipped him the bird as he got into his car and drove out of the parking lot.

A thought occurred to her. She might be stuck in the basement, but Jacob had to scrape dog shit.

She hiccupped out a laugh as she turned out of the station's lot.

He got to deal with dog hair.

And Monday morning, she would be investigating her first very own murder case.

8

I clicked the play icon on the computer monitor, sitting back and watching the video once again.

The news chopper caught the tail end of the highspeed chase, and the near perfect PIT maneuver executed by Officer Jacob Garcia. There was gunfire, then silence.

I held my breath, even though I already knew that not one of the bullets had found their mark. It seemed the street thug had spent more time planning his ridiculous wardrobe than he did at the gun range.

My pencil flew across the yellow notepad as I wrote down my observations. The way the fleeing man clutched his waistband in one hand as he ran.

I wondered why he didn't just wear clothes that fit, but if he had, the footage wouldn't have been quite as amusing. I'd seen the video enough to have the ending memorized, and Mister Street Thug came out looking like the moron he was. He was a waste of air, unworthy of the data used to store his most embarrassing moments for future generations to enjoy. But his capture was important to Ellie, and I had a vested interest in what drove her. If I had to study useless men who couldn't bother to match their plaid boxers to their shirts, so be it.

Ellie emerged from the passenger side of the battered cruiser, a vision despite the manly cut of the navy-blue uniform. She hit the ground running, forcing the man to lengthen his stride. He nearly lost his pants twice, and Ellie was catching up to him when he turned his head and focused on the railing. I could see the exact moment he made the decision.

I paused the video and recorded the time, scribbling more notes down before I pressed play again, but not before admiring Ellie's form frozen in a run, right foot poised to hit the ground. I noted that she'd managed to break free of the chains of wealth—she'd worked hard to be everything her parents were not.

She still possessed the gazelle-like grace she'd managed to emanate during her first appearance in the public eye at the tender age of three, but with hard work and grit, Ellie had transformed into a more authentic version of the person her parents trained her to be. She was perfection—ready to take action and get her hands dirty for justice. It was almost cute, the way she obviously cared for the wretched souls who walked the earth. As if they mattered.

In another instant, she would realize what the man intended to do and immediately take action. It was my favorite part, far superior to the action-packed vault over the railing and almost slapstick comedy that followed. This moment was the one when Ellie's tenacity showed through. She didn't mindlessly follow the hapless criminal over the edge. She assessed the situation, left on the ground any items that would drag her down to her useless partner's level, then she went for it. Those precious ten seconds were the epitome of who Ellie Kline was as a person, and I'd watched them until I had every nuance memorized.

Her French braid was tucked into a bun so smooth and neat that her hair didn't move when her hat flew off, and she plunged several feet to the water. Had she been prepared for the temperature? The local kayaker's club had recorded the water temperature at seventy-two degrees. Refreshing in the summer, but not quite comfortable in the fall. Would she fare as well in the same water without the benefit of the adrenaline that flowed through her?

Even with the volume low, I could hear the man the moment he began to scream. I waited, grimacing when the thug attempted to crawl onto Ellie's shoulders to escape the water. It was clear he didn't understand basic science let alone tell the head of a river turtle from the snout of a gator.

I leaned in, waiting with bated breath for Ellie to resurface, then watched the emotions play across her face as she found the source of the man's fear, then hid her obvious amusement. Right away, she knew it was a harmless turtle.

What neither of them knew was there was indeed a gator, buried in the soupy mud on the opposite bank, too busy soaking up the sun's October rays to be bothered with the two of them. The internet had yet to notice the mammoth beast, and I had every doubt they ever would. The added danger was inconsequential. Ellie would've handled the situation with the same grace she did everything, and the city would still be talking about her.

Her celebrity raised my hackles. Suddenly, Ellie Kline was the darling of Charleston. In the public eye for much of her life, I'd loved her for more than a decade. But now, Ellie Kline was trending online, and everyone wanted to know if she was single. As if she'd only just been discovered. As if my admiration didn't feed the glorious creature she'd become, even if it was from afar.

The video ended with the hysterical laughter of the buffoons videoing from the bridge, commenting on the pantsless thug and his harrowing flight from the redhaired goddess in blue.

I closed the tab and opened the news story, which I sent to the printer. The printing was done in a flash, silently and without a single smudge. In the center of another printout, an updated picture of Ellie several hours later, divine in a deep blue dress with her curls loose around her angelic face.

I carefully cut the picture out of one of two copies I'd printed, then I glued it to a square paper with the other photos of her I'd found plastered all over the internet in the last twenty-four hours.

Ellie stepping out of a god-awful yellow Mini Cooper.

Ellie and her oafish little brother climbing the stairs.

Ellie on the balcony in the arms of Charleston's most eligible bachelor.

The last picture had rocked much of Charleston, which amused me to no end. Ellie was a gorgeous woman, and Nick Greene was the son of very wealthy people. Like the prince suddenly swept off the market by a princess, the commoners seemed to think that was the only reason they didn't have a chance with royalty. It was painfully delusional.

If only stupidity was physically painful.

When I'd placed the new sheet neatly in the scrapbook, I thumbed through the pages and sighed. The only good thing about her sudden popularity was the plethora of material I was able to find online. In four days, I'd filled up two books. I had another empty one ready, just in case. I never knew when new pictures of Ellie would find their way to me.

I loaded maps on my computer and clicked on the street view of the building where she lived. In another tab, I opened up the virtual tour on the building's website and hit play.

The video was an amateur job, and the cameraperson had opted for bare feet instead of sensible shoes and a silent video. Each step came through the speakers, her breathing soft and gentle with the steadiness of someone who was Olympic fit. I didn't need to catch a flash of that red hair in the master bathroom mirror to know it was Ellie behind the camera, but I waited, holding my breath and eyeing the counter. At exactly sixty-eight seconds in, I paused the video and reached out.

I was careful not to smudge the monitor as my fingers hovered over a deliciously fat curl. The moment held so much for me. I could almost smell the two-hundred-dollar per ounce conditioner it would take to achieve defined curls that looked that soft. I longed to wrap the perfect tendril around my finger and tug until she whimpered. Would her nostrils flare with excitement? Would her eyes tell me to drop dead?

There were so many questions I needed answered.

I let myself enjoy the freeze-frame for a long moment before I finally let the video play again.

Her voice was measured, her diction perfect. There was only a hint of the natural Southern accent most of Charleston spoke with. Like the city's elite, Ellie had a way of speaking that set her apart and made her stand out from the unwashed masses. Every syllable dripped with class and education.

Every word spoke to my soul as she showed me her favorite corners of the apartment that looked like all the others, convincing me that the thousands a month for rent was a steal for the amenities included. Luxury in the heart of Charleston's French Quarter. And the owner's daughter living on the top floor.

She was right. Her building was worth every penny, and the people who lived there likely had no idea how very lucky they were. They were in the presence of greatness, separated from divinity by brick walls and clean lines of smooth steel. The world didn't deserve Ellie Kline, but I did.

A knock at the door came precisely when I expected it, but the interruption still enraged me.

"Yes?" I called, my voice distant and unrecognizable to my own ears. How I hated to put on airs for the masses, but I had a business to maintain. Playing nice with commoners was part of that.

"Your three o'clock just arrived," my assistant murmured through the door. "Do you want me to send them in?"

"Yes, send them in," I said without moving from my desk. "At exactly three and not a moment before, thank you."

Five minutes. Five precious minutes left with my queen. Then it was back to the workday, wasting my smiles on people who couldn't hold a candle to Ellie Kline.

I pressed my thumb on the thumbprint scanner that protected the bottom drawer, and it popped open. I pulled the drawer all the way out, smiling at the many scrapbooks I'd filled. Ellie's book belonged right in the front, but all the attention she was getting had me on edge.

Tapping my finger on the desk with each number I whispered reverently, I counted off the color-coded pairs. Thirty-seven books in all rested in the drawer. Eighteen lucky friends, and one who was not so lucky.

Ellie's books were soft blue, though I'd been tempted to choose a vibrant red to match her hair. But the other books were pastel, and I wanted her to blend in. I didn't want anyone to take notice—should the situation arise—to violate my time with Ellie. Besides, she didn't need gaudy trappings to earn my attention; she was my everything and more.

Her books slid in easily with the others, and I closed the drawer just as the doorknob turned, and the gorgeous face of my young assistant appeared.

"It's three, sir," he said with a soft voice that honored his status in my life. He was nothing. Without me, he would have no home and no life, and he knew it. He was my favorite so far, but they all started that way.

He looked nervous, so I forced myself to make eye contact and smile to put him at ease. The gesture worked, as it always did.

"Send them in," I told him. "And thank you."

Soft brown eyes lit up, and he all but preened. His full lips broke into a generous smile, every hint of the desolate street dweller he'd been now gone. He'd cleaned up nice, as they said, and he'd been particularly impressionable even from the start. I'd trained this one quicker than the rest, and even I was surprised by how thoroughly he'd changed.

But I didn't have time to dwell on my accomplishments or my dear, feisty Ellie. Duty called, and it was back to the grind for me. Young Ellie would have to wait until I was ready to play.

That's how it had always been. The moment would come when it was time. And when it was time, it would be as sweet as I'd dreamt it would be.

Patience was my virtue, and the best flowers were well worth the wait.

9

Ellie's low heels clicked on the tile of the wide hallway, the echo joined by the footsteps of officers coming into Charleston PD after an all-nighter.

Dressed in a smart navy pantsuit with a shirt that was a little more cream than yellow, she'd rounded out the look with nude pumps that were functional and fashionable. Her mess of red curls was pulled back in a no-nonsense bun at the nape of her neck. Two bobby pins on each side of her head tamed the little wisps at her temples, completing the look. It was one of the same styles she always wore her hair in at work, with the exception of her uniform hat.

Her head felt bare, but the sensation was nothing compared to the one she picked up from the eyes that watched her as she walked past. Some of her coworkers smiled and nodded, but she was met with more than a few glares broadcasting their jealousy.

She was starting to regret the choice to head for coffee in the breakroom when a pair of familiar brown eyes caught her attention.

Jacob smiled and hurried over to greet her. "You look

ready to kick some ass," he said as he motioned for her to join him to the side of the breakroom door.

"I figured you'd already be out and working with your new partner today," she teased, wondering why he wasn't wearing his uniform.

"I have the week off."

Concern mixed with curiosity. "Did you get reprimanded for what happened on the bridge?"

He shook his head. "I'll pick the K-9 up from the trainer later today. The first week with Duke is bonding, then several weeks of training. I'll be getting paid to hang out at home with the dog. It's a pretty sweet deal."

"He's going to live with you?"

Jacob shrugged, not seeming to mind the idea. "That's how this works. He's family now."

"I don't think I've ever seen you so happy." She offered him a saucy wink. "Come on. I need caffeine." At the breakroom door, she faltered for a second, then lifted her chin and shouldered her way through without a word to the beefy man in blue standing there with arms crossed, glaring at her.

"What gives?" Jacob asked him, but the other officer only grunted and moved into the hallway. Jacob stared at the man's back until he disappeared around a corner. "Don't let them get to you. Those of us who know you are happy for you."

They were standing shoulder to shoulder at the counter as Jacob poured them each a cup and Ellie ripped open enough sugar packets to make the brown sludge drinkable. "Thanks. Maybe I should've stopped for coffee on the way in."

"Why? You may have taken an unconventional route to get your promotion, but you still earned it. If they can't handle that, it's on them." He put his arm around her shoulder and gave her a friendly squeeze as she took a sip to test the coffee's flavor. "This is the happiest day of your life. Making detective is what you've always wanted, and you've earned it. If they want recognition for a job well done, maybe they need to be willing to jump into turtle-infested waters to get the bad guy."

Ellie snorted mid-sip, clearing her throat to keep from choking. "Stop it," she laughed.

"Have you seen the loop someone made of him climbing onto your shoulders and screaming? It's hilarious. You're viral now, and for all the right reasons." He pulled out his phone. "Then, there's this one."

It was a ten-second video of Ellie the moment she jumped off the bridge, complete with a soundtrack and a superhero cape.

"That's pretty good," she said after she caught her breath from laughing. "It looks like I was actually wearing a cape."

"I was pretty impressed myself." He scrolled through his saved videos. "Here's one of me."

In the gif, Jacob stood on the bridge, hands on hips, saying the same two words over and over. "Dammit, Ellie," video-Jacob repeated, shaking his head at the end of each loop as his dark gaze followed her vault over the bridge railing.

"No wonder you're so happy about your new partner."

"There are dozens of these," he mused, putting his phone back in his pocket. "You could waste a whole day on them."

"I guess I know what you did all weekend."

He snorted. "I'm much more exciting than that. I slept. I have a lot going on in the next few weeks."

She poured more sugar into her coffee. "Why so much training, though? I thought they started K-9s as puppies."

"The training isn't for the dog," Jacob laughed. "It's for me. To start with, I have to learn all the commands in French, and I have to practice taking down bad guys with a dog in the way."

"It won't be that much different," a voice called out from behind them.

Ellie's hackles raised on her neck, but her hand went to Jacob's arm, who had already tensed. She knew him well enough to know that he'd reached his limit.

"Don't," she whispered. "Just let it go."

Jacob was angry, but he nodded. "Let's get out of here." He gestured with his coffee cup toward the door. "I'll walk you to your office."

"You don't have to do that," she said. "I'm starting my day in the evidence locker downstairs."

"Then I'll walk you to the elevator."

She let him, smiling at the officers who offered their congratulations as they made their way through the maze of halls that eventually led to the service corridor.

Jacob stopped in front of the elevator, but he didn't press the button to summon the car. His eyes were soft, his full lips pulled down in a frown.

"What is it?" she asked.

He shrugged, meeting her eyes, a well of emotions swimming in them. "I wish people could be happy for you."

"Some are, and that's enough."

"It's not. You're just used to people disapproving of your choices. This is crap. You're a good cop, and you're going to make an awesome detective. You don't deserve this."

She touched his arm, then threw her arms around his neck and hugged him tight.

He froze for a moment then held her in the deserted hallway. When he let her go, he pursed his lips, then blew out a loud, slow breath that echoed in the narrow space. "When they assigned me the squad problem child, I thought this would be the best day of my life. You know, moving on and joining the K-9 unit. All Danver talked about was how I could prove myself by keeping you in line and making sure you didn't hurt yourself. I was ready to babysit you."

She huffed out a breath and reached out to push the elevator button. "Babysit?"

"Let me finish." His eyes were damp as he fought to hold his emotions in check. "But you, Ellie, you were a force of nature. I realized right away they'd misunderstood you. People are going to underestimate you because of who you are, but it's going to bite them in the ass in the end. Use that to your advantage, but don't let it get to you. You're a bad-ass cop, and you're going to be an even better detective." He flashed her a bright smile. "I believe in you. Have a good first day."

He patted her arm and walked away before she could react, jogging down the hall and disappearing around the corner.

When she stepped onto the elevator, she was blinking away the tears that threatened as it clicked—he'd come to the station that morning just to walk her in. That alone blew her away, and she had to dab at her eyes this time. But his words had bolstered her confidence, which had taken a hit when she'd been assigned to cold cases. She knew it was grunt work, a way to prove herself before they gave her more urgent cases.

She lifted her chin up high. She was going to surprise them.

With Jacob's words echoing in her head, she stepped out of the elevator and made her way to the evidence room. Her steps faltered when she rounded the corner, and through the glass partition, spotted a blonde woman at the desk. The woman looked up, gave her a welcoming smile that spread her red lips wide, and hit the buzzer that unlocked the outer door.

"You must be Detective Kline," the woman said warmly. "I'm Jillian Reed."

"Hi," Ellie said, still a little shocked.

Jillian was petite and wispy in stature with stick-straight blonde hair that fell to her shoulders and hazel eyes that were more gray than brown. Delicate, soft, and feminine. It was her eyes that gave her away. Ellie could see the woman's mind working, and she had no doubt that Jillian was whip-smart.

Ellie couldn't keep the grin from growing on her face as she responded to the other woman's warmth.

Jillian's laugh danced on the air like wind chimes. Ellie liked her right away. "Fortis didn't tell you I was a woman, I guess?"

"I'm sorry." Ellie's cheeks heated. "It's not you, it's just that—"

"Charleston PD is a total boys club, and we're like the only two women here? Yeah, I noticed."

Ellie chuckled. "I think it's a few more than just us, but yeah, he didn't mention it."

"Well, don't worry. I don't bite, and I'm happy you're here." She handed Ellie a small piece of paper with two six-digit numbers. "These are your specific codes. When you're done memorizing them, pop the paper in the shredder. You don't want anyone else getting ahold of your codes."

"Thanks." Ellie committed the numbers to memory and dropped the small square into the paper shredder beside Jillian's desk.

Jillian arched an eyebrow. "That was quick."

"I have a good memory."

"That's going to serve you well down here." Jillian nodded, looking impressed. "There's a lot of information to absorb. Did Fortis tell you what case you're starting on?"

"He said I could look around and see if anything jumps out at me."

Jillian clapped her hands together once, the sound echoing off the cinder blocks. Her face lit with delight, she jumped up and moved to the inner door that separated the evidence from her office area. "I have just the one, I think. You don't have to pick this one, but oh, it's been bothering me since I first heard about it, and I've never been able to stop thinking about it."

"All right. I'll take a look." Ellie followed Jillian, who was nearly bubbling with excitement.

"You'll need to put your code in. It's how they track who's in and out. I'm expected to access the rooms several times a day, but if there's a chance you're going to take any files out, you'll have to access the room yourself."

Ellie punched in the code, and the door unlocked with a beep.

Jillian breezed past her, muttering to herself and walking so fast that Ellie had to hurry to keep up. Names and dates were scrawled on each box until they entered the section that held victims who were never identified, where Jillian stopped. Here, the boxes all looked the same. Each was marked with "Jane Doe" or "John Doe" and a series of numbers that signified the date. There were several on the same date, Ellie realized. Those boxes had an additional number at the end, based on their order of discovery. To further separate the unknown victims, the location and time found were clearly marked.

"There are so many," Ellie said, her voice loud in the tomblike silence. Now that she was about to get her hands on an actual case, the number of cases waiting to be solved seemed insurmountable.

They were both silent for a moment. The weight of the suffering the victims must have experienced, and all the unanswered questions that needed unraveling lay heavy on Ellie's shoulders.

"It's overwhelming when you think about it," Jillian said. "So many families who don't know what happened to their loved one. They're just out there, hoping and praying. Waiting for a miracle."

Ellie sucked in a deep breath through her nose. "I guess I never thought about how many cases are never solved."

"Most people don't." Taking a white cardboard box from a shelf, Jillian set it on the table. She kept her hand on it, her hazel eyes locking with Ellie's. "But I do. They haunt me. I know that Cold Cases is supposed to be the rookie beat, to let you know that you're lowest on the food chain and all that. But you're here for a reason, Ellie. You can make a difference. Even if you only solve one of these cases, that's one less family left wondering where their loved one is at night."

"You really care about these victims."

Jillian nodded, stepping over to a file cabinet and removing a file. "When I took the internship here, and I found all these people just waiting to be identified, it changed everything for me. I was studying to be a librarian, and this internship was a stretch, but I was trying to find something that would make me stand out."

"Is there a lot of competition in that field?" Ellie asked.

"You bet. You wouldn't believe how fierce the competition is now that so many degrees are online. If you want to work for a big library, you have to have a hook. I thought this would set me apart, but it sent me in a new direction instead. I changed my major to Criminal Justice the next week, graduated, and took a full-time job here. I never looked back."

"So, why this case?"

Jillian gripped the lid of the white box with both hands. "I've read a lot of these cases, but this one really stuck with me. Young college-age woman found tucked in the woods at West Ashley Park. No missing persons report matching her description, and no leads."

"But there has to be a lot of cases like that, right? That's why they're Jane Does."

"You're right, but that wasn't all." She was still holding the box shut, and Ellie itched to open it, but Jillian was building up to something. Ellie could tell the clerk was bent on revealing the case in her own time. So Ellie waited, and Jillian finally continued. "This young woman was tortured, but according to the medical examiner, the torture was followed by a swift death."

"There wasn't a significant lag between the two?" Ellie asked, her interest piqued.

"No. And that's bothered me for so long. Why torture someone only to kill them right away?"

"Maybe she gave up the information the perp wanted pretty easily," Ellie suggested, eyeing the box. "If they didn't need her anymore, she would be a liability, right?"

Jillian shrugged. "Here's another thing: if she had such valuable information at her disposal, why has she never been reported missing?" Her fingers curled, fingernails hooking beneath the edge of the box lid. "Usually, victims are tortured for pleasure or information. If it was the latter, she should've been someone whose disappearance was well-publicized. But there's nothing."

Ellie couldn't suppress a shudder. "Can we be sure it wasn't for pleasure?"

"The quick kill at the end would dispute that."

Ellie tucked a strand of hair behind her ear. "I'm almost afraid to ask how she died."

"It's bad," Jillian whispered, her already light skin paling as she grimaced. "There are pictures, and it's not easy to look at. That's why I wanted to prepare you."

"Thank you, but I think I can handle it." She held out her hand for the box.

Jillian slid it across the table. "Don't say I didn't warn you."

In reverence, Ellie opened the box. At first glance, it was like any other evidence box, every item individually sealed in plastic bags. Each bag had an evidence seal in dark orange, which had to be initialed and replaced every time it was broken, but Ellie had no need. Everything was visible through the clear plastic, and opening them would only compromise what little evidence there was.

Each individual piece of clothing was sealed in its own bag, carefully folded so it laid flat. In addition to the actual clothing, there were photographs of each item, both on the victim and from several angles once it had been removed.

Ellie studied each piece carefully, then set them aside. "It's hard to tell what color the shirt was. That's a lot of blood."

Jillian flipped the bag holding the woman's shirt and tilted it at an angle until the bright light overhead caught it just right. "It's lavender."

"I see it now."

Next came the preserved biological evidence. A sizable amount of hairs, many of them with the roots. There was a note about the hair, which was a coppery golden brown so light it reminded Ellie of honey. The color wasn't natural according to the note, and there was no root growth. A recent dye-job. In the other bags, there were scrapings from underneath her fingernails, a DNA profile, and a rape kit.

Ellie took the copy of the medical examiner's report from the box, leaving the sealed original in its bag. She read it through, eyes widening as the details sunk in, then she looked up at Jillian with her mouth agape. "Decapitated?"

"One quick, clean cut between the C3 and C4 vertebrae."

Ellie frowned, studying the report again. "Wouldn't that take quite a bit of force?"

"Force, skill, and an incredibly sharp blade."

She blew out a slow breath. "At least that explains the blood loss."

Jillian shook her head and reached across the table to turn the page and point to the medical examiner's tight, messy writing. "See right here? The body showed several signs of shock, heavy blood loss that happened quite some time before the cause of death. She'd lost a significant amount of blood long before she was killed."

Ellie scanned ahead, then sucked in a quick breath. "Her hand was cut off at the wrist too."

Jillian nodded. "But look right below that."

"The fingers of that same hand were cut off first." Ellie shook her head. "This is horrifying. This poor girl."

"They estimated her age at twenty. Far too young to die."

Ellie scanned the rest of the report. "The rape kit came up with nothing."

"And there was no foreign DNA under her nails. The killer was meticulous, but here's where it gets weird."

Wasn't it already strange enough?

But as Jillian spread the crime scene photos out in front of her, Ellie's stomach turned.

"She looks alive," Ellie whispered. "Like she's lying in the woods taking a nap."

Jillian glanced up, obviously happy to have someone as enamored about the case as she was. "Not just that, but look how she's posed."

"You can't even tell where he's cut her. How big is the property where she was found?"

"Almost a hundred acres."

"That's not huge, but in the woods, I guess it's enough to

give the killer the time needed." Ellie leaned in closer to one of the gruesome photos. "How long was she out there?"

"She was found within twelve hours of being placed. Whoever killed her made no attempt to cover the body except to arrange leaves around her severed hand and neck to make it look like she was intact."

Ellie bit the inside of her lip and studied the photos once more. "There's no remorse here."

"I noticed that too."

Their eyes met, and Ellie nodded, her chest tight as she thought of the victim out there in the wilderness, exposed. "You've convinced me. This is the one."

"You're going to solve the case?" Jillian's face lit with hope.

"No," she said with a determined nod. "*We're* going to solve this case."

10

Ellie pulled up to her parents' house, parking in the long, circular drive in front of the sprawling historic brick mansion. She took a deep breath and closed her eyes.

She wasn't ready for Sunday dinner. After a long week, Saturday hadn't been enough time off to recharge. She was exhausted, more emotionally than physically, though the wide range of feelings she'd experienced this week made her feel like she was slogging through deep mud with each step.

An entire week had passed, and she still didn't know how she was going to break the news to her family. Wesley would be happy, and she was sure her dad would at least support her decision. But it was Helen Kline whose approval Ellie craved.

Rigid and set in her ways, Helen had never understood why Ellie wanted to make detective so badly, and she'd always brushed it off. No one in her family had expected her to make detective this soon, and Ellie dreaded the conversation. Still, she couldn't wait forever, and now that it was time for their weekly family dinner, she couldn't put it off any longer.

Eustace, the family butler for as long as Ellie could remember, opened the door before she could knock. She hugged him as she stepped into the foyer, inhaling the familiar scent of Old Spice.

"Lovely to see you, Miss Ellie," he said, wrinkled face cracking with a quick smile. His blue eyes were clouding with age, but the sparkle was still there. "I'm glad you could make it."

"I wouldn't miss it for the world," she said quietly, so her voice didn't carry from the massive foyer into the formal dining room. "What's for dinner tonight?"

"Braised beef gorgonzola. My own personal recipe."

Ellie barely suppressed a moan of appreciation. "Eustace, you never cease to amaze me. What on earth is Mother going to do when you retire?"

He winked. "Hire five more people, I imagine."

"I think it would take more than five people to replace you."

Eustace gave her a half-bow. "I was being humble."

Ellie squeezed the old man's hand then quickly kissed his cheek, just before her mother's voice echoed down the short hall.

"Eleanor?" her mother called out. "Is that you, dear?"

"You'd best hurry. Your mother is a bit impatient today."

"Isn't that every day?" Ellie laughed, turning toward the dining room, but Eustace was gone when she turned around, disappearing through a servants' door. Out of sight and out of mind as he went about his duties with the grace and speed of a man half his age.

Ellie rushed to greet her mother, who was straightening the place settings on the elegantly covered dining room table. She inhaled and let out a soft moan. "It smells delicious," she said as she followed her mother into the massive kitchen that was a chef's dream. "I don't know about you, but I'm starved."

"One would think you'd show up on time then. We've been waiting for you. Nicolas is here." Her dark eyes flashed.

Ellie caught herself before she groaned, and the sound came out as part sigh, part cough. "You know, you don't have to invite him to Sunday dinner every Sunday."

"Why not? He's practically family. And when you get married—"

"We're not even engaged," Ellie pointed out.

The truth was, it was more complicated than that, but explaining that to Helen Kline was pointless. The fact that neither Nick nor Ellie needed to define their relationship to be happy meant it was up to Helen's interpretation. And since Helen was thrilled at the possibility of a Kline-Greene merger, she chose to believe that Nick and Ellie's relationship was far more evolved than it was.

Before her mother could work up the "reasons you should be engaged and stop policework" pitch, Ellie sighed inwardly and laid it out on the metaphorical table. "Can we talk about this another time? I'm hungry and exhausted. And I'm sure Nick is tired of you pressing him about the subject."

Ellie hugged her mom tight, then linked her arm through Helen's, and they walked into the dining room together.

"Of course, dear," her mother said in a voice that assured Ellie that "another time" wouldn't be too far off, and smiled at Dan Jr. as he entered and pulled a chair out for her. "Thank you, darling," her mother said as she sat.

Ellie's father entered, greeted her, and sat in the chair at the head of the table, beside Helen's. As he picked up his water glass, his hand trembled slightly.

Ellie put her hands on her father's shoulders and kissed his cheek, speaking low into his ear. "How are you feeling, Dad?"

"I've been better." He chuckled, then coughed into a handkerchief with his initials delicately stitched on one corner. "But I'm happy to see you here, princess."

She sighed, kissed him again, then took her seat between Wesley and Nick. *Princess*. He was the only man in her life who had never slung the word like an insult. She'd never allowed anyone but him to call her that.

"Your father isn't feeling well at all," Helen said. "He's been going downhill since late last week." She looked pointedly at Ellie.

Ellie's stomach turned at the reference to her jump from the bridge, and when Nick's hand found hers under the table, she took it and held on. Helen's implication was clear—that the tension of Ellie's job was ruining her father's health—but Ellie wasn't about to take the bait. An argument at Sunday dinner was the last thing her father needed.

With a slight tremble to her lip that was the only sign Helen was fighting for composure, she glanced around the table and folded her delicate hands on the gleaming wood in front of her. Her wedding ring shone in the soft light of the grandiose chandelier that hung above the table. Her lips pursed, expression sad, she raised perfectly plucked eyebrows at her husband.

He nodded, gave her a cheerless smile, and slowly reached out to pat her hands. The effort appeared monumental, and the gesture she'd seen her father use to comfort her mother countless times ended in an abrupt fall of his hand onto hers. An instant later, Helen opened her hands to take his between her palms, protecting his dignity and giving the impression that it was intentional.

Like everyone else at the table, Ellie knew it was anything but.

"Your father has asked me to tell you all what happened at the doctor office Friday." She took a deep breath then sighed heavily before continuing. "Your father's health is deteriorating. He's had a series of mild strokes, which wouldn't have been as bad if he wasn't already in a fragile state. He'll need a transplant soon." Her forehead furrowed into a frown. "Which means that we'll be praying for another family's loss so that Daniel can have a new heart. It's not an easy place to be. And we're going to need you all to do your part to reduce his stress while we're waiting."

Everyone nodded, including Nick. Aside from that slight movement of her head, Ellie was frozen to her seat, her heart a wild jackrabbit in her chest.

Helen's returning smile was soft, equal parts scared and hopeful as she gazed at her children, and the one man she hoped would someday be her son-in-law. She'd made that dream known for as long as Ellie could remember. *No pressure or anything.*

When her mother's gaze settled on Ellie, she froze. *Here it comes.*

"I know you've made it clear that you're not giving up your job, but I'm hoping that you care enough about your father's health to tone it down a bit. You always were an adrenaline seeker, and you know how it affects your father's peace of mind. We want you to be safe, not running off and jumping from bridges. Perhaps you can ask your partner to take different assignments."

Ellie sighed. Her mother would never understand the chain of command, but now that was moot.

"I was hoping you'd be proud of me, and we could skip the guilt trip," she said, her voice wavering. She cleared her throat and continued, still holding Nick's hand under the table. "That was a major bust, and interest in working for the department has tripled with the publicity."

Helen's eyes lit up. "That's wonderful. Then they won't miss you. Of course, you'll need to give them two weeks' notice, but that won't matter once you—"

"I'm not on patrol anymore."

Her mother's mouth parted daintily, the closest she ever came to a mouth agape in shock. "You already quit? Eleanor darling, I'm so happy you've had a change of heart."

"I didn't quit police work. I got promoted."

Her parents blinked as one, then Helen gave her a tight smile. "A promotion is wonderful. Will you have your own desk?"

She thought of the tables that had been pointed out as her workspace. "And then some."

"Oh, Eleanor, I'm so proud of you. See, I told you there was a way to serve the city without putting yourself in danger. How many men will you be overseeing? How does that work?"

She met her mother's gaze full-on. "It's not that kind of promotion."

A dark look passed over Helen's face. She was no fool. But she was patient, silently waiting for Ellie to elaborate.

Ellie straightened her shoulders and took a slow, deep breath. "I put in for detective, and it's official."

"Detective of what?" Helen asked.

"Technically, Charleston calls it the Violent Crimes Unit, so we catch a little bit of everything. But you'll be happy to know I got the safest, most mundane assignment available. I'm working cold cases."

"Cold cases?" Helen's voice was strained. She let go of Daniel's hand and clenched her fingers into loose fists.

Ellie narrowed her eyes, watching the expressions playing across Helen's face. "Unsolved murders and kidnappings, assaults and the like are what Violent Crimes houses," she explained, realizing the description sounded worse than her beat job. "But I have the old dead-end murder cases. If it happened in Charleston and it wasn't solved, I'll be taking a look at it."

Helen glanced at her husband, eyes wide, ruby-red-stained lip caught between her teeth.

Daniel leaned forward as if he was about to stand up, but he paused to mop the shine from his face with a cloth napkin, then sat back.

Helen pressed her fingers down hard on the table, but not before Ellie saw the tremble.

What the hell? She'd thought they'd be happy.

"I'm not digging up bodies or anything dangerous. I'll mostly be searching the internet for new information, re-interviewing old leads, checking CODIS and other national databases to see if any new evidence matches what we have, and trying to identify victims so their families have closure. Of all the things I could be doing, it's the safest, and I still get to make a difference. Isn't that what you're always telling me you want me to do? Make a difference without putting my life in danger? Well, I found a way to do it."

"I don't think this is a good idea." Helen's voice cracked.

Blake turned in his chair next to Helen, his eyebrow arched.

Helen's voice never cracked.

What is going on?

"Why?" Ellie pressed. "Why isn't it a good idea to do my job and make a difference? I don't know what you want from me."

"We want you to quit putting yourself at risk."

"At risk of what?" She flung her free hand up in the air. "Some of these cases are older than me. Even if I *do* stumble upon a serial killer, they won't be in any position to run away from me, let alone harm me. What gives? Why can't you just be happy that I'm doing something I find fulfilling?" She couldn't hold in a sigh. "I thought this would put you at ease. No more jumping off bridges and wrestling half-naked thugs out of the water live on television. It's what you've always wanted."

Ellie slowly stood, gritting her teeth. She hadn't expected her mother to be elated about the promotion, but Helen's reaction stabbed an old wound. It was obvious her mother didn't want her to do anything that might be too gruesome or beneath the Kline name, but Ellie refused to give up on her dreams.

"Eleanor, sit down, please. We have a guest."

Ellie laughed. "Are you kidding me? Nick is here every Sunday. He's practically family. You say it yourself all the time. Now he's a guest? Is my job that distressing to you? Or is it the fact that I'm not like Blake and Dan, doing whatever you want to make sure they get their share of the fortune?"

Her older brothers' faces hardened in unison.

"I'm not like them. I want to build my own identity beyond 'Daniel and Helen Kline's only daughter.' Do you know what that means? If I do everything right, it's because your money got me where I am. But if I screw up? Well, that's because I'm just a silly little rich girl playing cops and robbers. I don't know why I expected my family to actually support my dreams."

"We want to support your dreams," Helen said.

"But not *this* dream, right?"

Helen shook her head. "That's not it. I just think you should leave this to the real detectives."

As soon as the words were out of Helen's mouth, Ellie could tell she regretted ever saying them. But it was too late, and even Blake and Dan had the good sense to sit in shocked silence at Helen's words.

Ellie lifted her chin, hot tears threatening. "I need some air." She turned and went straight out the front door.

The air had a cool breeze that spoke of fall as she ran down the front steps and between the two massive white pillars. Instead of heading for her car, she turned right, following the paved path that wound lazily around the Kline family's massive estate. The ground was sixty acres of picture-perfect gardens, tree-lined pastures, and one crystal clear stream fed by an underground spring cutting right through the middle of it all.

When she was little, this place had been everything to her. A magical world that held endless possibilities. As a teen, her home had felt like a trap, just like her parents' money. Then, Ellie had made the worst mistake of her life, ending with her father having a stroke that led to the heart attack that had nearly killed him. Only after that had this place been a sanctuary.

The only place she could be free from the curious gaze of anyone who knew her secret.

The wind curled around her, turning the hot tears to icy rivulets on her cheeks. She crossed the picturesque bridge over the creek and stood in the middle, staring at the Charleston skyline off in the distance. Nearby, the massive magnolia still held the simple tire swing from her childhood. She could smell the familiar fragrant flowers on the breeze, bringing back memories of her own childish laughter as she tried to swing higher until her tiny bare feet touched the sun.

Life was simpler then.

She didn't know that the rest of the world lived a different kind of life.

She hadn't known that people could be boundlessly cruel.

She smiled as Nick's footsteps sounded on the bridge. His cologne drifted up around her as he settled his dinner jacket on her shoulders.

If only her parents could be so supportive without saying a word.

11

Nick waited a beat before he stood, keeping his face passive when Helen and Daniel looked his way, though he was fuming inside. He wanted to tell them that her dreams mattered too. They were going to push Ellie away when all she wanted was for them to see her for who she was. He didn't understand how people who did so much for the community couldn't see that their own daughter wanted the same things they did, she just went about it differently.

Better, he thought, but he kept his feelings to himself. His own parents were like the Klines. Traditional and set in their ways, it had taken most of his thirty years for them to accept that Nick wasn't going to change. But Ellie was the only daughter, and with that came endless expectations.

"I'll go check on her," Nick said.

"Thank you." Daniel cleared his throat and gave a weak cough into his handkerchief.

Helen sat stone-faced beside her husband, a quiver at the corner of her mouth the only outward sign that she was fighting back tears.

Nick nodded, his jaw clenched as he left the table.

Wesley caught his eye and mouthed a silent "thank you," but Ellie's older brothers wouldn't look his way. They knew how he felt about their lack of support. Unlike Ellie's parents, Nick didn't owe the two brothers respect. Helen and Daniel Kline came from old money and old values that were hard to shake. Blake and Dan Junior didn't have an excuse.

The air was crisp, the breeze shaking the leaves that were just beginning to turn the oranges and reds of fall's vibrant colors. He knew before he turned for the trail where he would find her. Walking off her frustration was something Ellie had been doing for as long as Nick could remember. And with her quick temper and the independent streak that went against everything her parents wanted for her, she'd done a lot of walking over the years.

The sight of her on the white bridge that curved over the narrow creek took his breath away. She was awash in the silvery light of the full moon that rose behind her. Framing her face and tumbling over her shoulders, her hair swayed with the gentle wind as she stared unseeing at the shadowed outline of the tire hanging from a rope. It swung in the breeze, and for a moment, Nick could see the picture that hung in Mr. Kline's office in motion in his mind.

Six-year-old Ellie, hair wild and free and nearly brushing the ground when she stretched her legs out and leaned back, long legs stretched skyward, toothless grin wide and mischievous. Every time Nick had seen the picture, he marveled at how it captured her essence so perfectly. All spunk, bravery, and determination, she'd never let fear stop her from going after what she wanted. She was a little taller now, and she'd traded the tire swing for a badge and gun, but she was still the same vibrant hellcat who never backed down and never took no for a final answer.

And Nick was totally and completely head over heels in love with her.

Ellie wrapped her arms tight around herself and rubbed the bare skin of her arms with her hands as the chill in the air cut through her anger.

Making sure she knew he was there, he stepped onto the bridge, shrugging off his jacket and setting it on her shoulders. Silent, he stood stoic, rock-solid behind her. Close enough that she could lean on him if she wanted but giving her space if she needed to stand on her own.

She was quiet for a long time, the only sign she was aware of him the weight of her body pressing against his chest. Tense with frustration, he could feel her deliberate deep breathing. When she finally spoke, the conviction in her words was unmistakable. "I won't let my mother guilt me into giving up my dreams."

"And you shouldn't."

"Why can't she just say she's proud of me and leave it at that?"

"She means well. Our parents come from another reality, and Helen believes the best way to make a difference is to volunteer, donate, and then go home and forget about the troubles of the world." He shook his head. "My mother is the same way."

"But you're a man, so your mother's expectations for you are completely different. And you don't have a sister…" She leaned to the side so she could look up at him, a wry grin on her smooth face.

"That's true, but it doesn't stop her from voicing her opinion whenever the opportunity presents itself." He laughed. "Or when she makes her own opportunity."

"Has she been after you because of me?"

He shrugged one shoulder, and when she turned in his

arms to face him, he rubbed her back and held her close. "I made it clear to her a long time ago that her thoughts on our relationship should remain thoughts and nothing more."

"I bet that went over well."

"She knows when she's pushed me too far. Not that she's going to drop the subject. Ever. But now when she brings it up, it's a general comment." He kissed the top of her head, and she nuzzled against his chest. "I can't stop her from speaking her mind, but I can make sure she's doing it without your name on her lips."

Ellie gave a soft snort. "If only you could work your magic on my parents. Well, just my mom. Dad doesn't have the energy lately." She swallowed audibly. "I was so busy chasing my goals that I didn't notice how poorly he's been doing."

"Don't blame yourself. Your father hides it well. That's just who he is. He has his pride and his reputation."

"Still, I should've seen it."

He swayed gently, still rubbing her back in an effort to soothe her. But her pain ran deep, and it was going to take more than a hug to heal the scars that ran even deeper. "Beating yourself up right now won't change anything. Your father will be okay."

"I want to believe that."

"He's survived worse."

She shuddered, then nodded solemnly. "I know. But that doesn't make me feel any better." Her arms went around his waist. "I can't do this without him."

He cupped her cheek, gently tilting her face up so he could look into her eyes. He saw the tears that threatened, but that didn't stop him. She deserved honesty. "You can, and someday, you will. But that day isn't today. Everything you've done up until this point you've done without help from any of us. You are so much stronger than you give yourself credit for."

She bit her lip and nodded. A single tear spilled over, and he watched it flow down her cheek to her slender neck before he lost track of it in the soft moonlight. "I just thought this time my mom would be happy with where I'm at. I spend most of my day in the damn basement. You can't get much safer than that. I guess she's not really cool with the idea of me examining violent crime scenes, even if they are twenty years old."

"I don't understand that, either."

"Did you see the look she gave my father?"

He nodded. "I did."

"Sometimes, I feel like no matter what I do, they'll never get me."

She took his hand, and they walked back across the bridge, his coat sleeve coming to the midpoint of her hands. Though she was strong and capable, somehow, his oversized jacket made her look more fragile. Softer. His heart clenched, but he pushed aside his feelings of dread. She was right; she'd never been safer. So why couldn't he shake the feeling of unease that pressed so heavily on his shoulders?

"What do you suppose they're talking about?" Ellie mused when they were at the halfway point.

The path swung in a wide arch heading back toward the house, which rose like a sentinel on the soft swell of a low hill. It was imposing, opulent, and rich with family history, like so many other estates in Charleston. Though nowhere near the grandeur of Magnolia Gardens, it held its own enduring charm.

"Do we really have to guess?" he teased.

She squeezed his hand and let her head fall against his shoulder as they strolled along, in no hurry to go back to the house and face her family. "Marriage, kids, alliances between wealthy families." She scoffed. "They act like we're royalty."

"They're acting like parents. They may do it in their own out-of-touch way, but all parents have dreams for their kids."

"I guess."

"You know I'm right. Strip it down to the bare bones, and they just want to make sure you're taken care of." As soon as the words were out of his mouth, he wished he could take them back.

She stopped on the path, her anger clear even in the shadows the night cast on her face. "I can take care of myself. Of all people, *you* should know that."

He recoiled inwardly but held his ground. "I didn't mean it like that. I know you don't need anyone to take care of you. You've proven that time and time again. They just want you to be happy."

"I am happy."

That phrase from her mouth should have made him happy too, but it only stabbed. "I know that, which is why I don't push the issue."

"The issue?"

He blew out a long, hard breath. "Maybe I should stop talking. Every time I try to fix the last thing I said, I just make it worse."

"No, please. I want to hear it. What issue?"

"Our relationship." He gestured vaguely between the two of them. "Marriage, kids, whether we're even dating exclusively or not."

"Aren't we?"

He laughed. "If by exclusive you mean we're both not dating anyone, then sure."

Her shoulders shook as she laughed with him. "You're right. I'm sorry I haven't made time for you lately."

"I understand. You're busy, and you're working on yourself, your dreams." He only wished a life with him was on the top of the list. But he kissed her lips, then pulled back and tucked a soft curl behind her ear. "I get you, and I know that when you're ready, I'll be the first one to know. There's no hurry."

"Even with our parents pressuring us to get married?" She bit her lip, gazing up at him.

"Especially then. We're in this together." He cupped her cheek, and she leaned into his touch. "The only opinion that matters here is yours. I'm happy being with you the way we are. When or *if* you're ever ready to get married, we'll cross that bridge together then."

She pursed her lips thoughtfully, then smiled. "I don't deserve you."

"Actually, you do, and so much more. Ellie, I don't need a piece of paper to be happy. I have everything I need right here." He hugged her tight, breathing in her scent as she leaned against him. He'd always been patient with her, and he would just have to be for longer.

The world around them stopped, and for that moment, there was nothing but Ellie in his arms, the gentle breeze, and the hint of jasmine that clung to her skin.

When she moved out of his embrace, he wanted to pull her back, but he knew better. "I'm ready to go back inside."

"Are you sure?" He took in a slow, deep breath, holding back a sigh. "This is nice."

"You don't want them to think we ran off and eloped, do you?"

A hearty laugh burst from his chest before he could stop himself. He shook his head and put his arm around her as they walked toward the house. "That would be something, wouldn't it?"

"Mother would never forgive me."

"You're right, she would never get over that." He paused at the door, gazing down at her. "Let's get this over with."

She grinned at him, kissed him square on the lips then put her forehead against his. "I can't think of anyone I'd rather have by my side," she whispered.

"Funny," he said, his voice tender. "I was thinking the same thing."

12

"You're here bright and early on a Monday," Jillian said when Ellie walked into the basement office the next day. "You don't have to be here for another hour, right?"

"I couldn't sleep." She handed Jillian a cup of coffee she'd bought at the local donut shop, then gestured at the new desk in the space in the corner. "You getting a new office mate?"

"Yeah," Jillian smiled, "you."

"What? No, my desk is supposed to be upstairs."

"They put it in sometime over the weekend. There's a nameplate in the top drawer that says 'Detective Kline,' so I assumed it was yours."

Ellie hurried to open the drawer, and sure enough, a shiny new nameplate with her name on it rattled against the bare wood on the bottom of the drawer. "I'll talk to Fortis about it later. It's probably a mistake."

Jillian's face fell. "That's too bad. I was kinda excited to have company."

"I'm sorry." Ellie immediately felt terrible. "I didn't mean any offense."

"None taken. It just gets lonely down here, that's all."

Ellie glanced around the bright, artificially lit space. "I thought it would be annoying with people coming in and out all day."

Jillian shook her head. "Not as many as you'd think. I've gone an entire week without seeing a single soul. It's part of the reason I started looking at some of the cold case files to begin with. I can't open anything that's sealed, but I can run a search for everything the detectives logged in the database and go from there. It's not much, but it's better than staring at the wall."

"I guess it is." Ellie took a sip of her coffee and closed her eyes to savor the smooth liquid that was so much better than the sludge in the breakroom. "Speaking of looking into cases," she said when she opened her eyes again, "anything new on our Jane Doe?"

"I thought I'd wait for you. It's more fun that way."

"Let's get after it, then." Ellie turned the computer on and typed in her credentials; it was up and running in a matter of minutes. She took out her notes and started searching through the missing persons database.

While she was working, Jillian began her own search. "I looked a little over the weekend, but it's hard without the case file with me," she explained when Ellie looked over to see what she was doing. "There are more people turning up missing every year, so a lot of people turn to social media when the police can't help."

"I've seen that before. But most of the time, the person being shared was found years before. I'm sure that throws a wrench into things."

Jillian tapped her computer screen. "Isn't it mind-blowing that someone playing detective online wouldn't bother clicking on the article to check for updates *first*? But even accounting for all that nonsense, social media has helped bring countless people home when overworked police departments can't. Posting is worth a shot."

They worked in silence for a while, with only the clacking of fingers on keyboards filling the room as they searched hundreds of reports. Every few minutes, Ellie would glance at the copy of the picture that sat on her desk of the poor woman's face. Even with a notepad covering up the injury, Ellie couldn't wash the image of the clean cut partway down the woman's neck.

The notes pointed out that only a knife that was both heavy and extremely sharp could have resulted in such a clean wound. But quick didn't mean painless, and Jane Doe's blank, fixed stare had haunted Ellie's dreams since she'd first laid eyes on it. No matter how fast her death was, in the end, there was no mercy there.

And to think she'd gone nameless for all this time. Buried in a state funded cemetery with only a number to indicate her existence.

When the phone on her desk rang, crashing through the silence without warning, Ellie nearly jumped out of her skin. She was relieved to see that Jillian had jumped too. They gave each other embarrassed smiles.

"Detective Kline," she answered, savoring the words that felt exciting and foreign all at once. Someday, her new title wouldn't make her pulse quicken, but for now, she was enjoying the novelty.

"Come to my office," Fortis ordered, his thick, gravelly voice unmistakable.

Her stomach dropped. "Of course." The line went dead in her ear before she could say more. Setting the receiver in the cradle, she took a deep breath.

"Bad news?" Jillian said, having paused in her work.

"No, at least I don't think so."

"I'll wait for you if you want. Otherwise, I'm going to grab lunch."

Ellie glanced down at her watch, blinking her exhausted eyes a few times, and frowned. "I didn't realize we'd been at this for hours. Don't wait for me. There's no telling how long this might take."

They rode the creaking elevator together to the first floor, where Jillian got off and gave a tiny wave before she was gone. The car lurched upward, stopped abruptly, and jolted a little when the doors bumped open before it was completely lined up with the second-floor hallway.

Fortis waved her into his office from behind his desk.

At least he isn't scowling, Ellie thought, closing the glass door behind her, even though it did nothing for privacy and only slightly muffled their voices.

"That was quick," he said, offering her a seat.

She took it, sitting back and trying to look relaxed. The urge to ask if she was in trouble was strong, but Fortis was in a hurry and started talking before she'd found a comfortable position in the cracked leather chair.

"Jillian likes you." He smiled as his hazel eyes appraised her. "How are you liking Cold Cases?"

"It's…different."

"That department takes some getting used to. Here's a list of the cases I want you to start with. You can go in any order, but I'd like to get them cleared out first, if we can."

Ellie took the typed list. "The one I'm working on isn't listed."

This earned an arched eyebrow from him. "Are you still working on that Jane Doe?"

She automatically jumped to the defense of the helpless woman. "It's only been a week."

"Have you made any headway?"

No.

"Yes, but not much."

Fortis waved a dismissing hand. "Then go ahead and shelve it, and let's move on."

He started to turn, as if to end the conversation, but she couldn't abandon Jane Doe. "Why? What makes these cases more important? Aren't they all unsolved?"

His smile slipped, but he didn't let any emotion show. "This list is of the cases that have a lot of evidence. With all the advancements in technology, you can probably clear out half of them this month."

"That's a little ambitious."

He stiffened, but his demeanor remained cordial. "Do you have a better idea?"

Ellie knew that tone, but self-preservation wasn't as important as finding Jane's killer. "I want to see this Jane Doe case through."

He picked up a pen and thrummed it on the desk. "Do you have new leads?"

"No, but I haven't had a lot of time on it, and if I could just—"

"If you haven't made any progress in a week, it's time to let it go."

"Can't we account for learning? I'm working with systems I've never seen before, and I've finally started to hit my stride. I feel like I'm close to a breakthrough." Not feeling like she was convincing him, she played the guilt-trip card. "Don't you think this woman's family deserves to know what happened to their daughter?"

Fortis gave her a pitying look. "It's been years."

Ellie held his gaze, unwavering in her conviction. "Yes, a lifetime, sir."

Fortis sighed. "I'll level with you. You're the only detective I have on cold cases, and it's an election year. I need to have some progress to show. It sounds like this case is becoming a pet project you can't let go of. That's not how this is going to work. You hit each case hard, and when you hit a wall, you move on. We can't solve every cold case."

"Sir, if I solve this case, it's going to be huge. Don't you think the people of Charleston want to catch the person who decapitated a young woman and left her where children could've easily found her? I know I would feel better knowing that person is behind bars." She crossed her arms and sat back, drawing a proverbial line in the sand.

Fortis scowled. "We're not going to do this on every case, you understand? You work for me." He punched his chest with his index finger.

"One more week. If I haven't made serious progress by end of day Friday, I'll start your list first thing Monday."

"You'll start the list Monday, regardless," he countered. "This is only the start of your second week, and working one case at a time isn't what we do."

"Understood." She stood slowly and turned toward the door.

"Kline?"

She stopped and looked over her shoulder. "Yes?"

"Don't make this a habit."

"Yes, sir," she said and hurried out the door before he could change his mind.

She was halfway to the parking lot when she realized she'd forgotten to ask him about the desk. Shrugging, she decided she didn't care. Jillian was better company, and the evidence room was quieter than the bullpen where the other detectives gathered.

She grabbed lunch at a drive-thru and headed out to West Ashley Park. She was finishing the last bite as she parked her car and grabbed the running shoes she kept in the cargo area. Hurrying past the soccer fields and playground, she used a printed satellite image of the park to find the spot where Jane Doe's body had been dumped.

Placed, she amended, remembering the meticulous staging of the scene. *Displayed.*

Manicured open green spaces gave way to mulched trails bordered by thick marsh grasses. A large crane with a splash of red across its face stood in the shallow water, unbothered by her presence as it dipped its beak into the water, looking for fish.

Ellie was so entranced by the bird she almost missed the sign posted on a tree: A Fed Alligator is a Dead Alligator. Comparing the GPS on her phone to the crime scene printout, she suppressed a shudder when she realized she was standing almost in the exact spot. A few young palmettos had appeared since the body was found, but other than that, not much had changed in five years.

Standing in the very spot Jane Doe had been found, she could hear children shrieking with joy on the playground. The body had been only a few yards from the trail. There were so many places that would've hidden the crime for longer than twelve hours, maybe even forever. But the body had been carefully displayed right there, clearly visible from the walking trail and close to the water's edge—meant to be found. Whoever had done this knew the woman wouldn't be identified, or simply didn't care if she was—a fact that seemed so very callous.

It was the proximity to the playground that had Ellie trembling with barely concealed rage. This wasn't some remote mountain trail deep in the woods. Several houses in the nearby neighborhood were visible across the water, and in the space of five minutes, a mother appeared on the trail with her two kids. She pointed out the sign and reminded the children that the gators wouldn't bother them if they stuck close, then she smiled at Ellie and herded the kids on.

This is a busy trail. This body wasn't meant to be out here long.

The murderer had been expecting the body of the woman to be found quickly.

Why?

Ellie frowned. She suspected the killer had been hoping that gruesome sight was discovered by a child. It wasn't enough to torture the victim before she was killed, the perp wanted to terrorize the people of Charleston too.

Except, the people of Charleston had forgotten the girl in the park. They'd watched the news reports, read the articles, and worried. Then they'd gone on with their lives. Murder was part of modern life, and so many believed it was something that only happened to other people.

Jane Doe had probably thought that too.

There was nothing new for Ellie to discover at the dumpsite, but discovering how carefully the location had been picked gave her insight into the murderer's thought process. No shame. No fear. Absolutely no remorse. This wasn't a crime of passion, and it was clear the woman hadn't been tortured for information. All that left Ellie with more questions than answers, but she'd made progress.

She decided to stop at the M.E.'s office next, and had a copy of the official report in hand when she walked into the spacious office tucked in the back corner of the county coroner's building in North Charleston.

The dark-skinned woman behind the desk had thick, wavy hair that fell past her waist and deep red lips that spread into a quick smile. The tall woman stood when Ellie entered the room and held out her hand. "Afternoon, Detective," she said. "I'm Dr. Faizal. You can call me Moni."

"How did you know?" Ellie asked, sitting down across from Dr. Faizal.

"I would say it's the way you're dressed or even the badge on your hip that your jacket doesn't quite cover, but let's be honest." She leaned forward and smiled, dark eyes crinkling at the corners. "There hasn't been this much talk since Charleston got its first lady Medical Examiner."

"Jump off a bridge and get promoted to detective, and suddenly, everyone knows your name."

Moni laughed, and Ellie joined in, some of the tension that had drawn her shoulder blades together at the park releasing.

They drew a strange look from a man who walked past the open door carrying a file, and he was still staring at them when he disappeared from view. A few seconds later there was a thud, then the man cursing under his breath, followed by the unmistakable thwack of a stack of papers falling to the floor. One of the papers fluttered to a stop in the doorway, and when the man shuffled over to pick it up, he had a red circle right in the middle of his forehead where it had made contact with the wall.

Ellie clenched her jaw and managed not to laugh, but Dr. Faizal wasn't worried about the man's already bruised ego. "Do you need something, Tom?"

"No, sorry," he stammered and disappeared around the doorjamb.

"What was that all about?" Ellie asked.

"Some people are too nosey for their own good." She held out her hand and nodded toward the paper Ellie was clutching so tightly the corner had wrinkled. "Is this a case you're working on?"

"It is," Ellie said, handing the paper over. "I was hoping you could fill in some blanks for me. I know it's a five-year-old case, but I was thinking that you—"

"I remember this," Dr. Faizal said. "I'd never seen that level of brutality in my life. What a horrible way to die."

"My thoughts were that it was quick."

When Dr. Faizal glanced up, her eyes were solemn. "It was, but not the torture beforehand."

"It was my understanding that she was killed shortly after the torture."

Dr. Faizal scanned the report. "She was killed after her hand was cut off. But the state of her organs suggested that she'd lost quite a bit of blood hours before the final blow." She sighed, shaking her head. "The thing is, technically, though there wasn't much time between the torture and death, for the victim, it was an eternity. Mercifully, it also appeared that she was drugged and was probably completely out of it, if not in shock from the blood loss. If she hadn't been decapitated, she still would have died in a few hours, if she lasted that long."

"Is there anything else you can remember?"

"I'm sorry, but there was almost no evidence, other than the possible methods of torture, in this case. Which in and of itself is remarkable when you consider the shear strength and violence it took."

Ellie was already sure she knew what that meant, but she wanted to know what Moni thought of it. "Meaning?"

"This wasn't a first-timer. Whoever this was, they'd killed before. The knowledge and skill it takes to hit right between the vertebrae for a cut that clean isn't common."

"Plus, she wouldn't have sat still for it. She was probably moving…screaming, drugs in her system or not."

"Exactly. A nervous killer would've made a mistake." The M.E. tapped the file with a manicured fingernail. "This is a near-perfect crime."

"Near perfect?" Ellie accepted the report when Moni handed it back to her.

"The hair dye was the only thing that stood out."

Ellie flipped through the papers until she found the notes on the dye. "I see it right here. It was recent?"

"Very recent. I could smell the ammonia. Her hair was bleached shortly before her death."

Ellie's nose scrunched up, as if the smell of ammonia was in the air now. "Bleached?"

"No way she was naturally that color." The M.E. pulled up a file on her computer and turned the monitor around to face Ellie. "See her eyebrows? They're very dark, almost black. Her hair was likely very dark brown, if not black as well. It's tricky to get the hair to a light blonde when bleaching for the first time, which accounts for the odd copper-honey tone." She used her mouse to click to the side of the picture, on the young woman's hair. The picture reloaded, this time with darker hair. "She would've looked something like this."

Ellie stood, suddenly excited. She hadn't seen the dark-haired version of the victim before. Maybe she wasn't the only one. "Can you print that off for me?"

"Already done." After a few keystrokes, a paper appeared in the printer tray behind the desk. "Here you go. I know it's not standard procedure, but if you could let me know what you find, I'd appreciate it. This case has haunted me since they brought her in."

"I understand," Ellie said. "Thank you so much."

She could barely tear her eyes away from the newly brunette woman as she gathered her things and headed back to her car. She couldn't wait to show Jillian.

Maybe this was the break they needed to blow the case wide open.

13

Jillian had been gone for more than an hour when Jacob appeared in the doorway with a potted cactus, fighting to keep a grin off his face.

"Nice digs," he said, handing Ellie the plant. "I went up to the bullpen, but they said you were down here."

"I'm closer to the cold case files here." She shrugged and eyed the prickles on the cactus. They reminded her of Fortis when she'd gone head to head with him. "They acted like it was a mistake, but no one has done a thing to correct it, and I don't have the energy to argue. A desk is a desk, and I don't have to drag boxes upstairs or check out evidence if I'm inside the cage, so it works out. Although, this cactus might croak before it sees the light of day."

"Everything all right?" She shrugged again, and Jacob narrowed his eyes. "Spill it, Kline. It's six p.m., and you're still here, but you don't look happy about it. What's going on?"

"I thought I got a break in the case I've been working on." She frowned at the papers she'd been studying on her desk. "Except it wasn't a break, and now we're right back to where we were before."

"We?" Jacob's dark eyebrows shot up.

"Jillian is helping me. She's really good with the computer system, and she's a wealth of knowledge."

"Jillian. The evidence clerk?" He glanced around to make sure they were alone. "Are you sure?"

"Yes, why?" She scowled at him. "What have you heard?"

"Nothing, except Jillian has a reputation. She's like a guard dog. She doesn't like people in her space."

"It's not 'people' she has a problem with. You should see how the male officers flirt with her when they come downstairs. I'd be sick of it too."

Jacob lifted one shoulder, as if it couldn't be helped. "She's hot."

Ellie narrowed her eyes. "You say that, but it's obvious most of them think flattery will get them special treatment. If Jillian was a man, they wouldn't treat her like that."

"You don't seem to mind."

Ellie blinked, taken completely by surprise. "No one flirts with me."

Jacob snorted, his head falling back on his shoulders as he laughed. "Seriously? It happens all the time, you just don't notice."

She assessed his expression, trying to see if he was pulling her leg. "I think maybe you're imagining things. Anyway, Jillian is great when you treat her with respect, so I wouldn't listen to the rumors."

"Time will tell how long that lasts with you in her office all the time."

"Well, it's our space now, and we get along just fine."

"Why doesn't that surprise me? You up for a drink?"

She glanced up at him suspiciously. "Is that why you're here?"

"I came in to grab some paperwork before I start intensive training tomorrow."

"I thought you were supposed to start today."

He held his hands up. "It was pushed to tomorrow. I didn't ask why."

"All about the paid time off, right?"

"Hey, do you blame me? Maybe you could use a mini-vacation."

She grabbed her jacket off the back of the chair and waited for her computer to shut down before locking up. "Not sure I'll get one of those, but I could use a drink and fresh eyes on this in the morning."

"I can drive."

"Sure. I'll just leave my car here and take a service in the morning." She followed Jacob out through the side exit, whistling low through her teeth when he pointed the key fob at a powder blue Mustang with dealer plates. "New car?"

"It's a couple years old, but it's new to me."

"I didn't figure you for a Mustang guy, but it's nice. Where does the dog sit?"

He chuckled. "Duke gets the whole backseat to himself. He takes it all up too."

She slid into the passenger seat and leaned back, closing her eyes. When the victim's face popped up on the backs of her eyelids, her eyes snapped open, and she settled for watching the scenery fly by. Charlie's Pub was only a few blocks from headquarters, and so close to shift change that it was wall-to-wall police officers. A few greeted them, but just as many gave Ellie the side-eye and teased Jacob about the partner upgrade.

"Assholes," Jacob muttered, leading her to a booth in the back.

"Don't worry about it. It doesn't bother me."

"They'll get over it."

She shrugged out of her suit jacket, letting out a sigh as

she sank into the booth. "Or they won't. I'm not lying when I say I don't care."

"Some of them are still jealous of the attention you attracted."

"Like I jumped off a bridge for attention," she scoffed, arching her back and stretching, trying to shed the day.

"I know. And I've said as much to anyone who's confronted me about it. I'm sort of surprised no one busted my chops for letting you do the hard part."

"I think they're just grateful they didn't have to drag a slick, half-naked man out of the water. *That* was the hard work. You even lost a shoe."

"Funny," he grumbled, eyeing the paper menu that boasted some of the best deep-fried bar food that could be found in the South. "I couldn't get the smell of swamp water out of my upholstery."

"Is that why you got a new car?"

He looked at her dubiously. "Promise you won't be mad?"

"No, I don't promise," she said, following a comic scowl with a smile. "Come on, tell me."

"All right, but if you get mad…"

"I won't." This time she had to school her face so she didn't frown.

"When we were assigned as partners, I'd heard so many… stories, I was afraid my career would be over. So, I promised myself if my career survived working with you, I would buy myself a new Accord."

Ellie's eyes narrowed, sensing this was about to get worse. "You bought a Mustang."

"About halfway through our time as partners, I realized my life was in danger, so I changed my reward. I figure *living* through all that meant I deserved something special."

"Wow." Ellie tried to decide if that was a compliment or an insult.

"You promised you wouldn't be mad."

"No, I didn't," she laughed, "but I'm not mad. Actually, I'm kind of flattered."

A waiter appeared at their table, but before he could hand them the printed menu, Ellie waved it away. "I'll take a cheesesteak and fries with a rum and cola."

"I'll have the same," Jacob said. When the waiter was gone, he leaned forward to be heard over the crowd. "So, tell me about the case."

She laid the whole thing out, pausing when their drinks then food were delivered so the waiter didn't catch any of the gory details. Jacob listened with rapt attention, asking her questions a few times, but otherwise just hearing her out.

"It feels good to share that with someone," she said when she finally finished. "I can't tell my family because they would freak, and Nick doesn't really get it. I mean, he tries, but sharing the case with him might put him over the edge."

"That's the kind of thing you should only share with another LEO. Unless you've been a law enforcement officer, you can't really know how we can see this stuff day in and day out and still come to work ready to serve. It takes someone really special."

"Nick is special." She grimaced when she heard how defensive her own tone was.

"He's a good guy," Jacob admitted. "But my dad always told me, never marry someone who's not an officer. The marriage would be doomed from the start."

"Your mother was a housewife."

"Before that, my mother was a dispatcher. It's not the same thing, though a dispatcher is in touch with the horrors that happen to a beat cop. But they work crazy hours, too, so she quit to stay home with me. When I went to school, they were doing well financially, and she just never went back. She missed it, though." He took a sip of his drink and let it settle on his tongue before he swallowed. "She lived for Dad's stories."

"Nick would listen to me. But it wouldn't be the same, so I don't bring it up." She shrugged one shoulder and took a sip of her drink, letting the rum settle to the bottom of her stomach and do its magic. "It's not like we're getting married anyway."

"Is everything all right?"

She let out a long sigh. "Yes. He's perfect; completely content to wait until I'm ready and all that." She waved a hand in front of her face in a flippant motion, then finished the rest of her sandwich in two bites and went to work on her fries. "He's everything a woman could want and more."

"So, why don't you want to marry him?"

"It's not him." She looked into Jacob's probing brown eyes. "I don't want to marry anyone. At least, not right now."

"What about your parents? Are they happy you're working in a safer environment? Not many bridges in the cold case locker."

"Ha-ha. I thought they'd be thrilled, but no. My mother is freaked out by death, I guess, and my dad loves my mother, so he goes along with whatever she wants."

"I'm sorry." The waiter came back, and Jacob waved off his offer to refresh his drink before he continued. "I really thought they'd be happy."

"They're afraid I'll get hurt."

"Maybe I shouldn't have gotten you a cactus," he joked. "Too many barbs."

"Shut up." She laughed, rolling her eyes. "They're not that protective."

He screwed his mouth to the side and put his finger on his chin. The effect was hilarious, and she nearly snorted rum and cola up her nose. "I see you get my point," he said.

"Whatever."

"So, what did you think about the other case from West Ashley? Weird that two bodies were dumped there so close together, right?"

Ellie's lips parted, and she froze with her glass inches from her mouth. "What?"

"You're talking about the Jane Doe by the walking trail, right? There was another one found that same month."

She set her glass down with a sharp thunk, leaning forward. *Two in the same month?*

"In the same spot?"

He frowned. "No, but in the same park."

"Why aren't the two of them linked in the system?"

He pursed his lips and thought for a second. "I'm guessing because the cause of death was completely different. The body was hidden instead of displayed, and her head was attached to her body. At least, that's what I think the detectives said when a news anchor asked the same question."

Ellie leaned back in her seat, deflated. "Oh. Well, that doesn't sound like more than a coincidence."

"It doesn't, but there were some pretty strange things about both cases. Then there's the location. There are always people there, so whoever it was knew the area well, blended in, and were able to get in and out without leaving any evidence."

Ellie thought back to the path she had taken to the dumpsite. "Any shoe prints would be obscured by the mulch, right? It's not the best material for footprints."

"It may have been dry out and the path mulched, but isn't it unusual to leave nothing? No hair, no ripped clothing, no fibers. Nada."

Ellie could feel the case sinking deeper into her subconscious; talking it over with Jacob had been just what she'd needed. "The M.E. basically said the same thing. That she hadn't seen so little evidence in such a violent death."

"Same with Jane Doe number two."

"That still doesn't connect them. Are there any similarities at all? Even small ones that might not have seemed important at the time could mean something, with two bodies close to each other. How did she die?"

He shook his head, rubbing his hand over the side of his face. "I don't remember. It wasn't as gruesome as the first woman, so it wasn't discussed as much. If I remember right, the throat was slashed and stabbed, but I could be wrong."

She cocked her head to the side. "What if he tried to decapitate her too, and failed?"

"There's no way. If my memory serves me, the cuts were made in an entirely different place than when you aim to slice someone's throat. If you miss the artery, they could survive."

Ellie recoiled a little, eyes widening. "How do you know that?"

He gave her a wily smile. "You're not the only one who had dreams of making detective. It didn't pan out for me, but I watched enough crime dramas, learned more than I ever needed to know. Some of the most popular shows are horribly inaccurate, but the ones that really take time to research are worth the watch. If you want, I can give you my watch-list."

She held up her hands and shook her head. "Hard pass."

"Your loss."

"Do you know anything else about the case? How long between the first woman and the second?"

Jacob took a swig of his drink, his eyes going to the ceiling as he thought back. "Within the month, I think. And the second body was badly decomposed, but there'd been so much rain. Between that and the scavengers, time of death was hard to pinpoint."

Ellie's stomach lurched. "I'm glad she was dead for that."

"Me too. That's all I remember. They never figured out who she was, and a police sketch didn't lead anywhere."

"Maybe whoever did it heard about the first woman and decided it was a good place to dump a body."

"I think that's what detectives ultimately decided, but I can't be sure." Jacob took both their plates and stacked them on the edge of the table for the waiter.

"And you don't have any logical reason that the two are linked, besides location?" Ellie drained her drink and considered ordering another since Jacob was driving.

"That's right. And really, so many bodies are found in parks and in wooded areas that it could just be a coincidence."

"You don't sound like you believe that."

"I don't believe in coincidences." He downed his drink and set it on the table. "To tell you the truth, the detective assigned to the case dismissed everyone's concerns. I wasn't the only one who thought the two women might have been linked."

A rowdy group walked in, and as soon as Ellie saw the beefy cop who'd blocked her in the breakroom, she groaned. "Let's get out of here."

Jacob followed her gaze and nodded. "I have to be up early." He opened his wallet and tossed a twenty on the table. Ellie did the same, and they slipped out the door and headed to the parking lot.

As they were walking out, Ellie checked her watch. "I can't believe it's almost nine."

"Time flies in good company." His chocolate-brown eyes sparkled. "And you turn into a different person when you talk about a case."

"Is that a bad thing?"

He opened the passenger door, and she slid in, buckling her seatbelt as he started the engine. "Not at all. You light up.

It's amazing how your whole demeanor changes. I had my doubts, but I think this is your calling."

The compliment hit home, and she let it settle in, basking in its warmth. "Thanks. Maybe someday I'll get to work on newer cases."

"I didn't mean homicide as a calling." The low roar of the Mustang's engine fit Jacob perfectly as he made his way down the quiet streets toward her apartment. "Cold cases. When you talked about that victim, it was like her story lit a fire in your soul. I know you want the excitement and danger that comes with a fresh crime scene, but don't give up on cold cases too soon."

"Don't worry, Fortis isn't going to bump me up anytime soon." She leaned her head back on the headrest, smiling a little, surprised at how relaxed she was feeling now. "He's made it clear that I'm to follow the rules and keep my head down."

"Fortis is a good guy."

"He is, but I have a feeling Danver warned him I was trouble."

"Aren't you?" Jacob winked at her as he pulled the car to a stop at the curb in front of her building.

"You know what I mean," she grumbled in a warning tone. "Until I prove myself, I'll have to watch what I do."

"Or you can connect these two cases and solve them both."

His faith in her was like a ray of sunshine. She grinned at him in the glow of the streetlamp he always parked under. In or out of uniform, Jacob was a cop first.

"Thank you," she said.

"For what?"

"For believing in me."

He flashed her a grin. "Give 'em hell, Kline. Anyone who underestimates you is a fool."

She got out of the car and waved when she was safely through the locked entryway. Jacob didn't move, so Ellie hurried upstairs and turned on the lights in her place. When she opened the blinds and waved once more, he finally pulled away from the curb, satisfied that she was safe and sound.

Normally, his overprotectiveness annoyed her, but she was too excited now to care. The possibility of a second case rejuvenated her. That meant more evidence, which gave her a better chance of solving both crimes. Solving them wasn't going to bring either woman back, but somewhere two families waited for closure, and Ellie was going to bring it to them.

She wouldn't stop until she identified both of the women.

She would find their killer.

Justice would be served.

14

When Ellie arrived at Charleston PD early Tuesday morning, Jillian was just walking in the rear door.

"Late night?" Ellie asked her, handing over the coffee she'd brought her.

"You don't have to buy me coffee every morning." Jillian took a long, grateful sip.

"I know, but I have to get my own. Might as well get two."

"Thank you," she said as they walked to the elevator. "Really. I'm exhausted and short on sleep. It's taking a toll."

"I know the feeling. Can I do anything to help?"

Jillian shook her head. "Unless you can get Sam to stop snoring."

"Oh. I didn't know you were seeing anyone." Ellie held Jillian's cup as they stopped in front of the evidence room door so she could unlock the office.

"Sam isn't my partner." Jillian laughed, flipping on the light and picking up the picture frame on her desk. "Sam is my dog. Well, she's technically my brother's dog, but he's been saying he was going to pick her up 'next month' for the past two years, so I think she's my dog now."

"Aww." Ellie cooed at the photo. "How old is she?"

"Almost three. She's a mess. And the reason for the bags under my eyes."

"I see." Ellie slung her purse over the back of her desk chair and leaned back against the desk, savoring her fresh-brewed coffee. "She's a handful?"

"Energetic, friendly, sloppy, and always into something. I can handle that. But then she snores all night long."

"You have to draw the line somewhere." Ellie grinned so wide her cheeks hurt. She'd pined for a dog when she was a kid. Her mother had only waved a hand at all the priceless antiques in sight, and she had known there was no hope she would ever have a puppy. That hadn't kept her from asking, though, and frequently. "Maybe I could babysit once in a while. Or puppysit. Whatever it's called."

"You like dogs?"

"I love dogs." So had her brothers, and they'd even gone so far as to launch a united campaign for a dog in which they'd assessed the possible drawbacks and what they would do to prevent those. In the end, though, there were just too many valuable objects in their home to allow it to house a pet.

"Everyone says that until they meet Sam. She has a way of making people run the other way."

Ellie quirked up a brow. "It sounds like Sam and I have a lot in common. I may need to borrow her."

"I'll think about it. I'm not sure if I can sleep without her with me." Jillian pointed at the stack of papers on Ellie's desk. "Did you make any headway last night? That stack looks a lot bigger than it was when I left yesterday."

"I did. I found out a lot of things, and they led basically nowhere."

Jillian's smile slipped into a frown. "That's disappointing. I thought you'd find something."

"I found a lot of new information, but that's about all. I still don't have a suspect, though I do know a bit more about him."

"Are you sure it's a man?"

"Statistically, it's far more likely to be a man than a woman, especially when the victims don't appear to have a personal connection with the murderer." Ellie took a long draw of her coffee, steeling herself for the day and all the gruesome possibilities. "Then there's the dismemberment. That took a lot of strength."

"Yeah, I guess so." Jillian visibly shuddered.

Ellie took a seat at her desk, fishing the pictures of the dumpsite out of the stack of papers. "Here's where it gets interesting. I'm glad I went to the park because what the pictures don't tell you is how close this spot is to everything."

Jillian leaned in over her shoulder. "It looks remote in the photos."

"I thought the same thing, but look." She typed the address of the park into her search engine and pulled up the satellite image, pointing out the grassy spot by the water with her cursor. "Here's where the body was found, and here is the playground and the soccer fields."

"Wow."

"I know. They're right *there*. When I was looking over the crime scene, I could hear the kids. I was only there for a couple minutes before someone walked by, and on the way out, I passed three more people out for a walk. This is a high-risk dumpsite. Whoever did this was incredibly confident, bordering on arrogant."

Jillian's face reflected all the emotions Ellie had experienced at the horror of knowing how close people enjoying the park might have come to the killer. She shook her head. "Or he was incredibly lucky."

"I don't think luck has anything to do with it. There was

no sign of him being in a hurry at all, and the fact that it took twelve hours to find the body means he dumped Jane Doe right after the park closed since no one saw him enter or exit. Plus, he spent considerable time with the body."

"You're right. It's a whole lot of new information that doesn't move us forward."

"It doesn't." Rather than focus on that, Ellie preferred to stay positive. "But when we solve the case, it will all make sense."

Jillian's red-glossed lips spread in a generous smile that lit up her face. "I love the sound of that. *We*. No one has ever given me credit for helping."

"Your help has made all the difference." Ellie gestured toward the room where the cold case files were kept. "That's why I'm hoping you know where the other Jane Doe from West Ashley Park is."

Jillian frowned. "The other Jane Doe?"

"Jacob says there was another case not long after this one. The woman was about the same age and was left in the same general area."

"I don't remember that one."

"There wasn't long-term coverage of the first Jane Doe. The case stalled, and the media lost interest. I suppose that the second woman found revived the coverage, but in this day and age of crime fiction television shows and novels, people move on to the next thing pretty fast."

Jillian nodded, but Ellie could tell she was already thinking about the other case—mentally recalling the boxes in the vast section filled with Jane and John Does, in search of the case Ellie was talking about. Shaking her head, Jillian unlocked the door to the evidence room, heading for the cold case section without another word to Ellie, hands on hips, lower lip caught between her teeth.

Ellie followed and double-checked the date on Jane Doe

One's box, then she walked down the aisles checking boxes for a date that was close. Every time she found a similar time frame, she checked the dumpsite, only to come up empty. There were so many unidentified murder victims over the past twenty years, their bodies scattered throughout Charleston County, which covered over thirteen hundred square miles and held a population of just over four hundred thousand. Of all the victims, most were women. The stacks and rows of boxes were a sobering reminder that she was only one person, and despite her best efforts, many of the cases would remain unsolved. That knowledge should've discouraged her, but it propelled her onward instead.

Every victim in Cold Cases deserved justice, just like everyone else.

"I think I found it," Jillian called out from the far end of the middle aisle. "This one is in the wrong place entirely, but the date is a couple weeks after our Jane Doe."

Jillian set the box on the closest table, and Ellie carefully removed the lid. "This looks like exactly what Jacob was describing to me last night." She read the M.E.'s report, then handed it to Jillian.

Jillian's eyes flicked over the report. "The deaths aren't the same."

"They aren't, you're right. But in both cases, it appears the murder weapon was a knife. That's something."

"But dumpsite and the use of a knife isn't enough to link them, right? Makes it just as likely that they're not linked at all?"

"Are you sure you're in the right job? Maybe you should try for detective. Right, but it's worth looking into. Jacob said he wasn't the only officer who thought they might be linked." Ellie began to pull evidence bags out of the box. "But the detective assigned to the case dismissed their concerns."

Jillian searched for the name of the detective, and when

she found it, she huffed out a breath. "That's because he was set to retire. I remember this now. He half-assed this case like you wouldn't believe. I was mad, but there was nothing to be done. He put everything else he had on the back burner while he went after the man who murdered Franklin Lacey."

"Franklin Lacey." Ellie tapped her chin with her finger, tipping her head to the side. "Didn't his stepson hire a hitman to kill him, expecting to get the inheritance?"

"He did, and it backfired."

Ellie eyed the evidence bag that contained an article of the victim's clothing. "That's what happens when you're fifteen and don't understand how inheritance works. I know everyone was shocked when it turned out not to be the wife who hired the hit."

"That's the case Detective Jones retired on, so no one realized he let this and a few others languish when they didn't turn up leads right away."

"That's not the legacy I would choose to leave behind," Ellie said as she held up a sealed bag containing the victim's hair, the color of a moonless night. It was the hair samples that were the saddest. They made her almost feel a connection with the victim, as if the woman was still in the room, whispering clues that she could almost make out but not quite.

"Right? But that's burnout for you. There are more cases than detectives can handle, and sometimes, they choose the case that will make Charleston PD look the best."

Ellie thought back to the list Fortis had given her and cringed. "I'm already getting a taste of that. Fortis wants me to abandon the Jane Doe case and start on his to-do list."

Jillian rolled her eyes. "It figures. When do you have to ditch?"

Ellie could practically hear the tiny grains of sand flowing out of the hourglass. "I have until I clock out Friday."

"It's already Tuesday." A note of panic laced Jillian's voice.

"I know. That's why I spent ten hours chasing leads yesterday. This is important." She took the notes on Jane Doe Two back from Jillian with a sad smile. "We don't know Jane Doe One's name, but I know she deserves justice, and so does this one." Ellie gestured to the room at large. "They all do."

They were quiet for a long time as they each took one item out of the box, examined it, then passed it across the table. By the time they got down to the photos of the body, still stacked in the bottom of the box, Jillian was already looking discouraged. "Do you see anything that connects these two cases?"

"Nothing," Ellie admitted, feeling a tad discouraged herself. "They both have a note about a tan line where a watch had been worn on the wrist, but that's so common I'm sure half these cases are missing the watch they were wearing."

"Were they able to match the shape of the tan line to any specific brands?" Jillian asked. "Some lady's watches have very unique shapes."

Ellie looked back at the report and shook her head. "No. In fact, there was no attempt at a match noted for Jane Doe Two." Quickly, she flipped back through her notepad. "And Jane Doe One states no known brand matches the shape."

"That's something, isn't it?" Jillian brightened. "Maybe that's how they met their killer. Someone who sold knockoffs?"

"Seems like a stretch."

Jillian shrugged. "That's all I've got."

Reaching into the bottom of the box, Ellie braced herself for the gruesome pictures she expected to find.

And she was right to do so. The body was in horrible shape. Some of that was decomposition, like Jacob had said. But most of the damage to the body had been done by scavengers, not time in the elements, which made it hard to tell the woman's age or any other identifying features. The shape of her face was largely intact, though, and the accompanying police sketch seemed to match it almost perfectly. When her gaze landed on the hair, Ellie sucked in a breath and froze.

"What?" Jillian asked.

"Her eyebrows don't match her hair." Ellie pointed out the obvious difference in hue—her light-colored, almost blonde eyebrows, compared to her dark hair.

"So?"

"Her hair is dyed."

"A lot of women dye their hair." Jillian leaned over the photo to get a better look.

"But this woman's hair is dyed almost pitch-black, and judging by her eyebrows, her hair should be much lighter. It's not." Excited, Ellie dug through the pile of evidence bags lying on the table until she found the hair samples. "Look. This is just like the other victim. There's no root growth, so her hair was dyed right before she died."

Flipping through the pages of the M.E. report, Ellie scoured through the notes, looking for anything that mentioned a lingering smell. But her excitement quickly faded, and after reading over the notes three times, she sagged into a chair.

"No mention in the medical examiner's notes?" Jillian guessed.

"No. It's not clear how long she was out in the weather before she was found, but it was probably at least two weeks according to this."

Jillian pulled on a strand of her light blonde hair and wrinkled her nose. "When I dye my hair, that smell lasts for a week unless I wash it several times. The chemical that lightens the hair has a very distinct scent, and—" She stopped abruptly, her gray eyes lighting up. "But this woman's hair wasn't lightened."

"Does that matter?"

"You've never dyed your hair?" Jillian flicked amazed eyes to Ellie's head and gave her a mock scowl. "Right. You have the kind of hair many of us would kill for, so of course, you've never dyed it. Not all hair color works the same. Lighter colors work by bleaching the pigment, which leaves a strong odor behind for several days. But when you take someone whose hair is naturally light and darken it, the dye instead coats each strand with the color. Depending on the brand, going darker is gentler on your hair."

"What about the smell?"

"If the dye is ammonia-free and there's no bleaching, the smell isn't bad and tends to fade in a day or two."

Ellie's eyes widened. "So no one would have noticed a scent, with her being out in the weather, especially."

"Exactly."

"You know what this means?" Her heart rate picked up speed as she realized what it did mean. "These cases *are* connected. Why else would they both have fresh dye jobs, dumpsites that are really close to each other, and the same type of weapon?"

"I'm with you on the first two, but the first victim's death was very specific. I'm not sure I'm buying that it's the same guy."

Ellie loved the way Jillian wasn't afraid to state her opinion. She found that Jillian's opposing view actually sharpened her senses on the case.

"You think it's a copycat?"

Jillian scrunched her lips into an almost pout. "Possibly. It would explain the similarities."

"Not the dye."

Jillian tilted her head. "What do you mean?"

Ellie flipped through the detective's notes and pointed at a line halfway down the page. "The hair dye was never made public. Women dye their hair all the time, and Detective Jones never noticed that the two women had their hair dyed to match the other woman's natural color, one reason the cases were never connected."

"That's giving me chills. The killer dying the women's hair to match the other's original color somehow makes this whole scenario that much more sick. When you put it that way, how could it be a coincidence?"

"Exactly." Ellie slapped the file folder down on the table in triumph.

Jillian was quiet for a long time, eyes trained on the evidence spread out on the table. "But why dye their hair like that?"

The momentary triumph faded away, and Ellie shrugged. "I told you, this case has got me chasing my tail. Every answer I come up with only brings up more questions. But now that we *know* these cases are related, maybe something will stick out. At the very least, it made identification harder."

"How so?" Jillian rubbed her temples. "I have a feeling that has an easy answer, but my brain is just so full of the facts of the two cases that I can't see the murder for the blood."

Ellie quirked an eyebrow at her interesting comment. "If their families filed a missing persons report, the description was likely with their natural color of hair. If I'm looking for a blonde woman, I'm not going to waste my time looking through files where the woman has dark hair."

"And if your daughter's hair is so dark it's almost black, the police aren't going to show you sketches of blondes, or almost blondes."

"Exactly." Ellie's excitement was growing again. "And in

this case, the blonde was significantly taller than the brunette, so all the stats would've been wrong. It's an excellent forensic countermeasure." Writing feverishly, she noted every singularity, right down to the matching watch tan lines. When she turned the notepad around, she smiled at Jillian. "Taken separately, none of these things seem important. But now that we know the killer went to such great lengths to conceal the link between these two, we can change our approach."

"Is it enough to prove it, though?"

"It's closer than we were yesterday. We've made more headway in the past day and a half than I did all of last week." She reached into the box again, pulling out the sealed bag that held what was left of the victim's shirt. "This woman's shirt is lavender too."

Jillian took Jane Doe One's shirt out of the other box and used a magnifying glass to go over them side by side, then she laid them together so they were almost overlapping. "They're not just the same color. They were wearing the same shirt." She handed the magnifying glass to Ellie. "See? The fibers are identical."

Ellie nodded, then compared the other clothing items from each woman's box. "Same color jeans and underwear too."'

"Ugh," Jillian muttered. "The same underwear? Why does that make it worse when this is already about as bad as you can get?"

"I don't know, but I agree. It's so sadistic. And frightening." She shivered. "I wonder if they knew he'd dressed them alike. And they *knew* he'd dyed their hair. But this makes me wonder if they weren't abducted and held together, made into some kind of sadistic twins in the opposite."

"That's awful. Isn't it bad enough he was going to kill them?"

"No," Ellie said, going on instinct. It was almost like she could hear a voice in the back of her head, could almost see the first victim sitting, bound, across from the other victim. "I'm sure this was part of it. He didn't just torture them physically. The psychological aspect would've been important to him." She scribbled notes on the pad, teeth working her bottom lip. "Whoever this man is, he's deeply disturbed."

"It's almost lunchtime. What do you think about grabbing lunch and then checking out the second crime scene?" Jillian's eyes held a glimmer of excitement in them that Ellie had yet to witness. "I can be gone for an hour without anyone losing their minds. After that, people ask questions."

"That's a good idea." Ellie placed the evidence back into the boxes, careful not to mix anything up. "I'm going to shelve these side by side since the second case is in the same time period."

"That's where it *should've* been," Jillian confirmed, her expression grim as she turned to look at the rows of boxes. "I wonder how many other files are misplaced like that?"

"I'd be the last person to tell you how to do your job, but can you wait on looking into that?" Ellie shot Jillian a conspiratorial look. "So we can focus on this case? Checking and rearranging the files is a big job, and I only have until Friday. And I need your help. When this case is solved, and this monster is in a cage where he belongs, then you can rearrange to your heart's galore."

"You sound so sure we can solve this case by Friday. That's four days, counting today."

"I'm not." Ellie exited the evidence room and waited for Jillian to lock up. "The only thing I'm sure of is that I'm not going to give up until I find this man. As long as he's free, no one is safe."

15

The second Jane Doe's final resting place wasn't nearly as accessible as the first. Closer to the sinking wetlands that only wildlife could access, this site was well-hidden and far off the beaten path.

Ellie picked her way across the soft ground, doing her best to avoid the patches of mud scattered like landmines around her. More than once, she had to back out and readjust her course. Dry leaves and debris masked some of the softest places, making the trek more difficult.

Jillian stayed close but hovered between Ellie and the edge of the path. "How did he carry her out here with it like this?"

"She was dumped during a dryer month, which was probably intentional. The storm right before she was found was one of those freak thunderstorms that rolls in from out of nowhere and disappears just as quickly. It dumped a lot of water into the river in a very short space of time." Ellie looked up from the ground she'd raked her gaze over, assessing where to best carefully move to next. She shot Jillian a grin. "I checked the weather reports for that time period while you were in the bathroom at the station. When the water rises in the river, the ground here turns marshy, but before that, this was probably as stable as the walking path."

"*Marshy*? Is that the technical term?"

Ellie laughed. "You know what I mean. Make sure the ground is solid before you take a step."

"I'm staying right here. This is way above my pay grade."

"Mine too. I hope I don't fall because I didn't bring any towels, and I don't want to have to buy a new car," Ellie quipped.

Jillian scratched her nose. "A new car?"

"Remember that pursuit they caught on TV, the one ending on a bridge?"

Jillian shot her a droll look. "Is there anyone in Charleston who doesn't remember it? It was only two weeks ago, and it was all over the news for almost a week."

"You're right. It feels like a lifetime has gone by, but it was practically yesterday. My life has changed a lot. For the better, of course. Anyway, Jacob lost a shoe in the marsh, and his clothes got soaked. He couldn't get the smell out of his car and ended up trading it in."

"That's one way of dealing with it." Jillian didn't try to hide her amusement. "It is a horrific smell."

"I think he used it as an excuse to buy his dream car, but I don't blame him. The smell is nasty." Ellie's nostrils flared to emphasize the stench all around them.

Jillian smiled and nodded toward Ellie's feet. "You know what that sludge is made of, right?"

Ellie wrinkled her nose and turned back to scanning the ground. "Don't remind me." She shuddered. "We had to dig in the mud for a school project, and just a few inches down, the smell of decaying plants and long-dead sea life is overwhelming. I felt sick for days afterward." The wind kicked up, intensifying the scent around them, the odor clawing at her nostrils, making the memory so vivid she gagged a little. "There's nothing like that stench."

"Which is what makes this a great place to dump bodies. I bet more than one person walked down this trail and assumed the smell was just the marsh being extra fragrant that day."

"I'm sure you're right." Ellie glanced back at the picture of the crime scene on her phone, shoulders slumping. "This is as far in as I can get without sinking, but I don't think it matters. This dumpsite is so different from the other one, I can see why a connection was dismissed. The site is so far away from the trail, she wouldn't have ever been found if it wasn't for someone's dog breaking away and going nuts."

"Dogs do have an amazing sense of smell."

"This discovery was dumb luck, but the killer wanted the other girl to be found." Ellie shook her head. "That logic doesn't make sense."

"Nothing about these two cases makes sense."

Ellie nodded as she picked her way back to the trail, her arms out to keep from losing her balance. She was almost home free when her foot got stuck in the mud, and she gripped a sapling for purchase as she tried to yank her shoe free. When she couldn't get her foot out, she took the hand Jillian offered.

Jillian pulled as hard as she could. The boggy mud held Ellie tight for a moment, then let her go so fast she lost her balance, the release making a loud sucking noise that was almost obscene. She pulled on Jillian's hand, desperate to stay upright, but it only made things worse. Stretched out so she could reach Ellie's hand, Jillian's center of gravity shifted, and they tumbled with a loud *splat* into the mud.

"Damn it," Ellie sputtered as she tried unsuccessfully to

get up without smearing more mud than she already had on herself. "The smell is awful."

Jillian managed to get to her feet first, her blonde hair plastered to her head on one side, mud splashed across her cheek. She scrunched up her face. "Looks like you're going to need a new car."

Ellie shook her head. "Not just a new car. The smell will never come out of these clothes." She looked at Jillian, biting back a smile that threatened. "You're covered in mud."

"You don't say?" Jillian laughed, shaking her head. "You pulled me into it. What did you think was going to happen?"

"We can't go back to the office like this. If you want, I can take you home so you can grab a change of clothes."

"I live outside of McClellanville." Jillian drooped as she surveyed the damage. "It's an hour one way. Walmart?"

Humor that was entirely inappropriate for their location bubbled up into her chest as she pictured her and Jillian sashaying into the superstore. "What about my place? We're about the same size. You can just borrow some of my clothes and shower really quick."

Jillian nodded, then grimaced. "Maybe we should walk to your house. I don't want to ruin your car."

"It's fifteen minutes away, and I put some towels in the trunk after the last time. It'll be fine."

"If you say so."

They rode there with the windows down, terrycloth soaking up most of the dampness. Ellie sent the towels down the garbage chute before showing Jillian where the guest bathroom was. "When you're done, you can grab an outfit out of the closet, through those doors." She gestured to the guest bedroom.

"Your clothes aren't in your bedroom?"

"They are." Her cheeks heated a little. "This is the overflow."

Jillian snorted. "Overflow? Do you have clothes in every closet?"

"No," Ellie said with mock offense. "There's at least one closet where I keep the vacuum."

Jillian was still laughing, mumbling something about betting Ellie didn't even own a vacuum, when she closed the bathroom door.

As soon as the water turned on and Ellie was sure Jillian didn't need anything, she went to her room and stripped out of her pantsuit. It was going to take more than one pass with the body wash to get the reek out.

"Where's your car?" Jillian asked when they came downstairs thirty minutes later, changed and smelling much better.

"I had my detailer pick it up. He left me a loaner."

"Your detailer?" Jillian shook her head, her eyes wide. "You sure do lead a different kind of life."

She shrugged. "It's better than buying a new car, right? I'm kind of attached to mine." She held her arm out and pressed the unlock button on the key fob, then groaned when the headlights flashed on a miniature car. "I was hoping it wasn't the Smart car."

"It's tiny," Jillian commented. "Kind of cute in a red toy car sort of way."

Ellie stopped on the edge of the curb at what passed for a bumper on the car, planting her fists on her hips. "I'm not parking in the lot at PD."

"Don't be silly. It's great. Besides, it matches the look I've got going here."

She swung her gaze to Jillian, having not paid any attention to which outfit she'd borrowed. "And what's that?"

Jillian held out her arms, and the sleeves slid down until the fabric covered all but the tips of her fingers. "I'm thinking: toddler wearing her mom's clothes. You're more than six inches taller than me."

"You don't seem that short." Ellie gave her a once-over as she got into the driver's seat.

"I'm five-three. I'm not short, I'm *fun-sized*."

Their laughter filled the tiny car as Ellie darted out into traffic, making it to headquarters in record time and parking around the corner. They went through the side door and somehow managed to avoid running into anyone.

Jillian grabbed a bag out of the large bottom drawer of her desk, then disappeared. When she returned, she was wearing clothes that fit, and she placed Ellie's borrowed clothes, neatly folded, on Ellie's desk.

"Thanks. Luckily, I always keep a spare change of clothes here. It's the first time I've ever had to use them." She tried to give Ellie a withering look before a smile broke through. "That was quite an adventure."

"Too bad we're right back where we started."

"Yeah. I see what you mean about taking one step forward and a hundred back."

"I'm so frustrated." Ellie slapped the papers she'd started pouring over in Jillian's absence. "Something has to give eventually, but right now I just feel buried by all this new information. At least we have one thing we can do now."

"What's that?" Jillian stepped closer.

"We can search again with the correct hair color for each woman."

"That should help." Jillian went to her desk, firing up her computer. "I'll get right on it."

"I've been thinking about the watches too."

"What about them?"

Ellie lined up the two photos of the women's wrists. "Isn't it weird how they have the same tan line, but there was no brand of watch that matched?"

"A little," Jillian said cautiously, "but there's so many brands and models of watches. What are you getting at?"

"What if they were custom? Like, a best friend gift. What are the chances of them having the same exact watch that can't be traced if they didn't know each other?"

"If it was just any old watch, I would say high. But you're right, if the watch wasn't tracable, there's a chance it could be custom."

"It can't be a coincidence." Ellie turned back to the screen of her computer. "So, let's search for two friends who went missing at around the same time with matching watches, using the correct stats for each woman. You take social media, and I'll expand the search for friends reported missing in both the Carolinas and Georgia."

"That's a good idea," Jillian said, already focused on a newly opened search engine.

But chasing every possible lead in three states ate up half the afternoon, and their expanded search came up dry.

Ellie stood up so fast, her office chair rattled and almost fell over. "This is ridiculous," she mumbled. Pacing, she punched in her code to the evidence room. In the cold case area, she placed each box on its own table. She spread the contents out and stood between the tables, pouring over one item before going to the matching one from the other case. "Same age, same watch, same clothes, same dumpsite," she muttered as she paced between the tables.

One woman tortured. The other killed quickly.

But why? Why only torture one victim? It didn't make sense.

What about the second victim? Was she the one who'd had the information?

Maybe he was torturing her friend to force her to give it up. First, he'd cut the poor woman's fingers off. Then her hand.

How long had the torture gone on before Victim Two put a stop to it?

Ellie froze, closing her eyes. Something tugged at her subconscious, but every time she tried to grab hold of the thought, it retreated further into the recesses of her mind. "Victim Two put a stop to it," she whispered.

Victim One was tortured mercilessly, but Victim Two had been killed quickly. Her time of death was impossible to pin down because of weather and scavengers, but Ellie had a gut feeling the victim in the first Jane Doe case died first. So, what was she missing?

Kill the bitch.

The voice was a whisper in her mind, but it rocked her to her very core. She swayed where she stood, gaze flicking from one pile of evidence to the other. She could almost hear the whimpers of the first victim. She would've begged the man to stop. Or told her friend to tell him what he wanted to hear.

Everyone thought they'd be strong, but Ellie knew that in the end, most people were a lot more fragile than they realized. With blood loss and exhaustion thrown in for good measure, Jane Doe One was probably a hysterical mess before she died. But Jane Doe Two had low levels of ketamine and scopolamine—also known as Devil's Breath. One to paralyze and the next to take away the victim's inhibitions.

"Truth serum," Ellie muttered. A quick check of the first woman's autopsy showed no trace of ketamine or scopolamine, but Dr. Faizal had noted the presence of IV fluids known as crystalloids. Using her phone, she typed in the word and waited for the results.

She sat down with the notepad, writing down everything the article explained about crystalloids. Used to treat hypo volemic shock, the crystalloids were used to stabilize a patient who was experiencing catastrophic blood loss. Once the body lost fifteen percent blood volume, the organs began shutting down, and the patient went into shock.

Kill the bitch.

Ellie shook her head, ignoring the voice hissing the words in her head.

Movement caught her eye, but she didn't have to look up to know it was Jillian. "Look at this," she said, waving her over.

"I'm sorry. You've been in here so long muttering and pacing, I was starting to get worried."

"I've found something." She showed Jillian the toxicology report.

"They had different drugs in their systems. Is that important?" Jillian pulled out a chair and took a seat, looking over the report.

"He was treating Jane Doe One for hypovolemic shock."

"Hyper what?"

Ellie smiled, glad she hadn't been given a partner. She much preferred Jillian. There was a deep crevasse between Jillian's eyes, she was concentrating so hard on the paper in front of her. She was devoted if nothing else.

"It's a fancy way of saying she lost too much blood and was going to die."

"But he killed her. He kept her alive so he could kill her?"

"I know." Ellie pressed her fingertips into her temples. "That's what's so weird about it. Why keep her alive just to kill her anyway? Untreated, she would've died from the blood loss within the hour. But he kept her alive, and he gave the other woman ketamine and scopolamine."

"What are those?"

"A paralytic and type of truth serum."

Jillian's eyes lit up. "I was thinking he tortured Victim One for information, but he didn't need the information from *her*."

"Exactly." Ellie stabbed a finger at Jillian. "Whatever he wanted to hear, he wanted to hear it from the second victim."

"So, he tortured one to torture both?"

Ellie nodded. "I think he did."

"Sadistic bastard."

"And when he had what he wanted from the other woman, he put Jane Doe One out of her misery." Ellie's stomach turned over, and she suddenly felt confined, even sitting in the chair. She shot to her feet, shaking off the feeling of being trapped.

"That's awful."

"Put in that position, she'd basically be telling the man when to kill the other person." Ellie tensed, trying to silence the whispering in her head as it grew louder.

Say the words, a male voice hissed.

I won't say it. The female voice was thin. Scared, but defiant.

She dies either way, the man said.

I won't do it.

"Ellie?" When Ellie blinked her into focus, Jillian looked very concerned. "What are you thinking?"

"I don't know. I think he put all the responsibility for the friend's death on her as another layer of torture. When she gave him what he wanted to hear, he killed the first victim in one swift blow."

Jillian clutched her neck and swallowed hard. "I can't get that picture out of my mind. I don't get it. Why not just let the girl fade away? Her friend would still watch her die."

"It's not the same. Once she went into shock, she was probably drifting in and out. Left alone, she would've fallen asleep and died somewhat peacefully. So that was his point. Maximum fear. What if he made Jane Two choose her life over her friend's, then killed her anyway?"

"As if it couldn't get worse."

Say the words, the male voice demanded. Elongated, the hiss sounded more like a horror movie snake than a human.

Ellie shuddered, then forced the thoughts away. Imagining the horrors the victims faced wouldn't help her solve the case. She had to focus, because she was quickly running out of time.

"What now?" Jillian asked when Ellie started gathering the evidence to place back into the boxes.

"I need to talk to Dr. Faizal again. I need to know exactly how long these drugs last and what their effects would be. If I can establish a timeline, maybe all this will start to make sense."

"You can't make sense of a murderer," Jillian countered.

"Nope, but I can try. Somewhere, there's a man roaming free who tortured two women, who, if my theory about their watches is correct, were best friends. If I'm right, I need to find out why, and I need to know the details of how. Then I'm going to find the asshole and lock him up for the rest of his life."

"I hope you do." Jillian's voice was quiet, reverent. When she reached out to squeeze Ellie's arm, there was a slight tremble in her hand. "Now, I don't know how I'll sleep at night knowing this man is still out there."

"Thank goodness for Sam," Ellie joked, trying to break the tension that hung heavy in the air.

"I hope when you find him, he's already dead. That's the only way justice will ever be served, for him to be experiencing the agony of hell."

Ellie quirked up one brow at her new friend. "He might be the only one who can identify his victims."

"The world is safer if he's dead," Jillian insisted.

"Don't worry. If he gives me half a reason, I'll take him out myself."

16

I glared at the familiar number on the landline screen. I almost let it go to voicemail, but I knew it was inevitable that he would obsessively redial my number. I was in no mood for his nonsense.

"I thought I told you never to call me at home unless it was an emergency," I said coolly as I clicked the remote to pause my movie. "We're not friends."

"I understand, sir," the timid man stuttered. "But the girl is snooping around, and I thought you should know."

I bit back a curse, forcing my hand to uncurl from the fist it wanted to create. He was nothing like my street urchin. I needed to be patient. "Snooping where? On the internet? In the middle of the ocean? For something that has you so vexed, you are annoyingly vague."

"At the park," the man ground out.

"Don't get testy with me," I chided. "I've cut down better men than you for less. Are you absolutely certain she isn't just visiting the park like thousands do every month?"

"Twice in two days and *only* the two dumpsites."

I sat up straighter. "I'm listening."

"The second time, she brought along someone from the office."

"Describe him to me." I wanted to reach through the phone and snatch the details from his lungs.

"*Her*. Petite, blonde, giggly. She works at Charleston PD. I couldn't get close enough to hear what they were saying, but I—"

"Jillian Reed. She works in evidence."

"What was she doing in the park with Ellie?"

"I'd wager they were working, but that is purely speculation on my part." I drew the words out, toying with him. His feathers were so easily ruffled. "They won't find anything, so they're free to traipse around the park at their discretion."

"You're not concerned that she's apparently connected the two cases?" His tone was demanding, and for a moment, I was silent, envisioning the hundreds of ways I could teach him to be more respectful. "Did you hear me? Should we be concerned?"

A burst of red exploded behind my eye. "There is no 'we,'" I snapped. "*I* am not concerned. If you're afraid of young Ellie and her little gal pal playing detective, that's on you."

"No one else connected the cases."

"Arrogance," I explained. "The previous detective was after bigger fish, and two college girls weren't high on his list."

"What if Kline finds out their names?" The man's breathing was heavy and clearly audible. "If we're not careful, she could blow the whole thing open."

"You keep saying 'we.' I feel like there's a fundamental lack of understanding here. None of this is about you."

"B-but I'm involved. And what if there's evidence that implicates me…"

If only.

He was dry humping my last nerve. Pinning it all on him

would be satisfying, as would watching the live coverage of his inevitable suicide by cop. But I needed him, at least for now. His demise would have to wait.

"There's nothing for the girl to find. If Ellie manages to name them, it will serve to prove that she's more than the Kline name. There's no harm in that."

"Girl? She's not a girl anymore. She's a loose end that needs to be dealt with."

"Are you serious?" I snapped, jumping up from the couch. "Who do you think you are? Cross me again, and you'll find that I have better hiding places than West Ashley Park."

Blessed silence met my ear.

I waited, taking a deep breath and willing my heart rate to slow. It wasn't often that I allowed one of my followers to unsettle me, and he was pushing his luck. Still, it wasn't worth my time to deal with him.

Bored with his nonsense, I pushed the play button, and the movie started again. He remained silent, no doubt carefully picking his next words so he wouldn't give me an excuse to put him in one of my films. The thought made me chuckle. He'd die from sheer terror before I made the first cut of the knife. "You'd be a waste of storage on my flash drive," I muttered.

"Sir?" His voice was trembling. I could almost taste the fear through the phone. It was delicious.

I shook my head. "Nothing. I don't have time for your babbling. Leave the girl alone. She won't find anything worth the stress you're putting yourself through."

"Permission to keep an eye on her?"

"Aren't your eyes on her enough? It sounds as if you've been stalking her quite thoroughly."

He cleared his throat. "I was worried she was getting too close."

"There is nothing to worry about. I don't know how else

to make you understand, so I'm going to remove myself from this conversation. Keep your distance, and please let me know if there's anything *important* happening. Until then, good day."

I hung up without waiting for him to say goodbye, but try as I might, I couldn't get back into my movie. Not that I was worried about what Ellie might find. But having the case reopened presented more than a few challenges.

Which meant I would have to make some hard choices, and I was loath to even begin.

Like my office, everything in my home required a fingerprint to access. The painting in the library swung outward on its hinges as I opened it to reveal one of the many safes hidden throughout the house. I put in the combination, then completed it with my thumb jammed to the sensor. The safe clicked open, and I closed my eyes, inhaling deeply. I knew it would be impossible for any hint of their scent to actually linger, but the memories that rushed forth were so clear I could smell them.

The bracelets were nestled together on a pedestal, intertwined for eternity. The silver metal was cold in my hands as I carefully picked them up. Delicate script declared a timeless love on a wide metal plate, and on the back, their names and anniversary date were inscribed.

Tabitha's had Mabel's name listed first, and Mabel's was the opposite. Otherwise, the bracelets were identical. The bands were the same width as the plate, simple and plain, but it was the center of each plate that had caught my eye. An oval that resembled an old-fashioned picture frame held an etching of the two of them locked in a kiss.

I pressed the bracelets to my chest and closed my eyes. They'd been one of my favorites, though they hadn't reacted in a way I'd expected. But they'd been brave, and both had been defiant until the end. I so loved it when they struggled. The fight in them gave me life like nothing else did.

It was so interesting to watch. To witness. To examine and tear apart.

The bracelets had been in my wall safe since that day. I'd read dozens of books sitting in the chair beneath the oil painting of a crane picking its way through the shallows of the Ashley River. Their screams echoing in my mind were the most divine background music. Now though, I was going to have to make some changes. I couldn't risk the mementos being found in my house. They were the only thing that connected me to the women.

One by one, I gathered each item and carefully wrapped them in velvet cloths. I didn't need to catalog them. I had each one memorized so clearly that if I stopped to indulge, remembering was like a movie playing in my mind.

Next, I picked up a feminine tennis bracelet made entirely of cubic zirconium and indulged myself for a moment, closing my eyes. I could see the raven-haired vixen clearly, hear her voice as she demanded I kill her roommate the first time I'd asked the question. A record that had yet to be broken.

Would it ever be broken? Time would tell.

The stones dazzled, though it was fake. I'd considered presenting my raven girl with a real one before her death. But she was a coward and her friendship with her roommate as fake as the bracelet. I always told them right away that all they had to do to end the suffering was order me to kill their friend. So many balked and tried to avoid what was destined to happen, but not the raven-haired slut. As soon as I'd said the words, she'd blurted them back at me, forcing my hand. What had made the encounter special was all the juicy details she'd spilled as soon as her friend was dead.

I boxed everything up in a small ornate wooden box and

set it on the passenger seat. Once behind the wheel, I couldn't help reliving the flood of confessions that had spilled from her ruby lips. That was the best part. And her video had sold for far more than expected. Fans of snuff films didn't like death to come so swift and merciful as her friend's, but my darling vixen had spent hours spilling her secrets.

The bracelet had been a gift from the roommate's boyfriend, who she'd slept with until he dumped her roommate. Once he was available, however, she'd lost interest and moved on. The roommate never found out.

I'd mourned the possibilities that were never realized. Had I known the little tramp held so many secrets inside, I would've forced her to confess each and every one to her poor roommate before killing them both. But my raven earned herself a fitting death that had stunned even the most rabid fan.

She'd spilled her guts for hours on tape, and when she was done, I slashed her belly and spilled her guts a bit more literally. I could still feel her fear as she tried to scoop her innards back into their proper position. Still smell the erotic tang of blood as they slid through her fingers and tumbled to the floor.

My body quaked, bringing me back to the present. I forced my mind to less stimulating things, pulling into the bank parking lot, and adjusting my clothes to hide my growing excitement. Then I carefully picked up the box and walked into the lobby, catching the manager's attention.

I didn't have to spell out my needs, which was one of my favorite things about this branch of Charleston Bank and Trust. He led me to the safe deposit room, used his master key to release the box I'd had for over a decade, then whisked me into a private room with no cameras and left me alone with my treasures.

One precious prize at a time, I took every item from the wooden container and placed them in the safe deposit box. I spent a few minutes with each memory, promising my pretties that I would return often. Then there was only one piece left. My hands trembled as I reached in for it.

The necklace was the standard heart-shaped locket on a gold chain, but this one opened up to reveal Helen and Daniel Kline much younger than they were today. Ellie's first name was engraved on the front while a short message of undying love from her parents was on the back. She'd worn it religiously until she was fifteen, and then, it was mine. For twelve years, I'd held the locket against my throat, closing my eyes to remember the sound of her angelic voice from so long ago.

"I won't do it," she declared, glaring at me with eyes greener than the purest emeralds.

"She will suffer until you do." I gestured to the girl bound and sitting across from her. "Look at her. She's going to die anyway. Why would you force her to suffer?"

I'd worked on Ellie for what seemed like an eternity, increasing her medications until she was suggestable. She'd fought harder, but finally, I'd won. That moment had been pure sweetness. Twelve years later, I could still hear her innocence and the pain that pushed through the haze of drugs and exhaustion.

"Kill the bitch," she'd finally said, looking the other girl in the eye, just like I told her to, the words so sweet bursting from her full lips. *"Die, Bitch. Die."*

17

Jillian looked up when Ellie walked into their shared basement office Wednesday morning, cutting her eyes toward Ellie's desk. "Fortis left you a note. He's been down here already this morning."

Ellie handed Jillian a cup of coffee as she whizzed by without missing a beat. "It's not even nine yet," she grumbled. "Did he say what he wanted?"

"Nope. He just told me to let you know as soon as you walked in the door."

Ellie snatched the sticky note off the monitor and turned it around so Jillian could read it, rolling her eyes and slumping like she could fall asleep standing on her feet. She pitched her voice low, in a horrible impersonation of Fortis. "'As soon as you get here, come to my office.'"

Jillian giggled and covered her mouth, her eyes going to the door and widening.

"I don't think I talk like that." With the unmistakable voice of Fortis behind her, Ellie froze, her shoulders rising so they were almost even with her ears.

"I guess I should've looked behind me before I opened my

mouth." She treated Fortis to a dazzling, albeit apologetic smile when she turned to face him. "I just walked in the door."

"I know. I've been waiting for you."

"My shift starts at nine."

He checked his watch. "It's a quarter 'til. Didn't your parents teach you if you're early you're on time and if you're on time, you're late?"

"And if you're late, you're fired," she finished. "Yes, they did. I'm…on time?"

"My office, now," he ordered before turning and walking out of the room.

"That went well." Jillian's lips were pursed together, her brows in a worried line.

"You can laugh." Ellie took a long swig of coffee. "I can't believe I did that."

Jillian shrugged, raising her coffee in a toast. "If that's the worst thing that happens all day, it's not that bad, right?"

"We'll see if I still have a job when I'm done explaining myself."

Jillian crossed her fingers on both hands, turned back to her computer, and went to work.

Filled with dread, Ellie dragged herself into the hallway, taking the back staircase instead of the elevator. *Maybe if I give him a few minutes to cool off, he won't still be mad,* she thought, cringing. But if delaying by a few minutes backfired, and he was angrier when she got there, that would be bad too. Groaning, she took the last few stairs two at a time, hurried through the door, and rushed down the hallway.

She was out of breath by the time she burst through the door of the Violent Crimes Unit and caught sight of her reflection.

Five chairs swiveled in her direction, a few of the detectives stopping mid phone conversation, staring at her in surprise.

"Everything's fine," she said, smoothing her hair back from her face and willing her skin to return to a less mortifying shade of pink. "I'm just here to see Fortis." Resisting the urge to clap her hand to her mouth, she instead pressed her lips tightly together. She was a detective with Violent Crimes, so of course, she was there to talk to Fortis.

Everyone went back to work almost as quickly as they'd stopped, and when she dared look up again, no one was watching her. Placing one foot in front of the other, she took a few deep breaths through her nose. Her breathing was calm again when she wrapped her fingers around the cold brass handle of Fortis's office door.

Phone tucked under his chin, he pointed to the chair in front of his desk then turned back to the computer monitor. He nodded a few times, typing with only his index fingers, pecking at the keyboard with astounding speed. Then the conversation was over, and it was time to face the music.

Ellie sat ramrod straight in the chair, hands folded on her lap, ready to apologize.

But Fortis started talking before she could open her mouth. "Where are you with the Coggins case?"

"Coggins?"

His eyebrows came together over his nose. "The one on the top of my list. Did you have a chance to look at it yet?"

"Sir, it's only Wednesday. I still have the rest of the week to work on my Jane Doe."

To her relief, he nodded his agreement. "You have new information on that one?"

"Not much, but I'm making progress, and I think if I can just finish out this week, I can—"

"You're going to drive yourself into an early grave

obsessing like this. It's one case. There are hundreds. You've already spent more than a week on it, it's time to let it go."

Taking soft, even breaths, she kept her voice measured. "You gave me until the end of the week, sir." Despite her best efforts to stay calm, she could feel the heat crawling up her neck.

"I figured you'd get bored with that case by now and move on." He shrugged, waving his hand.

"You were humoring me?" Ellie sat forward in the chair. "She's a human being, and somewhere her family is wondering what happened to her."

He placed his elbows on the desk, leaning in, obviously enjoying the debate. "I wouldn't count on it. A lot of young adults set out to make their mark on the world and disown their families in the process. We don't even know if this female was from Charleston. She could be from anywhere."

"That doesn't mean she isn't worth the effort."

"You've put in effort," Fortis countered. "Quite a bit of effort. If you haven't found anything by now, what makes you think you're going to do better than Detective Jones did? He was one of the best and—"

"And he put this case on the back burner in favor of one that would bring him more attention when it was solved." Her lips were parted, chest heaving, sweat about to break out on her forehead. "If he'd been more focused on his job than retiring with honors, then he might've actually solved this case the first time around."

And the other one, she amended silently.

Fortis arched an eyebrow at her, and he didn't speak for so long, she was certain the next words to come out of his mouth would be the end of her career. Then a smile slowly spread across his face, and he shook his head. "Jones was a pompous ass who thought he could do no wrong, but you didn't hear that from me. I have no idea who gave you that information, but I don't doubt it's true. You have until the end of the week, but first thing Monday morning, I want you on the Coggins case."

"Yes, sir." She started to stand up, but he held up his hand, coming around the desk to sit on the corner, his expression softening.

"I'm not kidding about driving yourself into an early grave. You can't live for a case. Look into it, see if you can find new information, then move on. Otherwise, the stress will eventually get to you, and you're looking at putting your health at risk. I'm saying this from experience. I worked cold cases for a long time. You'll lose more than you'll win. If you can't set healthy limits, you're going to burn out."

"And I'm telling you from experience, I've survived far worse than this. I'm fine."

"Jumping off a bridge isn't the same," he scoffed, spearing her with his hazel eyes.

"That's nothing compared to escaping a kidnapping only to get hit by a police car. Jumping off that bridge was like a day at the water park."

Fortis blinked, his mouth going slack before he licked his lips and tilted his head. "Did you say you were hit by a police car?"

She was surprised by the question. "Yeah." When he looked at her expectantly, she went on. "I was in the hospital for a long time. I finished that semester of school at home while I recovered, but I'm fine now. It was an accident. I ran out into the street, confused by whatever drugs I was given. I ran right in front of him. He didn't have time to stop."

"Kline, why is this the first time I've heard about this?"

She shrugged, thinking it was odd that he didn't know. "I don't talk about it much. I was fifteen, and it just felt like a dream. The accident made it hard to remember anything, and I had heavy levels of drugs in my system. The doctor said

I shouldn't have been able to walk on my own two feet, let alone run."

Fortis stood up so fast the hem of his uniform jacket caught the pencil holder, scattering pens and pencils onto the floor. But he was already behind the desk, finger-pecking at the speed of light. After a moment, he sat back, shaking his head. "I can't believe it." He turned the monitor so she could see. "It wasn't my case, but I heard about it. I didn't make the connection because whoever filed the evidence away in cold cases spelled Kline wrong." He pointed to the file name: *E. Cline*. "See? That's probably why no one has ever approached you about it."

"Cold cases?" Ellie's eyes narrowed on the name as her heart began racing in her chest. "I don't understand," she said slowly, even though the puzzle was starting to slowly come together.

There was compassion in those hazel eyes. "You're still in the Jane and John Doe section. I'm glad you didn't come across it by accident."

It took her a second to get a breath so she could respond. "You're telling me that *I'm* in the cold case files?"

"Yes. Your case was never solved."

His words slammed into Ellie. If she hadn't already been sitting, she would've been knocked off her feet. She closed her eyes against the room as it began spinning out of control, leaned forward, and pressed her head against her knees.

There was a swish of fabric when Fortis knelt beside her and pressed a cold bottle of water against the back of her neck.

"I'm all right," she said, still folded in half, her voice muffled. "But I don't understand. What case?"

"Don't pass out in my office." He held the bottle against her neck. A single drop of condensation slid over her skin and dropped onto her slacks.

"I won't."

She took long, deep breaths and focused on the cold that spread from her neck down to her shoulders. The clock on the wall behind her ticked, and she silently counted each second. Slowly, the dizziness faded. When she was finally able to sit up, she took the bottle and drank half of it, then held it against her cheek.

"I'd love to believe you just got a little overcome by the Carolina heat, but I know better." His Southern accent took the gravity out of the words as he stood up and leaned against the desk again.

"I didn't know."

"You didn't know the case went cold?"

She shook her head, and the room spun again. "I didn't know I still had a case." Leaning back, she took another swig out of the bottle. "You don't have anything stronger, do you?"

He looked at her regretfully. "Not on the clock."

"Fine." Another sip. The clock continued ticking, unbothered by Ellie's world crumbling around her. "My parents told me that the kidnapper was dead."

Fortis just stared at her for a long moment. "To my knowledge, Ellie, that isn't true."

She shook her head, trying to understand.

"There wasn't a lot of evidence, and when you were hit, the paramedics compromised what little there was."

"IV fluids in the ambulance." She wrapped her fingers around the chair arm, focusing on pressing her skin against the edge of the corner of the arm until it was nearly painful. A sudden memory flashed in front of her eyes, of her jerking her arm away in the ambulance, terrified of what they might pump into her next.

"That didn't help." He spoke slowly, as if he were giving information to the next of kin of a victim. "Plus, in the ER, they had to cut your clothes off due to the road rash, and they were so tattered they just threw them away. By the time your parents were located, and it believed that you'd been kidnapped, the clothes were gone."

"It wouldn't have mattered. There wouldn't be enough evidence after the way it had been raining."

"That's right." He rubbed his chin with his thumb, silent for a moment. "If I remember right, you didn't know where you'd been taken, and there was no ransom demand." He met her gaze. "We never found where you'd been kept. Never had any ideas of who had held you. Your parents probably told you differently so that you'd feel safe."

It clicked then, the flack she'd gotten about taking this job. "This explains so much."

"Care to elaborate?"

"My parents should've been happy when I was assigned to cold cases. It's as far away from being in danger as I can be. But when I told them, the look they gave each other." She scoffed, rising from the chair as her strength returned on a wave of disbelief. "Man, why didn't I see it? They knew. Ever since that night, they told me that I had nothing to worry about. I never thought the case was unsolved, because why else would they be so calm?"

"Because they probably, truthfully, didn't think you had anything to worry about. After all, you've never been contacted by the person who took you again, right?"

Ellie nodded.

Fortis went on. "This wasn't my case, Ellie. Things were kept very hush-hush at the time, but if I had to guess, it was probably about ransom. A lot of kidnappings end in failure, believe it or not. They weren't able to contact your parents before you got away, so the kidnapper probably fled Charleston. People who kidnap children are usually cowards to begin with."

"It wasn't about money." She scowled, pacing to the door

and back. "I don't know where that theory came from. I've googled myself so many times, trying to find news stories about that night, but there's practically nothing except the fact that I'd been hit by a police car. The stories don't even name the cop who hit me."

"Do you remember anything from that night? Even the smallest bit of information could be what breaks the case wide open. Anything at all, no matter how insignificant it seems."

She shook her head. "And now that I'm trying to figure out why I'm so sure it wasn't about money, whatever I was feeling is gone. As soon as you said it was about ransom, I heard my own voice saying you were wrong. But I can't push past the blackness."

"I'm not surprised. From what I can remember, you were heavily drugged *before* you were hit, then at the hospital, they put you in a drug-induced coma to manage your pain."

"Too bad they couldn't take the memory of the actual pain away. When I woke up, the pain was awful." She grimaced, barely able to keep from cringing at the sudden recall.

"What do you remember about waking up?"

"Just that my parents were there, and my mom said no one would ever hurt me again." Ellie frowned, focusing on the plaque on the wall that declared Fortis's rank. "She didn't tell me then, but my dad was in the same hospital recovering from a stroke and a heart attack. But I was so out of it, I thought the man sitting in the chair was him."

"Who was it?"

"The officer who hit me." A headache began, her heartbeat throbbing through her temples. "I don't think I ever knew his name. I was in and out, but I know he stayed with me until they found my mother, but she was so distraught, and Wesley was so young, he took up a position outside the door and refused to leave."

"He probably felt awful." Fortis's eyes hadn't left Ellie one time. He'd barely blinked.

"I know he did. Mom told me he apologized so many times. Even though the dash camera proved that I ran in front of him from between two SUVs, he still couldn't forgive himself."

"That's tough."

"He was so dedicated. If I'm being honest, he's one of the biggest reasons I joined the force in the first place."

Fortis tilted his head to the side. "What's the other reason?"

"The kidnapping itself. I know that doesn't make sense since I don't remember it, but being kidnapped changed everything for me." Feeling steadier, she stopped pacing and propped her fists on her hips. "I want to get as many criminals off the street as I can. Doing so might not prevent every crime, but if one girl doesn't have to go through what I did because I took someone off the streets, then this will be all worth it."

"I can see why you're fixated on this Jane Doe. Your first case always seems special. And with her violent death, it's no wonder you're driven. But every box in that room carries a story much like hers. You have to be brutally honest with yourself and recognize when you've done everything you can. Then you move on."

"I promise, I won't be like this with every case. I just need to tell her family where she is and that she's not suffering anymore. It's the least I can do."

Fortis was thoughtful for a moment, then seemed to come to a decision. "I probably shouldn't do this, but I think you deserve to know everything you can about your case."

Ellie froze, amazed that she was even having this conversation. "Thank you. I can't believe my parents lied to me and that he's been free this entire time."

"Don't be too hard on them, Ellie. Like I said, they probably just wanted to protect you." When she only nodded, he went on, "Are you certain it was a man? It's rare, but it could've been a woman."

"I don't know how I know, but yes. I'm sure the person who kidnapped me was a man." She took a deep breath, then nodded again. "There's no doubt in my mind."

"You know you can't work your own case, right?"

"I understand." She dropped her gaze, hoping her immediate intention to go against his question wasn't clear.

"I should go to evidence and remove that box, but like I said, you deserve to know."

"What if he's been out there, watching me all this time?" She shuddered, her hand coming up to her mouth. She immediately shook her head. "Sorry, I'm being paranoid now. If he'd been watching me, he probably would have tried again."

"That's not a question I can answer. In all honesty, it's possible he died shortly after, or he ran as soon as you got hit by the squad car. If he was smart, getting out of South Carolina right away was the best thing he could've done. Short of never kidnapping you in the first place." Fortis shrugged. "If I could figure out the way the criminal mind works, we wouldn't be solving cases *after* the victim is murdered. I think it's been twelve years without incident, so he's either dead or long gone."

"Or very patient." A shiver passed through her again. "I need to see the files."

"You have to promise you won't take any evidence from the box." Fortis gave her a hard look, meeting her gaze. "I can't stress enough that this stays between you and me."

"I promise. I won't tell a soul, and I won't investigate it." She was tempted to cross her fingers behind her back, but she caught herself and crossed her toes the best she could in her shoes.

"Good. That's all I ask." Moving around the desk, he took a bottle from his drawer and set two green glass tumblers on the desk. He poured her a finger of bourbon then handed her the glass.

"I thought you said not on the clock."

"You're taking your lunch break." He raised his glass as if to give a toast and stopped himself halfway. "It's against the rules for you to work on your own case in any way, shape, or form, so I'm giving you an early lunch."

"Works for me." Throwing the smooth liquid back in one gulp, Ellie relished the way the heat settled in her chest, burning out and numbing the anxiety that had taken up residence. "Let's get this over with."

18

Ellie could feel Jillian's eyes on her as she followed Fortis into the evidence room, and on to the cold case locker. He quietly walked through the aisles until he found the square white plaque with the letter "C" to announce the contents of that row and the misfiled case box.

Ellie straightened her shoulders, tapping her fingers against her hip as she followed, trying to prepare herself for what she was about to see. But how could you prepare yourself to see the evidence of your unsolved kidnapping?

"There it is," Fortis said. Even at a low volume, his voice practically boomed through the utilitarian room. "Are you sure you want to see this?"

She nodded, then the click of footsteps behind her grabbed her attention, and she turned. She half-expected the kidnapper to be there, but it was only Jillian. She was standing ten feet behind them, hands clasped in front of her. Her face was pinched with worry, and the comforting smile she offered Ellie didn't extend to her eyes.

"You know," Ellie said.

Jillian nodded. "I thought you did and was just waiting for

you to mention it. A quick search of the files with your name came up empty, so I went with an alternate spelling, didn't take a genius. I can leave and mind my own business if that's what you want."

"Can you stay?" Ellie asked through the lump in her throat.

Jillian closed the distance between them and took Ellie's hand. "I'll stay as long as you need me."

Ellie didn't trust herself to speak, so she nodded instead.

Jillian turned her gaze on Fortis, squeezing Ellie's hand.

Fortis used a short stepladder to reach the box that was on the third shelf. In plain sight amongst the other cold cases, Ellie had walked past it every day since she'd started. The Jane and John Does that were violent cases but didn't fall under homicide were tucked into the back corner. She'd been close enough to turn and see her name on the box.

"Even if I'd seen 'E. Kline,' I wouldn't have made the connection," she said, more to herself than Jillian and Fortis. "It was here this entire time." Ellie stepped forward to take the box from him so he could grab the others.

But he shook his head and worked his way down the three steps. "This is the only box."

Ellie's lips parted in surprise. "How is that possible? Even my Jane Doe has two boxes."

"That's what I meant when I said there was almost no evidence." He turned away from them and blew the dust from the top of the box. It filled the space in front of him, so much like the haze that had settled on Ellie in Fortis's office when he'd told her about the case being cold.

Her heart clenched at the sight of what was obviously twelve years of dust. "No one has looked at it since I was a kid, have they?"

He shook his head. "I'm sorry. Usually with wealthy parents, there would at least be a cursory glance over the evidence every few years, but your parents never pressed the issue. They were content to have you home safe. They did hire a fulltime bodyguard for you, but they made it clear that our services weren't needed."

"I'm not surprised." Ellie never took her gaze from the box as he set it on the evidence room table, his hands still gripping the sides. "They never talked about the kidnapper, and whenever the subject came up, they alluded to the case being over and done. I never would have guessed he'd never been caught. I guess they were both so convinced this was about money, they never considered anything else as a possibility."

"The detective on the case exhausted every avenue, but even in the report it says that the likely motivation in the kidnapping was monetary gain." The phone on his hip beeped. He read the text message and scowled. "I have to take this. I trust I can rely on you to not do anything stupid with this?"

"Of course," Ellie said, then nodded to Jillian. "Jillian will make sure I don't step out of line, won't you?"

"Yep."

Fortis looked from Ellie to Jillian and sighed. "Why do I feel like I'm about to regret this?"

"I promised," Ellie offered.

"I'm counting on that promise." His phone chirped again, and he reluctantly let loose of the box and hurried out of the room.

Jillian's spine went stick straight before leaning toward the doorway so she could hear him leaving. When the outer door closed behind him, she turned to Ellie with a feral smile. "Tell me that promise wasn't a real promise."

Ellie held up her crossed fingers with a grin. "He's a fool if he thinks I'm going to sit around and wait for someone else to solve this case. They had twelve years."

"What about the Janes?"

Ellie frowned. "I'm not abandoning them. But I have to know what's in here. I have almost no memories of that night, and the memories I do have come in disjointed fragments that make no sense. Maybe something in here will tie the pieces together."

"Do you want me to look first?" Jillian's patient gray eyes studied Ellie.

"No. I'm okay." She took a deep, shuddering breath, then laughed. "I really am okay. I just had no idea this was here until a few minutes ago, and I've got to be honest, I'm completely overwhelmed."

Ellie sat down at the table and stared at the box for a long time without moving. Then she reached out but pulled her hand back just before she touched the lid.

Jillian raised her eyebrows, and when Ellie nodded, Jillian stood and placed her hands on the lid. "You can say no. Not a soul will think any less of you for not wanting to see this."

"Do it," Ellie said.

Jillian swept the lid off like a magician revealing her final illusion. Glancing into the box, her brows furrowed and her red lips turned down in a frown. "There's not much in here," she said as she slid the box across the table for Ellie to see. "No wonder they didn't solve it. A few pictures, a printout of text messages you sent your parents. That's really it."

Ellie peered into the box, shocked by the photos of her swollen and almost unrecognizable face. There was a toxicology report that wasn't ordered until the day after she was admitted. Texts retrieved from her parents' phones. One tennis shoe. "What the hell?"

"They botched this so bad, Ellie," Jillian murmured. "Why wouldn't the hospital assume you were running *from* something to run out in front of a car like that?"

"I don't know. But between the paramedics and surgery, it's no surprise the test results were inconclusive."

"You lost a lot of blood too," Jillian pointed out, tapping her finger on a line of the medical records. "This says you received a transfusion to save your life."

Ellie squeezed her eyes shut, trying to tamp down the rage that was growing inside her. "All they had to do was take a blood sample," she whispered angrily. "One sample that was untainted could've been enough."

"Or it could've been a complete waste of precious moments."

Ellie's eyes were still closed when she took a deep breath and nodded. "I know you're right, but there was that chance, and it's gone. They disposed of everything and kept one shoe."

"According to this, it's the only one you had. And your cell phone was never recovered." She handed the printout of the text messages to Ellie.

Ellie looked them over, then froze. "I didn't write this one."

"What?"

Ellie jabbed at the last message sent from her phone with her finger. "This one right here. I don't talk like that. I mean, I would never, *never* ask if I could stay a second night and use the words 'pretty please.'" She wrinkled her nose. "I was fifteen years old. I asked, and if they said no, I'd point out my good grades, or I found another way to bargain. What I didn't do was beg. I didn't write this."

"Do you think the kidnapper did?"

"It had to be him." She searched her memory, then blew out a frustrated breath. "Damn it. Every time I try to picture when and how it happened, I just come up blank. I know I went somewhere else because Nick saw me at the party when I'd told my parents I was staying at Amanda's."

"Did he see who you left with?" Jillian sat back down, alternating from looking at the photos of Ellie as a teen, and Ellie sitting across from her.

"No. He was about to graduate, and I was fifteen, so he kinda blew me off. When he came to check on me, I was already gone."

"Wow."

"Yeah. He's never forgiven himself for that." Ellie wondered if that was the reason he was so patient with her. Was it because he felt guilty? She brushed it off, unable to think of that with her very own almost empty cold case box sitting in front of her.

"It's not his fault, but I would feel the same." Jillian stared at Ellie steadily, as if willing her not to feel bad for Nick feeling bad. "If he was your friend and you were young and vulnerable, he would want to protect you."

"I was in way over my head, but it wasn't at the party. I didn't meet him there." Ellie bit the inside of her cheek, wracking her brain.

"Then where?"

Ellie thought hard, then scowled and threw her hands in the air. "I've got nothing. This is the most frustrating thing ever. I remember a few things here and there, but everything else is so fuzzy."

"So, talk me through it." Jillian leaned forward, tapping the table to get Ellie's attention. "Whatever you remember, just start talking. Don't worry about it being out of order or not making sense."

"Okay, yeah, let's try that." Ellie sat back in the chair, popping her neck. "So, I told my parents I was staying at Amanda's, but I ended up at a party instead. And at some point Friday night, I left the party and ran into the kidnapper."

"And your parents sent you a text Saturday afternoon."

"Right. The kidnapper apparently responded, which bought him some time. In fact, my parents didn't realize I was missing until Sunday evening when I didn't answer my phone, and they called Amanda directly. By the time they got ahold of her, I was already in surgery."

"So, a call to the police with your description would've been pieced together almost immediately."

Ellie nodded. "It was. My mom said there were about two hours between when she realized I was missing and when they were notified."

"Is that when your father had the stroke?"

Ellie pressed her lips together. "No. He had the stroke when he saw me."

"I'm so sorry." Jillian reached out and touched Ellie's hand, then looked into her eyes. Ellie's stomach clenched, and she looked away, but Jillian wasn't done yet. "It wasn't your fault, Ellie. You didn't kidnap yourself, and any parent would be beside themselves to see their child like that."

"I know. But knowing that it's not my fault and shaking this horrible guilt is harder than you would think. There were so many chances for someone to notice that I was missing, but everything went exactly the way the kidnapper wanted it to go."

"Except you escaped."

"That's the only thing that went my way." She shivered and rubbed her arms, almost feeling the cold rain from that night on her skin. "What if I hadn't gotten away? Would he have done something awful to me?"

"You can't do that. You'll drive yourself mad thinking about what if."

"I can't help it. Especially now that I know he was never caught. How many things can go wrong in one night? If I hadn't lied, I wouldn't have been at the party. And if Nick had told them I was at that party, they would've hunted me down and—" She sucked in a quick breath.

"Did you remember something?"

"No, but oh my gosh, why didn't I think about this before?" She was on her feet, all but running to the section where the two Jane Doe cases sat waiting to be re-shelved on Friday if she was unsuccessful. "The kidnapper dressed them, but did you look at their nails?"

"What?" Jillian said, jogging to keep up with Ellie's long stride. "What about their nails?"

"They both had fresh manicures and pedicures. Bright, festive colors, and no growth on the cuticle." She held the pictures up and showed Jillian, waving Jane Doe Two's photo of her lime green nails. "They were going somewhere."

"Okay. I am really not following you here."

"What if they're not reported missing in Charleston because their family doesn't realize they went missing *in* Charleston? If they were supposed to be somewhere else, they would report them missing there, right?"

"Maybe, but if they lived here, wouldn't they still make a report here?" Jillian frowned down at the photos of the women's hands.

"Not necessarily. A lot of coeds meet for summer and spring break activities, and they'll ride a train or a bus to another college before they leave. If they went to college somewhere else and they were on some kind of trip, they would be reported missing from their college and maybe even the place they were headed."

"Which means they could've been reported missing from *anywhere*."

"We have to broaden our search and start completely from scratch." Ellie tapped her foot on the floor, realizing how little time she had left on the cases, and how much work. "I'd be willing to bet my next paycheck their families reported them missing, but somehow we've overlooked it."

"What about your case?"

She shook her head. "I'm alive, and if that monster knows what's good for him, he'll stay gone. I've managed to live for twelve years without an answer, but these women have families who still don't know where they are. I can wait for closure."

In her pocket, Ellie's cell phone buzzed. She checked the caller ID and sent it to voicemail. "It's Nick. He probably wants to talk about the fundraiser he's heading up this month. I might have told him I would go."

"That doesn't sound too horrible. In fact, a date out to a fancy place sounds lovely." Her gaze took in the darkened corners of the evidence room.

Ellie's face lit up. "Maybe you could go instead. I'll even buy you a dress."

"Hard pass. I have this horrible condition where people say arrogant things in front of me, and I make this face." Jillian twisted her face into something between shock and horror. "It doesn't go over well at stuffy shindigs."

"I know the feeling." Ellie groaned when her phone buzzed again. "Man, he must be really excited to talk about it."

"The service sucks down here, though," Jillian pointed out.

"You're right." When Nick called back a third time, she answered, but all she could hear was crackling on his end. "You'll have to text me, I don't have a good signal," she said, then she hung up. "Hopefully, he'll figure it out."

"Maybe you should step outside, take a break and call him back."

"I'm sure it's nothing," she lied.

"I can put your case back on the shelf."

"I've got it." Ellie grabbed the box, and her phone vibrated again, this time with a text. "Oh good, he got the message." She balanced the box on her hip so she could read it.

"Does Nick have a friend? We could double date."

Ellie stared at the phone for a beat before the words sunk all the way in. The thunk of the box tumbling to the floor sounded distant and detached. She could hear Jillian calling her name, but her friend sounded like she was underwater and in another room. Then suddenly, everything slipped back into focus. "I have to go."

"Are you all right?" Jillian was already scooping up the pictures and evidence bags scattered on the floor. "Ellie, you're as white as a ghost."

"Can you let Fortis know I'll call him later?"

"Sure, of course. Ellie, please, what's going on?"

"My dad had another heart attack. They're taking him to Medical University of South Carolina." She swallowed hard. "Nick says it's not good."

Jillian set the box down on the table and grabbed Ellie's arm, ushering her out of the cold case area. "I'll drive you." She scooped Ellie's then her own purse off the desks on the way.

"What about the evidence boxes?" Ellie asked, glancing over her shoulder at the now closed and locked door.

"The people in those boxes are long dead. This is happening now, and I'm not going to let you drive yourself. They'll be here when I get back, and I'll take care of it then. If anyone loses their mind over it, I'll set them straight."

By the time they were in the hallway, the fog around Ellie had lifted. They bypassed the rickety old elevator for the back staircase, and when they burst through the side door into the bright autumn sunshine, it almost blinded Ellie. She jumped into Jillian's car, and this time, when Nick called, she was able to answer.

"I'm on my way." She was out of breath and struggling to get her seatbelt fastened as Jillian took the corner on squealing tires and flew down Lockwood Drive.

"I can come get you," he said as calm as ever.

Just hearing his voice made her feel steadier. "Jillian is bringing me."

"Good. Tell her to slow down. We don't need two emergencies in this family. Not today."

"I'll be there as quick as I can."

"I'll let your mom know." He hung up before she could thank him.

"We'll be there in five minutes." Jillian weaved between cars, going so fast it was like the other cars were standing still. "What did Nick say?"

"He said to slow down. We don't need another tragedy today."

Jillian eased off the accelerator but didn't slow much.

Ellie stared ahead, waiting for the hospital to appear in the distance. It was the only hospital near Charleston that performed transplants, and the best place her father could be.

Hopefully, the ambulance got him there before it was too late.

19

Ellie sat in the hard, cold chair beside her father's bed. She wrapped her hands around his hand, lying still on the white sheets, the monitor beeping a steady rhythm in the stark room. His hand was cool, his skin so pale that, when she'd first entered the room, she was sure he was already gone. But he was clinging to life and breathing on his own. It wasn't much, but it was something.

Leaning forward, she laid her head on the mattress, closed her eyes, and counted along with the constant noise of the heart monitor. One…two…three… Every time she got to one hundred, she started again. Her father's fingers twitched, but Ellie didn't bother lifting her head. He'd been in and out of consciousness all day, and so far, the twitching hadn't meant anything.

She heard Nick's footsteps before he spoke from behind her, his voice quiet. "Your mother is asking if you plan on coming to the cafeteria and joining her and your brothers for dinner. Or I can bring you something if you want to stay here."

"I'm not hungry." Her voice was muffled as she stirred, the

scent of disinfectant wafting up from the stiff mattress. "I could use some coffee, though."

"Here." She lifted her head, and he held out a plain white coffee cup with a brown cardboard sleeve. "One cream, one sugar, right?"

"Yes. Thank you."

He crouched in front of her, his large hand cupping her cheek. "I'll stay all night if you want me to."

"You don't have to do that."

"I want to."

She bit her lip, fighting back tears. Looking away and out the window, she cursed the sun that shone as if her world wasn't falling apart. "It should be raining," she murmu red.

Nick was still watching her when she looked his way again, his eyes searching hers. But when he reached for a tissue and tenderly dabbed at the tears that had trickled down her cheeks, it was her undoing.

She leaned against his chest, letting him take the coffee cup from her hand and set it aside before he gathered her into his arms and held her close. Kneeling on the floor next to her chair, he wrapped his strong arms tighter around her while she sobbed against his chest. He was silent, weathering the storm of rage and sadness that overtook her, with a calm like no other.

Swaying gently, he rubbed her back and tucked her head under his chin. Tears spilled down her cheeks, soaking his shirt as the pain ripped through her without mercy. "This is all my fault," she said between choked sobs.

He shook his head, resting his cheek against her hair. "It's not."

"If I hadn't lied to them, none of this would have happened. I never would've been kidnapped, and Daddy wouldn't have had a stroke. He's been struggling since that day, and it's all because of me. I did this."

"You didn't do this," he insisted. "You had no way of knowing what would happen. You were just a kid, Ellie. It was a fluke. No one blames you."

She scoffed, then hiccupped on a fresh sob. "Mother blames me. I know she does. How could she not?"

"Come on, Ellie. You know that's not true."

"She was so angry when she found out that I lied to them." She sniffled, wiping at her nose. "I heard her talking to Blake and Danny when I was in the hospital. She was mad at them for not telling her about the party, but they didn't know about it either."

"*You* didn't know. You snuck off to go to the movies with a boy. You didn't know he was going to take you to the party then ditch you when you wouldn't put out. That's not your fault."

Her brain and heart insisted that he was wrong.

"Daddy wouldn't be here right now if it weren't for me. And now we're sitting here, just waiting for him to die, or for someone else to die so he can live. How horrible is that? We either lose him or someone else loses everything, and *we* get Daddy back. Hoping that he gets a transplant means hoping someone else dies. It's not fair."

"It's not, you're right. None of this is fair, starting with you blaming yourself for something that happened twelve years ago. You made a mistake when you were fifteen years old, Ellie. None of us knew his heart was weak. Even your father didn't know. What if he hadn't been in the hospital when he had that stroke? He would've been at home and then..." He took a deep, shuddering breath. "Then he probably would've died. But he was at the hospital and got help right away. Healthy people don't just have a stroke, even when they're stressed. It was going to happen sooner or later, and as far as medical emergencies go, your father was lucky."

Air escaped Ellie's lungs with a whoosh. She was trembling, her heart racing, her eyes still filling with tears. "It doesn't matter how you explain it away, I still screwed up, and they've never let it go. They don't trust me to make big decisions or to live my life without fearing that something awful is going to happen. If I let them, they would probably wrap me up in a bubble and keep me there just in case."

"You can't really blame them for that. What happened to you is every parent's worst nightmare. You don't get over someone taking your child. You just don't. I know it drives you crazy, and you feel like they're still treating you like a child, but you should give them a little grace. They're trying to do better. They just love you so much."

"I wish they could be proud of me. I don't think that's too much to ask."

"It's not. Give them time. They'll see there's nothing to worry about. I mean, you're in cold cases. What could go wrong?" She stiffened before she could stop herself. Nick caught on immediately, pulling away from her so he could look her in the eye. When she tried to look away, his hand went to her cheek. "Ellie, what aren't you telling me?"

"Do you know what happened to the person who kidnapped me? Do you remember?"

He tilted his head, his eyelids narrowed. "I don't remember. I was only eighteen and graduating, so I guess I missed it while I was getting ready for college and stuff."

"Do you remember the trial?"

"No. But I was away at school." Nick's eyes were searching hers. He didn't know.

"That's not why you don't remember. There was no trial."

"So he pled out and spared you a trial? That was merciful of him."

"No, Nick. There was no plea and no trial." She shook her head frantically. "Mom and Dad told me that the kidnapper had been killed, then they somehow covered everything up.

But they never caught the guy. Whoever it was, he's still out there somewhere."

A soft gasp escaped Nick's lips, and his arms pulled her closer instinctively as he digested what she'd just said. "Are you sure?"

"Absolutely. My case was never solved." Ellie attempted to mop up her face with her sleeve. "There's not even a suspect."

"How is that possible?" Nick leaned back, his gaze going to her father. "And why didn't anyone investigate?"

"The paramedics and the hospital destroyed most of the evidence saving my life. They didn't know what I'd been through, so they treated me like any other pedestrian versus car. By the time anyone knew, it was too late." The moment she looked into the shockingly empty evidence box flashed through her mind. "There was almost nothing to go on. No witnesses, no physical evidence, and I have no memory of what happened except for bits and pieces that don't make sense. My case was shelved."

"Why didn't your parents hire an investigator themselves?"

"Because it was about money." Helen's voice was soft and flat as she stepped into the room and closed the door behind her. "They failed to get a ransom, and there was no need to drag our family through an investigation when there was no evidence." Her mother's dark eyes ran over Ellie's face. "I suppose that means you found your case?"

"I didn't. Fortis told me where it was." Ellie blinked up at her mother. "Why didn't you tell me the truth? This whole time I've been going about my life while that monster is out there somewhere."

Helen's bottom lip quivered, and a single delicate tear slipped over her cheek and ran down her throat. "He's long gone, whoever it was. We paid for round-the-clock security for years afterward, just to make sure." She turned her gaze to Nick. "We did hire a private investigator, but he found less than nothing, and he was also convinced the kidnapper had left town. We wouldn't have stopped looking if we didn't think she was safe." Helen sighed. "I hope you're not going to reopen the case. Your father can't take any more stress."

"Investigating my own kidnapping is a conflict of interest." Ellie was so cold, the same as this room, the same as her father lying still in the bed, the same as the evidence box that had told her nothing. The same as the rain on her skin that night. "I'm not allowed to, and after looking at what little the department has, there's really nothing I can do at this point."

"Good." Ellie tensed at her mother's response, but before she could think of what to say, her mother's eyes darted to the bed, and her lips parted. "Daniel?" she said, rushing to the bed.

"Water," her father croaked through cracked lips.

A nurse opened the door just then, a wide grin on his face. "I see you've finally woken up." He moved to the other side of the bed to fuss with the monitors. "Looking much better than you were a few hours ago. I'll get the doctor."

Daniel nodded, and he took a sip of the water Helen offered through a bent straw that reminded Ellie of the ones that came with a kid's juice box. He took several short sips, and when his thirst was quenched, he looked at Ellie, his voice just above a whisper. "Come here."

She did as he asked, standing beside her mother and holding back tears. "Daddy." The word came out as a sigh. "It's so good to see you."

"You too, princess."

There was a soft knock at the door, and a woman in a white lab coat walked into the room. Her smile was a brilliant white, her long brown hair braided over one shoulder and hanging down to her waist. "Your color is much better now." Clipboard in hand, she looked over the numbers. "As we discussed last month, you will need a transplant soon."

Last month!

Ellie stiffened. More lies? Where did it end?

Her eyes shot to her mother, but Helen was watching the doctor. When she caught Nick's eye, Nick shook his head, his message clear. *Let it go.* It didn't matter that her parents had led her and her siblings to believe that the transplant talk was more recent. At the end of the day, her father needed a new heart, and that was all that mattered.

"Will I be able to go home?" Daniel asked.

"I'm afraid not." The doctor gave him a sad smile. "Your health will need to be closely monitored. You can't afford to have another episode before a heart is available."

"How long do you think it will be?" Helen squeezed her husband's hand, as if to give him strength.

Ellie cringed. The weight of someone else's loss being her father's only hope wasn't lost on her. No matter how Helen phrased it, they were waiting for someone to die so Daniel Kline could live.

"It could be tomorrow, or it could be in a month. But Mr. Kline, you're near the top of the list, so as soon as a match becomes available, you will go to surgery." She closed the privacy cover on the clipboard. "Is there anything else I can help you with?"

Everyone shook their head, and the doctor was gone, the room plunged into an uncomfortable silence.

"How are you *really* feeling?" Ellie asked her father when the silence became too much.

"Never better." He winked at her. "I'm going to be fine. Don't you worry."

"We're all worried, Daniel." Helen patted his hand, then looked at Ellie. "Honey, I hope you can call your boss and let him know you'll need some time off. You should be with your family right now."

Ellie bit her lip and looked from her father to her mother and back again. "I'll spend every spare minute here, Daddy, but I need to work. I can't just sit here and stare at these walls."

"Eleanor, I'm not asking you to sit here all day, but you need some rest, and you need to be here for your family. Isn't that right, Daniel?" She looked pointedly at her husband with a gentle, practiced smile on her face.

"Helen, let the girl work. She needs something to keep her mind off all this." He coughed and pointed to the water on the table beside the bed. Helen held the cup for him, and after a few sips, he licked his lips and continued. "I know you want to keep her close, but it looks like I'll be here for a while."

"You don't know that, Daniel. We can probably go home with a nurse—"

"You heard the doctor. I'll be here until there's a heart available." His words were slow and measured, and obviously tiring him. "It could be tomorrow, or it could be two months from now. Ellie can't put her life on hold until I'm better. That's ridiculous."

"Families stick together when times get tough, Daniel," Helen insisted. "She needs to be here with us."

Nick shifted on his feet and clasped his hands together in front of him. His shoulders were stiff, and Ellie could see the vein throbbing on his temple.

She cleared her throat. "I'm sorry, Mom, but I'm not going to step away from work. Who knows how long it's going to be. Like Daddy said, I can't just walk away until then."

"Eleanor Elizabeth Francis Kline, please think of your

father." Helen's eyes turned hard, suddenly the disciplinarian mom she'd been in Ellie's youth.

"I am, Mom. I promise. You heard what they said. He needs rest and for things to be calm so he can focus on staying well." She took her mother's hands in hers. "I will be here the instant you need me. Now that I made detective, my schedule is a lot more flexible. I'll tell Fortis what's going on and let him know that I'll be in and out. It'll be all right."

"How are you going to keep going like that?" Helen frowned, worry surfacing in her eyes.

"I'm fine. I really am." She gave Helen what she hoped was a reassuring smile. "If things get to be too much, I'll take vacation time. But right now, I'm no use here."

Nick stepped forward. "I'll be happy to relieve you when you need a break, Mrs. Kline. Between Ellie and me, we'll make sure Mr. Kline is never alone."

"Danny, Blake, and Wesley can help too," Ellie added.

"Your brothers are so busy." When Ellie pulled away, Helen hurried to amend her statement, but the damage was already done. "They don't have the flexibility you have."

"Meaning their jobs are important." Ellie forced her voice to remain low and calm, but inside she felt rage growing.

"Leave her be, Helen," Daniel said. "I'm tired already, and I need to rest. What I *don't* need is someone sitting in this room and staring at me while I do it." He gestured at the large sofa against the wall across from the hospital bed. "There's a pullout bed in there. Nick, if you would pull that out for Helen, I would appreciate it." He reached out with shaking hands, and Helen met him halfway. He squeezed her hand, then pulled it to his cheek and sighed. "I need you here with me, Helen. Everyone else should go about their lives until we get this sorted. It'll be like it was before we had children."

Helen laughed and kissed Daniel on the forehead. "Fine,"

she sighed. “But don’t expect me to sleep on those scratchy sheets.”

“I wouldn’t dream of it.” Daniel relaxed back into the pillow with a grin.

“Write a list of what you need, and I’ll pick it up,” Ellie offered quickly.

“Thank you.” Helen opened her arms, and Ellie stepped into her embrace.

She inhaled the soft scent of her mother’s perfume and closed her eyes. “I love you, Mom.”

“I love you more. Please be careful,” she whispered, so low that Daniel couldn’t hear. “Your father’s heart can’t take any more stress, and to be honest, neither can I.”

“I will, Mom,” Ellie promised. She’d made so many promises today, and she already knew she’d break the first. Could she keep this one?

Helen wrote a list out on the hospital notepad in perfect, flowing cursive and handed it to Ellie. Ellie hugged them both one more time and left with Nick close behind.

They were on the elevator when Nick held out his hand. “Give me the list, and I’ll take care of it.”

“She’s not going to like that.”

He shrugged. “It’s a long list, and you’re going to have to buy everything to fit that bed, so it’s not like you can just go home and find it in your closet. I know how you *love* shopping.”

She wrinkled her nose, convinced, and handed the list over before fishing in her purse for her wallet.

He held up his hand. “You can owe me one.” He pulled her close and tilted her chin up for a soft, quick kiss. “That’s a good start.”

She rolled her eyes. “Make sure you keep the receipts.”

“I’ll think about it.” He put an arm around her as the door

opened on the first floor. "Do you need me to drive you back to work to get your car?"

"Sure." After the stress of the day, she didn't mind being tucked to his side for a while longer.

In the deserted parking garage, he hit the button on the key fob, and headlights flashed ahead of them. They were shiny and brand-new, yet another luxury vehicle in the long list of new cars Nick had purchased.

Ellie arched an eyebrow at him. "This has to be a new record."

He shrugged, eyeing the sexy lines of the vehicle. "I like this one."

"It looks just like all the others you've had."

He opened the passenger door and held it for her. "Yeah, but it's what's inside that makes all the difference."

He was still holding the door when she stepped forward, and one arm snaked around her waist, pulling her against him. A surprised chuckle slipped from her lips, quieted by his kiss. This time, the kiss was deeper, more passionate than before.

Her heart quickened, and she wound her arms around his neck, kissing him back with quiet urgency. When she finally pulled back but remained wrapped in his embrace, she was breathless and smiling. "You must really like this one."

"I do, but you know me; once I find the right one, I'm smart enough not to let her get away."

Ellie had a feeling he wasn't talking about cars anymore.

20

"I hear you got a new partner."

Jacob looked up from the gym's bench where he sat tying his shoes and glared at the officer standing in front of him. Like him, the man was dressed in black track pants with white stripes and a black athletic shirt with his name stitched over his heart. On the opposite side was the name of the Krav Maga studio in neat block letters. Jacob didn't recognize the man, but that didn't mean anything. Ever since he'd been paired up with Ellie, everyone seemed to know who Jacob was.

"I did," Jacob said coolly.

The officer was buff, his light blond hair cut short, and he bounced on the balls of his feet. He wore a shit-eating grin on his face that matched the expressions of the three meatheads standing behind him with their arms crossed.

"Bet you like cleaning up after a dog better than that last hot mess, right?" the man pressed. "You deserved the upgrade."

"Funny, I told your girlfriend the same thing."

The man blinked, and pink color crawled up his throat.

Pressing his lips together, he narrowed his eyes and took a threatening step forward. "You better watch yourself," he said through clenched teeth.

"I'm sorry, was that too much?" Jacob feigned concern. "I guess if you can't take it, maybe you shouldn't be dishing it out." He shrugged one shoulder, keeping his expression innocent. "I suppose I should've known a man who needs to bring his friends to trade insults can't handle being challenged."

The man's hands clenched, and he leaned in as if to take a step forward. But something through the front glass of the gym caught his eye, and he froze, then a slow smile spread across his face. "Speak of the devil, and she appears. Must be nice to have that kind of money to spend on a flashy car while the rest of us make an honest living."

"Are we done here?" Jacob punctuated his bored tone with a well-timed yawn. "I don't know about you, but I came to the gym to work out."

"I'll see you on the mat," the blond retorted. "Unless you're too scared to partner with a man."

Jacob laughed. "Honestly, buddy, I'd love to see you take her on, but I'm sure she came here for a real workout. You wouldn't want a woman handing you your ass in front of all your friends, would you?"

"Everybody partner up and take a spot on the mat," the instructor called out.

When the man and his followers turned, Jacob used the distraction to slip away. He jogged to the door and opened it for Ellie with a welcoming smile. "The bullshit's already nice and deep in here. You ready to spar?"

She nodded, but she wore a frown and barely met his gaze. "Hell, yes."

Jacob pursed his lips. "Is something wrong?"

"Nothing that kicking your ass won't fix."

"Good thing you're already dressed for the mat then."

Ellie glanced sharply up over his shoulder, but Jacob didn't bother following her gaze. "Ignore them. He's just mad because I made him look like an idiot in front of his entourage."

She grimaced. "I know him. He asked me out last year."

"No wonder he was putting on a big show for his friends." Jacob snorted. "Oh man, that makes it even better. Come on, let's get this done."

"I hope you're ready, because I'm not going easy on you today."

"Let's go, people," the instructor urged, nodding pointedly in their direction.

Jacob jogged to the mat with Ellie right behind him, and they immediately transitioned into jumping jacks to warm up with the group. The blond man looked over at them a few times, but every time Jacob caught his eye and flashed a wide grin, the man turned away angrily.

"We're going to start with palm-heel strikes. Get your targets, and let's go."

Jacob grabbed one of the black foam-filled targets and put his hands in the loops. "Ready?"

Ellie nodded and hit the target with the heel of her hand. Left. Then right.

Jacob held the target in front of his center, the power behind her strikes more intense than usual. "Let it out," he said in a low voice.

Ellie doubled up at his words. Left, right. Left, right in quick jabs, pivoting her body with the motion then getting back into fighting stance. When it was time to switch, Jacob handed her the target and got into position.

Even though she was just holding the target for him, Jacob could see the fire in her eyes. The urge to ask her what had happened was strong, but he'd known Ellie long enough to have learned that she would talk when she was ready and not a moment before.

They worked through the moves individually as a group, progressing to elbow and knee strikes until they were completely warmed up. Jacob watched Ellie turn into a beast before his eyes, and by the time they were ready to spar, Ellie was all but breathing fire. The frown that had marred her forehead when she'd walked in faded and was replaced with a genuine smile that reached her emerald green eyes.

"Targets down," the teacher instructed. "Let's practice grappling."

"Oh, boy." Jacob groaned, retrieving his mouthguard. "I have a feeling I already know how this is going to end."

"At least you're wearing protective gear." Ellie shrugged her shoulders as the rest of the class cleared the mat. "Guess we're first up."

"Great," Jacob teased.

They both got into fighting stance as the instructor shouted, "Go!"

Jacob blocked each of her strikes, catching her palms and trying to get his own strikes in between. Ellie was on fire. Focused, she moved on to kicks, catching him off guard more than once. When she used a leg sweep to take him off his feet, he hit the mat hard and rolled before she could deal the final blow, which would end the fight. She might be fueled by rage and ready to take him down, but he wasn't going to let her win that easily.

He was on his feet again, and this time he got a front kick in past her defenses. She grinned, arching a single eyebrow and bouncing on the balls of her feet.

"She's enjoying this," one of the other students muttered loud enough to be heard.

But Jacob kept his eyes on Ellie. He knew better than to take his focus off her, even for a split-second.

When she gave him an opening, he took it. He had her in a bearhug with her arms pinned before he realized that was exactly where she wanted him.

She stepped hard on his foot then did a reverse kick to his shin and thigh. His grip loosened, and he was rewarded with an elbow strike to the stomach, then to the face. He winced, but she was coming at him, facing him, striking him hard with the heel of her hand, then her elbow again. When she kicked him, he instinctively backed up. His move gave Ellie a chance to make space between herself and her "attacker," ending the fight.

But she didn't take it.

She came at him again, a blur of knees, elbows, and hand strikes. When he hit the mat again, she was on him so fast he didn't have time to roll out of the way. Her knee was in his back, pinning him to the mat.

"That's enough, Kline." The instructor walked up to them, ready to intervene.

But Ellie was in control, despite her fury. She stood and held a hand out to Jacob. They were both breathing hard when he got to his feet, but another pair was already taking the mat, and all eyes were on the partners getting ready to spar.

Jacob took the towel Ellie handed him and mopped the sweat from his brow. "Good job," he said when he finally caught his breath. "I hope you feel better."

They walked to the door and stepped outside to let the cool afternoon air dry the dampness from their skin.

"I'm sorry about that. It's been a long, frustrating day." She looked back at the windows that made up the entire front of the gym. The group was still focused on the pair fighting it out on the mat. "I'm sorry if I made you look bad."

He shook his head. "Any man that's intimidated by a strong woman isn't a real man. I knew what I was getting into when I stepped onto the mat." He wiped his face and took a long drag on his water bottle. "I do wish I'd let you take on Prince Charming instead, though."

"I would've enjoyed handing his ass to him." She grinned, her gaze searching out the blond in the circle inside. "He did *not* take my rejection well."

"I believe it," Jacob said, thinking back to the earlier conversation with him. "As long as you're feeling better, that's all that matters."

She bit her lip, her attention divided between him and whatever was on her mind.

Still, he didn't press her for information. "You ready to go back inside? I didn't get a chance to hit the weights yet, and I could use a spotter."

"Sure."

He followed her in, ignoring the stares that tracked them as they made their way to the back room. His focus was on Ellie and getting through his workout. Everything else was just background noise.

❄

Ellie clipped her damp hair up off her neck and used a towel to wipe the steam from the mirror. The ladies' showers were empty, so she'd taken her time washing away the sweat and the grime from her workout, then wrapped herself in a towel so she could air-dry for a few minutes before getting dressed. She glanced at her arm, noting a bruise was already starting to darken where Jacob had gotten in a good shot. She was sure he was covered in bruises.

Finger-combing her spiral curls, she got dressed. She was sore and tired, but it felt good to get all that stress worked out of her system. Exactly what she'd needed after the day she'd had. It seemed like a lifetime since Fortis had called her into his office. So much had happened between then and walking into the gym, it seemed almost unreal.

But her father's health issues and the looming transplant to save his life were all too real, and no amount of sparring could make that go away.

She stuffed her dirty clothes and towel into her bag and slung it over her shoulder. The gym was a flurry of activity as she hurried down the hall toward the parking lot, and when the door closed behind her, the loud music was instantly deadened to a low, pulsing beat.

Jacob was waiting for her by her car. "You look refreshed," he said when she stepped onto the sidewalk.

"That was just what I needed to get my mind off everything, thanks."

"I was thinking about a late dinner."

She shook her head. "I'm not hungry. Really, I just need to get home."

His smile slipped a little, but he recovered so quickly she wondered if she'd imagined it. "I understand. Is there anything I can do?"

"This was enough." She gestured to the bruise forming along his jawline and sighed. "I guess I should tell you what's going on."

"You don't have to."

"I know." She took in a steadying gulp of air. "My father's health is failing. He needs a heart transplant, and he'll be in the hospital until that happens."

"That's rough, I'm sorry." He stepped closer, pulling her in for a hug. "How is your mom handling it?"

"By suggesting my job is keeping me from keeping vigil at my father's bedside."

"You can always take vacation time."

"I don't want to. I can't stay pent-up at that hospital for weeks on end. It's just too much. Daddy understands."

Jacob's dark eyebrows shot upward. "He's awake then?"

"He is. He's just too weak to get out of bed."

"Are you sure he's not saying it's okay so you don't feel guilty?"

Ellie considered for a moment then shook her head. "Daddy isn't like that. He doesn't always understand me, but he gets that I love my job. I wish my mom could do the same, but she's so set in her ways she really can't see things beyond her own experiences."

"I can see why you're so stressed."

She thought about telling him about the cold case file and everything else, but she decided against it. Her father's health issues were enough. There was no use opening that second can of worms.

"She agreed with him eventually, but I could tell she would rather have me there with her and Daddy to keep an eye on me."

"Are your brothers staying with him too?"

"Are you kidding?" she scoffed, throwing her hands up in defeat. "I guarantee she didn't give them the same talking to. Because *they* have responsibilities."

"I'm sorry you have to deal with that."

"Thanks, I appreciate it. Everyone has to deal with family dynamics. I just wish she'd get over it already."

Jacob tried to imagine her family dynamics and failed. "You *are* her only daughter."

"That's Wesley's fault." She laughed at the joke she'd told before. "If he'd been born a girl, I'd be home free."

Jacob chuckled, shaking his head. "You don't honestly believe that, do you?"

"You're right, I don't. But at least it would be a little easier."

He bumped her with his hip. "I'm sure she's proud of you, even if she doesn't always know how to express it."

"I wish I could be so sure. But my dad stepped in, so there's that."

"It's something, at least."

"Yeah, I was a little surprised. Daddy usually sides with her no matter what, but he was so calm about it." She frowned before she continued. "It's like knowing how fragile life is made him realize that we can't just let life slip by us, you know?"

"I understand completely. Your mom will figure it out. And in the meantime, at least she's nice about it."

Ellie agreed. "I just wish he wasn't hurting so bad. And my mom looks so worried. They're both usually pretty relaxed, so it's weird to see them like that."

"I'm sure it is." He looked at his watch. "I have to get going. Duke has a schedule, and if I mess it up, he gets destructive."

"Duke sounds like my kind of guy." Ellie laughed, and Jacob's eyes reflected her humor.

"Call me if you need to talk," he said. "And if there's anything else I can do, don't hesitate to ask."

"Thank you. I'll let you know."

She watched him drive away as she got into her car and turned the radio all the way up. Picking a station that was upbeat, she sang along as Guns N' Roses belted out "Sweet Child o' Mine" as she backed out of the parking spot and made her way home. It was after dinnertime, and the streets were almost empty, so she made it home in record time, stopping to pick up takeout on the way. She took the stairs, and by the time she opened the door to her apartment, her mouth was watering over the scent of orange chicken and chow mein.

Her phone chirped at her as she sat down to eat. When she read the text from Nick, she smiled.

Your mom is settled, and your dad is resting comfortably. She told me I was her new favorite son. Not sure what your brothers are going to think about that. He included a winking emoji at the end, drawing a laugh out of her.

She set down her chopsticks and typed in, *Thank you for staying with them. I'm doing much better. Kicked Jacob's ass at Krav Maga and grabbed Chinese takeout.*

Poor Jacob.

She was smiling as she sent him one last text. *He survived. I really appreciate you for helping with my parents.*

Anytime, he responded with a smiley face. *Sweet dreams.*

She was still smiling when she took the last bite of her dinner and cleaned up the kitchen. The day had started off rough and gone downhill from there, but in the end, she'd been reminded that she was surrounded by people who loved her and understood what she needed to feel safe when her world was out of control. She resolved to take Nick out to dinner to thank him. He deserved a medal for dealing with her life, but he would have to settle for filet mignon instead.

She didn't bother getting undressed when she crawled into bed more than an hour earlier than her normal bedtime. She was exhausted, and she still had so much work to do before the weekend. There were only two more days until the workweek was over, and she'd promised Fortis she would shelve the Jane Doe case if she hadn't made headway by then. That didn't give her much time, and she was determined to give the unnamed families closure. It was the least she could do after their violent deaths had snuffed out two vibrant lives. In fact, it was the *only* thing she could do for them.

That and bring their killer to justice.

21

"You look like hell," Jillian said when Ellie dragged herself into the office bright and early Thursday morning. "Maybe I should've brought *you* coffee."

"I'm fine." Ellie forced a smile. "I overdid it at the gym last night, and I'm a little more sore than I expected."

Jillian smiled back, hers looking more natural. "At least you know you gave it your all."

"Thanks. I needed to work through my feelings."

"About your dad?"

"About my dad, about Nick, about my mom." She set Jillian's coffee on her desk. "And about my own cold case. My whole life, really. Things aren't going the way I'd hoped, and now I have just today and tomorrow to try and figure this case out before I have to step back and work on something else. I was feeling really overwhelmed, but I think I managed to get all the kinks out." Ellie yawned, covering her mouth and looking longingly at her already empty coffee cup.

"I didn't touch mine yet, you want it?"

Ellie gladly took the proffered cup, gulping the hot liquid as quickly as she dared. She burned her tongue, but in a few minutes, when she started to feel human again, she knew it was worth it. "Did you make any headway with the Jane Does after I left?"

Jillian shook her head. "Sorry. Detective Finnigan is preparing to testify next week so he was in and out of here all day looking up stuff for his case."

"I bet that was annoying."

Jillian rolled her eyes. "You have no idea. But, I did go through a bunch of searches this morning to see if these girls pop up together. So far, I've come up dry. I tried extending the searches, but if you go out too far, it comes back with too many hits to weed through. Slows the computer way down."

"Did you mark off where you've searched so far?"

"I'm already one step ahead of you. I have a list, and it's organized by website and by region." Jillian presented the neatly printed list with a flourish and a goofy smile that made Ellie laugh.

"Thanks, Jillian. I'm going to get started." Hanging her purse on the back of her chair, Ellie straightened the papers on her messy desk. "I think we're on to something with the theory that their families don't know they disappeared in Charleston."

"At least we have a new perspective. That's something, isn't it?"

"It is, but it makes it more complicated. When it was only Charleston, we had a small sample area and a limited number of people. Now that these two women could be from anywhere and could've been headed to any number of destinations, it's going to be that much harder." Ellie frowned as Jillian nodded her agreement. "And if their families don't know they disappeared together, that's another strike against us."

"*If* they really were together," Jillian pointed out. "We

don't have proof that they were killed by the same person, and even if they were, what if he picked them up separately?"

Ellie nodded. Maybe she'd been going with her gut feeling a little too much. "You're right. We can't even say for sure whether they ever ran across each other. He could've killed one then grabbed the second girl later."

"Or we could have multiple killers using the same dumpsite."

Ellie's mouth dropped open. "Don't you dare put that out to the universe. I know I can't prove it yet, but I'm telling you, I *know* these cases are related."

"They don't have the same cause of death, only one woman was tortured, and they were dumped in two entirely different fashions. Sometimes, more than one killer is drawn to the same place when disposing of a body, could be because of the previous dump. Plus, multiple serial killers can be active in the same place at the same time." Jillian shrugged and propped her chin on her hand. "It's not unheard of, even in a place like Charleston."

Ellie plopped down in her chair and groaned. "Web searches are not my favorite thing, but the theory is the only lead we have right now. Until we can figure out who these women are, it's going to be next to impossible to figure out who killed them with the evidence we have."

"Then let's get after it," Jillian quipped, her fingers flying over the keyboard.

Ellie typed in keywords from her own list, then scrolled through the results. With every combination of words that came up empty, she made a note and kept going. She'd started with just a few, added more to the list, then tried different combinations. The results varied so wildly, Ellie's head started pounding. She rubbed her temples, glaring at the computer screen. "There are so many people listed as missing on social media that aren't even in our database."

"I know. How does that happen?"

"Sometimes friends and coworkers are the only ones who know someone has disappeared and they don't really know what to do. Or they're afraid to go to the police for whatever reason. And could you imagine if every boss that was ghosted by an employee filed a missing persons report?"

Jillian groaned. "We'd never get out from under all those reports."

"I think it's usually obvious when that happens, though."

Jillian paused in her typing. "You would think so, but I worked with this one guy that was super dependable, driven, and an all-around great coworker. He just stopped showing up one day, and nothing at work changed. He left there one afternoon like he always did every day, and the next morning he was just gone. I was really worried, but my boss said it happens all the time. Then he showed me a picture of the guy checking in on his social media account. He was out on the lake *fishing,* and his status announced he'd taken a job offer from a rival company starting that Monday."

"He didn't bother giving notice?" Ellie asked.

"Nope. He had to have known he had the job for a week or two, but he kept it a secret. Then he got tired of working and just took a long weekend before he started his new job. No one even batted an eye at it."

"I guess it's good that more of those cases aren't reported."

Jillian shook her head. "We would have entire police departments chasing their tails for no reason."

"That explains some of them, but what about the ones posted by family?" Ellie had a hard time believing family members would just go on, never digging deeper into the disappearance of their loved one. "Surely they know their loved one is actually missing. I get that social media is like the modern-day missing poster, but that's not enough, is it? Why would they post online and not go to the police?"

"You'd be shocked at how many missing people are found by online sleuths. And some of those families did file a report first. But when the police point out evidence that suggests their loved one left on their own, a lot of families don't want to believe it. It's not a crime to walk away and start a new life."

"Unless you're already a criminal."

"And that accounts for some of the others," Jillian added. "If you do a quick search of some of these missing women, they have someone in their household with an active warrant. If someone is hiding from the police, they're not going to call us to their house to look for clues in a disappearance."

"It just breaks my heart. With cameras almost everywhere and the power of social media, we should be able to find most of these people in days, if not weeks. There's no reason for someone to stay missing unless they *want* to. Even then, it's next to impossible to erase your electronic footprint."

"You would think." Jillian's fingers resumed typing.

"I wonder how many people are never reported missing in any capacity. Even with this many listed here, there still seems to be more Jane and John Does waiting to be claimed than families looking for their loved ones. It's sad when you think about it."

"I try not to think about it too much. You can't make people care about each other."

"You've got that right." Ellie tilted her head in agreement as she thought about the rows of unsolved cases. "Thank you for helping me with this. I'm not sure I could get through so many without your help."

"Don't mention it. It's nice to have something to occupy my time between waiting for people to check out evidence and ask me questions like I'm a walking encyclopedia. It feels like some of them have never seen a computer before."

"I know the feeling." Ellie laughed, rubbing eyes that were already starting to get tired. "I'm not sure what they would do without you either."

"The world would screech to a halt." Her silver eyes twinkled when she said it with a flourish.

"That's probably truer than you realize. Doesn't that stress you out?"

Jillian's shoulders lifted a fraction. "Not one bit. It's nice to be needed. It's also nice to finally dig into a case rather than just be the gatekeeper."

"That's what I'm going to call you now, Gatekeeper. Like on Ghostbusters." Ellie laughed, and Jillian shuddered in response and made a growling sound like Zuul, the Gatekeeper, while miming turning a key in the lock before throwing it away.

They went back to work, keyboards clicking the only sound for a long time. Even divided between them, it was a lot of ground to cover.

"I can see why Fortis was worried about me getting attached to cases," Ellie said, breaking the long silence. "I've found several I want to write down already so I can investigate on my own later if they don't end up on his list."

"There are people who make a good living doing just that."

Ellie scrunched her nose up. "I'm afraid to ask how they make money."

"Rewards."

"I'm sorry I asked."

Ellie's eyes were dry and gritty when she leaned back in the chair hours later and let out a moan of frustration. "It's almost lunchtime. I don't know about you, but I'm starting to get discouraged."

"There's a reason cases go cold."

"Not our case, though. We can't blame it on normal circumstances. It wasn't worked thoroughly because Detective Jones had already mentally checked out before the bodies were found. On the bright side, maybe we'll crack it wide open, and they'll let me work current cases."

"Cracking a case isn't like it is on the movies."

Ellie shot Jillian a hard look, wondering if she was getting hangry, the universal word for hungry-angry. "I know that, but I think we have a better chance than normal on this case. It's not like he tried that hard, right? There's plenty of new information to discover. We just have to know where to look."

"Except, whatever evidence was still there when he dropped the ball is gone now. Washed away or just lost. If we'd had the case in the first forty-eight hours, it would be different. I don't think there's anything about this case that gives us an advantage over Jones, no matter how incompetent he was."

Ellie rolled her eyes. "Whatever you say, Miss Optimistic."

They both laughed.

"Fine. I'll stop being a realist if you stop trying to convince yourself this is going to be easy."

"I know it's not."

"Good." Jillian's face was serious, her eyes worried as she glanced at Ellie. "I don't want you to get your heart broken over these women. I want to find out what happened to them, too, but we have to accept that we may never know the truth."

"As long as I know I did my best, I can accept that." But Ellie wasn't so sure that was true. She was determined to see this case through, even if that meant defying Fortis and working it long after her time was up. The two women drew

Ellie to them in a way she couldn't explain. She was invested now, and completely obsessed.

Is that a bad thing? Everyone deserved justice.

Her computer gave a low, audible click to let her know the search was done. "Oh, good. Only a hundred more search results to wade through. That's not going to take forever."

"Maybe we should go to lunch and come at it again with fresh eyes. After a while, all the pictures and faces start looking the same."

"You're probably right." Ellie sat with her chin in her hand, scrolling through the pictures of missing women, her eyes starting to glaze over.

"I'm hungry, and I don't work well when I'm hungry."

"You're not the only one." Ellie filed that bit of information back for later. "Let me finish up this group, and I'll get lunch with you. I'm almost done." Her sigh was heavy as she scrolled on. "There are so many women that are never fo—" Her hand froze on the mouse. "Holy crap."

"What?" Jillian shot up from her desk and hurried to stand beside Ellie. She peered down at the screen and went rigid. "Oh, wow."

"I think that's them." Ellie clicked on the post on a missing persons website and scanned through all the pictures. "Roommates Tabitha Baker and Mabel Vicente. Both twenty-two and founding members of Students With A Purpose. It looks like they were active in the community and online until they disappeared." Ellie read through the description, her brow furrowing. "That's strange. They weren't even reported missing until three months *after* the women's bodies were found."

"That is weird. Maybe it's not them."

"These cases are definitely related to each other. They were last seen on the same day, and they lived together and

—" She sucked in a quick breath. "They weren't just friends. It says here they were longtime girlfriends."

Jillian leaned in closer behind Ellie. "Where did they go missing from?"

"Let me see, oh there it is." Ellie whistled low beneath her breath. "No wonder they didn't come up on any police database. It says here they were attending an outreach program to build filtration systems for villages that don't have access to clean water." She looked pointedly at Jillian. "In Ghana."

"There's no way to transport a body that far without someone noticing, so they obviously didn't make it to Ghana. Or if they did, they were taken as soon as they returned home. Is there any other information?"

"Not much, but their next of kin are listed here. Both families live just outside of Charleston." She wrote down the phone numbers and addresses for both women. "One of these is almost an hour away, but the other one is in Lincolnville."

"That explains why they didn't hear about the bodies dumped at West Ashley Park."

"Not really. Everyone was talking about that case, and even after the police announced they'd exhausted their leads, people still wondered." Ellie compared the pictures of the women to the police sketches from the evidence. "Even though the pictures don't look that much like the composite sketches, usually families come forward if there's even the slightest possibility it's their child."

"I'm sure there's an explanation. People don't just stop caring about their daughters." Jillian frowned. "Unless it's because they were dating. I've heard of families disowning their kids when they come out."

"Still doesn't explain why they wouldn't come forward when the bodies were discovered. Death has a way of letting us know that life is too precious to waste."

"Sorry, but not always." Jillian pursed her lips, like she was about to impart something on Ellie that she'd been sheltered from. "I've seen some crazy things since I started working here. I'm just warning you that you might not get much out of the families."

"Well, I have to try. Wanna come with me?"

Jillian's face fell in disappointment. "I wish I could, but I have other things I need to be working on. I can't leave for that long anyway."

"Just thought I'd offer, I know you really care about this case."

"Only one of us is actually a detective," Jillian teased. "But you shouldn't go alone. Maybe you can tell Fortis, and he'll have one of the other detectives go with you."

"No way." Ellie shook her head. "I'm not going to let one of those other guys take credit for solving the case when we worked so hard. Besides, it's not like I'm interviewing a suspect. They're grieving families."

"You never know." Jillian gave her a warning look.

"You watch way too many crime shows. I'll be fine."

"Want me to cover for you?"

"You don't have to. Just tell Fortis you don't know where I went if he asks you."

Jillian shot her an *are you crazy* look. "Be careful, all right? You know what the statistics say about women who are murdered?"

"I know, I know. Most women are murdered by someone they trust. I'll keep my eyes and my ears open. If I have any issues, I'll call the department."

"If you haven't come back by five, I'm sending in the cavalry."

Ellie checked her watch. "It's not even noon."

"That's right. You should have plenty of time to interview them both and get home by then."

"I'll call you." Ellie grabbed the evidence collection kit from the large bottom drawer of her desk and sent everything to the printer—the missing person post and the addresses of both families. On the top of the printed out pile were the composite sketches and her notes from the scene.

"You'd better." She had her purse and was locking up by the time Ellie had everything she needed. "Please be careful," Jillian told her again when they parted ways out in the parking lot.

"I will," Ellie promised one last time. Then she got into her car and headed down the highway toward Lincolnville. "Promises, promises."

She'd be careful, but she wouldn't let anything stand in her way of finding justice for these women.

22

The little house on Calhoun Street was painted white with blue trim. Surrounded by manicured trees and a blanket of green grass without a weed in sight, it looked more like a picture out of a magazine than a place real people lived. But when Ellie knocked on the door, a tall blonde woman with striking blue eyes answered. "Can I help you?" she asked, her tone pleasant.

"I'm Ellie Kline with Charleston Homicide Division," she said, trying to keep her voice soft. "Is it all right if I come in?"

The woman's eyebrows knitted together, and her forehead furrowed. "Who are you looking for? This is the Baker residence." She laughed uncomfortably. "I'm pretty sure I don't know any murderers."

"I just have a few questions." Ellie glanced over her shoulder for a moment, scanning the neighboring houses, then turned back to Mrs. Baker. "It will only take a minute. I just don't want to feed the rumor mill. You know how some neighbors love to gossip."

Mrs. Baker looked past Ellie, then sighed and nodded. "Miss Harris is the worst, and she's already watching us through the curtain. I'd rather not deal with the fallout of that woman's wild imagination." She stepped out of the way, waving her inside. "Come on in."

Ellie followed her through the house to the living room and sank into a plush loveseat.

"Like I said, I'm not sure how I can help you. I don't really know anyone that would do that sort of thing. I mean, well, I —" she sputtered, waving her hands as she perched on the edge of the couch. "I'm sorry, I really don't know why you're here."

"Actually, Mrs. Baker, I was hoping you would look at a picture for me."

"A picture?" She tilted her head, and her forehead wrinkled again. "I'm not sure I understand."

"It's actually a police sketch." Ellie took a deep breath. "I'm working a cold case, and the woman hasn't been identified. I'm trying to find her killer, and I came across your missing person's ad online."

Mrs. Baker paled. "Where was this woman found?"

"In Charleston."

A relieved smile spread across Mrs. Baker's face. "Oh, I can save you the trouble right now. You see, my Tabitha went to Ghana, and that's where she disappeared. I'm traveling there again in a few weeks. I have some promising leads, and I think this time I'm going to find them."

Ellie's heart clenched in her chest. "How many trips to Ghana have you made?"

"At least one every year since she disappeared. This will be my sixth time, my first since my husband died."

"I'm sorry for your loss." Ellie's stomach was in knots, and the urge to get up and leave was strong. Mrs. Baker had already gone through so much, and Ellie was about to deliver another crushing blow. But she straightened her shoulders and took another deep breath, determined to see this through. "I do need you to look at the sketches, just so I can rule out Tabitha."

"Sure, of course." The woman gave a wide smile, but it slipped as a thought dawned on her. "These aren't crime scene photos?"

"No, ma'am," Ellie assured her. "Just a sketch like you would see on a poster. It says she had darker hair here, but we think that might be a mistake."

She took the picture of the second Jane Doe out of the stack and handed it to Mrs. Baker.

"Then, it can't be my Tabitha." Mrs. Baker took the paper with no more reverence than if Ellie was handing her a grocery list. "My Tabitha has blonde hair like me. I'm sorry you wasted a drive out here, I wish you would've called first, I could have saved you the..." She glanced down at the photo, and her face went slack.

Ellie held her breath, watching the woman.

She swayed where she sat, mouth agape, her fingers shaking as she ran a finger over the sketch. "No," she whispered, tears welling in her eyes. "Oh god, please, not my baby. Please, no." She stood, and her knees buckled.

Ellie jumped up and caught her before she hit the floor. Guiding her back onto the couch, Ellie moved to sit beside the trembling woman.

"It's not her," Mrs. Baker screamed at Ellie. "It's not her. This is *not* her. She's in Ghana. Why are you doing this? Tabitha went to Ghana with Mabel, and they got separated from the group. She's there, waiting for me. I have to go get my Tabitha. She's waiting for me." Mrs. Baker curled into a ball, clutching the sketch. The thick paper crumpled in her hand, shaking violently as Mrs. Baker fought to hold on to her last shred of hope. "This is a mistake. This can't be real."

"I'm sorry," Ellie said quietly, afraid to touch her for fear she would shatter even further.

"You're wrong. It's not her." Mrs. Baker's voice was angry now, her words clipped. "You need to look at the woman again and fix this."

"Is there someone I can call to come sit with you?" Ellie soothed. "You shouldn't be alone."

"It's not her," Mrs. Baker whispered in a wheedling tone, the police sketch clutched to her chest. "It's not my Tabitha."

But Ellie could see reality setting in, and she knew Mrs. Baker was beginning to grasp the truth. So Ellie sat there, quietly letting the woman work through her grief and give up the little glimmer of hope that had helped keep her sane through the years.

When her sobs quieted, Ellie placed a comforting hand on Mrs. Baker's arm. "Do you have something I can take for a DNA comparison, and maybe a photo?"

"DNA?" She blinked, then whispered the word again. "DNA?"

"I'll need definitive proof the victim is your daughter."

She shook her head, her face crumpling as she glanced down at the sketch again. "It's not Tabitha."

"All right," Ellie said patiently. "Something that might still have her DNA on it would help me rule her out."

"Okay, sure. Rule her out." Mrs. Baker stood unsteadily and walked to the doorway as if floating in a haze.

Ellie's heart was broken as she followed the woman through the house, her evidence collection kit held discreetly against her leg.

The door snapped and creaked when Mrs. Baker opened it, the stale air taking Ellie's breath when they walked into the large bedroom. When Ellie saw what was on the other side of the door, it knocked the rest of the wind out of her.

"Tabitha moved her stuff home before their trip." Mrs. Baker smiled tremulously. "It was supposed to be a six-month trip, and there was no reason for the girls to pay for a lease while they were gone, so they moved back into her room for a few weeks."

"They?"

Mrs. Baker took a deep breath. "Mabel's parents were a little hesitant to accept the girls weren't going through a phase, so Mabel decided to stay here."

"I understand," Ellie said quickly, poking her head into the adjoining bathroom. "Do you know which toothbrush and hairbrush are Tabitha's?"

"Of course. If it's lime green, it's Tabitha's. She adored the color, even though Mabel and I both found it ridiculous." Mrs. Baker's laugh started low then jumped a few octaves at the end. It was clear she was holding on to her sanity by a thin thread. "Nothing matches lime green, but Mabel was a good sport."

"I'll just be a minute." Ellie ducked into the bathroom and closed the door behind her.

Using a permanent marker, she cataloged the items she took: Two toothbrushes and hairbrushes stored in separate bags, a plastic tumbler for rinsing after brushing, and a pink razor that looked like it had seen better days. Then she picked up a small frame in between the double sinks and took it back into the bedroom. "Can I take this? You'll get it back, I just need to make a copy."

"I have a copy you can have." Mrs. Baker plucked the frame out of Ellie's hand. "I'll print it off for you." Mrs. Baker's gaze landed on the bags clutched in Ellie's hand, then she left the room without comment.

Ellie moved around the bedroom, looking, but careful not to touch anything. Until she had proof that the body found in West Ashley Park was Tabitha Baker, the room technically wasn't a crime scene. Still, she didn't want to contaminate any possible samples. The case had been botched enough already.

"It's ready!" Mrs. Baker called out.

Ellie followed the sound of the woman's voice, leaving the door open behind her. She found Mrs. Baker in the kitchen with a tall glass of amber liquid in her hand. The older woman pointed to the counter where the picture sat on the clean surface. "I thought a bigger one would help, so I grabbed you an eight-by-ten. We had those made right before they left on their trip. Mabel didn't know it, but Tabitha planned on popping the question once they landed in Ghana. We warned her against it. Foreign countries can be a dangerous place to be open with things like that, but Tabitha wanted to do something bold."

"She sounds like an amazing woman." Ellie studied the woman, finally seeing the real her, with gorgeous blonde hair and eyes that sparkled. Dark-haired Mabel sat next to Tabitha, all of her limbs intact.

"She was amazing." Mrs. Baker downed a swig of the alcohol and stared off into the distance.

Ellie noticed Mrs. Baker used the word "was" this time, and her heart broke a little more. Far from admitting it out loud, Mrs. Baker had clearly already started to accept Tabitha's death. In her eyes, there was a deep sadness that was more profound than anything Ellie had ever witnessed. And the quiet acceptance of a fate she'd fought against for so long left Mrs. Baker looking years older than she had when she'd first met Ellie at the door.

Desperate to tear her eyes away from the grieving mother, she looked down at the picture and did a double-take. "Mrs. Baker, did Tabitha and Mabel have matching watches?"

"They're not watches, they're bracelets." She opened a drawer filled with odds and ends, handing Ellie a magnifying glass. "Thank goodness for the junk drawer." She sighed. "Look closer and you'll see they have a wide silver plate with the words 'I love you for always' inscribed in the front. In the middle is a picture of the two of them."

Leaning close to the picture, the magnifying glass enlarged the details in startling detail. She could clearly see the words etched on the silver plate and felt her excitement growing. "Thank you for your time, Mrs. Baker. Are you sure I can't call someone for you?"

Mrs. Baker shook her head. "There's no one," she said quietly. "I'll be all right."

"I can stay with you for a little bit if you'd like."

Mrs. Baker stared at Ellie with eyes cold as steel. "Not to be rude, but I wish you'd leave."

Ellie recoiled inwardly, but she managed to stop herself from reacting in response to the woman's harsh words. She'd just found out her daughter was more than likely murdered; the least Ellie could do was not take her words personally. Ellie forced a gentle smile and gathered her things. "I'll leave my card on the table by the door."

Mrs. Baker nodded without looking at Ellie.

Hurrying through the house, Ellie tossed a business card on the small coffee table then let herself out. She caught the curtains fluttering in the window of the house across the street and made a split-second decision. Crossing the empty road, she knocked on the door and waited impatiently.

The door opened a crack, and an older lady peeked through the gap with the chain still attached.

"Miss Harris?"

"Can I help you?"

"Mrs. Baker is going to need a friend," she said without explanation. "Please keep an eye on her and don't leave her alone."

The door closed, and there was the sound of the chain sliding. The woman threw the door open wide and was out of the house and off the porch so fast she wasn't much more than a blur of gray and white house dress. When Miss Harris knocked on the front door across the street, Mrs. Baker answered, then wailed and collapsed into the neighbor's open arms.

Clearly in her element, Miss Harris ushered Mrs. Baker into the house and shut the world out. The sound of Mrs. Baker's sobs through the closed windows tore at Ellie's heart. Tears stung her eyes as she struggled to keep her emotions in check.

When Ellie drove past the house, she could see the outline of the two women through the whisper-thin white lace on the front window. They were sitting side by side with their arms around each other while Mrs. Baker leaned on the older woman. She couldn't bring Tabitha back, but Ellie felt better about leaving now that Mrs. Baker wasn't alone.

In the center console, her phone flashed an icon that told her she had six missed calls. It was no surprise they were all from Fortis. Groaning, she dialed Fortis's direct number, and guiding her car toward the highway, she held her breath while waiting for him to answer.

"Where are you?" he asked without preamble.

"Lincolnville."

"You need to let me know if you're following a lead outside the office like that." He paused, his breath shuddering as he inhaled. "Before you leave to question anyone outside the precinct. Is that clear?"

"Yes, sir."

"Good." He sounded surprised, like he'd expected her to argue. "Did you find anything?"

"I have a positive match on the names."

"Names?"

"There were two Jane Does found close to one another during the same timeframe." Her fingers tingled, itching to get the DNA to the crime lab.

"I didn't know there were any connected cases still in cold cases."

"These weren't previously connected."

He was silent for a moment. "What made you connect them?"

"A hunch and a bunch of little coincidences."

"Were you able to get a DNA sample?"

Ellie took a turn and merged onto the highway. "I have samples for both victims. I also was able to get a recent photograph, and I can tell you without a doubt that these victims are the same women. The mother of victim one confirmed the police sketch was her daughter."

"How was she when you left her?"

"Her neighbor is with her. She's distraught, of course, but I got the feeling she was expecting something like this." She blew out a loud breath. "I was less prepared than she was."

"Was that your first notification?" Fortis asked, his tone softening.

"No, but when I've notified before, the relatives were in shock." She cleared her throat and swiped at the tears that had spilled over her cheeks. "It's a surprise, and they're not prepared, so they just listen and nod. But Mrs. Baker just lost her husband, and she's been traveling overseas to look for her daughter for the past five years. She thought she was missing in a foreign country, and she still had hope she would find the woman and her girlfriend, so when she saw the sketch, she just lost it."

"You never know how people are going to react, which is why we always send two people to notify."

Ellie nodded in total agreement. "I'm sorry, sir."

"What's done is done. How long until you're back?"

She did a mental calculation, buying time to construct an argument for this case. "Twenty minutes. Sir?"

"Yes?"

"I'm sorry I didn't notify you before I chased this lead, but I need a couple more days on this. This was a big break, and it's only a matter of time before I solve it. I want to bring this monster to justice and get him off the streets."

"Remember what I told you, Kline? You can't make this personal." Fortis's volume grew louder as he continued. "Just because you have bodies and names doesn't mean you'll find out who did this. The case went cold because there was a lack of physical evidence, not because we didn't know who the victims were."

"But this is closer than we've been on this case." Ellie didn't bother mentioning Detective Jones. She was on thin ice with Fortis as it was, and putting another detective down was not the way to ingratiate herself with her new department.

"And the case could stay cold. I want to make sure you're prepared for that possibility. This is real life, and things aren't always wrapped up in nice, neat little bows at the end."

"I know that, and I am prepared." She gripped the steering wheel, not near ready to give up the fight for these women. "I just need a little more time to make sure I've done everything I can. Mrs. Baker deserves closure."

"Did you talk to the other family?"

"Not yet. Tabitha and Mabel were living in the Baker's house for a few weeks before they were supposed to travel abroad." She forged on, wondering if he would see through her but not really caring. "I got the distinct impression the Vicente household wouldn't be as welcoming, due to the nature of the women's relationship, so I decided I should talk to you before I go there and maybe take someone with me."

He chuckled. "I hope you don't think I buy that."

"I wouldn't dream of it." Ellie smiled at her own quip, but her muscles were tensed to the breaking point.

Fortis's full, rolling laugh came over the line. "You're

something else, Kline. But good call. If they weren't accepting of their daughter's relationship, there's no telling how they're going to react to the news."

She waited, her lips pursed together, steeling herself for his refusal.

"One more week," he finally said.

It took a minute for the words to sink in. She grinned. "Yes, sir. One more week."

"Then you're on my list, you got it? And you get a week per case unless you make some significant headway in that first week."

"Got it, sir."

"Good. And Kline?"

The way he said her name made her want to squirm in her seat. "Yes, sir?"

"Excellent work."

23

Ellie's bedroom was pitch-black when a loud knock at the front door had her on her feet before she was fully awake, reaching for her service revolver. She glanced at the clock, shocked it was only four in the morning. Heart racing, she crept through to the living room without turning any lights on, gun at her side. There was another knock, then the handle jiggled.

Time slowed to a crawl as the doorknob turned slowly one way, then the other as Ellie waited for the door to be kicked in. She knew would-be robbers often knocked first to make sure a dwelling was empty before they picked the lock or broke down the door and let themselves inside. She raised her gun, pointing the barrel center-right at the door. When they did, she'd have one hell of a surprise for them.

Frantic knocking jolted her pulse into overdrive. "Ellie!" a familiar voice called through the door.

The air whooshed out of her lungs, and her shoulders sagged with relief. It was Jacob. She lowered the gun. But as soon as the realization hit, the relief was replaced by dread.

Nothing good could come from Jacob pounding on her door before sunrise.

"Coming," she called out, slipping her revolver into the nearest drawer and running the last few feet across the apartment. She checked the peephole out of habit, then yanked the door open and came nose to nose with her former partner. "What's going on?" she demanded, already shaking from the adrenaline that had flooded her veins.

Jacob smiled, his eyes glassy. "They have a heart."

She stared at him for a beat, then her knees went weak. He pulled her against him and entered the apartment. It only took a few steps before she regained her footing. Stepping out of his arms, she grabbed her purse and fished in it for her keys.

"Nick sent me to pick you up. He's already on his way to the hospital with your mother."

"I thought she was at the hospital." Ellie shook her head. Nothing Jacob was saying was making sense. "Where was she?"

"Home. Nick stayed at the hospital so she could go home and shower, and she fell asleep." He was talking fast, almost sputtering and far from calm. "Luckily, he was there when the doctor came in, so he called me, then rushed to your parents' house to pick her up." She'd never seen Jacob like this. "Get dressed and pack a bag. I brought the cruiser, so we'll be there in no time at all, just hurry."

His urgency had her springing into action, the last bit of fog that had clung to her brain slipping away. "A heart!" she cried, a little too loudly for the middle of the night, but she didn't care. By some miracle, her father had finally been matched with a donor. That was something to shout about. Her neighbors would get over it.

She packed the necessities in record time and rushed out of the apartment so fast she almost forgot to lock the door.

Jacob caught her arm. "Slow down there. They're prepping the OR and the donor, so it's going to be a bit before they're ready for your father. We have time. Lock your door and watch where you're going. We don't need another family member in the hospital right now. I don't think Nick could handle it."

Ellie laughed, turning back to carefully lock the door. "I thought you were going to say my mother, but you're right. Poor Nick has got his hands full."

"Tell me about it. I'm glad *he* went to get your mom, and I got stuck with you. I don't think she likes me very much." At street level, he opened the side door for her and disarmed the cruiser, opening the front passenger door.

Duke was stretched out in the back, snoring softly. When his nose caught the scent of someone new, he lifted his head, gave a soft *woof*, and looked at Jacob. Though the dog was built like a German Shephard, his hair wasn't quite as thick. She could barely see his face, other than his teeth, in the back seat because his facial markings were so dark.

"She's all right," Jacob assured him.

His master's words were enough for Duke, who went right back to sleep.

"What kind of dog is that?" Ellie turned in the front seat, noticing how his back was a brindle color, glinting in the light of the street lamp.

"Dutch Shephard." Jacob flipped the lights on but left the siren off, so he didn't wake up the entire neighborhood. "Don't worry. He's trained not to kill, just subdue." He flashed her a grin.

She glanced back at the dog again. "That doesn't make me feel much better."

Jacob shot through the streets, eating up the distance to the hospital. "That was quick, right? Didn't they just put your dad on the list?"

She shook her head. "That's what I thought, but apparently, my parents kept this from us for over a month." She frowned, watching Charleston zip past, deserted at the early hour. "I don't know how the registry works, but on Wednesday, the doctor told us he got moved near the top because it was so urgent. After that, it's just a matter of waiting for a donor."

"Don't they have to match?" Jacob's voice was calm, despite taking the freeway on-ramp with squealing tires.

"Daddy's AB negative."

"So what are the odds of him matching someone?" Jacob gunned the engine on the empty highway.

"Pretty high. He's universal." Ellie held on to the door handle, a smile coming to her face. She had to admit she missed the highspeed chases with Jacob. But this was even better.

"I thought O was universal."

"O is a universal *donor*, but they can only receive organs from other type O donors. Daddy is a universal *recipient*. A, B, AB, and O are all options for him. Doesn't matter if they're positive or negative."

"I had no idea."

"I'm sure that's how he got matched so fast. There are a lot of factors, but if the donor is a type the other people on the waiting list can't match with, they move down the line. Daddy was already near the top." She sat up a little straighter when she spotted the lights of the hospital in the distance, and the reality of the situation hit her. "There it is."

"You sound sad." He reached across the console and squeezed her hand.

"It's not that I'm sad, it's just that someone suffered a huge loss tonight and they still cared enough to donate." She sniffled and wiped at her eyes with the back of her sleeve. "We'll probably never know who they are, but they're giving me my dad back. There's nothing we can do to repay them for their sacrifice."

Jacob pulled up to the front of the hospital and parked under a tree. Rolling the windows down a little, he looked in the back of the car and sighed. "I think I got a broken one."

Duke snorted in his sleep, and his paws jerked, but he didn't wake up.

"He's kind of cute when he's asleep."

Jacob shot her a dirty look and locked the doors as they got out, and they hurried through the lobby and onto the empty elevator.

"Is Duke going to be all right?"

"The windows have wire screens so he can't get out, and it's not going to get to seventy before midmorning. He'll be fine for a few hours, but I'll come check on him in a little bit." He checked his phone and held it up for her to see. "And I have a K-9 Cam installed."

"A K-9..." She snapped her lips shut and held in a snort of laughter. She knew Jacob had already received enough flack about his new partner, so she fought to summon a serious expression as she looked at the video feed. Sure enough, Duke was still passed out in the back, chasing rabbits in his sleep. "It even has a temperature reading on the screen."

"It's a new program they're rolling out soon. We get to test the prototype."

"Exciting," she teased.

"Not as exciting as being partnered with you. Even on his wildest day, Duke is no Ellie."

She pursed her lips, tilting her head to the side with a mock frown. "I'm not sure if I should be offended."

He laughed as the elevator let them out on their floor. "You shouldn't be. Don't tell Duke, but you'll always be my favorite partner."

She didn't have to point Jacob toward her father's room.

It was the only one with the door open and all the lights on so early in the morning. A team of a half dozen medical professionals stood outside the door, each with a different level of excitement on their faces.

"That's the transplant team," Nick said from behind them. Carrying a tray of paper coffee cups, he took one out and gave it to Ellie, then handed the whole tray to Jacob. "There's one there for you. Can you take the other two to Wesley and Helen? There's cream and sugar in the room."

"Sure," Jacob said before disappearing into her father's room.

Nick pulled her into his arms and inhaled deeply. "I missed you. How are you holding up?"

"I'm good. Did they take Daddy back yet?"

"Not yet. That's why the team is waiting in the hallway. They don't want to get him too riled up before they take him."

"I'm sure he's already stressed out."

Nick shook his head. "They gave him a little something to take the edge off. That's why I'm glad I caught you, cause he's a little loopy. Still your dad, but I wanted to make sure you were prepared."

"Thank you. And thank you for sending Jacob."

"I didn't want you driving yourself, and your mom didn't answer her phone. I found her passed out on the couch from exhaustion. She didn't even lock the door."

"I'm glad you went to get her." She kissed him on the cheek then nuzzled against him for a second. "I don't know what I would do without you."

"Come on, they're going to take him soon. Let's go see your dad."

When they walked in, the scene was eerily calm. All of her brothers stood to the side of the room, trying to stay out of the way. Helen's hair was a mess of flattened curls on one side, her makeup was smudged under her eyes. She hovered over her husband, who was so quiet, Ellie wondered if he was asleep.

Ellie untangled herself from Nick's arms and went to her mother. "Mom." It was one word, but it was all she had to say for her mom to turn and dissolve into her embrace. She held her mom close, silent tears flowing like rain from both of them.

Over her mother's shoulder, she could see her father. He was smiling, but his gaze was distant and a little hazy.

"They gave him the good stuff," Helen said, turning to smile at her husband. "It's happening soon now."

Ellie nodded and moved to the side of the bed.

Daniel took her hand and brought it to his lips. "My princess." A loopy smile told her he wasn't feeling a bit of anxiety. "You've never looked so strong."

"I love you." Her voice was raspy with the tears she was holding back for his sake.

"I love you more," he countered. "Don't let your mom get stressed out. She's always worrying about shit." Ellie stifled a laugh when the word slipped out of his mouth. Her father never swore. He caught her strangled expression and chuckled. "Life's too short to be uptight, Ellie. Chase your dreams, and don't worry about what society thinks you should do. You do what *you* want to do." He jabbed her chest with his finger to drive home the point.

Ellie chuckled, not even wanting to know what her mother thought of his epiphany. "You're going to be so embarrassed when you remember all this."

Daniel winked at her. "Not a chance in hell, cupcake."

There was a soft swish of fabric, and the blurry-eyed doctor who had seen them on Wednesday was at the bedside. "Hello, Ms. Kline," she said with a warm smile before she addressed Daniel. "Are you ready?"

"As ready as I'll ever be." He gave her a thumbs-up.

"Good, because it's time," she declared, stepping back so everyone could hug Daniel before he went to surgery.

Helen lingered for a moment, then moved back and let each of her children have a turn before she hugged him again. Jacob remained in the corner when Nick stepped forward to shake his hand.

"Get your ass over here," Daniel said to Jacob.

Jacob did as he was told, leaning over the bed and hugging Daniel carefully. Ellie wasn't standing close enough to make out what her father whispered in Jacob's ear, but Jacob listened intently, then nodded before the doctor moved to Daniel's bedside. The transplant team came in and whisked Daniel and his hospital bed toward surgery. They were gone in a matter of seconds, and the empty spot where her father had been filled Ellie's heart with dread.

She looked at her watch. It was four thirty-six in the morning. Only thirty-six minutes had passed since Jacob had woken her up. Her whole world had changed in the space of a half hour.

He's going to be fine, she told herself, looking to the doctor for reassurance.

"He won't be out of surgery for at least nine hours," the doctor said. "There's nothing you can do here for now. After surgery, he will be intubated for at least twenty-four hours and visitation is strictly limited to decrease risk of infection. Mrs. Kline will be notified as the surgery and recovery progresses, but there's no reason for you to wait here."

Danny rested a hand on their mother's shoulder. "We can stay in shifts if it will make you feel better."

Blake stepped forward. "I'll take the first shift."

Helen looked at her sons, her face pinched with worry. "I could use some rest," she said, looking down at herself. "Maybe a shower first."

Ellie hugged her brothers and her mother, then took Nick's hand as they all walked out together.

When they reached the parking lot, Danny took Helen to his car, Wesley and Blake following. Nick was still holding her hand when Blake walked back into the hospital, taking the first shift to wait for their father's surgery updates.

Nick pulled her close and kissed her for the first time since she'd arrived at the hospital, and she realized he looked exhausted.

"Are you going to be all right?" she asked him.

"I'm fine. I just need some rest. Is it all right if Jacob takes you home? I don't know if I can drive to your house."

"Of course. Do you want us to drop you off at your house?"

"Not unless you're staying," he teased. "I'm right around the corner. I'll be fine. I just need to know that *you're* taken care of."

"I've got her," Jacob said. "You get some rest and let me know if you need me to bring a pizza by later."

Nick shook Jacob's hand, grinning. "They have this new fangled thing called delivery now. I dial a number and pizza appears like magic."

"Funny." Jacob laughed. "I'll make sure she gets home safe."

Nick hugged her one last time, then he jogged over to his car and sped away.

Jacob raised one eyebrow then shrugged. "I'm sure he can afford a ticket for speeding."

"Let it go, Garcia." Ellie gave him a teasing push.

When they got into the car, Duke was sitting up and looking around.

"Am I allowed to pet him?"

"Technically, when he's at work, he's not allowed human

contact, and we are in his vehicle. But since it's not work hours quite yet, I'll cut him some slack."

"And he won't take my arm off?" She peered at Duke warily.

Jacob shrugged. "Take your chances." He gave the command to relax, and Duke turned into a different dog. When Ellie reached her hand out for him to sniff, he immediately licked her clear to her elbow, panting in the way a dog did when he wanted attention and couldn't wait. Jacob shook his head. "You're going to ruin my partner."

"It's the least I can do."

Behind the wheel, Jacob gave her a knowing look. "I don't suppose you're *actually* going home?"

She scratched the dog behind his ears, making his eyes roll back in his head. "Sitting at home would be just as bad as sitting at the hospital."

"Where to?"

"Work sounds good." She looked down at the sweats she'd pulled on in a hurry. "After I go home to change first."

He snorted. "Work sounds good? Only to you."

❄

By the time early afternoon rolled around, Ellie was starting to regret her decision to work on so little sleep. Jillian had ordered pizza for a late lunch, and Ellie was sitting at her desk eating, hoping it would revive her when Fortis walked in.

"Are you serious?" he boomed, hands on his hips. "I didn't believe it when they told me, but here you are, plain as day."

"I can't sit at home and wait for the call." She dropped her half eaten slice onto the paper plate. She looked at the clock. It was now officially nine hours and fifty-eight minutes since she'd left the hospital. Not that she was counting.

"Well, you can't sit here and wait for it, either. Especially since you aren't answering your cell."

Her hand went to her pocket, and she patted around, then dug through her purse. She pulled her phone out, and sure enough, the battery was dead. She was even more tired than she thought. "Crap."

"Don't worry. Nick had enough sense to call the office. Your dad's out of surgery. Everything went well."

Ellie clapped her hand over her mouth and sagged in the chair, relief flooding through her. She couldn't stop the tears that welled into her eyes.

"I'm not trying to tell you how to live your life, but you shouldn't be here," Fortis continued. "If you can't stand to be home and you need to talk to someone, Dr. Powell is in today."

"The department shrink?" She cringed, sitting back in the chair. "I'll pass."

"I'm not ordering you to talk to him, but it would probably help. Regardless, I can't have you here. You should really take a few days off, but I know you better than that already. I'll settle for you going home now and getting a jump on the weekend."

"But—"

"I'm not taking no for an answer." Fortis's light-colored eyes pinned her to the desk chair. "Take the rest of the day off and come back on Monday, or I'll give you a mandatory two weeks. Your choice."

"All right, I'll go home."

"Let's go." Fortis jingled his keys in his pants pocket.

Ellie's mouth dropped open. "I can catch a ride."

"You don't think I'm that stupid, do you?" he quipped. "It's either me or Danver. Your choice."

She shook her head and grabbed her things.

Jillian handed her the box of pizza and hugged her. "Call me if you need me."

"Thanks," Ellie murmured, suddenly exhausted.

Fortis drove her to her apartment, then parked the car and turned in his seat so he could look at her straight on. "Do you need me to help you carry your things up?"

"I've got it."

He nodded. "I'm glad your father's okay."

"Me too."

"If you don't feel like coming in Monday, I'll mark you down for vacation time."

She raised her chin. "I'm coming to work."

"I knew you'd say that." He smiled, a hint of pride on his face. "I don't have to follow you to your door to make sure you actually go in, do I?"

"No, sir."

"Good. You get some rest, Kline. People need you, but you need to take care of yourself first."

She nodded, quickly exiting the car and dragging herself through the door and into the elevator. Dropping her things on the kitchen table, she shoved the pizza box into the fridge. By the time she got to the bed, she was too tired to take off her shoes. She let out a long sigh as she collapsed onto the mattress. Whether she needed a vacation or not, she couldn't take it. The spirits of the murdered women demanded justice, and Ellie was the only one listening.

She was asleep the second her head hit the pillow, but her dreams were plagued with images of the two dead women.

Tabitha and Mabel stood together in the dark, calling Ellie's name.

24

Ellie's hand was on the evidence room door when Jillian yanked it open, grabbed her elbow, and ushered her over to the desk.

"You're never going to believe what I found." Jillian typed quickly on her keyboard, then gestured at the screen with a triumphant grin on her face. "Steve Garret."

"I'm not sure who that is," Ellie said slowly as she took in the empty cups and plates scattered about the office. "Jillian, did you even go home this weekend?"

Jillian glanced at the papers in piles on her desk and shrugged. "There's a chance I clocked in at like four this morning, but I couldn't sleep." She rolled her chair back and forth on the balls of her feet, grinning. On the corner of her desk, three to-go coffee cups rattled softly when the ventilation system kicked on.

"Jillian, how much coffee have you had?" Ellie asked, still holding a cup in each hand as she did every morning. "You're positively buzzing."

"Those three, plus my first trip to the breakroom. I'm not sure how many I drank before I dragged myself downstairs."

"I can see that. I don't think I've ever seen you so..." She searched for the right word. *Hyper, bouncy, scattered.* "On fire."

"I've been thinking about this all weekend. I mean, the going to Ghana thing. How none of the other people in the group noticed the women were missing. That sort of thing."

"It was a large group."

"And they were all strangers."

Ellie's eyes widened, and she stepped closer to the computer screen. "All of them?"

Jillian used the mouse to open several tabs, lining them up until they fit side by side, filling the screen. "There were fifteen people on the trip, all around the same age, but from all over the East Coast. Except for Mabel and Tabitha, *none* of them knew each other before the trip."

"That's weird." Ellie grabbed her notebook and wrote down the names and ages of everyone on the screen. "Usually, these groups work together and travel together." She leaned forward and read the notes Jillian had taken. "None of them had any overlap?"

"None that I could find."

She squinted at the only male in the photos. "And there's only one man on the trip? That's odd too."

"That's Steve Garret. Lives in Charleston. He's the key to all this."

She turned to Jillian, hoping in her caffeine buzz, she'd turned into a genius. "Why do you say that?"

"Look at his social media page during that time." Jillian scrolled through Steve's page. "See?"

"His pictures are all selfies, and the rest are candids of the women. They're all working, but he seems to be documenting the entire thing and nothing else." Ellie tapped her fingernail on the desk. "Notice anything?"

"I did. I haven't seen Mabel or Tabitha in any of these pictures."

"Not even in the group picture." Ellie pointed at a name on the screen. "He's tagged everyone on the trip, but what about this account? It's not any of the women. Can we find out who this account is and why he would tag them?"

"A deleted account. I checked."

"Of course," Ellie scoffed. "Is this the only trip he's done like this?"

"I wondered the same thing, so I looked it up. He did a few, but this was the last one."

"Weird. Sounds like we should pay Mr. Garret a visit."

"We?"

Ellie shrugged. "Fortis did say not to interview anyone alone again. He didn't say I couldn't take you."

Jillian laughed, grabbing her purse. "Are you sure he didn't?"

"My desk is here, and every detective needs a partner. It seems like it's obvious that you're it. If I'm wrong, I guess I'll have to apologize for the misunderstanding."

"I feel like you do that a lot."

They stepped onto the elevator, and Ellie shot her a wry grin. "It's easier to get forgiveness than permission."

Jillian jabbed at the button. "I'll have to remember that one." The door opened, revealing an empty hall with a straight shot to the side door that led to the parking lot. "Come on," Jillian said. "Let's go catch a bad guy."

The single-story house had little more than a two-foot-wide strip of yard going around the entire thing. Bent and rusted, the chain-link fence had seen better days, as had the rest of the neighborhood.

Ellie picked her way up the stairs and pushed the doorbell. When nothing happened, she knocked and stepped back, one hand resting lightly on her holster.

"Are you sure anyone lives here?" Jillian whispered. "It doesn't look like it."

"I hear someone moving around." Ellie wrapped her knuckles on the rough wooden door. Several paint chips shook loose and fluttered to the porch. Ellie watched them land on a wide gap between the floorboards before they slipped in between and disappeared into the darkness.

"That's not creepy *at all,*" Jillian muttered.

It took Steve Garret a full minute to answer the door. He looked disheveled, his short brown hair sticking out every which way, his eyes hazy. He smacked his lips and swallowed, and when he finally spoke, his voice was gritty with sleep. "Can I help you ladies?"

Ellie flashed her badge. "I'm Detective Kline, and this is Reed. We need to talk to you if you have a minute."

He blinked, looking over Ellie's shoulder then back at her with his eyebrows furrowed. "They pay that well at Charleston PD? I've never seen a cop who drove an Audi before."

"Look, we can do this here on the front steps, but I'm sure you don't want your neighbors thinking you're a snitch or something." Ellie gestured with her head at the nearest house. "This doesn't look like the kind of place where snitches last long, and they'll have us made for cops in a hot minute."

"Comin' inside won't change that." He scratched his arms, then sniffed, still peering through the partially open door.

"Your neighbors know you sell?" Ellie asked.

Steve looked like a deer caught in headlights.

"I'll take that as a yes." She pulled a crisp hundred-dollar bill out of her wallet. "Then we're just two gals looking for a party."

He eyed the money for a second, and his hand snaked out and grabbed it before he stepped back to let them in. "Most customers are in and out pretty quick."

"Five minutes."

"Fine." He closed the door and locked it behind them, gesturing at a couple of large beanbag chairs stitched to resemble legless chairs. "Have a seat if you want."

"I'll stand," they replied in unison.

"What do you want?"

"We're here about a trip you took a little over five years ago."

Steve nodded, sniffed, and rubbed the back of his hand across his nostrils. "Ghana? Man, that was something. We had the best time." He paused, the whites of his eyes flashing. "I didn't do nothin' illegal there, I swear. I was a different person back then."

"Cocaine?" Ellie asked.

"It's a helluva drug." Steve chuckled, scratching his arm again. "But I guess that's not why you're here."

"We're wondering about these women." Ellie handed him a copy of the picture of the two together. "Do you remember them?"

He squinted hard before shaking his head. "I don't, but there are a lot of things that are sort of fuzzy these days."

Ellie forced a smile, her shoulders tensing. She shot Jillian a look and knew the other woman was thinking the same thing. It was going to be next to impossible to get anything useful out of this junkie, especially when he was in desperate need of a fix. "Mabel and Tabitha. They were a couple. They were the only ones who signed up together."

He started to shake his head and stopped, his face a mask of concentration. "Wait. The names ring a bell. I think they were on the register and were the ones who didn't show. That happens a lot. People get all stoked about helping others, then as the trip gets close, it starts to sound like work."

"So, they were signed up to go but didn't show up?"

He scratched at his neck before moving to claw at his

cheek. "I think so. I think they were at the first meeting. There were a lot of people on that trip."

"Just fifteen."

"No. There were like, twenty, I think. Me, Katarina, and the three guys from the volunteer tourism group, and the guide and stuff."

"Katarina?" Ellie pressed at the new name.

To her surprise, Steve blushed, scratching himself even harder. He inhaled deeply and let out the long sigh of a man dissed by a woman. "Man, that woman was something else. Flirted with me hardcore. Then we got back, and she didn't return my texts." His eyes were glossy with unshed tears when he looked back at Ellie. "Straight up ghosted me. It's like we didn't share a love so deep that it crushed my soul when I called and her phone was disconnected."

"I didn't see anyone named Katarina in the pictures."

"That's because she had a contract." When Ellie arched an eyebrow, he explained. "Modeling. She signed with a big agency, and part of her contract was that she couldn't be photographed by anyone until her campaign debuted. Every time a camera came out, she found a way out of getting her picture taken."

Ellie glanced at Jillian, who was writing so fast the tip of her pen on the paper was a blur. "Go on," Ellie said to Steve. "Where did you recruit Katarina from? For the trip, I mean."

"I didn't recruit *her*. She's the one who approached me and offered me a job organizing the volunteers for the trip. It was a sweet gig, and it paid bank." He pursed his lips together. "She brought me cash. You know, so I didn't have to claim it on my taxes." Steve's lips parted, and he let out a little breath. "You're not with the IRS, are you?"

"We have no interest in your financials," Ellie assured him. "But why isn't Katarina on the roster anywhere? And did Katarina bring the tourists to you, or did you find them?"

"Katarina wasn't a guest. There was no reason to write her name down. But she gave me all the names and told me how to word the email so people would be interested."

"Do you still have the email from her?" Ellie glanced around for a laptop, not having any luck.

"From her? No. She didn't *email* me. She stood over my shoulder, telling me exactly what to write. It was hard for her to communicate in writing, and I wanted her to be happy. English wasn't her first language, and she didn't want her email to sound stupid."

"So, she came here?"

"No. I went to her apartment." He looked down at his hands, closing his eyes for a long moment before he opened them and continued. "We made love, and she told me about the trip she was organizing, but she needed help. I told her she didn't have to pay me, but she insisted that her bosses had deep pockets."

Excitement caught in Ellie's chest. "Do you remember where her apartment was?"

"Yes, but it doesn't matter. Everything was gone when I went over there. I asked a couple people if they knew where she'd gone, and no one had any idea who I was talking about."

"I hate to sound rude, but are you sure you went to the right place?" Jillian asked, pausing in her notetaking.

Steve laughed, snorted, then coughed and scratched the back of his head. "I get it. You don't believe the junky, right? But I was clean then. Katarina *made* me this way. She came out of nowhere, and suddenly my life was complete. She even promised I would have a job when we got back." He scoffed and looked close to tears.

"But you didn't?" Ellie didn't like the sound of this Katarina.

"We were going to host people in locations all over the

world. Doing good and making a difference. Together." Steve let out a shuddering breath. "I was going to marry her. When she disappeared, I spiraled bad. I lost my house and my car, and I ended up here." He gestured around the room. "Started selling when shit got real bad, and I couldn't get my job back."

"Where did you work before?" Jillian held the pen poised, having forgotten she was technically the secretary on this run.

"In a great job in tech. Everything I dreamed of my entire life, and I worked really hard to get where I was. But man, when she offered me all that dough…" His grin was lopsided, a touch of sadness in his eyes. "I flipped my boss off on the way out the door. Seven grand a month *and* an all-expense-paid vacation every six weeks? I was ready for it."

Ellie fought to not roll her eyes. "What about the other excursions you hosted?"

He shrugged. "I guess that's how they found me, but those weren't for Katarina. That was just volunteerism, man." He pounded his chest once with a closed fist. "You know, from the heart. I did it because I wanted to do some good in this world. But shit went downhill when greed got in the way." The fingers of his left hand were trembling, and a nervous twitch had started at the corner of his eye.

"And you didn't get any pictures of her? Or maybe the modeling campaign he told you about?"

He shook his head, sadness welling into his eyes.

"Could you describe her if I sent over a sketch artist?"

He lifted a shoulder. "Yeah."

Ellie nodded at Jillian and took a step toward the exit. "You've been a great help." She handed her card to him. "If you think of anything else, give me a call, okay?"

"How will you pay?" Steve said as Ellie reached the door.

Ellie turned and frowned. "Pardon?"

"If I give you info over the phone, how are you going to pay me?"

"We'll figure something out."

He nodded, and Ellie hurried Jillian out of the dilapidated house and down the uneven walkway. They were on the highway before either of them spoke.

"He wasn't serious, was he?" Jillian's face was aghast. "What a creep. And did you hear the way he talked about that Katarina girl?"

Ellie narrowed her eyes as she drove. "Do you think she was real?"

"I don't know, but I know he was hurting really bad. You think he does more than just cocaine?"

The last time Ellie checked, cocaine didn't make a person itch like a dog with fleas. "Maybe meth, but I didn't see any marks on him to suggest he shoots up."

"Do you think he's telling the truth?"

Ellie shrugged, taking the Lockwood Drive exit and letting out a long sigh. "I don't know. His story is wild, and he's all over the place. At one point, he was probably a fine, upstanding citizen."

"Do you think he killed them?"

"I don't know that either. But I think there's more he's not telling us, and he was involved somehow."

"Agreed," Jillian said.

When they went through the front door, Fortis was walking down the main hall toward the entrance. He stopped, eyes narrowed. "You're something else, Ellie. I hope this little trip was worth the trouble?"

Ellie gave him an innocent look. "You said to never go alone again."

"I'll have to be more specific next time. Find anything?"

"Yes, sir. Our victims didn't make it out of the country. They were killed before the group left."

"Who'd you talk to?"

"The group leader." Ellie breathed in through her nose, pressing her lips tight. "He's a junky with a wild story about how he ended up on the trip in the first place. I'm not sure how much we can believe, but I'm certain Mabel and Tabitha never made it on board the plane. Not that Steve Garret was paying enough attention to notice. They were on the register, but he can't remember seeing them at all aside from the first meeting."

"You think he did it?"

Her instincts were telling her there was more there, but that Steve wasn't a murderer. "Hard to say. I think he knows more than he's letting on."

"Well, keep on him, maybe he'll crack." Fortis headed toward the door again. "And Kline?"

"Yes, sir?"

"Excellent work." His gaze caught on Jillian, and he smiled. "You too, Reed. Thanks for keeping her out of trouble." His laughter echoed through the hallway as the front door closed behind him.

"That went better than I expected," Ellie said.

Jillian smiled, blowing out a breath. "What's next?"

"Well." Ellie led the way onto the elevator. "First, we're going to verify everything Steve Garret told us. Then, we're going to find this mystery woman."

"Do you think she really exists?"

"I don't know, but if she does, I'd bet she can tell us the cold truth."

"And if she doesn't?" Jillian pressed the button to the basement multiple times, as if that would get them moving faster.

"Then Steve Garret will have to answer for that. And if so, we'll bring him in."

25

"Thank you so much for your time," the man said, lingering in the doorway with a wide grin on his face.

"That's what I'm here for," I responded. "I'll see you in two weeks."

My patient paused. "Is it possible to move to weekly appointments?"

"You don't need them," I assured him. "In fact, I think once a month would be better."

"I'd really rather come once a week."

I felt the familiar tingle of anger running up the back of my skull, but I made sure my smile remained firmly in place. "You've made some impressive headway. Let's not ruin it."

Sadness swept across his face, then barely contained rage. "Did I do something wrong?" he demanded.

"Not at all." I remained calm, cool, completely in control.

"I'm the client, aren't I?"

"Of course," I assured him.

"I would like to see you once a week. That's how this works."

I sucked in a deep breath just as my assistant appeared,

his soft brown eyes wide, mouth tight. "Gabe. Please make sure to update Mr. Pritchard's address. I'm not sure it's correct as we're having some billing issues. He's only approved for twice a month. Let's see if we can get him a more regular schedule."

I longed to slap the satisfied look right off Pritchard's face, but Gabe didn't miss a beat. He swooped in with his perfect smile and gently took Mr. Pritchard's arm, leading him away from my office. "Let's get all your information squared away and make sure things are in there correctly, shall we?"

"Yes, thank you." My client allowed Gabe to lead him out in the hall, nodding in my direction.

As Gabe walked away, I marveled at how he'd learned to anticipate my every need. It was the only reason he'd lasted as long as he had.

Shaking with rage, I poured myself a shot of dark bourbon and downed it. I closed my eyes as the heat spread down my throat, and let out a sigh. Pritchard wasn't the first to sink in adoration at my feet, but his obsession was unwelcomed. I chose my consorts carefully, and the oily, peevish man was useless to me.

The phone rang and an all too familiar number flashed on the screen. "Speaking of useless," I muttered. "What?" I demanded when I snatched the phone out of the cradle.

"She went to talk to Garret today."

I sat up straight, my heart quickening, as close as I came to feeling unsettled. "Why would she do that?"

Ernest scoffed through the phone. "Why else would she? She must know something."

"Did you listen in on their conversation?"

There was silence, then his voice was hesitant. "The little weasel is paranoid or something. None of the bugs we planted work."

"Why wouldn't you bring this to my attention before now?"

"W-when we tested them, they worked fine. I'm not sure when things changed, but the bugs could just be malfunctioning."

"All of them?" I was barely able to get the words out from between my clenched teeth.

"Yes, sir."

"He's likely using a signal interrupter. That works on a variety of devices. It's doubtful he even knows about the planted bugs."

"Sir?"

I began to pace, pissed that I was forced to explain. "A signal interrupter will prevent things like baby monitors and short wave satellites from picking up his conversations. It's preventative only and is a broad spectrum tool. If he knew about the actual bugs in his house, he would've removed them or worse. Don't worry about it. He doesn't know."

"All right, but Ellie still went there today and spent quite a bit of time inside. That can't be good."

I poured another shot of bourbon, refusing to be bothered by this news. "His name was bound to come up in an investigation."

"I'm not worried about *him,* so much as what he might say."

"Such as?" I asked.

"About Katarina?"

I closed my eyes as the name rang through my brain. "What would he tell Ellie about her that would yield any information?"

"I don't know. But they were in there a long time and if he didn't tell them about Katarina, then why were they in there for so long? What else could he have been telling them?"

"They?" I paused with the shot glass nearly to my lips,

wondering if I should risk making myself fuzzy around the edges.

"Jillian Reed was with her again."

"Reed is a desk clerk, not an officer, much less detective." The mousy little librarian turned desk jockey didn't seem like the type to risk her neck. But then, I hadn't thought the rebellious redhead with the bouncing curls would make detective.

I licked my lips, envisioning the way her hair had stretched and coiled like perfect, fiery springs with every movement of her head. She was luscious, bold, and I longed to share the same air with her again.

"Did you hear me?"

I blinked, scowling. "If you wouldn't mutter, there would be no issue." I injected my voice with disdain to cover up the fact that my mind had wandered. "Say it again. This time without sounding like you've a mouth full of marbles."

"As far as I know Reed hasn't made officer, but she's still helping Ellie. If you don't want to deal with Ellie, perhaps Jillian could stand to—"

"Don't!" I snapped, then I lowered my voice, checking the doorway. "I will tell you when and if I want you to do anything." I gave a snort of disbelief. "If you haven't noticed, everything you touch turns vile. Don't make a move on either woman. I'll take care of this."

"Sir, I-I'm..." He tripped over his own tongue like a bumbling buffoon. "I'm sorry."

"Altered behavior is the only apology I'll accept. I've more important things to consider than your constant attacks of conscience." I paused and sighed dramatically. "Perhaps you're not the man I thought you were."

"That's not true," he hurried to say. Backed into a corner, he could agree with me and prove he was incompetent, or he could argue with me and prove the same. There was no right answer.

Glee rushed through me, and for the first time since I'd woken that morning, I felt pure joy. He remained silent and I remained superior. It was the one thing that I loved about him. "You'll await my instructions. Until then, try not to trounce around Charleston in a panic. It's unbecoming."

I hung up before the boot licking could commence. If I wanted my ego stroked, Gabe was far better at it than any other.

I sat in the chair for some time going over my options. For once, the sniveling loon was right about Ellie. She was getting far too close and something needed to be done. The fact that she went to Garret meant that she was on the right track. As much as I enjoyed observing her without getting my hands dirty, action was needed.

The man I dialed answered on the first ring. "Sir," he said, his voice brisk. I imagined him snapping to attention.

"The time has come to make good on our debt."

"Understood."

I relished the feeling of being in command, and paused for a moment to let the tension build. "I need you to take care of a little problem for me."

"I'm listening."

"There's a mess that needs cleaning. A man by the name of Steve Garret." I rattled off Garret's address. "It needs to look like an accident."

"I can do that, sir."

"But before you kill him, give him a message for me. Tell him 'Dr. X sends his regards.' Nothing more. Just that."

"As you wish." The clipped words were music to my ears.

"It should be done quickly before he spooks and takes off."

"I understand."

"I knew you would." I allowed myself a smile, thankful now I hadn't taken that second shot so I could feel the anticipation of my plan being carried out.

Gabe poked his head in just as I hung up. He didn't say a word, but simply waited to be invited in.

I let Gabe think the smile was for him. "Did you get the information from my client that I asked for?"

He nodded. "Updated in the system."

"Are you through for the day?"

He took a step forward. "I can stay if you need me."

"Whatever would I need you for?" I retorted with absolutely no inflection in my voice.

Pain flitted across his sweet face, but he didn't sulk or fire back at me. A simple nod and he was gone.

He really was the very best.

I waited until I heard the turbo engine of his little sports car fire up outside the window. His world was so different now than it had been when I found him begging on the street corner. The cardboard sign in his hand had flopped in the wind, black marker dripping in the constant drizzle of the dreary fall day. Not a second of hesitation had shown on his face when I rolled down the window and told him to get in.

That day had changed his life. Mine too.

The fact that I delighted in hurting him should be obvious to him, but there were things Gabe craved more than my approval. A warm place to sleep and an endless supply of food was at the top of the list, surely. He'd never asked whose name his apartment was under, or who had the groceries delivered to his door. Being a kept man obviously agreed with Gabe. He never questioned me, and he never asked for anything more.

Another bit of perfection crossed my mind, so I dialed her number. Her voice was sweet, and despite her age, she sounded no older than a college freshman.

"I need your assistance," I said when she answered.

"Anything." She was breathless to do whatever I bid.

I explained briefly, and with every breath, I could hear her excitement growing.

"Shall I deal with Steve?"

I chuckled. "Not to bother. I have a consort dealing with that."

She made a sound of disappointment. "Oh poo."

"Patience, my sweet. You'll have a prize of your own soon."

Her giggle was soft, like gossamer wings. "I cannot wait."

"What I need you for is far more important."

"Yes?" I imagined her chest heaving, nostrils flared and eyes wide like an animated doll.

"You are such a delight. I need you to call this number and leave an anonymous tip."

"That's all?" She giggled again. From anyone else, the habit would've annoyed me like nails on the proverbial chalkboard.

"Our friend Steve has let the cat out of the bag, so to speak. I need you to throw Detective Kline off the case. Here's what you need to do."

She listened intently as I explained exactly what I needed her to say.

When I was done, she let out a quivering breath. "That sounds fun."

"Good. No need to call back. I trust you'll do what I need done in a timely manner."

"Gladly," she chirped, like a bird on a string.

"I look forward to our next endeavor together." The little titter of joy that bubbled up from her delicate throat brought a smile to my lips. "And puppet?"

"Yes."

"Do choose another name. Katarina has run its course."

I didn't need to wait for her answer to know she would do that exactly.

The building was quiet when I disconnected the call. I walked to the window and peeked through the blinds. The only car that remained in the lot was mine. Sleek and stylish, it was a sophisticated tan that whispered money rather than shouted it. Success without the fanfare. It was imperative that my clients see me as worthy of their trust without jealousy raising its ugly head. To achieve this was a delicate balance, but it was only one of the many careful ways I'd curated my image through the years. The quiet doctor with a warm smile and a kind heart who never earned a second glance when things went askew. The image was what made me so good at my job.

But I'd taken a chance I shouldn't have, and the books in the locked drawer filled the room with the voices of the lost.

Taunting me.

Begging for my demise.

As if Ellie Kline had the slightest chance of finding me.

I knew I couldn't keep the books in my office any longer. Sighing, I retrieved two collapsible storage boxes and sneezed when the cardboard dust made by the lasered cuts reached my nose. One by one, I loaded the books into the boxes until the drawer was empty.

Staring into the abyss that was now my drawer, rage filled me as quickly as a strike of lightning. I kicked the drawer front and it bounced on the hinges then slid to a close and locked on its own. Pain shot through my foot, but I ignored it. It wasn't fair. First my trinkets, and now my scrapbooks. These would go in a safe at my home inside a hidden room. Even if they turned up in an investigation, having scrapbooks of murder victims didn't link me to any crime.

Eventually you'll have to destroy them, a voice nagged in the back of my head.

I grimaced, stacking the boxes on top of one another and taking the handles of the lowest box. By some miracle, all the books had fit perfectly, with room for another if Ellie proved to be more than two books could contain. Different colors, they were a rainbow of beauty and pain.

My muscles flexed beneath the fabric of my shirt as I carried the boxes out the door. Balancing them between my thigh and the wall, I fished in my pocket for my keys. When they fell to the floor, I cursed under my breath.

"I got it." I nearly jumped out of my skin when the woman appeared from around the corner.

"Janice, hi," I said, forcing the surprise and concern from my expression. "Don't worry about it. I'll manage."

"Nonsense, let me help you." She scooped up the keys and locked the door then shoved them into my pocket. "I'll call the elevator for you."

I held back a sigh, forcing a smile. "If only my real neighbors were as courteous as my office neighbors. What are you doing here so late? I didn't see your car."

"My husband dropped me off this morning and took it to get serviced." Her grin was wide, eyes twinkling with sheer delight and endless optimism. I loathed her. "It's one of the many perks of having a mechanic in the family."

"I'll bet."

The elevator bell dinged, and she stuck her arm in front of the door to hold it. "I'm assuming you're going down."

"Of course."

She stood between me and the door, looking over her shoulder to smile at me for no reason at all. I squeezed past her, and on the way down, every time the back of her head faced my way I imagined bludgeoning her right there and leaving her carcass on the floor. A chuckle escaped from me, breaking the silence and giving me a startle. I coughed to cover the noise but the dimwit didn't seem to notice.

"Don't you just love Mondays?" she gushed. "There's something about a new week crammed with exciting possibilities that just makes me want to sing."

"You're a peach," I lied.

The doors finally opened, and once again, Janice blocked the sensor, ensuring my safety. Just when I thought I was rid of her, her heels clicked behind me on the tile floors covered with far too many coats of wax. "There you go," she announced as she squeezed by me to open the outer doors.

"Thank you, Janice."

"I can get the trunk if you'd like."

"No need. It's operated by my foot."

"That's amazing. I wonder if my husband can have that installed in my car. Oh, that would sure help when I have too many things in my hands. There's something about putting them down and picking them up again that makes them feel so much heavier, wouldn't you say, and—"

"There he is right now." It was a blissful moment as her car turned into the parking lot and there was silence for a moment.

"Right on time! I sure am the luckiest woman alive, but you know, he says he's the lucky one." Her dreamy smile made me want to vomit.

"I bet he is." I wondered if her husband ever thought about having the mechanic "tweak" her brakes. "Well, thank you for the help."

"No problem."

I walked over to my car and swung my foot under the rear bumper. The trunk popped open, and I lowered the boxes inside carefully before snapping it closed. When I turned, Janice was only a few feet from me. I jumped and instantly hated her for it. "Can I help you?"

"I just wondered what you were taking home. I mean, are you supposed to take patient files home with you?"

"They're not files. It's research."

"Oh." She furrowed her brow, and her husband lightly tapped the horn to get her attention. "What kind of research?"

I forced my hands not to reach out and grab her around the throat. Giving a cheerful laugh, I said, "If I told you, I'd have to kill you. Isn't that what they say in spy movies?"

Her mouth snapped shut, and for a moment I thought she was going to run to her husband in a panic. But then she threw her head back and emitted a sound that was somewhere between a braying donkey and a dying cat. Saliva clung to her buck teeth, and I imagined a million vile ways for her to die before she closed her gaping mouth and wiped the tears from her eyes.

"You're so funny. I'll have to remember that one." She put her hands on her hips and wagged her head in a mocking fashion. "'If I told you, I'd have to kill you.'"

Anger filled me, exploding out the top of my head, and blackness crawled around the edges of my vision.

Another tap of the car horn brought me back to reality.

But nothing surprised me as much as the quick hug around my neck she gave me before she bounded off like a wounded gazelle in her clumpy heels. Ungainly, tragic, and far too ugly to kill.

I raised a hand and waved to her husband. As he kissed her on the lips, I nearly gagged at the thought of her skin touching mine. The ride home would take far too long and the water would never be hot enough to rid me of the feel of her. I would have to try anyway. I needed her scent off me, even if I had to burn my clothes and scrub a layer of skin off to do it.

I wondered if she knew just how repulsive she was.

26

After Monday's excitement, Tuesday was almost mundane. After visiting with her dad, and liking the new color in his cheeks, Ellie dragged herself into work on a dreary Wednesday morning that insisted upon spitting rain and turning cooler. The look on Jillian's face said they were both feeling that midweek, no-new-lead slump.

"Should I pretend to be surprised that new information in this case led to another dead end?" Ellie asked with a wry smile that faded into a grimace. "I'm starting to wonder if Jones didn't give up on this case with good reason. This is frustrating." She sat down in her chair and kicked her foot to spin it around, head back, eyes closed. When it puttered to a stop just two turns later, she sighed and looked over at Jillian. "Any hits on the tip line we set up?"

"Not one. Social media is the same, though I'm not surprised about that."

"Why?"

"Even anonymous names can be easily traced online through their IP address."

"We can trace the phone calls too, but if they block their

number or use a burner phone, we can't. The paranoid ones will go to extra lengths to make sure they stay anonymous. People aren't always willing to put themselves out there." Ellie lifted her hands and let them fall back on the arms of the chair.

Jillian scrunched her lips and puffed out her cheeks. The air sent her thin bangs straight up where they hung for a minute before settling back on her forehead. "What about tracking down the others on the trip? Maybe we should try that?"

"I'm not sure what that would accomplish. No one knew each other, and Tabitha and Mabel never even made it on the plane. We could ask them about Katarina, but I'm not sure she exists."

"You're right about this being nothing but frustration. Two steps forward and ten back. It's like every clue leads to nowhere."

Ellie snorted. "Glad I'm not the only one feeling stuck." Opening the top drawer of her desk, she pulled out the list Fortis had written for her. "I guess I could look at Fortis's wish list."

"Are you really going to admit defeat?"

"Of course not." Ellie looked up sharply. "But there's no use pounding our heads against a wall all day again. Yesterday was bad enough. We'll set this aside, and I'll look at another case while we wait for something to click."

"I guess I could do *my* job," Jillian said. "My backlog is basically nonexistent, but I have some things I can work on that are slightly more exciting than watching paint dry."

"That's the spirit. Glass half shattered and all that." Ellie smirked at her friend, who she was beginning to think of as her partner in crime—or in fighting crime. God, she needed more coffee.

Jillian looked confused. "I believe you mean half full."

"Whatever. I guess I'll track down number one on Fortis's list and see what's in the box." She stood up and was halfway across the room when her phone rang. "If that's Fortis, can you tell him I'm in the cage working his list?"

Jillian spun in her chair and picked up the phone on Ellie's desk. "Detective Kline's desk. She's in the evidence locker at the moment. Want me to grab her?"

Ellie gave her a thumbs-up as Jillian's brow wrinkled.

Jillian nodded, then waved frantically for Ellie to come over. "Hold on, she's right here. Go ahead and patch the caller through." She smiled up at Ellie, almost giddy. "They got a tip. It seems like a strong lead."

Ellie ran the last few steps and pressed the phone to her ear just as the caller came on the line.

"Hello?" a young woman's voice said. "Detective Kline?"

"Speaking. Can I help you?" Ellie dug through the drawer for a pen and started to write on a blank page in the notebook. Nothing came out, so she flung the pen, grabbing another and scribbling a circle in the corner of the page until the ink flowed.

"I have information about the missing girls."

"Tabitha and Mabel?"

"Yes," the woman said, her voice breathy and fragile. Punching the button to raise the volume, Ellie still struggled to hear her when she continued. "They came to the plane for Ghana, but the man turned them away."

"What was this man's name?"

"Steve Garret." The woman paused only for a second. "He told them their money was no good and they argued. I couldn't hear everything, but they left and the one was crying."

"How long was this before the flight took off?"

"Maybe one hour." Her voice lowered, as if she were telling a secret. "Then they disappeared."

"And you're sure it was Mabel and Tabitha?"

"It was the girls in the picture online. I remember them very clearly."

Ellie's heart quickened. They hadn't released Steve's name. The lead felt good. "So, they fought with Steve, then the two of them disappeared."

"No, not two. All of them."

Ellie frowned, wishing the caller would be more specific. "All of who?"

"Steve and the two girls."

Ellie caught Jillian's gaze. "Steve went with them?"

Jillian's mouth dropped open.

"There was a lot of yelling, then they calmed down after Steve said something to them."

"What did he say?" Ellie tapped on the notepad, willing the woman to get to the details she needed.

"I couldn't hear them, and I didn't want to look like I was trying. But they nodded, and when he pointed to the door, they all went out together."

"Did Steve come back right away?" Frustration welled up in Ellie, to know that this woman might hold the information they needed, if only she could have heard the conversation.

"I don't remember when he came back. We boarded the plane a little bit later, but there was some mechanical issue. They left us on the tarmac for a long time, and I was so tired that I fell asleep. When I woke, the plane was about to take off. Steve was there and the girls were not. No one seemed to care, so I went back to sleep and didn't wake up for hours."

Jillian had moved to stand over her shoulder, reading the notes as Ellie recorded everything the caller was saying. When Ellie wrote the last part, Jillian gasped.

"Do you remember what Steve was wearing?" Ellie wanted to see if there was a possibility that his shirt was ripped or maybe dirty, but she didn't want to lead the tipster and have her tell her what she thought she wanted to hear. She hoped her questions would jog the caller's memory if there was a tear or some other sign the women had fought back. "Was it the same as what he wore when he first arrived?"

There was a long pause and then the woman's soft voice was back. "I'm not sure. I didn't really look at him. He made me uncomfortable. He flirted with everyone, and when I asked him to stop, he kept at it."

Steve was starting to sound like a lot more than a harmless dopehead. "What about Katarina? Did she seem like she was flirting with him, or was it all on his end?"

"Katarina?" the woman repeated. "There was no one named Katarina."

"There wasn't? Are you sure?" Had Steve been lying?

"Yes, I'm certain of it. We all worked very hard together in Ghana, and I remember everyone from the trip. They became like sisters to me. There was no Katarina."

"Can you tell me if Steve hung out with anyone in particular, then?" Ellie asked.

"Just another man, but he didn't tell us his name."

"A man in Ghana?" Ellie rapidly wrote that down, then realized how quick she was to grasp at leads, that was how badly she wanted this case solved. She would be crushed if she had to shelve her very first cold case as a detective.

"No, before we left. They were together every minute until the plane left, but the man didn't come with us. When we flew home, the man was there again." The woman sucked in a breath over the phone. "He was very quiet and a little odd."

"How so?"

"I'm not sure how to explain it. Just scary. Very still, with dead eyes and no smile. I was glad he didn't come with us."

Ellie noted that down, thinking that would just about cover half the mugshots ever taken. "Is there anything else you can tell me?"

"I'm sorry. That's all I remember. I wish I could help you more." Her breath caught, and she sniffled softly.

"You've done more than enough," Ellie assured her. "Thank you for calling."

When she hung up, Jillian was watching Ellie's face, waiting. "So? Was it a good tip?"

Ellie beamed. "She had information we didn't release, including Steve's full name."

"That's promising. Could you tell anything about her? Was she one of the others on the trip?"

"She spoke with an odd cadence like English was her second language, but she was very clear about Steve's odd behavior. I'm not sure which volunteer she would be." Ellie flipped through the notes on each traveler. "I didn't see where anyone was an immigrant."

"Was her accent strong?"

Ellie shook her head. "No. I can't really explain it. It was her word choice more than anything, but it's possible that's just how she speaks. Regardless, she gave me enough to know for certain that Steve lied to us. There was no Katarina. Just another man, and that man didn't go with them."

"That's strange."

"It gets weirder." She recapped the rest of what the caller had told her about Steve disappearing then boarding sometime later.

"Do you think he helped the other guy get Tabitha and Mabel to a secondary location?"

"If he did, it had to be close. If Steve can prove he was at the plane when they were abducted, we can't pin it on him." Ellie gritted her teeth. "I knew he was lying about something, but I didn't think he was a willing accomplice."

"What now?"

Ellie sat back in her chair, thinking through her next move. "I don't want to call Steve just yet. It'll spook him, and I need to verify a few things before I run with this."

"How are you going to do that?"

"I'll make a few calls to the other women on the trip. Maybe we'll get a few that can corroborate what our tipster said."

"You want help?" Jillian's voice was hopeful.

Ellie shook her head, giving her a *sorry* look. "There aren't that many. Besides, don't you have exciting filing work to do?"

"Don't remind me." Jillian groaned and skulked back to her own desk.

❄

Ellie set the receiver in the cradle and leaned back in her chair. "Well, that was pointless," she muttered.

Jillian walked back into the room. "Anyone corroborate the caller's story?"

"Yes and no."

"I'm almost afraid to ask what that means."

"No one remembers either way." Ellie scribbled on the corner of the notebook page.

"Oh. That's not what I expected." Jillian rubbed her temple. "So the case is staying consistently murky."

"Basically. But it's enough to justify bringing Steve in to speak with us."

"Is it? You think he'll come quietly?"

Ellie shrugged, not relishing going back to Steve's rank abode. "I'm not sure, but I don't really have enough to compel DNA or anything like that."

Jillian quirked a brow. "He doesn't know that."

"True. But I'll need an unmarked car to pick him up in. There's no way he's riding in the back of my car."

"Which means you have to tell Fortis that you suspect him?"

"Exactly." Ellie sighed and scanned her notes as she thought about going to Fortis with the little she had. "I'm not sure I have enough just yet."

"Run a background on Steve and maybe have him picked up for something else."

Ellie's eyes lit up. "You're a genius."

"I know."

Ellie rolled her eyes and typed Steve's information into the database along with his address. She got a hit almost instantly and her eyes went wide.

Jillian hurried around the desk to take a look. "Whoa. Are they really enforcing this?"

Ellie's fingers flew over the keyboard, and when the results loaded on the screen, she laughed. "Probably just as a reason for contact and to pile on charges. But it's right here. Excise tax on unauthorized controlled substances."

"Okay, but why is that even on there?"

"Probably a clerical error. See right here? He pled no contest and got off with community service two years ago. Everything else was dropped but this charge. I doubt it was on purpose, but it's still there."

Jillian tapped her red lips. "You think Fortis will go for it?"

"For bringing in a viable suspect on a bogus charge? Probably not." Ellie debated her options, toying with one that was the most obvious.

"But you're not going to ask Fortis, are you?"

The hell with it. "No, I am not."

"Ellie, I can't pretend I didn't know this time. If I lose my job, I don't have anyone to help me with bills."

"Don't worry about it." She ignored the last part, used to everyone assuming she went to her daddy for mad money. "I actually had another plan."

"I'm afraid to ask."

"Don't." She grabbed her purse and slung it over her shoulder. "I'll be back in a little bit."

"What do I tell Fortis if he comes by?"

"Tell him I didn't tell you where I was going."

Jillian chewed on her bottom lip. "He's not going to like that."

Ellie shrugged. "He will when I've got my guy."

"Be careful, Ellie," Jillian called out as Ellie gathered her things and headed out the door.

Ellie turned and smiled at her. "Don't worry, I've got this."

"I know you do," Jillian said with an exaggerated frown. "That's what I'm afraid of."

Ellie was still smiling when she pulled out her cell phone and called Jacob as she pushed through the side door. "Where are you?"

"Good morning. It's nice to hear your voice too, Kline." There was a sharp whine in the background and a shushing noise from Jacob.

Ellie smiled, wondering if she'd interrupted doggy potty time. "Sorry. I need a favor."

"Is your dad okay?"

"Yeah, he's doing well, but that's not what I need."

Jacob groaned into the receiver. "I have a feeling I'm not going to like this."

"Come on, Jacob. I just need someone with a cruiser to help me bring a person in."

"Is there a bridge involved? I'm still a little traumatized."

"Quit messing around." Ellie mentally scrolled through

her other possibilities but knew that no one but Jacob would agree. "Can you pick me up or not?"

"Sure. Where are you?"

"At the side door. Are you close?"

"Right around the corner. Be there in a minute."

She hung up the phone, and a moment later, his cruiser braked to a stop in front of her. "I see Duke is resting," she said as she got in and looked in the back. "Hard morning chasing criminals, huh, Duke?"

Duke sat up and barked, startling her and making her wonder if the cute puppy persona was all to lull a person into thinking he was just that, a cute puppy.

"I didn't think about what we're going to do with Duke when we pick the offender up."

"You can drive, and I'll sit in the back with the perp." He looked over at her with a wide grin, showing off his pearly white teeth. "You're sitting in my partner's seat."

Ellie couldn't help but stick her nose in the air at his suggestion that she'd been replaced by a dog. "Fine, that'll work." She rattled off the address, and Jacob started to log it in.

"What are we picking him up for?"

"G. S. one of five dash one thirteen."

He looked at her, tilting his head. "What is that? Jaywalking in a school zone?"

"Excise tax on a controlled substance." She didn't mention that the charge was two years old.

Jacob did a double take at her. "Seriously? They tax that?"

"Yep."

"Well, I'll be." Jacob hit the highway without logging their reason in. "Let's pick up our guy and ask him why he's behind on his drug dealer tax." He chuckled, shaking his head. "And I thought jumping off a bridge was bad."

"If you're scared…" Ellie gave him a challenging look.

"Are you kidding? I can't wait to see this guy's face when you tell him why you're bringing him in."

"You think he'll come quietly?"

Jacob's grin spread wider. "I hope not. Duke hasn't gotten to chase anyone all week."

27

"The house looks deserted," Jacob said from the walkway, surveying the tiny weedy yard and rusted chain-link.

Duke stood beside him, eyes intent on the door, his flanks quivering.

"It looked like this Monday too." Ellie picked her way up the rickety steps and knocked on the door. When there was no answer after a second knock. She tilted her face close to the wood, careful not to touch the peeling paint, and called out Steve's name, listening for a response. "Can Duke walk around the building or something?"

"And do what, exactly?" Jacob said from the walkway.

"I don't know. Alert for drugs?"

"He's not a drug dog."

Ellie frowned, eyeing the dog, wondering if he had to pee. He certainly looked like he was about to pop a screw loose or something. "Then what does he do?"

"He chases bad guys and holds on to them until I get there."

Ellie's eyebrows went up, and she rolled her eyes. "So he's

the dog version of me. I guess when you start getting older, you need a partner who can do the hard work for you. At least your dog has never dragged you off a bridge after a suspect."

"You've never dragged me anywhere." Jacob puffed out his chest, his forehead wrinkling into a frown.

"It's only Wednesday."

"Very funny." He cracked a grin. "As much as I'd like to give you probable cause to gain entry into the house, Duke doesn't do any of that. I guess you'll have to come back another—" He put his hands on his gun belt as she dragged an old, half rotted chair across the porch. "Ellie, what on earth are you doing?"

Ellie climbed up on the chair, standing on her tiptoes and feeling along the frame of the door. Her hand touched something wet, and her stomach turned, but then her fingertip hit cold metal. She managed to pluck the key from the carnage of an old bird's nest and presented it to Jacob with a brilliant smile. "Why do they think no one will look there?"

Jacob gave her a disbelieving look. "You can't just unlock his door, Ellie."

"I'm just going to make sure he's okay. Think of it as a welfare check. When we came by Monday, he was acting like he felt ill."

"He's probably a junky you woke up before he could get his morning fix." Jacob glared at her. "I'm not going to watch you do this."

"Then turn around."

He threw his hands up in exasperation. "You know nothing you find will be admissible in court, right?"

"I've already been in his house. There's nothing in plain sight that's helpful. And he didn't live here when the women went missing." She cupped her hand to her ear and leaned toward the door. "Did you hear that?" she asked in an exaggerated whisper.

"This is about the two cold cases? Ellie," Jacob warned, "do you have any idea—"

Duke let out a growl, his powerful haunches tensing.

"I heard something," she lied, ignoring Jacob's narrowed eyes, "and so did Duke. It sounds like someone moaning." Sliding the key into the lock, she turned the doorknob and opened the door a fraction. "Mr. Garret!" she called out. "Are you in need of assistance?"

Jacob grumbled to himself, but he made no move to stop her. She stayed on the threshold, pushing the door inward. It creaked and shuddered, shedding paint chips on the floor as it swung open. Her eyes widened, and she turned and motioned to Jacob.

"No way." He shook his head, feet planted on the cracked concrete walk.

"I think you need to see this."

Throwing up his hands again, he commanded Duke to stay where he was and climbed the stairs. "Whoa," he said when he was beside Ellie, surveying the inside that was now in worse condition than it had been. "Did it look like that on Monday?"

"No. And unless he was wrestling his own demons, someone was here." The beanbag chairs that had been arranged in the living room were scattered. A lamp was overturned, papers lying everywhere.

"You know, you have probable cause now to at least check the rooms to make sure he's not lying dead somewhere in the house."

Ellie's heartbeat started racing. "Can you call it in?"

"Call what in?"

"I'm not going to risk compromising the crime scene. It may be the only link we have."

Jacob frowned down at her. "Crime scene linked to what? The two women?"

"Steve's accomplice. I don't have a name or a description."

Jacob looked doubtfully back at the ransacked room. "I don't think he's in there."

"I know that." Ellie huffed and took another look around, pointing up at the ceiling. "But look. Have you ever heard of that brand of smoke detector?"

"So it's an off-brand. So what?"

"Steve worked in tech before he quit to work for Katarina."

Jacob popped his neck, a sure sign he was losing his patience. "Who is Katarina?"

"Long story. Anyway, don't you think he has a few too many alarms for a two-bedroom shack?" She pointed at another on the living room ceiling.

"He lives in this shithole. Maybe he's worried about fires."

"What about the fabric plant and the clock just sitting on the fireplace mantle? You don't think it's weird that the clock is pristine when the rest of the house looks like this?"

Jacob zeroed in on the fireplace and nodded. "Okay, I see it. They could be cameras."

"Exactly." She looked at him expectantly, then arched an eyebrow.

"Fine." He tilted his head and spoke into the radio affixed to his shoulder, then he gave her an annoyed look. "There, you happy?"

"Not really."

Jacob couldn't keep his lips from turning up in a small smile. "Why am I not surprised?"

"My only link to this case might be gone. If he didn't catch his partner on camera, then I'm stuck at square one."

"He was probably just robbed."

She glanced around the neighborhood. That was a

distinct possibility, but something told her there was more to it. “I don’t think so. There’s more to this.”

“If you say so. This could have just been another junky looking for a fix.”

“Or it could be a lead that actually cracks the case.” She sighed and sagged against the doorframe. “I just want to give Mabel and Tabitha the justice they deserve.”

Jacob grabbed her shoulders and leaned forward so they were eye to eye. “Ellie. These families have been searching for their lost daughters for years. You gave them closure. Or at least they’ll have closure when the DNA tests confirm. If nothing else comes of this case, that’s not your fault. It was mishandled from the start. The fact that you were able to figure out who both Jane Does are is a damn miracle. Sometimes enough is good enough.”

Ellie pressed her lips together in a firm line. “Not for me.” Why was everyone always trying to keep her in a neat box, telling her that she’d done enough?

“You’ll drive yourself batty if you don’t learn to take the losses and celebrate the wins.”

“Their deaths are loss enough. I’m not stopping until I find their killers. The cases wasting away in neat white boxes deserve justice like the rest of us. And with technology growing every year, a lot of those cases will be solved eventually.”

“Okay, but does it have to be you?” She knew he was only reminding her that she’d been walking a fine line for a while now.

“I’m the only detective who cares enough to keep fighting for them. Do you know the last time they had a detective dedicated to cold cases?”

“Yeah, whenever they had their last rookie detective.” Jacob’s brown eyes softened. “Ellie, they gave you cold cases to keep you out of trouble.”

"Don't you think I know that?" she barked, stepping back until his hands dropped off her shoulders. "But that doesn't change anything. Victims of crime deserve to rest in peace. Especially these two."

"Why them? There are hundreds of unsolved cases that fade away and are forgotten. What's so special about these women that you're willing to risk everything to find the truth?"

I don't know, she thought miserably but stood her ground.

"I don't expect you to understand. You never saw things the way I do anyway." He winced, and she immediately regretted snapping at him. "I'm sorry. You didn't deserve that. I just don't want their suffering to be for nothing."

"You've done more than anyone else has for their cases," Jacob said softly. "I know it doesn't seem like much, but there are two families that have been hurting who will get to bring their daughters home for a proper burial. You did that. You should be proud of that accomplishment, and you managed it with almost nothing to go off of. You did more with this case than anyone else. It's enough, Ellie."

"No, it's not." Brakes squeaked, drawing her attention to the street. "The cavalry is here. I can catch a ride back if you need to leave."

"And miss all the excitement?" He smiled, his easy manner back just like that. "No way."

❄

"YOU CAN COME IN NOW, DETECTIVE," one of the first arriving officers said from the doorway, stepping out of her way with a nod. His footsteps were hollow on the front stoop as he took his position just outside the crime scene tape, facing the small crowd that was starting to gather on the street.

The weight of the moment wasn't lost on Ellie, but she

had work to do. She'd been waiting almost an hour to get into the house and have a look around.

The living room had sustained most of the damage, but it was clear as she walked through each room that whoever Steve had struggled with had ransacked every room.

Looking for what?

Was Jacob right about it being another junky looking for Steve's stash? Or maybe it had been a straight-up robbery. Not as common as people were led to believe, but it was possible that the perp had been looking for money and nothing else.

She scanned the walls and the wood floors, all covered with a thin layer of filth, and shook her head. Unless they knew what Steve did for a living, *no one* would assume this house hid money. No. This was about Steve. Either the drugs he was selling, or it was about his involvement in the death of Tabitha and Mabel. Ellie was willing to lay money on the latter.

"Detective Kline, you'll want to see this," a voice called out from the back of the house.

Following the hallway, she stopped at the last door on the right, where a small group of crime scene techs stood around a computer monitor.

"That looks pretty new," Ellie commented.

"It's state-of-the-art." The tech was excited, her nostrils flared and eyes wide. "But that's not what I wanted to show you." She clicked on the mouse with her gloved hand and moved to give Ellie an unobstructed view.

"Fifteen cameras?" Ellie couldn't help but show her surprise at the multiple screens, all pulled from different sections of the house, both inside and out. "This guy took paranoid to a new level."

"With good cause," the tech said. "This is early this morning, about three."

The crime scene tech clicked on the play icon, and the video started.

A shadow appeared on the doorstep in the form of a person.

Steve opened the door, and even though the video was a little dark, she could see the instant that Steve recognized the man. Steve attempted to shut the door in the man's face.

But the man was on him in seconds. He grabbed Steve by the arms and stepped inside, kicking the front door shut with his foot.

Another camera picked up the scuffle, in which Steve was clearly outmatched. Holding his hands out in surrender, Steve backed into a corner and sunk to his knees.

"He's begging for his life," Ellie said. "That has to be his accomplice." The man was about the same height as Steve and had a balding hairline, but that was about all she could make out in the darkness of the room.

"They definitely know each other," the tech said.

The intruder backhanded Steve, and Ellie and the tech winced as one. Steve collapsed in a heap, motionless and twisted at an uncomfortable angle.

"That wouldn't be enough to kill him," Ellie said. "But look at him. He's out cold."

The tech pointed at the monitor. "Watch this. It gets better."

The man was quick on his feet, sure of what he was doing. Going from room to room, his every move was caught on the hidden cameras in the darkness, the only light coming in from the windows.

"He's throwing things around, but he's not taking anything," Ellie mused.

"Yep. Our guy wants this to look like a robbery, but he didn't take a thing. He's clearly a professional."

"He looks so calm." Ellie thought about the man Katarina

had described. Someone who was quiet and scary with dead eyes would be this mechanical. "There's no way this man is a junky or a thief."

"I noticed the same thing right away. I would lay money he was hired to kidnap our missing person." The tech struck a single key with a flourish, grinning at Ellie. "And there's your still-shot of the suspect. I'm guessing he didn't know about the cameras because he looked right at this one." It was a full-on front shot of his face.

Ellie held her cell phone up and took a picture. "The quality isn't that great, but it's something. And it's more than I had. What happened to Steve?"

"Unfortunately, the video only shows the man carrying him out to the car. And the cameras only picked up the side panel of the car, and there was no license plate." She pointed at the frame that covered the street. "For all his paranoia, he missed a prime opportunity to place this camera better."

"It's one more roadblock in a case that's proven to be nothing but obstacles." Ellie held up her phone. "But this is more than we've had to go on since we started. Thanks."

"Don't thank me." The tech laughed. "Thank Steve Garret. If it weren't for his tech know-how and paranoia, we wouldn't even have this."

"True," Ellie said. "Now, all we have to do is figure out who has Steve."

"Find anything good?" Jacob asked when Ellie emerged from the house. He was standing on the walk with Duke, outside the boundary made by the crime scene tape. "I was starting to think you weren't coming out."

Duke gave a short whine under his breath as if to concur.

She laughed and held out her phone to show him the picture. "Just this. It's not much."

"Send that to me, and I'll get a BOLO sent out."

"Thanks," she said, getting in his car and sending the picture to his cell phone.

"Where to now?" he asked as he loaded Duke up.

"PD. I want to run this man's picture through facial recognition and see if I get a hit. It's a longshot, but it's better than no shot."

"Any idea where Steve Garret ended up?"

"No clue. He was knocked out when the man took him out of the house. The camera didn't pick up the rest. We don't even know if he put him in the trunk. The officers are going to question the neighbors, but Steve's neighbors aren't exactly the type that will care either way."

Jacob chuckled. "That is true." Jacob fell silent until he pulled up at the police department and parked, giving her a long look across the front seat of the cruiser. "I know you don't need one more person in your life telling you to be careful, but Ellie, please be careful. My gut is telling me that there's more to this than there appears."

"Mine too."

"Good. Don't let your guard down."

She gave him a soft smile, glad at least that, even though Jacob was worried, he wouldn't try to stop her. "I won't."

His lips were tight when he nodded, and she could tell that he was really worried. But she couldn't abandon the case, whether she was in danger or not. The women's murders ate away at her every moment of the day, and there was no way she could rest until she found the man who'd taken an unconscious Steve Garret from his home in the dead of night. Finding him would be vital to unraveling the case.

She could feel it.

28

Ellie groaned as the pictures flashing across the computer screen slowed then stopped. *No Match* flashed on the screen once, then hung there in bold red letters, taunting her.

"I guess it wouldn't be fun if this case didn't have a great new lead that led nowhere," Jillian grumbled sarcastically. "An email came across right before you walked in with a 'Be On the Lookout' so hopefully someone will see our Mr. Garret and pick him up."

"Could we be that lucky?" Ellie took a sip of her soda.

"Probably not."

"Kline, a moment," Fortis said from the doorway.

Ellie almost startled but caught herself in time. "I guess you heard about my person of interest on the case."

"No, I hadn't. Did you get a name?"

"Not exactly."

"What does that mean?" Fortis ground the words out impatiently. "Did you run him through facial recognition?"

"I did." She flicked her eyes back to the computer screen and felt herself wilt a tiny bit. Damn it.

"Let me guess—more of nothing."

Ellie grimaced.

"Look, I'm not here to bust your chops about the cold case. I've got two out with the flu today and another looking like hell. I need you to take a case. Cut and dry, out on Rivers Avenue, in the woods. Homeless man found him, probably an overdose."

"Is it suspicious? Homeless people overdosing in the woods there happens all the time."

"Kline, look." Fortis pursed his lips, frowning at her. "I know it's not ideal, but it's an open and shut case. You just have to be there to make sure all the evidence is collected in case the medical examiner comes back with something different than OD. You don't have to take anyone with you."

"All right," she said.

He handed her a set of keys. "Don't wreck it."

"I can't take my own car?" She kept her palm open, as if the key was contaminated. She hated to think what cruiser would be used as an extra. Probably one that smelled like vomit.

"Not in that neighborhood."

She used the opportunity, wondering if her wish came true she would be given a moped instead of a sedan since her desk had been stuffed in the basement instead of the department office. "Maybe you should assign me an unmarked car."

"We don't have any extras. This is the one we use when the others are in the shop. It's a little dated, but it gets the job done."

She grimaced. "Does it have shag carpet?"

"Not anymore." Fortis grinned. "I had it parked next to your car. It's kind of a greenish color. Call me if you have any problems. When you're done with this one, you can get started on that list."

She decided not to argue with him. "I'll let you know when I get back."

"You don't have to do that. Just put your report on my desk when you're done." He hesitated in the doorway, his eyes showing an emotion she couldn't quite place. "And I thought you'd want to know right away, the DNA results came back. Tabitha Baker and Mabel Vicente were positively identified."

Her breath caught, and it was like the weight of the world was lifted. She wanted to shout with joy and cry at the same time. But Fortis was still standing in front of her, waiting. She swallowed back the tears that welled up suddenly. "Thank you, sir."

He nodded and left her sitting at her desk with the keyring hanging from her finger.

She jumped up from her chair, and Jillian shot her wide smile as she grabbed her purse and went out the side door to the parking lot. She froze. A seventies-era moss-green Ford sedan was parked beside her car. With chrome in places she had forgotten cars could have chrome, it resembled something her grandfather would have driven, if her grandfather hadn't driven a Cadillac.

"He wasn't joking," she muttered to herself. "At least I'll be safely encased in metal." The door hinges creaked loudly, and when she sat on the velour seat and pulled the door shut, it fell back open. Gripping the handle with both hands, she pulled with all her might, slamming it closed so hard the car rocked. "Geez Louise. This is the reward I get for identifying the victims of my first case? I'd hate to see what the prize will be when I solve it."

The steering wasn't any better, but the engine was quieter than she'd expected and had a response that she had to admit she loved. She arrived at the scene in no time, having burned more gas than her car would in a week. Guiding the behemoth off the road and onto the hardpacked dirt, she parked near the coroner's van and got out after she switched shoes.

"We're waiting on your say to move the body," the coroner said, looking impatient.

"How long has it been there?"

"A couple hours at most. Rigor is just starting to set in, located primarily in the neck and face at this point." He checked his watch. "I'd say about two hours based on that and body temp, but it's hard to tell." He looked up at the sky. "Weather's been warm to cold, plus the rain, and rigor can start setting in as early as one hour."

"It's all right," she assured him. "I know figuring out the time of death in the field isn't as easy as the TV makes it look."

He grinned and took a pen from his pocket. "Sign here, please. And congrats on the promotion."

She flashed him a smile and signed her name, giving the clipboard back. "Thanks. Where is the body?"

"Straight through there against a tree." He gestured toward the tree line. "There's an officer watching the other residents of the homeless camp."

"Thanks." She picked her way over the uneven ground and sidestepped around withering vines that crept across the path before spotting the very young officer standing with his arms resting on his belt, looking in every direction except the body.

"You can head to the road if you want," she told him. "I'll only be a minute."

He was gone so fast, he was little more than a blur of uniform blues.

Ellie smiled in sympathy, and carefully went to the corpse leaning against the tree. The man's hair was matted and wet from the rain they'd had earlier in the day. Other than his skin being unnaturally pale and the needle still sticking out of his arm, he looked like he was sleeping. Except, the weight of his head had turned his face downward, his joints having gone so slack that his neck was bent at an awkward angle no living person would be able to sleep through.

Careful not to move the body, Ellie crouched down and used one gloved hand to move the hair away from the man's face. Steve Garret's lifeless eyes stared back at her, blue lips lax, and the beginnings of a bruise where the mystery man had punched him in the face.

"This was no overdose," Ellie muttered.

"What?" the coroner said, body bag in hand and a stretcher held between him and his assistant.

"This wasn't an overdose," she repeated, louder and even more certain this time.

"How can you be sure?" He squinted at the man against the tree.

"I know this man." Ellie stood and spread her feet wide in a stance that said she wasn't going anywhere until this was treated as a homicide investigation. "He didn't shoot up, and I have evidence of foul play that I can't discuss right now."

The coroner assessed Ellie, then the corpse, an annoyed expression on his face. "But he's got a needle hanging out of his arm."

"You're right, but I think it's staged. He does cocaine. I just talked to this man the other day. No marks on his arms."

"I didn't look for signs of older marks yet."

"Don't worry about it. If I didn't know this man, I would've thought the same. That's why we investigate every suspicious death." She gave him what she hoped was a reassuring smile. "We're going to need a crime scene team out here. Can you call it in? My radio is in the car."

The coroner stared at her, and when he nodded, the men turned back the way they'd come.

Ellie looked around her feet, careful to step where she'd

already left footprints. As she was scanning the soft layer of dirt that had already dried from the light rain earlier in the day, a pair of prints caught her eye. The toes were facing the body, but it wasn't just that. The impressions were deep, as if the person had stood there for quite a while, and the soles seemed to be in perfect condition.

A quick once over of the area confirmed that her suspicions were correct. All the prints that appeared to be from curious onlookers were farther back, and the impressions left by their soles showed signs of excessive wear. Only one set of prints was different, and that set went into the woods on a path.

Hand resting on the butt of her gun, she took off at a slow lope, careful to run beside the prints and never on them. The trail narrowed but was still wide enough for two people even when the woods got so dense that she could no longer hear the traffic sounds from the street beyond. She hesitated, but when she looked back over her shoulder and saw how far she'd come, she pressed on.

You've got this, she told herself. She would *not* be afraid.

It was one man, and she had the element of surprise.

The trees thinned then dropped away, the path leading to a street. Ellie tried to follow the muddy footprints, but the asphalt had been washed clean by the rain. There were no houses on the street and only a handful of buildings. Wherever the man was, he was long gone.

"Damn it," she said under her breath.

Undeterred, she set off down the road and across the street, pushing open the door of a print shop and walking up to the counter. "Did you see anyone come out of the woods over there about an hour or two ago? It could've been up to four hours ago."

The man stared back at her, eyes heavy with boredom.

"You'll have to be more specific. Junkies stumble out of the woods all the time. It's a quiet place to get a fix."

"Okay, but this man wouldn't be stumbling." She showed him the photo on her phone.

He chortled. "I mean, come on. I can't see anything on that."

"White male, mid-thirties, muscled but not big, balding."

"Lady, you just described half of Charleston."

She leaned against the counter, waving the phone. "Please look again. This is important."

"I'm sure it is. But I didn't see nothing, and I'd appreciate it if you'd stop scaring away my paying customers."

She looked out the front of the store at the empty street and the parking lot without a single car in sight. "What customers?" She turned back just as the office door closed and locked behind the man. "Great," she muttered, pushing out the door and heading toward the next business, grateful she'd had the foresight to change into her running shoes.

The motel was one of those pay by the hour joints. Commonly referred to as a no-tell motel, it looked every bit the part. Even in the light of day, it was seedy looking. She shuddered at the mental image of a bug-infested pigsty so cheap the ten-dollar-an-hour hookers wouldn't bat an eye at sharing the space with more than just the Johns.

Straightening her shoulders, she headed for the tiny, dingy office. She used her foot to push the door open so she didn't have to touch anything, thankful that the door appeared to swing both ways. Or the hinges were broken. She turned her attention to the young man sitting behind the counter. When he saw her, he tensed and looked around nervously.

"I'm not here for that," she said, flashing her badge. "I just need to know if you've had any clients who showed up in the past few hours and left in the last hour or two."

He squinted at her badge, then gave her the side-eye. "This is a pay by the hour establishment. Everyone that got here a couple hours ago is already gone."

True enough.

"Okay, but I'm looking for two guys."

"That's not uncommon."

"Fair enough," she said, pushing away the mental image that comment brought on. "The first guy." She showed him a picture of Steve Garret from his social media page. "He's about five years older than this, but he looks about the same."

"Never seen him," the motel clerk said. "Hey, Eddie, come here a minute, would you?"

"Sure," a man called out as he came through the door behind the counter. "What's up, I'm just about to—" The balding man froze and stared at Ellie.

It was the man from the video footage.

"You…" That was all she managed to get out before he tossed the boxes he was carrying at her and took off out the back door.

Ellie sidestepped the boxes and went out the front, angling to cut the man off as he ran across a field toward another wooded area to the north. His long legs stretched wide, eating up the ground, pristine black combat boots pounding the ground in the steady rhythm of a man who ran often.

He was fast, but Ellie was in excellent shape and almost the same height as the stockier man. The wind whipped at her face and drew tears from her eyes as she chased after him across the uneven dirt of the empty lot.

"Stop, police!" she ordered.

He didn't so much as hesitate. Sights set on the trees ahead, he was clearly of a mind to lose her in the woods.

But Ellie wasn't planning on going down easily.

She kept her eyes locked on the spot where he disappeared into the trees, adrenaline propelling her faster than she'd ever run before. Rushing headlong into the trees, she wasn't prepared for the blow that caught her in the side of the head and knocked her clean off her feet.

Her tailbone hit the ground first, and her teeth clacked together. Pain shot up her spine and rattled through bones that suddenly felt brittle. She silenced the cry that threatened to escape, blinking to clear the haze of agony clouding her vision.

When she drew in a breath and wiped at the tender spot on her head, her hand came away bloody. Dizzy and more than a little light-headed, it took her a full second to make sense of the sticky red liquid. Pushing past the haze, she forced her lungs to draw in deep breaths in an attempt to catch the wind that was knocked out of her. But she didn't have time to wait until she felt better. The man was getting away. She couldn't let him get away.

Get it together, Ellie.

Through eyes that were struggling to focus, she watched the man run through the woods like a jackrabbit as she stumbled to her feet and took off after him on legs that felt like lead.

With every step, the pain lessened, and within a few yards, she was back up to speed, though more cautious. He'd caught her by surprise. It wouldn't happen again. Wary of another attack, Ellie slowed when she came to an area that was dense with foliage.

But she spotted him through the trees, and he was starting to slow down. She saw why when she followed and the trees grew more sparse, revealing a natural stone wall surrounded by trees growing so close together that nothing could pass through.

Recognizing the dead end for what it was, he turned and advanced on her, fist balled up and ready to strike.

Still a little dizzy from the head blow, Ellie readied herself, her hand going to the gun at her side...but it wasn't there.

Muscle memory was a beautiful thing, but her muscles had clearly forgotten that she no longer wore the duty belt low on her hips. Since making detective, she'd had no reason to draw her weapon, and she'd not taken the time to practice drawing from the shoulder holster she now wore.

And the man was advancing fast, too fast for her to reach inside and retrieve her gun.

Ellie centered herself, but unlike the suspect, her palms were open, her feet centered in classic Krav Maga fighting stance. Slowing her breathing, she focused on centering herself. She could do this. She would do this. She...

Before she could inhale a second breath, he charged.

She held her position. When he extended his arm to hit her, she crouched, striking the side of his knee with her palm before ramming her elbow into the underside of his chin.

He grunted and staggered, shook his head and roared. "You'll pay for that," he spat, eyes wild. His punch grazed her cheek and sent her sprawling to the ground.

She was on her knees in an instant, but he was already behind her. He clamped his arms around her chest and squeezed. Just as he lifted her off her feet, she stomped down on his foot. Quickly throwing her head back, her skull connected with his cheek with a loud crack. It wasn't the nose shot she'd hoped for, but he groaned, and his gripped loosened.

Using her elbows and knees to pommel him, she managed to slither out of his grasp. She was dizzy, and her blood-matted hair ripped away from the skin of the side of her face with every movement, reminding her she was already wounded.

Trying to put distance between herself and the man, she

ran toward the rock wall so that when she turned, he would have the trees behind him. But the move meant trapping herself in the process. She went for her gun again, fumbling with the unfamiliar snap. If she survived the next few minutes, she swore she'd head straight to the shooting range and practice until her arm fell off.

She'd only taken two steps when a strong hand wrapped around her hair that had fallen from its bun, and her head was yanked back violently. This time a cry of pain did escape her lips, and she went down hard, flat on her back. She struck him repeatedly as he fumbled for her weapon, but he was too close for her to get any power behind the hits. In disbelief, she rolled out of the way as her gun cleared the holster, and he squeezed off a shot. The bullet buried itself in the ground where she'd been l ying on her back only a second before.

She didn't try to run, surprising them both when she leapt to her knees, and her elbow caught him in the throat.

He squeezed off another shot that went wide.

Her hands were on his wrists, trying to wrestle the gun from him, but he managed to hold on to the trigger. The third shot tore through her arm and sent searing flames into her shoulder. But there was no time to focus on the pain or check to see if she was mortally injured.

The man was taking aim again. And at point-blank range, any shot could kill.

Making one last grab at the piece, she shoved his hands upward instead of pulling.

The move put him off-balance, and he stumbled backward, taking her with him.

The gun went off, sending shock waves through her body.

But this time she didn't feel any pain. Oh god, was it so bad that she was numb to it?

Or had the bullet gone wild?

She froze, staring into the man's eyes, which were glassy with shock. He'd taken the bullet. Looking down, she saw that blood was pumping from between his fingers, pressed to his upper abdomen.

He was going to die, and she would never be able to tell the families of the two women why they had been taken.

"Why did you kill Tabitha and Mabel?" she demanded, her voice distant past the ringing in her ears.

"Doctor Ex—" His breath caught, and he licked his lips. "Doctor."

"Why did you kill them?" she shouted, enraged that death would get in the way when she was so close to the cold truth of two heinous murders. She was shaking. Covered in blood. Head pounding, chest on fire with each inhale. In the distance, she heard someone shouting her name, but she focused on the man. "Tell me why you killed them."

"No," he said, the light in his dark, cold eyes fading.

She wanted to shake him, but she was too weak.

"Please..." She had to know. She had to put these women to rest.

"Doc..." The man's jaw went slack on the word, his breath caught on the exhale, but his chest didn't rise again. It never would.

The world spun, and it started to get dark. She forced her eyelids open wider when she heard barking.

Duke appeared, whimpering and pushing at her arm with his cold nose.

"Over here!" Jacob shouted in the distance. "Ellie, say something!"

"Help," she croaked, wavering even as she was sitting on the ground.

Jacob skidded the last few feet on his knees, face pale with worry. "You're shot."

"I-I n-noticed." Her teeth had begun to chatter. She was so very, very cold.

"You're going to be okay," he murmured, ripping open the snaps on his uniform shirt and casting it aside. He tugged his white tee over his head and folded it quickly. "You're going to be okay."

"W-why are you g-getting undressed?" she wondered vaguely. "G-god, Jacob, I-I d-didn't r-realize you were so r-ripped—" She hissed when he shoved the fabric against the wound near her shoulder. "Oh…t-t-that."

Was the sun setting already? The world around her was growing so dark.

"Don't flirt with me now, Ellie. Do you know what day it is?"

She tried to think. "Wednesday." She gasped with the pain that surged as he pressed down to stem the flow of blood. "Hurts."

"I know it does."

The pain had her mind clearing to a sharpened point. "D-don't call my parents."

"Wouldn't dream of it."

"My d-dad can't take any m-more right now." The dark that had toyed with her before loomed over her again.

"Don't close your eyes," Jacob ordered, shouting into her face.

"You sound so far away." Her own voice came out feeble, not like her. She wasn't feeble. She was a badass. One who had survived a kidnapping and was now cleaning up Charleston's old fourberie.

"The ambulance is coming. Can you hear it?"

Sirens wailed in the distance. "Don't put me in the bus with that scumbag."

"He's dead."

"G-good. He killed Tabitha and Mabel."

"Stop talking." He looked over his shoulder. "They're here. Hold on just a little longer."

"I'm so tired."

"You lost a lot of blood."

"I think that's from the bullet." She snorted, impressed with her own detective skills.

A paramedic appeared at her side and took over holding the shirt against her wound. "Let's get her loaded up," he ordered.

Ellie winced when they turned her on her side to slide the backboard beneath her, then she was strapped in, and they were running down the trail as fast as they could over the rough terrain. The jostling proved to be too much for her, and every time she blinked, she lost time. When she opened her eyes, she was in a new place.

Blink

"I'm right here with you, Ellie." It was Jacob's voice, but he didn't sound like himself. "We're not far from the hospital."

Blink

"Twenty-seven-year-old female with a GSW to the shoulder. We're two minutes out. Patient has lost a lot of blood."

Blink

"Get me five units of blood and an OR ready, stat!"

Blink

"Ellie, if you can hear me, this is Dr. Avery. You've been shot. You should be getting sleepy. Count backward with me, you don't have to speak. Five...four...three...two..."

Blink

29

Beep.

Beep.

The beeping was so annoying, it encouraged Ellie to lift her heavy eyelids open.

There were voices too. But they blended together for a moment before she was able to pick out the familiar ones.

"She's waking up," her mother said a little breathlessly.

There was a shuffling of bodies as someone leaned over the bed.

When Ellie's eyes finally opened all the way, and her vision cleared, her mother was holding her hand.

Helen kissed her knuckles and took a deep breath. Eyes glassy and cheeks wet, she forced a smile. "Oh, honey. There you are."

"How long was I out?" Ellie croaked.

"A couple hours," Wesley said from behind Helen. He smiled at her and winked. "Don't milk it. You're going to live. Won't even have any long-term damage, we've been told."

"Thanks, little brother." She laughed and immediately cringed. "That hurts."

"Dr. Avery says you're going to make a full recovery, but you'll have to take it easy."

Helen bit her lip. "Honey, you're a hero. But now that you've solved those murders and the girls will be laid to rest where they belong, maybe it's time to accept that this job is just too risky."

"I'm fine, Mom." Ellie tried her best to actually look fine from a hospital bed. "But, thank you for worrying about me."

"It's a mother's job." Helen gave a soft laugh. "If I could just turn it off, I would. It would make life easier."

"Where's Daddy?"

"Recovering nicely. He should be able to come home by the end of next week." Her mother seemed to relax a little thinking about it.

"So soon?"

Helen patted her hand. "You and your father have more in common than your spirited personality." She bit her lip, shaking her head. "Your father is driving the nurses batty, so I'm hiring a home health team, and he'll take the east wing of the house until he's stronger. The risk of infection is actually lower at home than in the hospital."

"Good, then I can go home too."

She started to fumble for the button that would sit the bed up, but Nick was there with a stern expression on his face. "You have to stay overnight. The bullet missed all the nerves and only nicked the brachial artery, but you were lucky. It could've been a lot worse, and you shouldn't push it. If Jacob hadn't shown up..." He looked to his left, and Ellie followed his gaze, delighted to see Jacob standing against the wall. Nick cleared his throat. "He saved your life."

"Why were you even there?" Ellie asked. "You came out of nowhere."

"Fortis. He called me not long after you left and asked me to head your way."

"I thought it was open and shut." She frowned. "He said I didn't need anyone."

Jacob nodded, pushing off the wall and coming to the side of her bed. "Yeah. He said as soon as you left, he got a bad feeling about it."

"Good thing." Nick's fingers stroked her hair away from her face. "The doctor said even the tiny nick would've been enough for you to bleed out if Jacob hadn't been there so fast. Ellie, you would've—" His voice broke, and the room fell into a heavy silence.

Fighting back tears, Ellie smiled. "But he *was* there, and I'm going to be okay."

Helen opened her mouth, then closed it with a sad smile. "Thank goodness for Jacob." But Ellie knew it had taken Helen all her willpower not to demand she quit her job.

It's not much, but it's progress, she thought. When she caught Jacob's gaze, he winked at her. He knew exactly what she was thinking.

"We should let you rest," Jacob said, breaking the silence. "I'll bring Duke by when you're feeling a little better."

"Well, as soon as they let me, I'm out of here."

"I know where you live," he teased.

The line of people walking by her bed to say goodbye was a blur, except when Jillian popped down to kiss her cheek.

"You get all the rest you need now." Jillian wiped the lipstick she'd left on Ellie's cheek off, blinking back tears.

When the door closed, only her mother and Nick remained.

Helen cleared her throat and sighed. "I know I don't say this enough, but I'm so proud of you."

Ellie's lips parted in shock, but she managed to collect herself. "Thank you. I know you have your reservations about my job, but you have to understand, being on the force is like—"

"An extended family," Helen offered. "I know. I see that now." She smiled and lifted a delicate shoulder. "I don't know how you feel about having people see you like this, but the waiting room is wall-to-wall police officers. I didn't have enough words to thank them for their support, but I did my best."

"Really? There are that many?" She glanced at Nick, then back at her mother. "They've been here the entire time?"

"Most of them," Nick said. "They've been rotating who picks up calls, and I'm pretty sure the hospital is permanently out of coffee, but they're here."

"Can I see them?"

"Are you sure you're up to it?" Helen's forehead wrinkled. "I'm not exaggerating when I say that every officer in Charleston has been in that waiting room."

"Yes, I'm definitely up for it."

It took almost an hour for every officer in the hospital to have a turn wishing her well and shaking her good hand. Helen left to be with Daniel, but Nick stayed with her, holding a straw to her lips when her throat was parched and adjusting the bed when she needed it. When the last officer left, Ellie nodded to the doorway. "Who's out there?"

"Security detail," Nick said. "They'll have someone stationed until you're released tomorrow. Just in case."

"I thought he was dead." Her pulse quickened, but Nick already had her hand in his.

"He is. It's standard. They said the guards are about watching your back when you can't watch your own."

Ellie smiled. "If I'd known it would take getting shot to get them to treat me like an equal, I would've done it a long time ago."

Nick nearly choked on a barking laugh. "If your mother heard you say that," he warned.

"I know. Send them in here, will you?"

"Of course."

When Nick returned with the two officers who had been in the hall, both took off their hats, but the large man with the wide shoulders and perpetually dour expression hung back.

"I know you," Ellie said after the other officer shook her hand and scurried out of the room and back to his post. "You're—"

"The jerk from the breakroom?" he finished. He looked smaller with his hat in hands as he nervously twisted the stiff material. He kept his eyes lowered, and Ellie almost felt bad for him.

Almost.

"I was going to say 'Officer Smythe,' but okay." She flashed him a wide smile. "Thank you for having my back today."

The grin that spread across his face was awkward and magical all at once. She could tell he didn't smile often, but it was worth the effort. "I'm sorry we got off on the wrong foot."

"Tomorrow's a new day."

"If there's anything I can do to make it up to you..."

"Actually," she said with a grin. "There is something you can do."

❄

NICK HELPED Ellie into her dress blues the next morning, carefully adjusting the sling on her arm with a worried look on his face. As a detective, she didn't wear a uniform anymore, but somehow the blue seemed right for what she had to do today.

"You know if you don't feel up to this, no one is going to blame you."

"I'm fine," she said. "Now, help me with my hair."

"How about we leave it loose and down?" Standing behind her, looking into her eyes in the mirror, he finger-combed her curls. "I think this is perfect."

"It's unprofessional, and I look like a wild woman."

"And it was that wild streak that made you the stubborn, relentless person you are."

She sighed. "All right, you've convinced me."

He kissed her forehead, and she breathed in his clean scent. He was also dressed in his best, determined to stay at her side just as he had done since she was shot six days ago.

Truth be told, she'd needed the mandatory time off, both to heal and because of the investigation following an officer involved shooting. She had four days to go, and as tired as she still was, she was itching to get her fingers on the next case...after she'd officially laid this one to rest.

She still couldn't believe her mother had not only approved but suggested she stay with Nick while she recuperated.

"*Your* house?" Ellie had gasped when Nick had told her. "Scandalous."

He'd laughed. "Don't get any ideas. I'm not that kind of guy."

"That's a shame." She winked at him. "Light exercise helps with recovery."

"Maybe I could be persuaded. But not until your arm is healed."

"Fair enough."

And true enough, he'd been a gentleman the entire time, although she wasn't sure how she felt about that. But as he opened the passenger door of his Cayenne, then scooped her up and sat her in the seat with a tender kiss. "There's more where that came from if you behave yourself."

"Don't count on it," she teased.

"Trust me, I'm not."

Their light-hearted mood turned solemn as they pulled up to the church.

The Baker and Vicente families were already seated when Ellie and Nick walked into the back of the chapel.

Mrs. Baker spotted them right away and waved them over.

On the front pew in the next aisle, a grief-stricken woman in head-to-toe black sat beside a tall man with thick, dark hair. They were stone-faced, mouths set in identical thin lines.

At the front of the church was a large print on an easel of Tabitha and Mabel together, young lives cut short far too soon captured in a moment of bliss. On the marble alter were two urns with delicately carved patterns, side by side. Their names were etched into the metal, along with their birthdates and date of passing.

Ellie knew it was too soon to have the bodies that had been exhumed from the state-funded cemete ry cremated. It would take several more days before the women's ashes were placed inside the containers, but she stared reverently at the two names just the same.

Ellie choked back tears and plastered a kind smile on her face just in time to take Mrs. Baker's hand in greeting.

Tabitha's mother said, "I'd hug you, but I hear you had a bit of a go of it last week."

Had it only been six days? Ellie thought, surprised by everything that had happened since she'd first called on Mrs. Baker at her home.

"I'm fine," she said quietly. She looked around the chapel, at all the lovely flowers that had arrived for the memorial service. "Are those Mabel's parents?"

She nodded.

"Have you talked to them?"

"Yes," Mrs. Baker whispered quietly. "It's hard because they have so much guilt for not accepting the girls together. And now that Mabel and Tabitha—" Mrs. Baker drew in a quivering breath. "Now that it's too late, they both have some regrets."

"Most of us do." Ellie rubbed Mrs. Baker's arm in acknowledgment. "Excuse me."

She slipped by Mrs. Baker and made her way through the crowd to pay her respects to Mabel's parents.

"Are you the one who found my girl?" Mr. Vicente asked after Ellie introduced herself. "When I think about all that time she was close by. We had no idea. I should've felt something. I should've known something bad had happened."

"There's no way you could've known," Ellie assured them both. "But you're here now, and that's what matters."

"It's a small blessing they were together at least." Mrs. Vicente dabbed her eyes with a lacey handkerchief. "I wish we could find some way to honor that now." She reached out and touched Ellie's cheek. "Thank you for caring about our daughters. They deserved to have justice and you gave that to them."

Before Ellie could think of what to say, Mrs. Vicente gestured around the chapel and sighed. "And all this. I don't know how you got the city to pay for it, but it's too much. We're the only family Mabel had, and Mr. Baker died and left Mrs. Baker alone." She let out a heavy breath. "Most of the girls' friends have started families and moved away. These are the only people we have left."

Ellie looked at the meager crowd spread across the chapel. Seeing it made her heart hurt, but she had to hide the smile that threatened to peek through. Ellie hadn't paid the final expenses for both girls to have their loss marked by a handful of near strangers.

The door in the back of the room opened, and Officer

Smythe stepped into the doorway. Dressed in his dress blues with white gloves, his hat tucked under his arm in respect, he waited until Ellie nodded before he walked into the room.

Mrs. Baker and the Vicentes gasped in unison as officers walked in step, filling up every last pew, with more than a dozen officers left standing in the back. The room that had felt sullen and empty moments before was filled to overflowing with officers who had come to pay their respects to the young women who had spent the last five years waiting to be identified.

Hot tears suddenly streamed down Ellie's face, to be the one to finally bring the two young women peace. She turned to go stand with the others, swiping at her tears, when Mrs. Vicente took Ellie's hand and tugged gently. "You belong in the front with the family. If it weren't for you, we wouldn't be here today."

Ellie nodded, not trusting herself to speak. Mrs. Baker sat down next to her, and nestled between the grieving mothers, the tears flowed freely.

For the first time in a long time, Ellie felt an overwhelming sense of calm. She'd stuck her neck out and defied her superior officer, all for this moment. With Nick behind her and the families of two young women who would never be called Jane Doe again surrounding her, Ellie knew what she was meant to do.

30

Fortis beaconed her to his office the moment she showed up to work the following Monday, ten days after her release from the hospital.

"How did you enjoy your vacation?" he teased. "I bet you're itching to get your desk moved and get to work."

She'd thought she was about to be given a lecture about working on the first case of his list he'd given her. "Moved?"

"You know, upstairs? Out of cold cases, and out of the evidence room." He gestured toward a man on the other side of his glassed-in office, who was carrying what resembled her desk chair. "Of course, you'll have to see the department shrink for a bit before you'll be cleared to carry a weapon again, but that's just protocol. You can work on fresh cases until you finish your stint with the head doctor. Light duty. That's what you want, isn't it?"

She shook her head. "No, it's not."

His smile slipped. "I thought you were all about proving yourself so you could get out of there." He thumbed toward the basement. "You caught the captain's attention, and he's more than pleased with everything you've done. Hell, I think he'd give you my job if you asked for it at this point."

"With all due respect, I'd like to stay in Cold Cases."

Fortis lowered his voice, glancing at the outer office. "This isn't about your case, is it? I could lose my job for letting you get into it."

"No, it's not." She took a deep breath. "I know that cold cases are the ones that no one wants to catch, but sir, when I solved that case and got to see those families *finally* bring their loved ones home to rest, something about it felt right. I want to do that for more people. All the people in the back corner of that locker deserve to have justice."

"If you turn down this offer, I'm not sure when another will come up. There's a chance you'll be stuck in Cold Cases for a long time."

"I hope so," she said. "Now, is there any way someone can take my things back downstairs? I have a lot I can be working on until I'm healed enough for the field again."

"Sure." Fortis sat back with a warm smile. "But you still have to see the shrink."

She groaned and blew a stray strand of curly red hair away from her face. "Fine. I guess I'll get it over with."

"That's a relief. I thought that would be a bigger fight with you."

"Don't worry, the fact that I'm going willingly doesn't mean I've changed." She shot him a grin. "I'm still the same old Ellie."

Fortis's laugh filled the space, echoing off the ceiling tiles that did almost nothing to deaden the sound. "That's what I was afraid of."

Ellie left Fortis, and after finding the psychiatrist's office. She'd come to make an appointment and had been surprised to be told that the good doctor could see her right away.

Might as well get it over with.

After introductions, the blond Dr. Powell sat in an armchair across from her with his legs crossed, hands folded over his knees, a placid smile on his face. Pen and paper sat on the end table beside him, but he made no move to use either.

"So, where shall we start?" Ellie shifted uncomfortably in her seat. His constant, unwavering eye contact was making her self-conscious.

His blue eyes assessed her, as if he could read every move she made. He seemed to thrum a nervous energy just beneath the surface, as if he might bubble over at any moment. "Well, I'd be lying if I said I didn't know something of your story, so why don't we start with the incident on the bridge?"

"That's not when I got shot," she protested.

"You're right, it's not. But it seems to me that everything you do and all the ways you put yourself in danger all stem from the same need. Am I close?"

Ellie bristled. "I'm not putting myself in danger. I'm chasing suspects and capturing criminals."

"And you're jumping off bridges into gator-infested waters and running after murderers without backup. That's not exactly safety conscious work there, even if you have inspired half of Charleston to apply to wear the badge." He smiled and wrote something in illegible chicken scratch, humming to himself. "Very nice, actually. You're better PR for the department than all the commercial spots combined. But that doesn't explain why you're always the one in the thick of things. Danger seems to follow you like a lost hellhound."

"Luck of the draw." The smile she gave him felt forced, even to her. "The perps we end up chasing are the ones we have to catch. I don't get to choose who jumps off a bridge and who surrenders peacefully."

"Have you considered taking a more careful approach?

You know, like your former partner." He checked his notes. "Jacob Garcia. I took a peek at his file, and he hasn't jumped off a bridge or followed a murderer into the woods with no backup, and somehow, he's been on the force for several years longer than you have. He's also never been shot." Dr. Powell looked over the rims of his glasses at her. "You don't find that even the slightest bit odd?"

She shrugged. "Not really."

"Shall I go over a few other officers and their stats?"

"Are you allowed to do that?"

"I'm allowed to peruse any file and make recommendations as I see fit." He blinked at her, totally nonchalant. "It's what I do."

Ellie pursed her lips. "I thought we were going to talk about me getting shot and whether I'm still having nightmares or not."

"Most people have nightmares after a near-death experience. I'm not so much concerned about that as I am about the reckless behavior. We want you to be safe. Many of your fellow officers were upset to find out that you'd nearly died. How does that make you feel?"

"I'm not one of those women who likes to talk about my feelings."

"You should try it." He chuckled. "You might find you really do like it. If you don't want to talk about how supported you felt when the entire department showed up to hold vigil during your surgery, maybe you want to tell me what you went through that makes you feel like you're invincible."

She blinked back hot tears and tried to tamp down the sudden rush of anger in her chest. That was the trouble. She wasn't invincible. Not even in the least. "I'm surprised you don't know already, after looking in my file."

"Your file doesn't tell me what makes you tick. It only tells me what you do that breaks protocol."

"Okay, I guess this is a safe space, right?" She didn't want to, but she guessed explaining what led her to become an officer would get this guy off her back faster. And the quicker she was out of here, the quicker she could be working another cold case.

"Nothing you say leaves this room."

"Okay." She took a deep breath, ready to get it all out in a rush. "Well, you probably already know that, when I was fifteen, I wanted to go to the movies with a guy who was a senior, but I was a freshman. My parents said no, so I told them I was staying the night at a friend's house, and as soon as my mom dropped me off, he picked me up."

"There's nothing overly rebellious about that. It's human nature to defy our parents for young love."

She didn't need a lecture about young love and rebellion. "Yeah, well, it didn't go as planned."

"Going behind our parents' backs rarely does."

It was hard not to roll her eyes, but she managed not to. "He took me to a party instead. There was drinking, and I was uncomfortable. Things got out of control, and I ended up walking through Charleston in the middle of the night, not sure if I should go home or to my friend's house."

"Did your friend know she was your alibi?"

"No. That's why I decided to find my way home and sneak into my room. My parents were up and out of the house by six a.m. most days, so I thought I could get away with saying I got a ride home early or something."

He nodded, making a note. "What happened?"

Her chest swelled as she sucked in a deep breath, and sagged when she let it out. "That's where it gets hazy."

"Were you drunk?"

"No."

"Did someone drug you?" Powell stiffened minutely but his expression didn't change.

"It's possible, but that's not what happened." The deep dark of that night flashed before her eyes, and she swallowed, blinking until the light of the room pushed it back. "I was walking, and someone offered me a ride. The next thing I knew, I was in this dark place, begging for my life."

Dr. Powell leaned forward, clearly intrigued. "How did your parents find you?"

"I escaped."

"Wow." Powell's eyes went wide and his gaze sharpened on her. "That's impressive. How did you manage that?"

"I don't know, which is what haunts me. I can't remember much at all." Sometimes, she wished it wasn't that way, that she could just remember so she would know there was nothing she was missing. So she wouldn't feel so lost. So… crazy. "Just a few scattered memories here and there. Nothing that makes sense."

"How did you get ahold of your parents before you were recaptured?"

"I didn't. I was running, looking over my shoulder and screaming for help. I must've been closer to the road than I thought because the next thing I remember, I was in the hospital recovering from being hit by a squad car. That's the moment I decided I wanted to be a police officer."

"I don't know what to say." Powell nodded, glancing over his notes. "I can see why you feel invincible. After an experience like that, mortality seems like a distant issue and not something that can happen at any time."

She shook her head, laughing softly. "But I don't really feel that way." Did she? "I don't think about it. I just react and get the job done, then sometimes afterward the adrenaline crashes and I realize how badly I could've been injured."

"Do you feel some kind of regret at those times? Maybe a little fear?"

"A little." She tried not to smile at the exhilaration she'd experienced in those instances. "But mostly, I guess I just feel like I've done something that someone else wouldn't, and that feels good."

"Tell me, Ellie, do you feel guilty for what happened to you? You do realize that nothing you did *made* that person kidnap you, right?"

To her horror, emotion burned into her face, and she swallowed hard to force it back down. "I do understand that, but I still feel responsible for it." Guilt dug away at her stomach even as she said the words. "If I hadn't lied, I would've been safe at home. My parents never would have had to worry."

"Teenagers sneak out and they lie, Ellie. Those are natural, normal things for a girl of fifteen."

"Logically, I realize that, but convincing myself that it wasn't all my fault is not that easy. And then there's my dad's —" She stopped short, refusing to go there. "Anyway, I feel bad."

"You don't have to tell me what you almost said, but I can tell you'd like to get it off your chest. This is a safe space, Ellie." He leaned forward, setting the notepad on the table and pressing his hands together. "You can be honest with me here. And with yourself."

She caught her quivering lip between her teeth and forced away the tears that threatened. "My dad had a stroke when he found out what had happened to me. It caused significant damage to his heart, and he's been on heavy medication since, just to keep him healthy. He's not the man he was before I was kidnapped, and that eats away at me."

"I can imagine it does."

"A couple weeks ago, he had to have a heart transplant. It

was awful, waiting for someone else to lose a loved one so my dad could live."

Someone's going to die, Ellie, you choose when.

Ellie pushed the creepy voice out of her head and focused on Dr. Powell. "You're right, though. I'm not careful with myself because taking chances makes me feel good." She stood and wiped her hands on her pants. Her shoulder tugged, but it was less painful than it had been the week before. "I hate to chat and run, but I have to leave soon. I haven't seen Jillian, and I'm supposed to be on light duty, so only half-days this week."

"Self-care is important care. You do what you need to do to get healthy." Her hand was already on the door when he said, "And Ellie?"

She stopped, ordering herself not to give away any more of herself. She'd already spouted off like a soda bottle shaken and opened too fast. "Yes?"

"Thanks for stopping by."

31

Ellie fussed with the bandage on her arm, trying to roll her sleeve down over it. She scowled at her reflection in the mirror.

"It looks fine." Jacob stepped forward, fixing the sleeve. "Everyone in Charleston knows you got shot."

She scowled at her shoulder. "I want to look like a responsible officer."

"*Detective*," Jacob corrected. "And you could wear a nun's habit and they would still know who you are."

"That's what I'm afraid of." She half-grimaced, half-smiled as Jacob helped her into her jacket.

"You're going to do great. I promise. No one is here to judge you. It's an annual fundraiser, not a big to-do."

"The Chief of Police is going to be there. Jacob, aren't you nervous?" She pressed one hand to her stomach, trying to quell the nerves.

"He's there every year. Now breathe. Do I need to call Nick and have him take the night off so he can hold your hand?"

Ellie glared at him as his brilliant smile grew wider. "No, you don't. He had his own fundraiser already scheduled. I appreciate you being my plus one."

"I wasn't going to let Smythe have the honor. Plus, this was my only way to get in."

"I thought it was just a silly fundraiser?" she mocked.

"It is, but it's nice to be invited, even if it is only because my ex-partner solved two cold cases in one day."

She checked her hair that was pulled back in a sleek bun. "It wasn't a day, but thanks."

"You ready to go?"

"Would it be weird if I hid in the evidence locker all night?"

"It would, but you do you." Jacob held open the door, one eyebrow up in question.

"I always do." She grinned and tipped a pretend hat at him as she went out into the hall, leading the way to the police department's foyer.

Outside, simple white lights wrapped around the handrails leading up the stairs to the front entrance. The potted palms and entryways were lit up as well, giving Charleston PD a festive look.

"There are a lot of cars here," Ellie said, eyeing the parking lot. "I hope they're not all packed into the breakroom."

"You'll see. They open the accordion wall between the breakroom and the group rooms for things like this. It makes a large space for gathering."

She took the arm he offered, hiding her sling against his jacket so it wasn't so obvious. They worked the room, indulging everyone they met with the same short recap of Ellie's injury and the cases she'd solved.

Chief Marcus Johnson spotted them from across the

room as he sipped from a delicate flute of champagne. He flashed Ellie a wide grin and held it up for a toast to her.

Something tugged at her memory, but she pushed it aside. Ever since Dr. Powell had convinced her to open up about her past, odd images had been bubbling to the surface at the worst times. Now wasn't the time for a memory to crop up out of nowhere.

As he reached her, Johnson's large hands covered hers, his skin a rich, deep sepia. "Detective Kline," he said warmly. "It's nice to see you. You too, Jacob." He shook Jacob's hand vigorously. "I'm glad you both could make it. Tell me, Ellie, how is your father? Is he home yet?"

The question caught her off guard. Everyone else had asked about her gunshot wound, but Chief Johnson seemed more concerned with her family life. She instantly liked him. "He's doing great. They released him a week early with a home health team. He's out of quarantine sometime this week. All he needs is an all-clear from the doctor. I think he'll be happy to be free to roam the house. He's been confined to one wing of the house and is more than a little stir-crazy."

"I bet he's itching to get outside."

"He is."

Someone called out to the chief, and he gave a soft groan. "I'd love to stay and chat, but duty calls. Tell your parents I send my regards and thank them again for always supporting our officers in blue."

"I will."

"That was interesting," Jacob said.

"I'll say. It was like he knew me."

"In all fairness, you have been on television twice in the past six weeks. That's a lot for one officer."

"All right, fine. You're right." She jumped at the sudden vibration in her jacket, then laughed. "My cell phone buzzed.

I hope that's not Nick telling me the auction was a bust. He loves this car that's being sold." She took out her phone and frowned at the screen. Answering, she shoved one finger into her ear so she could hear. "Jillian, what's up? I'm at the fundraiser."

"I know," Jillian said. "I'm in evidence."

"Jillian, it's eight o'clock."

"I know. I got wrapped up in something and lost track of time. I can't explain over the phone. You need to come down here."

Ellie glanced around at the glittering lights, feeling a moment of disappointment. She shrugged. She got enough of glitter and glam at the fundraisers her mother pried her to. "I'll be there in a minute." She hung up and turned to Jacob. "Want to go downstairs with me?"

Jacob snorted and took a swig of his drink. "Why does that sound so dirty when you say it like that?"

"Hurry, Jillian is waiting."

He choked, coughing and pounding his chest with his fist. "I'm not sure I'm up for this."

"Stop being such a man," she teased as she hurried him to the service hallway.

"I'm not sure what else you expect me to be."

"Be more like Duke."

"Sure." Jacob huffed, trying to look insulted. "I'll remind you, Duke is not a bloodhound. What's going on?"

"Jillian must have found something."

He frowned down at his drink. "We're off the clock."

"I'm salaried. I'm never off the clock."

Jacob rolled his eyes, sighing as he threw back the remaining contents of his glass. "Whatever. The chicken they serve is usually dry anyway."

Jillian met them at the evidence office and ushered them to the back room where the cold cases were stored.

"What are these?" Ellie asked, looking down at the white boxes lined up on two tables.

"A hunch. You said you couldn't get ahold of all the women on the Ghana trip, right?"

"Right."

"Well, first, I looked at the women you couldn't reach. There were two of them. Then I got to thinking about other trips like the one Mabel and Tabitha were supposed to go on. I started running some of our Jane Does against missing persons who went missing while doing charity work overseas. I found three, total."

"Three that match our Jane Does?" Ellie asked.

"No. Three pairs of missing women. I grouped each pair together." Jillian placed her hands on two boxes. "The first two are from a trip that was headed to Peru then Costa Rica for six months. Then another pair of missing women from the Ghana trip. That's all I have so far, but that makes six victims."

"There are seven boxes," Jacob pointed out.

"That's mine." The words were out of Ellie's mouth before she could stop them. In the silence that followed, she could almost hear the puzzle pieces click into place.

Seven boxes.

One was missing.

She knew that now with a certainty she would never question.

Jacob's jaw dropped. "As in, your case from when you were abducted?"

Ellie swallowed hard before inclining her head just a fraction. "I just found out recently that it was never solved."

"But how can that be true? You were rescued. How did they not find the guy?"

"There were a lot of mishaps between when I was rescued and when my abduction came to light. I was hit by a police cruiser and unconscious for days after I escaped. Then I had no memory, and my parents told me the kidnapper had been killed, so…"

Jillian leaned forward, over the table. "There's more."

"How can there be more?" Jacob lamented, glancing from Ellie's evidence box to the others and running his fingers through his hair.

"In every single one of these cases, one body is mutilated and one is a quick, clean kill."

Tell me the words or I take off another finger!

Ellie shook herself away from the voice, her heartbeat jumping sky-high. "Anything else?"

"I haven't had a chance to go through everything, but I'm thinking if your case had been solved, maybe no one else would've died." Jillian clapped her hands over her mouth. "I'm sorry, that came out wrong. I'm not saying I wish you would've died."

"No, I understand," Ellie said quietly. She slipped the lid off her box, and one by one, took everything out, still sealed in the plastic bags. "I keep remembering things. If I could have forced myself to remember, would these women be dead?"

"You can't think like that, Ellie." Jacob shook his head emphatically. "You're not responsible for these six deaths."

"Seven."

"Why do you say that?" Jacob frowned down at the boxes.

"They all come in pairs, right? So somewhere, there's a dead woman who still hasn't been found."

He glanced up at her sharply. "How can you be sure?"

Say the words.

Ellie shuddered, her jaw clenched against the voice that wouldn't shut up. "There was blood on me that wasn't mine. Arterial spray. It was a fine mist, but it was there." Her eyes swept over the boxes again. "This means that

Eddie Bower was only a small cog in a much larger machine."

"That only happens one way," Jillian said, her eyes huge.

"I know." Ellie drew in deep breaths in an effort to quell the panic that was growing in her chest. "So, she had to be the first to go. Why did he spare me?"

"You didn't give him a choice," Jacob said vehemently, eyeing the boxes then piercing her with his determined stare. "Ellie, you can't beat yourself up for being strong."

"Sure I can." She picked up a bag out of her white box, and froze, placing the notes on the table and reading them slowly at first, then again until she'd read them ten times. "Whoever the woman with me was, she was the one who was tortured. All because of me."

Say it, Ellie. Put her out of her misery.

"It's not your fault," Jacob insisted as he leaned over so he could read the notes she held tightly against the table. "What's this?"

"The officer who hit me stayed with me until my parents were found. I was talking, even under sedation. Screaming, really. He wrote down everything I said."

Jacob's brown eyes bored into hers. "Ellie, you can't blame your—"

"It's right there." She stabbed her fingers at the words. "It says right here that 'I told her to die. I told him to kill her. I couldn't stand to hear her screams anymore.'" She looked up, staring into Jillian's eyes before turning to stare into Jacob's, the horror of what she had suppressed for so long slowly coming to light. "I said it with my own mouth, even though I have no memory of any of that."

"You were being held against your will. You had to survive."

"Not at someone else's expense, Jacob. Not like that."

Tears rolled down Ellie's face as she started to move her hand to reveal the words she'd covered up.

But something else caught Jacob's attention first. "Do you see who the notes were taken by?" he asked, wide-eyed.

"Officer Marcus Johnson." She was frozen to the spot. "That's why he looks so familiar. I thought it was because he's on TV all the time, but it was *him*."

A memory of lying on the cold, wet asphalt and the policeman kneeling over her, frightened, burst in front of her vision.

"Chief Johnson. Chief Johnson is the officer I ran out in front of."

"What is under your hand?" Jacob tried to push Ellie's hand away from the paper, but she wouldn't budge.

She trembled, and the voice was like thunder inside her.

Say the words, Ellie. Say the words I need to hear.

"I can't do it," she whispered, eyes squeezed shut so tightly the tears couldn't escape. But when she opened her eyes, Jillian and Jacob were watching her, waiting.

"What does it say?" Jacob pressed gently.

"The one thing he needed to hear to put the poor woman out of her misery." Ellie's throat was thick with unshed tears, forgotten terror lurking just beneath the surface of her mind. "It was all I had to say to make him stop the torture, and I couldn't take it anymore. I finally said it."

Jacob swallowed, glanced at Jillian.

Jillian took a step toward Ellie. "You can tell us. We won't judge you. And we can find this person, make sure justice is served for good."

"Justice," Ellie whispered, closing her eyes.

She balled her fists up and took a shuddering breath, then opened her eyes and licked her suddenly dry lips. She fought back the memory as the basement room tried to turn into that cold, dark room full of so much pain.

"All I had to say was, 'Die, Bitch, Die.'"

The End
To be continued...

Thank you for reading.
All of the Ellie Kline Series books can be found on Amazon.

ACKNOWLEDGMENTS

How does one properly thank everyone involved in taking a dream and making it a reality? Here goes.

In addition to our families, whose unending support provided the foundation for us to find the time and energy to put these thoughts on paper, we want to thank the editors who polished our words and made them shine.

Many thanks to our publisher for risking taking on two newbies and giving us the confidence to become bona fide authors.

More than anyone, we want to thank you, our readers, for clicking on a couple of nobodies and sharing your most important asset, your time, with this book. We hope with all our hearts we made it worthwhile.

Much love,

Mary & Donna

ABOUT THE AUTHOR

Mary Stone

Mary Stone lives among the majestic Blue Ridge Mountains of East Tennessee with her two dogs, four cats, a couple of energetic boys, and a very patient husband.

As a young girl, she would go to bed every night, wondering what type of creature might be lurking underneath. It wasn't until she was older that she learned that the creatures she needed to most fear were human.

Today, she creates vivid stories with courageous, strong heroines and dastardly villains. She invites you to enter her world of serial killers, FBI agents but never damsels in distress. Her female characters can handle themselves, going toe-to-toe with any male character, protagonist or antagonist.

Discover more about Mary Stone on her website.
www.authormarystone.com

Donna Berdel

Raised as an Army brat, Donna has lived all over the world, but no place has given her as much peace as the home she lives in with her husband near Myrtle Beach. But while she now keeps her feet planted firmly in the sand, her mind goes back to those cities and the people she met and said goodbye to so many times.

With her two adopted cats fighting for lap space, she brings those she loved (and those she didn't) back as characters in her books. And yes, it's kind of fun to kill off anyone who was mean to her in the past. Mean clerk at the grocery store...beware!

Connect with Mary Online

facebook.com/authormarystone
goodreads.com/AuthorMaryStone
bookbub.com/profile/3378576590
pinterest.com/MaryStoneAuthor